Vonvalt drained the last of his ale.

"On our way here," he explained, "we were told a number of times about a witch, living in the woods just to the north of Rill. I don't suppose you know anything about it?"

Sir Otmar delayed with a long draw of wine and then ostensibly to pick something out of his teeth. "Not that I have heard of, sire. No."

Vonvalt nodded thoughtfully. *"Who is she?"*

Bressinger swore in Grozodan. Sir Otmar and I leapt halfway out of our skin. The table and all the platters and cutlery on it were jolted as three pairs of thighs hit it. Goblets and tankards were spilled. Sir Otmar clutched his heart, his eyes wide, his mouth working to expel the words that Vonvalt had commanded him to.

The Emperor's Voice: the arcane power of a Justice to compel a person to speak the truth. It had its limitations – it did not work on other Justices, for example, and a strong-willed person could frustrate it if on their guard – but Sir Otmar was old and meek and not well-versed in the ways of the Order. The power hit him like a psychic thunderclap and turned his mind inside out.

Praise for
Richard Swan and
The Justice of Kings

"A stunning piece of modern fantasy writing."
—RJ Barker, author of *The Bone Ships*

"*The Justice of Kings* is equal parts heroic fantasy and murder mystery. Sir Konrad Vonvalt's fierce intellect and arcane powers will make you long to follow in his footsteps, but it's his young clerk, Helena, who brings heart and dazzle to the story. Together they're a formidable team, and Richard Swan's sophisticated take on the fantasy genre will leave readers hungry for more."
—Sebastien de Castell, author of *Spellslinger*

"*The Justice of Kings* is utterly compelling, thoroughly engrossing, and written with such skillful assurance I could barely put it down. The characters feel so real I swear I suffered every horror and hangover alongside them, and their world—though we see just the smallest portion of it here—feels vastly complex, poised on the brink of a disaster I can't wait to watch unfold."
—Nicholas Eames, author of *Kings of the Wyld*

"A fascinating look at justice, vengeance, and the law—great characters, compelling, and wonderfully written. A brilliant debut and fantastic start to the series."

—James Islington, author of *The Shadow of What Was Lost*

"A marvelously detailed world with an engrossing adventure from a unique perspective."

—K. S. Villoso, author of *The Wolf of Oren-Yaro*

"A fantastic debut."   —Peter McLean, author of *Priest of Bones*

"Swan crafts a strong, dynamic character in Vonvalt. . . . This promises good things from the series to come."   —*Publishers Weekly*

"Murder mystery meets grimdark political fantasy in this first of a trilogy. . . . An intriguingly dark . . . deconstruction of a beloved mystery trope."   —*Kirkus* (starred review)

"The world of the Empire of the Wolf is a rich and interesting one. . . . Readers will enjoy the world building, Sir Konrad and his crew, and the unique touches to a familiar fantasy tale."

—*Booklist*

THE
JUSTICE
OF
KINGS

Book One of the Empire of the Wolf

RICHARD SWAN

orbit

orbitbooks.net

Copyright © 2022 by Richard Swan
Excerpt from *Book Two of the Empire of the Wolf* copyright © 2022 by Richard Swan
Excerpt from *The Pariah* copyright © 2021 by Anthony Ryan

Cover design by Lauren Panepinto
Cover illustration by Martina Fačková
Cover copyright © 2022 by Hachette Book Group, Inc.
Map by Tim Paul
Author photograph by Robert Lapworth

Orbit
Hachette Book Group
1290 Avenue of the Americas
New York, NY 10104
orbitbooks.net

First Paperback Edition: August 2022
Originally published in hardcover and ebook in Great Britain and in the U.S. by Orbit in February 2022

Orbit is an imprint of Hachette Book Group.
The Orbit name and logo are trademarks of Little, Brown Book Group Limited.

The Hachette Speakers Bureau provides a wide range of authors for speaking events. To find out more, go to www.hachettespeakersbureau.com or call (866) 376-6591.

Library of Congress Control Number: 2021940495

ISBNs: 9780316361484 (trade paperback), 9780316361583 (ebook)

Printed in the United States of America

LSC-C

Printing 3, 2023

THE

JUSTICE
OF
KINGS

The
Sovan Empire
at its greatest extent

Enos Seaguard

Rill

Baquir

Tolsburg

Denholtz Muldau

Leyenswald Jägeland

Schwanstadt

Walderstadt

Grozoda Venland

Annholt

Grallstein

Grall Sea

N
W E
S

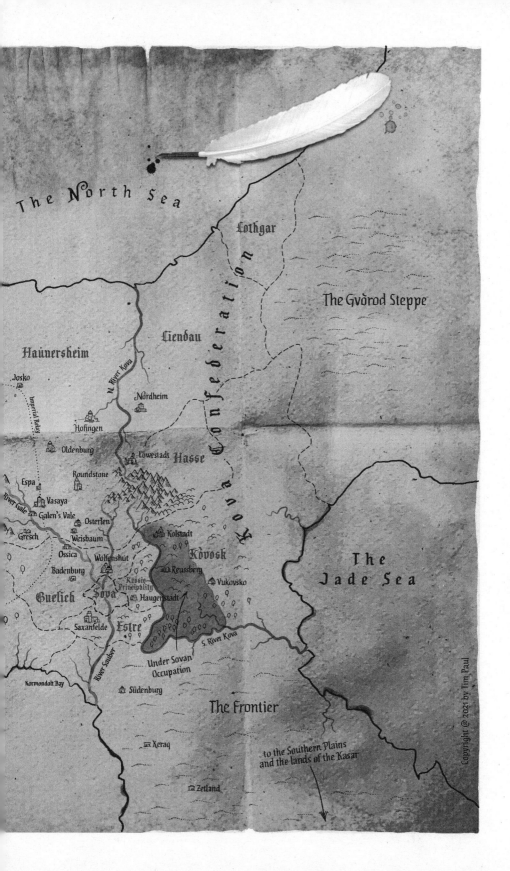

Table of Contents

I

The Witch of Rill

*"Beware the idiot, the zealot and the tyrant; each
clothes himself in the armour of ignorance."*

FROM CATERHAUSER'S THE SOVAN CRIMINAL
CODE: ADVICE TO PRACTITIONERS

It is a strange thing to think that the end of the Empire of the
Wolf, and all the death and devastation that came with it, traced
its long roots back to the tiny and insignificant village of Rill.
That as we drew closer to it, we were not just plodding through
a rainy, cold country twenty miles east of the Tolsburg Marches;
we were approaching the precipice of the Great Decline, its steep
and treacherous slope falling away from us like a cliff face of
glassy obsidian.

Rill. How to describe it? The birthplace of our misfortune
was so plain. For its isolation, it was typical for the Northmark
of Tolsburg. It was formed of a large communal square of
churned mud and straw, and a ring of twenty buildings with

wattle-and-daub walls and thatched roofs. The manor was distinguishable only by its size, being perhaps twice as big as the biggest cottage, but there the differences ended. It was as tumbledown as the rest of them. An inn lay off to one side, and livestock and peasants moved haphazardly through the public space. One benefit of the cold was that the smell wasn't so bad, but Vonvalt still held a kerchief filled with dried lavender to his nose. He could be fussy like that.

I should have been in a good mood. Rill was the first village we had come across since we had left the Imperial wayfort on the Jägeland border, and it marked the beginning of a crescent of settlements that ended in the Hauner fortress of Seaguard fifty miles to the north-east. Our arrival here meant we were probably only a few weeks away from turning south again to complete the eastern half of our circuit – and that meant better weather, larger towns and something approaching civilisation.

Instead, anxiety gnawed at me. My attention was fixed on the vast, ancient forest that bordered the village and stretched for a hundred miles north and west of us, all the way to the coast. It was home, according to the rumours we had been fed along the way, to an old Draedist witch.

"You think she is in there?" Patria Bartholomew Claver asked from next to me. Claver was one of four people who made up our caravan, a Neman priest who had imposed himself on us at the Jägeland border. Ostensibly it was for protection against bandits, though the Northmark was infamously desolate – and by his own account, he travelled almost everywhere alone.

"Who?" I asked.

Claver smiled without warmth. "The witch," he said.

"No," I said curtly. I found Claver very irritating – everyone did. Our itinerant lives were difficult enough, but Claver's incessant questioning over the last few weeks of every aspect of Vonvalt's practice and powers had worn us all down to the nub.

"I do."

I turned. Dubine Bressinger – Vonvalt's taskman – was approaching, cheerfully eating an onion. He winked at me as his horse trotted past. Behind him was our employer, Sir Konrad Vonvalt, and at the very back was our donkey, disrespectfully named the Duke of Brondsey, which pulled a cart loaded with all our accoutrements.

We had come to Rill for the same reason we went anywhere: to ensure that the Emperor's justice was done, even out here on the fringes of the Sovan Empire. For all their faults, the Sovans were great believers in justice for all, and they dispatched Imperial Magistrates like Vonvalt to tour the distant villages and towns of the Empire as itinerant courts.

"I'm looking for Sir Otmar Frost," I heard Vonvalt call out from the rear of our caravan. Bressinger had already dismounted and was summoning a local boy to make arrangements for our horses.

One of the peasants pointed wordlessly at the manor. Vonvalt grunted and dismounted. Patria Claver and I did the same. The mud was iron-hard beneath my feet.

"Helena," Vonvalt called to me. "The ledger."

I nodded and retrieved the ledger from the cart. It was a heavy tome, with a thick leather jacket clad in iron and with a lockable clasp. It would be used to record any legal issues which arose, and Vonvalt's considered judgments. Once it was full, it would be sent back to the Law Library in distant Sova, where clerks would review the judgments and make sure that the common law was being applied consistently.

I brought the ledger to Vonvalt, who bade me keep hold of it with an irritated wave, and all four of us made for the manor. I could see now that it had a heraldic device hanging over the door, a plain blue shield overlaid by a boar's head mounted on a broken lance. The manor was otherwise unremarkable, and a far cry from the sprawling town houses and country fortresses of the Imperial aristocracy in Sova.

Vonvalt hammered a gloved fist against the door. It opened

quickly. A maid, perhaps a year or two younger than me, stood in the doorway. She looked frightened.

"I am Justice Sir Konrad Vonvalt of the Imperial Magistratum," Vonvalt said in what I knew to be an affected Sovan accent. His native Jägeland inflection marked him out as an upstart, notwithstanding his station, and embarrassed him.

The maid curtseyed clumsily. "I—"

"Who is it?" Sir Otmar Frost called from somewhere inside. It was dark beyond the threshold and smelled like woodsmoke and livestock. I could see Vonvalt's hand absently reach for his lavender kerchief.

"Justice Sir Konrad Vonvalt of the Imperial Magistratum," he announced again, impatiently.

"Bloody faith," Sir Otmar muttered, and appeared in the doorway a few moments later. He thrust the maid aside without ceremony. "My lord, come in, come in; come out of the damp and warm yourselves at the fire."

We entered. Inside it was dingy. At one end of the room was a bed covered in furs and woollen blankets, as well as personal effects which suggested an absent wife. In the centre was an open log fire, surrounded by charred and muddy rugs that were also mouldering thanks to the rain that dripped down from the open smoke hole. At the other end was a long trestle table with seating for ten, and a door that led to a separate kitchen. The walls were draped with mildewed tapestries that were faded and smoked near-black, and the floor was piled thick with rugs and skins. A pair of big, wolf-like dogs warmed themselves next to the fire.

"I was told that a Justice was moving north through the Tolsburg Marches," Sir Otmar said as he fussed. As a Tollish knight and lord, he had been elevated to the Imperial aristocracy – "taking the Highmark", as it was known, for the payoffs they had all received in exchange for submitting to the Legions – but he was a far cry from the powdered and pampered lords of Sova. He was an old man, clad in a grubby tunic bearing his device and a pair of homespun trousers. His face was grimy and careworn and framed by white hair and a white beard. A large dent marred his forehead, probably earned as a younger man when the Reichskrieg had swept through and the Sovan armies had vassalised Tolsburg twenty-five years before. Both Vonvalt and Bressinger, too, bore the scars of the Imperial expansion.

"The last visit was from Justice August?" Vonvalt asked.

Sir Otmar nodded. "Aye. A long time ago. Used to be that we saw a Justice a few times a year. Please, all of you, sit. Food, ale? Wine? I was just about to eat."

"Yes, thank you," Vonvalt said, sitting at the table. We followed suit.

"My predecessor left a logbook?" Vonvalt asked.

"Yes, yes," Sir Otmar replied, and sent the maid scurrying off again. I heard the sounds of a strongbox being raided.

"Any trouble from the north?"

Sir Otmar shook his head. "No; we have a sliver of the Westmark of Haunersheim between us and the sea. Maybe ten or twenty miles' worth, enough to absorb a raiding party. Though I daresay the sea is too rough this time of year anyway to tempt the northerners down."

"Quite right," Vonvalt said. I could tell he was annoyed for having forgotten his geography. Still, one could be forgiven the occasional slip of the mind. The Empire, now over fifty years old, had absorbed so many nations so quickly the cartographers redrew the maps yearly. "And I suppose with Seaguard rebuilt," he added.

"Aye, that the Autun did. A new curtain wall, a new garrison and enough money and provender to allow for daily ranges during fighting season. Weekly, in winter, by order of the margrave."

The Autun. The Two-Headed Wolf. It was evens on whether the man had meant the term as a pejorative. It was one of those strange monikers for the Sovan Empire that the conquered used either in deference or as an insult. Either way, Vonvalt ignored it.

"The man has a reputation," Vonvalt remarked.

"Margrave Westenholtz?" the priest, Claver, chipped in. "A good man. A pious man. The northerners are a godless folk who cleave to the old Draedist ways." He shrugged. "You should not mourn them, Justice."

Vonvalt smiled thinly. "I do not mourn dead northern raiders, Patria," he said with more restraint than the man was due. Claver was a young man, too young to bear the authority of a priest. Over the course of our short time together we had all had grown to dislike him immensely. He was zealous and a bore, quick to anger and judge. He spoke at great length about his cause – that of recruiting Templars for the southern Frontier – and his lordly contacts. Bressinger generally refused to talk to him, but Vonvalt, out of professional courtesy, had been engaging with the man for weeks.

Sir Otmar cleared his throat. He was about to make the error of engaging with Claver when the food arrived, and instead he ate. It was hearty, simple fare of meat, bread and thick gravy, but then in these circumstances we rarely went hungry. Vonvalt's power and authority tended to inspire generosity in his hosts.

"You said the last Justice passed through a while ago?" Vonvalt asked.

"Aye," Sir Otmar replied.

"You have been following the Imperial statutes in the interim?"

Sir Otmar nodded vigorously, but he was almost certainly lying. These far-flung villages and towns, months' worth of travel from distant Sova even by the fastest means, rarely practised Imperial law. It was a shame. The Reichskrieg had brought death and misery to thousands, but the system of common law was one of the few rubies to come out of an otherwise enormous shit.

"Good. Then I shouldn't imagine there will be much to do. Except investigate the woods," Vonvalt said. Sir Otmar looked confused by the addendum. Vonvalt drained the last of his ale. "On our way here," he explained, "we were told a number of times about a witch, living in the woods just to the north of Rill. I don't suppose you know anything about it?"

Sir Otmar delayed with a long draw of wine and then ostensibly to pick something out of his teeth. "Not that I have heard of, sire. No."

Vonvalt nodded thoughtfully. *"Who is she?"*

Bressinger swore in Grozodan. Sir Otmar and I leapt halfway out of our skin. The table and all the platters and cutlery on it were jolted as three pairs of thighs hit it. Goblets and tankards were spilled. Sir Otmar clutched his heart, his eyes wide, his mouth working to expel the words that Vonvalt had commanded him to.

The Emperor's Voice: the arcane power of a Justice to compel a person to speak the truth. It had its limitations – it did not work on other Justices, for example, and a strong-willed person could frustrate it if on their guard – but Sir Otmar was old and meek and not well-versed in the ways of the Order. The power hit him like a psychic thunderclap and turned his mind inside out.

"A priestess . . . a member of the Draeda," Sir Otmar gasped. He looked horrified as his mouth spoke against his mind's will.

"Is she from Rill?" Vonvalt pressed.

"Yes!"

"Are there others who practise Draedism?"

Sir Otmar writhed in his chair. He gripped the table to steady himself.

"Many . . . of the villagers!"

"Sir Konrad," Bressinger murmured. He was watching Sir Otmar with a slight wince. I saw that Claver was relishing the man's torment.

"All right, Sir Otmar," Vonvalt said. "All right. Calm yourself. Here, take some ale. I'll not press you any further."

We sat in silence as Sir Otmar summoned the terrified maid with a trembling hand and wheezed for some ale. She left and reappeared a moment later, handing him a tankard. Sir Otmar drained it greedily.

"The practice of Draedism is illegal," Vonvalt remarked.

Sir Otmar looked at his plate. His expression was somewhere between anger, horror and shame, and was a common look for those who had been hit by the Voice.

"The laws are new. The religion is old," he said hoarsely.

"The laws have been in place for two and a half decades."

"The religion has been in place for two and a half millennia," Sir Otmar snapped.

There was an uncomfortable pause. "Is there anyone in Rill that is not a practising member of Draedism?" Vonvalt asked.

Sir Otmar inspected his drink. "I couldn't say," he mumbled.

"Justice." There was genuine disgust in Claver's voice. "At the very least they will have to renounce it. The official religion of the Empire is the holy Nema Creed." He practically spat as he looked the old baron up and down. "If I had my way they'd all burn."

"These are good folk here," Sir Otmar said, alarmed. "Good, law-abiding folk. They work the land and they pay their tithes. We've never been a burden on the Autun."

Vonvalt shot Claver an irritated look. "With respect, Sir Otmar, if these people are practising Draedists, then they cannot, by definition, be law-abiding. I am sorry to say that Patria Claver is right – at least in part. They will have to renounce it. You have a list of those who practise?"

"I do not."

The logs smoked and crackled and spat. Ale and wine dripped and pattered through the cracks in the table planks.

"The charge is minor," Vonvalt said. "A small fine, a penny per head, if they recant. As their lord you may even shoulder it on their behalf. Do you have a shrine to any of the Imperial gods? Nema? Savare?"

"No." Sir Otmar all but spat out the word. It was becoming increasingly difficult to ignore the fact that Sir Otmar was a practising Draedist himself.

"The official religion of the Sovan Empire is the Nema Creed.

Enshrined in scripture and in both the common and canon law. Come now, there are parallels. The Book of Lorn is essentially Draedism, no? It has the same parables, mandates the same holy days. You could adopt it without difficulty."

It was true, the Book of Lorn did bear remarkable parallels to Draedism. That was because the Book of Lorn *was* Draedism. The Sovan religion was remarkably flexible, and rather than replacing the many religious practices it encountered during the Reichskrieg, it simply subsumed them, like a wave engulfing an island. It was why the Nema Creed was simultaneously the most widely practised and least respected religion in the known world.

I looked over to Claver. The man's face was aghast at Vonvalt's easy equivocation. Of course, Vonvalt was no more a believer in the Nema Creed than Sir Otmar. Like the old baron, he had had the religion forced on him. But he went to temple, and he put himself through the motions like most of the Imperial aristocracy. Claver, on the other hand, was young enough to have known no other religion. A true believer. Such men had their uses, but more often than not their inflexibility made them dangerous.

"The Empire requires that you practise the teachings of the Nema Creed. The law allows for nothing else," Vonvalt said.

"If I refuse?"

Vonvalt drew himself up. "If you refuse you become a heretic. If you refuse to *me* you become an avowed heretic. But you won't do something as silly and wasteful as that."

"And what is the punishment for avowed heresy?" Sir Otmar asked, though he knew the answer.

"You will be burned." It was Claver who spoke. There was savage glee in his voice.

"No one will be burned," Vonvalt said irritably, "because no one is an avowed heretic. Yet."

I looked back and forth between Vonvalt and Sir Otmar. I had sympathy for Sir Otmar's position. He was right to say that Draedism was harmless, and right to disrespect the Nema Creed as worthless. Furthermore, he was an old man, being lectured and threatened with death. But the fact of the matter was, the Sovan Empire ruled the Tolsburg Marches. Their laws applied, and, actually, their laws were robust and fairly applied. Most everyone else got on with it, so why couldn't he?

Sir Otmar seemed to sag slightly.

"There is an old watchtower on Gabler's Mount, a few hours' ride north-east of here. The Draedists gather there to worship. You will find your witch there."

Vonvalt paused for a moment. He took a long draw of ale. Then he carefully set the tankard down.

"Thank you," he said, and stood. "We'll go there now, while there is an hour or two of daylight left."

II

Pagan Fire

*"The vainglorious and boastful initiates
should be weeded out of the Order at the
earliest opportunity. To be a Justice is to
be a patient and rigorous administrator of
the law. Tales of swordfights and horseback
chases, while loosely rooted in fact, are to be
discouraged and dismissed as rumour."*

MASTER KARL ROTHSINGER

Within a few minutes we were back outside in the cold and
rain while a lad fetched our horses. Then we rode on into the
fading light. I pulled my waxed cloak around me, trying to keep
the worst of the rain off my clothes, but neither Bressinger nor
Vonvalt seemed to be bothered by it. Claver, hunched in his
saddle, looked bedraggled and wretched, but he was clearly
savouring the prospect of frightening the local pagans.

In spite of what Sir Otmar had said, we did not make for

Gabler's Mount. Instead Vonvalt took us directly into the woods, down an old huntsman's path half-lost under the ferns.

"Sir Konrad?" I said. My voice sounded meek and aristocratic, and I hated myself in that moment. Despite years of hard travelling, I had still grown soft. Gone was the feral refugee growing up on the streets of Muldau. I was turning into one of the nobles I had despised for so long.

He turned. The black beard which he wore in the colder months of the year glistened with rainwater.

"What is it?" he asked. His horse, a big Guelan war destrier called Vincento, plodded to a halt.

"Isn't Gabler's Mount to the north-east? This is north-west."

Vonvalt nodded. "I know," he said.

"The old man was lying," Bressinger said. "Sending us off in the wrong direction."

"Doubtless to be ambushed." Claver sneered.

"Oh, I don't think so," Vonvalt said mildly. "Misdirection, rather than murder. He hasn't had the time – and certainly doesn't have the gall – to organise anything like that. No." He gestured to the ancient, mossy trees. "The Witch of Rill is in these woods."

We moved on, into that groaning, hundred-mile forest. The last of the light had long drained from the sky. I shivered as the cold sought out my damp clothes and sapped the last of the heat from my bones. I was desperate for a fire for some warmth – or, more importantly, light – when my silent prayers were answered. Ahead, perhaps a quarter of a mile away, was a flicker of orange.

Vonvalt and Bressinger were talking in low voices ahead, so I called out to Claver instead. "Did you see that light?" I asked.

"I saw it," he said, and sneered. "Pagan fire. Draedists have always been drawn to its corrupting influence. They dance around it like lunatics. 'Tis a shabby practice."

I could see people moving around the fire as we approached. Vonvalt made no attempt to conceal himself or otherwise approach subtly. Instead he rode on with purpose. I could see now that there were maybe fifteen or twenty peasants encircling the fire, which itself burned in the centre of a small glade. Near the fire was a stone altar which was sheltered by the overhanging branches of a nearby tree. Behind the altar was the witch, an elderly woman wearing a crude wooden mask and some dark, threadbare robes. She stood so motionless that I thought in those first few moments that she might be a statue.

"Madame witch," Vonvalt called to the woman. "Kindly remove your mask."

Screams penetrated the chilly night air. The pagans whirled to face us with expressions of exaggerated shock. Whatever ritualistic dancing had been going on before was brought to a sudden, dramatic stop.

I thought that the witch would defy Vonvalt, but she brought her hands up to the wooden mask and removed it, and set it carefully down on the altar. I had half been expecting the mask to conceal a monster's face, or at the very least someone grotesquely disfigured, but I was simultaneously disappointed and relieved to see that she was simply a regular old woman. Her expression was neutral as she eyed us. It was in that delicate moment of inaction that Claver decided to assert his religious credentials.

"You desecrate the Creed of Nema!" he erupted. No one had been paying the holy man much attention, but now he had a glut of it.

Vonvalt whirled about in his saddle, his expression thunderous.

"That's quite enough, Patria," he snapped.

"Justice Vonvalt, these people are heretics!" Claver continued, genuinely baffled. He exercised himself into a fury. "Avowed apostates! Look at this pagan nonsense! This cultish ritual! It makes a mockery of the laws of Sova!"

"I, and I alone, will decide what makes a mockery of the laws of Sova," Vonvalt said. His tone was as cold as the evening air. "Kindly be quiet, or I will have Bressinger take you back to Rill." He turned back to the peasants and gestured to the fire. "You all know it is illegal to practise Draedism," he said. "The law is clear."

"How did you find us?" the old woman asked. Her reserve had hardened to defiance. It heartened her flock. I watched their bodies subtly recalibrate from flight to fight.

"It is the eve of the month of Goss," Vonvalt said. He pointed to a break in the clouds, where the moon waned to a thin crescent.

"We do not recognise the Imperial calendar," the old woman said.

"But the Book of Lorn demands this . . . " Vonvalt gestured to the fire " . . . ceremony on the eve of Goss, yes? The fire of Culvar burns and by its light and heat the Trickster is banished."

"You use the names of the false saints. The saints of the Autun. The Book of Lorn is a simulacrum of the Book of Draeda. A poor one at that."

"But the ritual is identical," Vonvalt remarked, as if he might convert her on the spot. He shrugged. "In any event, it is how I found you."

A stand-off ensued. The old woman would not – could not – fold and abandon her beliefs simply because Vonvalt had told her what she was doing was illegal. She knew it was illegal. And of course, Vonvalt was bound by his oaths and the law to prosecute her – but he, too, was unwilling to do so.

"Sir Otmar has already agreed to pay your fine," Vonvalt said eventually. "Simply renounce Draedism and I will leave you all in peace. No one need die here tonight."

"Otmar would never renounce his beliefs," the old woman said harshly.

Claver exploded. "You damn him with your words! He is a Draedist!"

"Be quiet!" Vonvalt snapped.

"This whole village should be burned to the ground and its heretic peasants along with it!"

"Nema's blood, man, will you shut up!" Vonvalt shouted. "Dubine, get him out of here."

"With pleasure, sire," Bressinger said, and pulled his horse – a large brown courser called Gaerwyn – around.

"I do the Goddess's work!" Claver shouted. "Do not touch me! I will see Nema's work done here!".

Bressinger pulled up alongside the priest and snatched the reins from his hands, leading the horse away back down the huntsman's path. I half-expected Claver to dismount and charge back into the fray. Instead, faced with Bressinger's unshakeable impassivity, the priest lapsed to silence.

Vonvalt turned back to the old woman. "You are Sir Otmar's wife," he said.

"Lady Karol Frost."

"My lady, are you aware of the consequences – the consequences which the law forces me to put in motion – if you refuse to renounce Draedism?"

"I am aware."

"You would consign yourself to death?"

"I would."

"You would consign these people to death?"

"Every man and woman here can make their own decision."

Vonvalt sighed, annoyed. He was about to speak again when something remarkable happened: the wooden mask began to rise up off the altar and levitate in the air.

I shrieked. The peasants gasped. The mask, an ugly, rough-hewn thing, rose smoothly and stopped a fathom above the altar. It hung there, the firelight dancing off its features, watching proceedings with an unmistakable hostility.

Everyone froze. For a few moments I was unable to catch my breath. The old pagan gods, furious at this Imperial interruption, were here in the glade. A horrible sense of vertigo washed through me. Murderers, thieves and rapists, Vonvalt could deal with; the wrath of the elementals, he could not.

Vonvalt pulled his short-sword from its scabbard. The blade sang in the night air. Lady Frost screamed, for despite her stern comportment and staunch belief in the old gods, even she could not help but be terrified by the cold gleam of steel.

Immediately the closest peasants surged forwards, a trio of burly men who shouted and jabbered in the ancient Draedist tongue. They reached out with frantic, grasping fingers, trying to get to Vonvalt's leg to pull him down from his horse.

"Get back, damn you," Vonvalt said, more irritated than angry. Vincento reared up, front legs cycling. The big black destrier planted a hoof directly into the chest of one of the Draedists with enough power to crack his breastbone and sent him flying. A second pagan lost his left arm below the elbow to Vonvalt's sword. The idiot screamed, wide-eyed, and fell backwards, clutching the spurting stump.

The third Draedist was in the process of rethinking this ill-advised course of action entirely when Bressinger's horse battered him to the floor from the side. The man tumbled in between the creature's hooves, dazed and beaten, but not killed.

"*Stop this at once!*" Vonvalt roared. This time he used a hint of the Emperor's Voice, and immediately the commotion died away. Lady Frost remained by the altar. The three peasants who had attacked Vonvalt lay on the floor, groaning and whimpering. Bressinger was already dismounted and was tending in his rough and unsympathetic way to the man who had lost his lower arm. The other Draedists stood in a loose, horrified gaggle. Some way off, I was aware of Patria Claver, watching these sorry proceedings from where Bressinger had left him. After a little while the priest turned away and headed back to Rill. I wish with all my heart that I could say it was the last we saw of the man.

Vonvalt's face was a mask of displeasure as he surveyed the

scene. After a few moments, he gently urged Vincento over to the altar and stopped there. Then he whipped his sword through the air in a wide arc. The mask dropped out of the air, clattered off the old stone and fell unceremoniously into the mud below.

"Thread," Vonvalt said. "Black thread, anchored to a hidden pulley." He sheathed his sword with callous indifference.

The spell was broken. Whatever further mischief the peasants had been about to mount in the name of religious fervour died along with the illusion.

Lady Frost looked wretched. She began to sob. I didn't feel bad for her. It was a damnable thing to do, a spectacle which she had evidently planned for later on in the evening's festivities.

"Go back to your homes, now," Vonvalt said to the assembled pagans. "Every person here will come to me in the morning and renounce, or so help me it'll be the noose for the lot of you."

The peasants practically fell over themselves as they dispersed, scattering into the cold, dark woods.

"How is he, Dubine?" Vonvalt called down to Bressinger.

Bressinger shrugged. "With a decent surgeon he might live."

Vonvalt looked at Lady Karol. "You will arrange for this man's care," he said. "If he dies, I will hold you to account."

The woman nodded, her eyes flicking between the armless pagan and Vonvalt.

Vonvalt sighed and shook his head, then pulled Vincento around so that he was facing me. He absently patted the horse's neck. "Helena, back to Rill," he said quietly. "I want to prepare for court tomorrow morning. It's going to be a busy day."

⁓

We rose early the following morning. Again, it was cold and grey, and I wondered if the sun ever touched Rill.

We unloaded our equipment from the Duke of Brondsey's cart: ledgers, statute books, a quill and ink, fresh rolls of parchment, a collapsible trestle table, Vonvalt's wing-backed leather armchair, fresh wax and stamps, a shield-sized device of the Sovan Empire mounted on a five-foot pole, and various warrants of office that people were entitled to inspect. We set them up in the centre of the public square.

The village slowly rose with the sun, and the smell of cook fires filled the cold air. For most of the peasants, breakfast would be a thick porridge flavoured with whatever was to hand, and a mug of ale, though there was a distinct smell of frying bacon emanating from the Frosts' manor. Vonvalt, Bressinger and I had eaten a few cold crusts of pie in the inn, and my stomach was already growling.

"Our friend the priest left, then?" Vonvalt asked as he settled himself into his armchair. I sat on a small stool next to him. As his clerk, my job was to take down a note of what was said during proceedings.

"Aye," Bressinger replied from his right. "Some time in the night, though not before giving me an earful."

"Thank you for not waking me."

"He is not happy with the way you are dealing with the Draedists."

"It is not his business to be happy about it."

Bressinger gave Vonvalt a reproachful look. "His interest in it was unnaturally keen."

"His interest in the entirety of my affairs has been unnaturally keen since he joined us. I am glad to see the back of him. The only thing that vexes me is that he did not leave us earlier. He is clearly capable of travelling alone."

"You do not think it odd?" Bressinger said.

"Of course I thought it odd. But the man is odd." Vonvalt shrugged. "I expect he will beat us to Seaguard, then? Off to persuade the margrave and his men to part with their lives on the Frontier."

"I expect so."

"He is a fool, Dubine. Put him from your mind."

"A dangerous fool."

"Indeed."

"And with powerful friends, if he is to be believed."

"*If* he is to be believed," Vonvalt said. He was about to say more when the day's first customer approached the table, a peasant of middling age, wearing rough homespun clothes and a wool cap. He shuffled over to Vonvalt, intimidated by our little temporary court, though to me it looked very shabby.

"I'd, uh," he started, and then snatched off his cap. "By your leave, my lord, I'd, uh, like to . . . " He leant in close. Vonvalt, with infinite patience, for he was on official duty now, bent forwards accommodatingly. "I'd like to, uh . . . renounce?"

Vonvalt nodded sagely. "I accept the renunciation." He opened one of the heavy ledgers and began writing. He took and noted the man's details. In the margin, he wrote the fine, which was a penny and which he would collect from Sir Otmar. "Do you have any grievances for the Emperor?"

The man shook his head vigorously. "No, my lord, nothing."

Vonvalt nodded again. "Then that is everything."

It went much the same with the remaining villagers. One by one, those we had seen in the forest – and some others, too – approached us and quietly renounced. It was the only business of the day. Usually we dealt with all sorts, especially since it had been years since the last Imperial Justice had passed through. There were always thefts and assaults to deal with, as well as more serious crimes – murders, rapes, treason. But on that cold, wintry day in Rill, there was only the quiet rejection of pagan faith.

Vonvalt closed his ledgers for lunch and sent me off to get him and Bressinger some bread, cheese and ale from the inn. When I returned, I was stunned to see Lord and Lady Frost standing in front of the table. Sir Otmar had a bag of coins in his hand. I hurried back in time to hear the last of the charges Vonvalt had decided to indict them with: incitement to blasphemy.

"We're not guilty of the charge," Lady Frost said in that sneering way aristocrats – even minor ones – do. "We pay the fine only to protect our people."

I sat back on my stool and began to furiously scribble the words down.

Vonvalt took the bag of coin from Sir Otmar and passed it to Bressinger, who began to count them.

"I will make a note that the next Justice to pass through Rill should find a shrine to Nema. Somewhere *prominent*," Vonvalt said dourly.

"And how exactly shall we do that?" Lady Frost asked.

Vonvalt nodded towards the woods. "There are plenty of deer in those woods. Send a hunter today. Keep the skull. Have it blessed by a priest. Fashion an altar in the Imperial style. It is very simple."

Bressinger finished counting the coins. "There's five marks here if there's a groat," he said quietly.

Vonvalt looked at the Frosts. There was a long silence. "The fine is a penny per blasphemer," he said. "Or would you like me to add a charge of attempted bribery to this ledger, too?"

Sir Otmar, reddening, snatched back a handful of the coins. His wife cuffed him sharply.

"Fool," she muttered, and stalked off.

Once she was out of earshot, and the correct fine had been paid and stored away carefully in our strongbox, Vonvalt addressed Sir Otmar.

"Sir Otmar, I like to think I am a fair man. The Empire grants me a great deal of discretion in dealing with matters such as this." He paused, thinking of the right words. "I hope you realise that this could have gone very differently. A different Justice on a different day ... " He let the words hang. Sir Otmar, who had half the fire of his wife, nodded meekly.

"I know, my lord. I am indebted to you."

Vonvalt waved him off. "I am not a fool, Sir Otmar. I know full well what will happen when I leave this place. What I am telling you is, you must be more careful."

"I appreciate the candour, my lord," Sir Otmar said, and bowed.

We watched him go in silence. Then, when it was apparent that the day's business was done, Vonvalt closed the ledger.

"I have a bad feeling about this place," he muttered, and stood. "A bad feeling indeed."

III

Galen's Vale

*"With the crime of murder, one must be sure of the
security of the conviction before the sentence – that
of execution – is carried out. To take a life is severe;
to take a second in recompense is doubly so."*

FROM CATERHAUSER'S THE SOVAN CRIMINAL
CODE: ADVICE TO PRACTITIONERS

The rider found us a few miles outside of Galen's Vale, a large
and wealthy merchant town in the Southmark of Haunersheim –
being the country that lay to the east and south of my native
Tolsburg. Rill was now a distant memory, several hundreds
of miles, two handfuls of towns and a month and a half of
travel away.

The air was colder and drier down here than it had been in
the shadow of the Tolsburg Marches, and swirled with flakes of
snow. Bressinger had tried to lift our spirits with an old Jägelander
folk song he must have learnt off Vonvalt, but I couldn't join in

because I didn't understand the words – he sang neither in Old Saxan, being the common dialect of the Empire, nor Tollish, my native tongue – and Vonvalt didn't join in because he was prone to silence on these long journeys. He sat hunched in his saddle at the head of our caravan.

The rider was a young lad of the town watch, muscular and full of cocky self-regard. I was immediately self-conscious of my shabby appearance, hunched as I was under my waxed cloak and smelling like the Duke of Brondsey. In the event, I needn't have troubled myself; he didn't spare me a second glance.

"Lord Sauter said there was a Justice coming down the Hauner road," I heard him call out to Vonvalt. He wore a mail hauberk and coif that framed a face ruddy from the cold, and was capped with a kettle helm. His surcoat was blue crossed with mustard-yellow and embroidered with the Galen's Vale device.

"Justice Sir Konrad Vonvalt," he said, no longer bent over in the saddle. "This is my taskman, Dubine Bressinger, and my clerk, Helena Sedanka."

The guardsman touched his helmet. He looked distressed. "Sires. Miss." My heart leapt as he briefly locked eyes with me. "Your timing is opportune. There's been a murder, not two days ago. Lord Bauer's wife. Half the town is up in arms."

"And the other half?" Bressinger murmured to me.

"Be silent," Vonvalt snapped. He turned back to the lad. "It is a rare thing for a lord's wife to be killed."

"'Tis unheard of in the Vale, sire. And neither hair nor hide of an explanation."

"It was not Lord Bauer?" Vonvalt asked. It was a fair question. It was normally the husband.

"As far as I know, the man is not under suspicion."

"I see," Vonvalt said, rubbing his chin. "Strange."

"Aye, sire, 'tis that. When we saw your caravan from the Veldelin Gate, Lord Sauter commanded me to escort you in with all haste."

Vonvalt turned back to me, and briefly took in the sorry bedraggled sight that I was. The Duke of Brondsey snorted and hee-hawed behind me, trembling with the cold.

"I will ride ahead with you," Vonvalt said to the watchman, then turned to Bressinger. "Dubine, take Helena into town. See the horses are stabled and sort our lodgings."

"Sire."

"Where is the body of Lady Bauer?" Vonvalt asked the lad.

"In a physician's house – Mr Maquerink. He attends to official medical matters."

"I will see the body first, before it ripens too much for anything useful to be deduced."

"As you wish."

They sped away ahead, their horses kicked to a canter. I watched them go.

Bressinger turned his horse and covered the gap between us. He must have been able to read my mind, because he said, "A boy like that is no good for you, Helena."

My face flushed. "What are you talking about?" I asked hotly.

Bressinger smirked. "We'd best get moving before the weather closes. Remember what I taught you about cloudreading?"

I nodded to a bank of low, dark clouds to the east. "Snow," I said, sulking.

"Come on then. And this time join in with my singing."

"I don't know Jägen," I said.

Bressinger paused with such deliberate drama that I had to laugh. "Nema's blood, Helena, you're as deaf as a timber. That wasn't Jägen; it was Grozodan. I hope you're not confusing my country of birth with that of our esteemed master."

"No," I said, chortling away. "Not with a poncy name like Dubine, anyway." I deliberately pronounced it the way Vonvalt pronounced it, Du-ban, rather than the way everyone else did outside of Bressinger's native Grozoda, Du-bine.

"I'll cut that tongue out of your head if you don't mind it," he said. "Now, listen in, or the next couple of miles are going to go very slowly indeed."

✍

We arrived at the town itself at midday, entering through the Veldelin Gate, which watched the southern approach. Galen's Vale was in Haunersheim, though Tolsburg and Guelich had both tried to claim it over the course of its tumultuous history. It was a town that was very much a product of its location, both geographically and politically. Guelich, after all, was the realm of Prince Gordan Kzosic, the Emperor's third son, and any large town within striking distance of a royal invariably functioned as both a fortress and a temporary palace.

It was a large walled town, built into the slopes of the Tolsburg Marches and cut in two by the River Gale. The surrounding foothills, long and shallow tracts of green, were fertile and well cultivated, and produced enough cabbages, peas, broad beans, onions and potatoes to feed the town and generate a trade surplus – though that was not the real source of the place's wealth. The River Gale was both wide and deep, and ran all the way to Sova itself, albeit circuitously. It made Galen's Vale a busy trading hub, and generated enough in merchant tax revenue to provide for a decent town watch, well-kept and patrolled roads, a large temple to Nema the God Mother (that had once been a temple to Irox, the bovine pagan god) and an impressive, fortress-like kloster that occupied a commanding position further up the hill.

The streets thronged with merchant traders, guildsmen, watchmen, commonfolk, lords and ladies. We picked our way through them, anonymous even as we sat high above them on our horses. I noticed that the ground was cobbled for the most part, though still muddy, and the roads had closed shit-ditches, one of the better Sovan imports that was yet to reach much of the outer Empire. Fortunately the cold, as it had in Rill, helped keep the smell to a minimum, though the familiar stench of woodsmoke, piss, offal and shit still managed to pervade the air.

The town's buildings ranged from thatched daub cottages to towering brick-and-timber town houses. The temples, of which there were dozens, were rendered in large yellowing blocks of stone, stained by generations of woodsmoke and festooned with crude idols. Flowers and other trinkets lay scattered about their steps, most trampled into muddy oblivion. Beggars wailed into the cold air, refused alms and sanctuary in equal measure.

By virtue of his position, Vonvalt was entitled to be hosted by the town's most senior councilman. This was usually the mayor or the local justice of the peace, but could often be the town's most senior priest, or some other lord or knight. Without express instructions as to where to take up lodgings, Bressinger decided to make for Mayor Sauter's residence, which turned out to be a huge brick town house with attractive timber framing.

"Think this'll do," he said gruffly as we pulled our horses to a stop outside its iron gates. We both dismounted, and Bressinger approached the guardsman posted by the entrance.

"Yes?" the guard asked in a manner befitting his trade. He was clad in the same armour and surcoat as the other town watchman had been.

"I am Dubine Bressinger," he said. "This is Helena Sedanka. We are employees and associates of Justice Sir Konrad Vonvalt." Bressinger showed the man his Imperial seal.

"Ah, yes, sire," the guard said, bowing. "We've been told to expect you. I'll have the boy take your horses and mule. Are you both well?"

"We're fine, thank you. We're looking for the town physician's residence," Bressinger said.

"There's more than one, though I suspect you're after Mr Maquerink," the guard said. He pointed back the way we had come. "Apothecary Street. Two roads down, on your right. You'll see the signage easily enough."

"Thank you," Bressinger said. The ostler, a filthy boy redolent of horse shit, appeared and began to lead our animals away.

"Lord Sauter said you were to be provided with victuals on arrival," the guard called after us uncertainly. "Will you not take some food or wine?"

"Later, thank you," Bressinger said. I felt my spirits sink. My stomach felt as empty as a sacked granary.

"As you will," the guard said, nodding, and we made our way on saddle-sore legs to find where Vonvalt had got to.

❧

The physician lived a comfortable existence on Apothecary Street, surrounded by other learned medical men, barber surgeons and astronomers. The road here was cobbled, too, but not rutted like the traders' roads that branched off from the market square. Mr Maquerink's house was marked out by a large wooden sign daubed with a blue star, which was the common Imperial mark for a licensed physician. Bressinger pushed his way in to the front room, where the smell of blood and death hung heavy in the air. Through the translucent windows at the back of the house I could hear wild pigs rootling through the physician's trade waste.

"Dubine?" Vonvalt called from somewhere below. We both turned to our right and saw a staircase descending into the bowels of the residence.

"Sire," Bressinger called back.

"Come downstairs."

We obliged, and found ourselves in a single large room which spanned the length of the house. A number of stained trestles were lined up, with more stacked against the walls. Candles – wax, not tallow – burned with a herbal scent that was completely powerless against the smell of decay. Vonvalt and the physician were stood next to the only occupied trestle at the far end of the room, the former with a kerchief of lavender pressed to his nose.

"Mr Maquerink has just been explaining to me how the body was found," Vonvalt said as we approached.

"Yes, well, Tom Bevitt's boy found her by the Segamund Gate outflow, caught on a sunken root," the physician said. He was a stooped old man, grey-haired and moustached. It was as though a lifetime of caring for others had drained his own life force. He was beggar-gaunt, a far cry from the plump physicians and apothecaries I'd seen before. "'Tis a miracle in itself; the undertow is powerful. Few things that enter the Gale are seen again."

"Who did he tell?" Vonvalt asked.

"He didn't need to tell anyone. The screaming raised half the eastern closure. The town watchmen fished her out. Brought her here."

"And no one has touched the body?"

"No one, milord. Save myself, of course, but that was just to arrange her." He gestured. "And to take a look at that wound."

I looked where the physician pointed, compelled by morbid curiosity. Not that the sight of a corpse particularly fazed me; I was an orphan of the Reichskrieg, after all, well-acquainted with the sight of the dead. Although Tolsburg was vassalised by the Sovans before I was born, it wasn't until I was perhaps ten that the after-effects of the war – the shortages of food, the infighting, the last of the uprisings – had calmed down enough that some semblance of normal life could resume. There had been plenty of fighting and death to go around in those early years of my life, and that was not just in Tolsburg. In my nearly two decades, three large countries – the kingdom of Venland, and the duchies of Denholtz and Kòvosk – had all been tamed by the Sovan Legions. Taking into account Vonvalt's native Jägeland, which sat to the west of Tolsburg, and Bressinger's native Grozoda to the south, both absorbed thirty years before when those men were adolescents, as well as the original Sovan territories – Sova, Kzosic Principality, Estre and Guelich – it was the largest the Empire would ever be, with nearly a hundred million Imperial subjects living under the watchful eyes of the Two-Headed Wolf.

The woman on the table was probably in her early forties, death-grey and clad in a green dress with expensive cloth-of-gold piping. The water that she had been fished from had not been kind to her remains, but even my unpractised eye could tell she hadn't drowned.

"That's a serious blow," Bressinger remarked, "and not with a bladed edge."

"You have a good eye for corpses," the physician said. I watched Bressinger and Vonvalt exchange a brief look.

"Quite," Vonvalt said dourly.

We all stood in silence for a few moments.

"Who is the sheriff?" Vonvalt asked.

"That would be Sir Radomir Dragić," the physician said.

"He knows of this?" Vonvalt asked.

"Of course," the physician said. "All of Galen's Vale knows about it. Lord Bauer is a well-known man; his wife was well-liked."

"Is Lord Bauer popular?"

The physician hesitated. "Well-known," he confirmed.

"And what is the sheriff's reputation?"

"An effective lawman, though as sour a man as you are ever like to meet – and a drunkard to boot."

"I am yet to meet an effective lawman who was not so," Vonvalt remarked as he edged closer to the corpse. I saw how he was careful not to get close enough to contract a pox. Corpses were known to exude noxious vapours in the same way a fire emits smoke.

"A single blow to the side of the head," he murmured. "Applied with some considerable force."

"Yes, milord," the physician said. "A killing blow for certain. Look how the skin has split and parted, and the skull has broken. A club or some other blunt weapon, wielded by a strong arm."

"How can you tell it was not done with a blade?" Vonvalt asked.

It was a question he certainly knew the answer to. He was simply testing the old physician.

Mr Maquerink gestured to the wound with his index finger. "A sword or axe would have cut the skull as surely as the skin, and with a clean incision. This has been smashed like a block of granite. You can see from the pattern of the fractures in the bone, and the way the skin is burst open, rather than hewn."

"You have experience of such wounds?"

"You'll be hard-pressed to find any medical man in Galen's Vale who has not had first-hand experience of such, thanks to the Reichskrieg."

Vonvalt nodded. We all stood looking at the corpse, as if staring at it for long enough would yield up its secrets. But it was clear there was little more to be divined. Lady Bauer had been struck a vicious blow that had probably killed her outright. As the most senior Imperial lawman, it was within Vonvalt's gift to conduct the investigation, and subsequent trial, by the Sovan Law of Precedence.

"Is there anything else remarkable about the body?" Vonvalt asked quietly.

"Nothing, milord," the physician confirmed. He gestured again to the wound. "*Ve sama horivic.*"

It is as you see it. The words he spoke were High Saxan, the language of the governing classes, but it was a common enough phrase that no one needed a translation.

"Murder, then," Vonvalt said.

"Aye," Bressinger said quietly next to him.

Mr Maquerink looked nervously at Vonvalt. When he spoke, his voice was pregnant with worry. "Will you use . . . your power, on her? I've heard it said some Imperial Magistrates can converse with the dead."

Vonvalt eyed the corpse. He shook his head gently. "No," he said. He looked up and down the length of Lady Bauer's body, sadness in his eyes. "The body is too decayed. Dead too long."

He paused, thinking for a moment. "Stand back," he murmured, and everyone quickly obliged. He held out a hand, his fingers splayed, his arm pointing at Lady Bauer's head. His face took on a slightly pained aspect as he assessed the chances of a successful séance. After a few seconds, his hand dropped. "No. No, I will not even try it."

"Who knows what manner of things have their claws in her now," Bressinger muttered.

Vonvalt looked at him sharply. "Guard your tongue. That is not for bandying about."

Both Mr Maquerink and I exchanged a look of alarm. Before anything more could be said, Vonvalt spoke. "Thank you, Mr Maquerink," he said. He took a few steps back. "I am finished here. You may have the body prepared for consecration and burial."

"Aye, milord."

"You will write a report? To document your findings."

"Aye, milord."

"Very good. Dubine, where are we lodging?"

"With the mayor, sire."

Vonvalt turned back to the physician. "Will you have the report sent to me there?"

"As you wish."

Vonvalt took one last look at the body. There was a pause. "All right. We shall leave you be."

We left the physician's lodgings and stepped out into Apothecary Street. The clouds had drawn in since we had been inside the physician's house, as if our collective mood had pulled them down on top of us. They formed a low ceiling of grey, leaving the town in an uneasy twilight.

"I want to meet Sir Radomir," Vonvalt said, eyeing the clouds. He added, not entirely convincingly, "There is still plenty of daylight left."

"I'll warrant he's in the town watch house," Bressinger said. "We passed it on the way in, near the Veldelin Gate."

"I remember," Vonvalt said, nodding absently. "This way, then. Keep up, Helena!"

Vonvalt walked quickly. It was one of his habits. Given his powers, and his conspicuous bearing and badges of office, he tended to draw lots of attention. The Emperor's subjects were a superstitious mob, and we would almost always amass a following wherever we went. Some sought justice of a kind Vonvalt could not provide; others wanted him to channel his powers so that they could speak to lost loved ones. More still were simply caught in his thrall. Vonvalt exuded an otherworldly aura that some were more sensitive to than others. These people often formed a motley collection that trailed us like camp followers shadowing an army. They normally kept twenty or thirty paces back, shambling after us in various states of anxiety and catatonia. If we spent any length of time in a building we could expect to find various trinkets left on the threshold as offerings: flowers, candles, idols. Vonvalt had long since grown used to this; indeed, I'm not sure he even noticed it any more. For my own part, even after two years, I still found it disconcerting.

We were fortunate in that Galen's Vale was a merchant town, and that lords and moneyed men of business moved through the streets wearing all the trappings of wealth. It meant Vonvalt was less conspicuous than he might otherwise have been. Nonetheless, we walked with purpose.

The watch house was in the southern closure. Galen's Vale, like most other towns in the Empire, was segregated along traditional guild lines. The watch house was in the district given over to the maintenance of law and order, which meant that it shared a street with the courthouse and the town gaol. It was a two-storey building, framed with old black timbers and fronted by an extravagant number of latticed windows. A pair of large chimneys belched black smoke into the frigid air. In front was a stockade, currently unoccupied thanks to the Wintertide amnesty.

We passed a haggard and miserable-looking guard standing by

the front door, and entered. Vonvalt immediately strode to the front desk, jolting a bored serjeant out of his reverie.

"I am Justice Sir Konrad Vonvalt of the Imperial Magistratum," he announced.

"An E-Emperor's Justice?" the serjeant stuttered, touching his forehead. The man's jaw worked for a few moments in silent excruciation. "I-I'd heard rumours but I didn't believe it. We've not had a Magistrate here for years. You've come down by the old Hauner road?"

Vonvalt grunted. "I want to speak to Sir Radomir."

"Y-yes, of course," the serjeant said. "I'll have one of the lads fetch him."

"No need," Vonvalt said. "He is upstairs?"

The serjeant swallowed. "Top floor, milord." He looked uncomfortable. "He's . . . not a man who will take well to being interrupted. May be best if I have you announced."

Vonvalt smiled thinly. "I shouldn't worry, serjeant," Vonvalt said. "He will not mind being troubled by me."

We walked up the creaking stairs. Candles lit the way, dozens of them – some wax, most tallow. Given I was clad in heavy woollen clothes and a thick cloak, I soon began to sweat. Sir Radomir's chambers were on the top floor, easily identified by the "Sheriff" painted on the door in Saxan. Vonvalt rapped sharply on it.

"I said I was not to be disturbed," came a severe voice from beyond.

"Open this door in the name of the Emperor," Vonvalt said loudly.

I heard a muffled "Nema's blood," then footsteps. A bolt was withdrawn, and the door pulled open. Air, rank with alcohol fumes and carried on fire-heated air, gusted out.

"You must be the Justice we've all heard so much about," Sir Radomir sneered. He was a tall man, as tall as Vonvalt, with stern, gaunt features and cropped, greying hair. His face was marred with a livid wine-stain birthmark. He wore white breeches and a blue-and-yellow doublet, and a small dagger was strapped about his waist.

"I am," Vonvalt remarked. His face was a mask of distaste.

"Lord Sauter has hurried you into the town, I see."

"He has."

There was a pause.

"I am a busy man, Justice," Sir Radomir said impatiently.

"Then it is just as well that I do not require a great deal of your time."

Another pause. Sir Radomir's hands were as bound as anyone else who faced off against an Imperial Justice – but, as with many others, that did not mean he had to like it. And, like everyone else, he was wary of Vonvalt's powers. Even in somewhere as metropolitan as Galen's Vale, it was hard to completely rise above the old wives' tales and silly peasant rumours that followed Justices everywhere like a cloud of noxious vapour.

"Who are these two?" Sir Radomir asked, indicating us with his chin.

"This is my taskman, Dubine Bressinger, and my clerk, Helena Sedanka."

"A Grozodan and a Toll," the sheriff said with a sneer.

"What of it?" Vonvalt asked sharply.

Sir Radomir jabbed a thumb at his own chest. "I fought the Tolls for two years in the Marches."

Vonvalt made a show of looking down at me, then back to the sheriff. "My clerk wasn't born when the Reichskrieg reached Muldau, Sir Radomir. Or is it in your nature to fear nineteen-year-old girls?"

The sheriff shrugged, not taking the barb.

"Sir Radomir," Vonvalt said through his teeth. "I appreciate that my presence in Galen's Vale may not be welcome. But I am here to see justice done, as surely as you yourself."

Sir Radomir sighed theatrically. He dallied for a further few moments before relenting. "I suppose you'd better come in then – before you let all the heat out."

We followed the man into his chamber. It was surprisingly well-appointed, with expensive-looking wooden furniture, a large, only slightly mouldy rug, and a cast-iron fireplace where a large log fire burned. The fittings did not suit Sir Radomir, who looked like he had come from very humble beginnings. I wondered what his story was, and how he had come to be ennobled.

We decloaked in the fierce heat and sat before the desk, opposite Sir Radomir himself.

"Lord Sauter has tied himself up in knots about Lady Bauer's death," the sheriff said. He gestured to a pair of pewter tankards in front of us, though there was wine on the desk. "Will you take some ale?"

"We're fine," Vonvalt said. "Was Lord Sauter close to the Bauers?"

"Lord Sauter is close to those who would make him wealthy," the sheriff said, though he appeared to regret his candour. "Which would explain how he was able to spend any time with Lady Bauer. She was poor company for sure." He sighed again, picked up his goblet and took a long draw of wine. "I will speak plainly with you, Justice."

"I fear you already have," Vonvalt said.

"She used to be a fine woman. Then she lost her son to a pox and her daughter to the kloster and she changed. Her mind changed. She was melancholic and ill-tempered. People will say kind things about her now that she is dead, but by Nema was she sour."

Bressinger stirred. Vonvalt spoke quickly.

"Losing a child is a cruel thing to endure," he said. "Arguably the cruellest. You cannot fault her that."

"I know that," Sir Radomir replied dismissively. "This was different. I don't know. It did not seem to be just that. She was preoccupied, and not solely with grief."

"What do you mean?"

Sir Radomir thought for a moment. "No. I do not know. Call

it a lawman's intuition. I never got to the bottom of it. Probably never will, now she is dead." He sighed mightily. "'Tis no good for a lady to be murdered – I realise that is as obvious a statement as you're ever likely to hear."

Vonvalt inclined his head. "I take the point."

"Half the town is up in arms. The commonfolk die or are killed frequently, of course – it is normal in a place such as this. But a lord's wife . . . this news will reach Baron Naumov in Roundstone, if it hasn't already. Perhaps beyond. If it crosses the Guelan border and reaches the Prince's ears, we'll be in real trouble. Last thing I want is a royal snout rootling about the town. Nema knows we have enough wild pigs off Apothecary Street."

"You would do well to guard your tongue," Vonvalt said sharply, but the sheriff waved him off, unfazed. Vonvalt pursed his lips. "What more do you know? Have you spoken with Lord Bauer?"

Sir Radomir gave Vonvalt a sour look. "I've been keeping order in Galen's Vale for ten years, Justice. Yes, I have spoken to Lord Bauer."

"What has he said?"

Sir Radomir took another long draw of wine. His lips glistened in the firelight as he set the goblet down. "The man was convinced a business rival is responsible for the crime."

"Is that so?"

"It is."

"He has named the man?"

"He has."

Vonvalt cleared his throat, as he sometimes did when he was trying to control his temper. "Sir Radomir, I would assist you with this matter."

"Justice, the Emperor already has a faithful subject right here in the Vale capable of investigating this matter. That subject is myself."

"I might have guessed."

"I do not like being usurped."

"Do not exaggerate. You are not being 'usurped'," Vonvalt said. "The Law of Precedence accords me the right to take over the investigation. It is a matter of legal administration, not an indictment of your abilities."

"I am still not happy."

"Few ever are, Sir Radomir; take solace from the fact that, like all others before you, you have no choice in the matter. I can present you with my warrants of office if you so wish."

Sir Radomir grimaced. I had not seen a lawman so unhappy to release a case before. Many were pleased to be rid of the burden of investigative work, much of which was thankless and, ultimately, fruitless.

"I would have you assist me closely," Vonvalt said. "You are clearly a man who takes pride in his work. I have no desire to make an enemy of you."

"You will share the credit? If we find the man?"

"And accept sole responsibility should the investigation fail."

"That is a rare concession."

"I am not a vain man, Sir Radomir. I am only interested in seeing justice done."

Sir Radomir eyed Vonvalt, wrong-footed.

"We shall see."

"Tell me the name of the man, Sheriff. I'll not ask again."

"Zoran Vogt," Sir Radomir said. "Bauer's business rival. The pair have a long history. They are like squabbling children."

"A criminal history?"

"I have suspected the pair of them of misdeeds in the past, but I have not been able to prove anything. Many use the Gale for illicit trading. The river flows to Sova itself."

"They work together?"

"Apparently, though you'd not know it from the way they carry on. They are all alike, these new lords. 'Merchant princes', people call them. They or their fathers profiteered from the Reichskrieg and earned themselves knighthoods in the process. Now they consider themselves above the law."

"*De jura nietra iznia*," Vonvalt murmured in High Saxan.

"'No one is above the law'," Sir Radomir said. "Do you seek to impress me with your grasp of courtly language, Sir Konrad?"

"*Enough!*" Vonvalt snapped, his voice booming through the room like a thunderclap. I looked sharply at him. He had used the Emperor's Voice, or a hint of it. Bressinger looked alarmed. Sir Radomir visibly blanched. His throat worked for a second as he tried to speak. His eyes widened as he cast them about the room, visibly panicked that he seemed to have lost the power of speech. He looked for all the world like a man who has just realised he is drowning.

"Nema's blood, Justice," the man rasped after a few moments. He absently pressed a hand to his heart, and steadied himself with the other against the table. "Faith, that is quite a power."

"And one I seldom have cause to use," Vonvalt said, his voice steel. "I am tired, Sir Radomir, and I am not a little weary of your insolence. I have given you all the slack I am prepared to, given you are clearly a man who champions the cause of justice. But I will not brook further disrespect. I have told you I am here to assist. A woman, a lady, no less, has been murdered. You would do well to remember that. I am not your enemy here."

Sir Radomir took a few moments to gather himself, which largely involved several large mouthfuls of wine. He refilled his goblet and set it down.

"What else would you like to know?" he asked, his voice a little hoarser.

"Tell me about Bauer and Vogt's relationship. You say they have a history?"

Sir Radomir nodded. "Vogt filed a report with us a few years ago. He complained that Lord Bauer had deliberately sabotaged a large shipment of grain that he was sending downriver. Vogt had purchased the grain on credit; the loss of it left him in a precarious position."

"He has recovered?"

"He has. But he believes the incident cost him a knighthood, on top of a significant amount of coin." Sir Radomir snorted. "He may well be right."

Vonvalt thought for a moment. "But the complaint is a number of years old?"

"The incident with the grain shipment is certainly at least two years past. We keep records, per Imperial ordinances. I can have them retrieved from the archive."

"That would be helpful, thank you."

"Other than that, Lord Bauer cannot conceive of who would want his wife dead."

"Except perhaps Lord Bauer himself," Vonvalt said. "In my experience, where a woman is murdered, the blame often lies with her husband."

"Aye, that is my experience too. I have cautioned Lord Bauer that he has not escaped my suspicions. But for all I do not like the man, instinct tells me he did not commit the murder."

"No?" Vonvalt asked.

"As I said, Justice, I have kept order – or something approximating it – in Galen's Vale for ten years. I was a lawman up at Perry Ford before that, and I've been a soldier." He nodded to Bressinger. "You and your man here, you fought in the Reichskrieg?"

"We did," Vonvalt said.

"Then you will know what killing does to you. How it changes your mind. You cannot kill another human being and fail to be affected by it, even if they are an enemy. Lord Bauer may have a grim countenance, but he is no murderer. He hasn't the manner."

"I see," Vonvalt said. Despite their initial and mutual dislike, I could see Vonvalt was beginning to respect Sir Radomir.

"Of course, I do not have your powers," Sir Radomir said.

"No, but I find that professional instinct is often more than enough," Vonvalt said. "Did Lady Bauer have any enemies that you are aware of? Had she had an affair, perhaps? Or maybe she came across some information she shouldn't have?"

Sir Radomir shrugged. "If she did, not a whiff of it has crossed my desk. I have tasked my men to keep an ear to the ground, but..." He shrugged again. "... I confess, Justice, I am not hopeful. There is no explanation for it. It vexes me no end."

"I can well imagine," Vonvalt said absently. I could tell that already the matter was troubling him. He rose after a while. "That is all for now. Thank you for your time, Sheriff."

Sir Radomir stood. "'Tis no matter. I hope we can shed some light on it soon. I have not come across a killing like it in all my years as a lawman. Not even in Perry Ford were lords' wives killed."

"It is a rare enough thing in Sova itself, Sheriff," Vonvalt said, "and when it does happen, one cannot take two breaths before the culprit is turned out." He looked out the window. Darkness was closing in rapidly. He looked back to Sir Radomir. "Two days since Lady Bauer's murder and nothing to show but an overripe corpse. We must act quickly if we are to get to the bottom of this."

IV

Lord Bauer

"Only a Justice may compel a man to speak
where it is not in his interest to do so."

FROM CATERHAUSER'S PILLARS
OF SOVAN CIVIL LAW

We left the watch house and made our way to Lord Sauter's residence. The clouds had finally broken, and the air swirled with snow. I was grateful for the town's wealth, and its cobbles; wading through muddy slush with cold, soaked shoes was a miserable business.

"He's a hard man," I heard Bressinger say to Vonvalt.

Vonvalt grunted. "I did not care for his manner," he said, "and he is a sot to boot. But he speaks plainly. There is value in that."

We walked quickly through the cold. The market had closed at some point in the past hour and the streets had all but emptied, leaving only the odd watchman to amble across the cobbles. One challenged us as strangers; the rest recognised Vonvalt for what he was. By the time we reached Lord Sauter's residence, the light had all but faded and the temple bell was tolling, signalling the beginning of the curfew and the closing of the town's gates for the night.

"Sir Konrad," the guard said, stumbling to his feet as we approached the residence. It was fronted by a fence of wrought iron, the only entry a large gate secured by a pair of brick pillars. "Lord Sauter sends his regrets; he has been called away on an urgent matter and cannot attend you tonight. He has made arrangements for you to be taken care of in the meantime."

"Very well," Vonvalt said as we were admitted through the gate. I could tell he was secretly pleased; the idea of making polite conversation – or worse, talking shop – for another few hours was not a pleasant prospect. For Vonvalt it was wearying, but for me, a junior clerk who was expected to sit in silence but still look interested, it was almost fatally boring.

We were taken through the front door and shown into a large entrance hall. The interior of the house was as impressive as the exterior. What little light there was filtered through stained-glass windows, littering the floorboards with random spots of colour like flame flickering through a handful of jewels. The heat was almost oppressive and suggested a number of stoked hearths burning in multiple rooms. The walls were thick with tapestries and the floorboards were piled with rugs. The furniture looked expensive; indeed, some of it had clearly been imported from foreign lands, judging by its style. It was a house of ostentatious wealth.

We were shown by servants to quarters on the top floor. Vonvalt was given a large bedchamber with a dual aspect in the corner of the building. One window looked out over the river in the distance and the other down a wide guild street, though there wasn't much to see of either. The snow was falling thickly, and the darkness seemed to overwhelm the town's street lanterns as though it were black smoke.

Bressinger and I were given a room down the hall to share which was separated from Vonvalt's by another locked chamber. I was disappointed to see that there was only one bed in our chamber, though unsurprised; Bressinger and I had had to share in the past, and for all I liked the man, he was a loud and fidgety sleeper. In the event, he left to go whoring not long after we had arrived, and he did not return until the morning.

I was looking forward to a hot meal and then getting my head down for some sleep, but Vonvalt bade me join him in his room shortly after we had settled. My heart sank. Over the course of the past year I had grown increasingly weary of our lives on the road and disillusioned with my apprenticeship as a Justice's clerk. I was in no mood for one of our evening study sessions.

"Sit down, Helena," Vonvalt said as I entered his chamber, gesturing to a comfortable-looking armchair. Vonvalt, who had stripped out of his overcoat and jacket and now wore a simple shirt and breeches, was relaxed on a window seat, smoking his pipe. I knew that he would have arranged to have a bath prepared for later in the evening. He took every opportunity to wash that he could.

"What do you think?" he asked, looking out of the window.

"About what?" I asked. I was in too bad a mood to conceal my impudence.

A flash of irritation passed over Vonvalt's face. "About matters generally," he said. "Sir Radomir. Lord and Lady Bauer. Have you formed any preliminary views?"

I started to sigh, but stopped myself halfway through. Vonvalt was a patient man, but sighing – that was insolent. Even in my bad mood I recognised that. Still, like many before it, there was plenty of scope for this session to be long and dull. There was no precedent, no structure to follow; they varied in length and content. Sometimes they were lessons, in which Vonvalt would sit and teach me for an hour on subjects as diverse as jurisprudence, history and the Reichskrieg (though mercifully never mathematics, which he was no good at). Other times Vonvalt would seek to engage me in a debate, where I was invariably thrashed and left feeling hot with anger and resentment. Occasionally we simply conversed. Vonvalt was human, after all, and liked to be companionable once in a while.

My dislike of our learning sessions stemmed, I think, from two places. The first was that I was developing a genuine disinterest in Vonvalt's practice. I found much of it drudge work. Touring the fringes of the Empire turned up all manner of crimes, but almost all of it was petty and low-level. Anything that was more important or exciting Vonvalt tended to deal with entirely alone, on account of my inexperience and relative youth. And as an impertinent young woman, I resented this.

The second was something I did not realise until much later, and that was a fear of disappointing Vonvalt. He had saved me from a wretched existence on the streets of Muldau. I owed him everything, including my life. Since it was clear that he sought to mould me in his own image so that one day I might join the Order, I felt compelled to repay that faith with conscientiousness and diligence. When I considered that I had failed, I felt unworthy and reacted with bad grace, which in turn led to further resentment.

To look back now at how I felt and acted makes me feel ashamed, but – of course – I was just a girl. The young and inexperienced must be given their leeway.

"I think Lord Bauer killed his wife," I said flippantly. "What the sheriff says about Vogt being somehow responsible is a fantasy."

"You would deny Sir Radomir's instincts?"

I shrugged. "I did not put much stock in anything he said. The man is a bigot. You heard how he referred to me and Bressinger."

Vonvalt waved me off as though I were a cloud of pipe smoke. "Most people mistrust their next-door neighbours, let alone those from another country. As a Hauner, Sir Radomir is emblematic of the common Sovan. Our tolerance of other cultures and creeds remains the exception, not the rule – at least, this far outside of Sova."

"It doesn't mean it's acceptable." Being referred to as a Toll so dismissively had irked me more than I had realised. Vonvalt, in referring to me as an exception, was being far too generous in his assessment. He had been drafted into the Legions and killed fellow Jägelanders, and then Grozodans, and probably not a few Tolls before being taken in by the Order as an initiate, yet he did not let any of that cloud his judgment. To him, everyone was a Sovan, because everyone was subject to the common law. For me, while our work had shorn me of some of my bigotry, I still disliked Hauners like Sir Radomir and – Nema help me – Jägelanders like Vonvalt as much as the next Toll. After all, Jägeland, Haunersheim and Tolsburg had been at one another's throats for centuries before the Autun had pitched up. Hating one another was normal. It was hard not to be coloured by the swamp of prejudice when you were anchored to its bed.

"I am not saying it's acceptable, I'm saying it's endemic," Vonvalt said. "Come, now, do you suggest you are fully above it? We have toured some – and I do mean some – of the Empire, Helena, but there is much more to the world than Sova's conquests. What about men of different skin colours and textures? I have seen merchant ships on the River Treba staffed with men with skin as black as pitch. The Kasar from the south are wolf-men. Look at the Emperor's Warden, he is a Kasar." He took a draw from his pipe. "And everything in between. I will grant you that your wayfaring has given you an insight into the many peoples of the Sovan Empire, but all those people look alike, more or less – and act alike, for all their perceived differences."

"Dubine is dark-skinned," I said. "And I am close to him."

"Dubine is a Grozodan," Vonvalt scoffed. "He spent too long in the sun in his youth. He is not dark-skinned – not in the way you mean. How would you fare in the company of a man from the Frontier?"

"It wouldn't bother me at all," I said.

"Quite," Vonvalt murmured. "The point is, it does not follow that Sir Radomir's bigotry should cloud his lawman's instincts with regard to Lord Bauer. Even if it reflects poorly on his character."

"What if the suspected person was a foreigner?" I asked.

Vonvalt thought for a moment. "It doesn't matter. The Magistratum is very clear: the law is to be applied equally to all persons within the borders of the Empire – and any person who, outside the Empire, nevertheless submits, voluntarily, to its jurisdiction." He was retreating to quotation, something he usually did when he was on weaker ground. In fact, I was certain he was wrong. The question was whether he was being naïve, or just pretending to be to draw me into the argument.

"But you can agree that what the Magistratum ordains should happen, and what happens in practice, are often two different things."

He took another long draw on his pipe. "Naturally, Helena," he said. He had to agree, since the truth of what I'd said was patent. "That is the whole point of our existence."

I gritted my teeth. A year ago I would have given up at that point. Vonvalt's tone was designed to make me feel foolish, and was a typical lawman's trick. But I knew, largely thanks to his tutelage, that he had merely sidestepped the issue.

"I'm not talking about the purpose of a Justice," I said hotly. "I am talking about the application of the laws of Sova. A lawkeeper may adjudge a foreigner, or anyone he does not personally like, for that matter, more harshly than the law permits, on account of his physical characteristics."

"And that is the purpose of the common law, and precedent. That is why we record all of our findings, and why they are sent back to the great Law Library so the clerks can check that the law is being applied consistently."

"A process which can take months and sometimes years!" I

cried. "Small comfort to the man who has had his head removed for a crime which, but a week later, may not warrant it!"

Vonvalt all but shrugged. "One of the great strengths of the common law is that it can change over time, to remain in keeping with social mores. Name a better system. Certainly the laws of Tolsburg were as shabby a collection of ordinances as ever existed."

I felt my will to continue debating wither on the vine. I knew nothing of the laws of Tolsburg, since they had fallen into irrelevance, and Vonvalt had an answer for everything, even the most apparently incontrovertible of statements.

"I don't know," I said, wearily. The session had started as a conversation and had strayed into a debate on legal ethics. Vonvalt was clearly in one of his odd and combative moods, and I was often its first victim.

Vonvalt sighed, and a great cloud of pipe smoked flowed from his mouth. It was clear that he too had taken no satisfaction from our session. "In the morning I want you to fetch the town records kept since the last Justice's visit. I expect it will be Resi August, since we seem to be moving in her footsteps, however old they might be. Then you can get the records from Sir Radomir about the complaint lodged by Mr Vogt against Lord Bauer. Bring them into this room, and have the servants bring up a larger table, too. You can make a start on reviewing them."

"All right," I said, powerless to refuse, but brimming with resentment.

Vonvalt looked at me for a moment. "I'm going for a bath. I'll see you downstairs for dinner."

"I'm not hungry," I mumbled, a patent falsehood.

He paused for a moment. "Good night, then," he said, in no mood to indulge my sourness, and extinguished his pipe.

I pressed myself to my feet and left, glad to be out of his company. I made my way to my and Bressinger's room and flopped down onto the bed. I lay there for a while, waiting until

I was sure Vonvalt had made his way downstairs; then, eventually, I undressed and climbed under the covers, and snuffed out the lamp.

~

We rose with the sun, which meant longer in bed in those dark winter months. After weeks on the road, in and out of inns and impromptu campsites, suffering freezing cold temperatures and the constant threat of wild animal attack and robbery, Lord Sauter's luxurious guest bed was a welcome change. Servants had been up early too, stoking the hearths; warmth from the ground floor had already filled my chamber and made throwing the covers off considerably easier than it might otherwise have been.

Bressinger returned shortly after I awoke, reeking of beer. I studied him as he tramped about the place. He was a handsome man, there was no doubt about it – more so than Vonvalt, whose naturally downturned mouth rendered his face into a permanent mask of displeasure. Both men were dark-haired, though Bressinger's – which he wore in a ponytail – was darker, as were his eyes and skin. His most distinguishing feature was his moustache, which I did not much care for, and was certainly not a common styling outside of Grozoda and perhaps parts of Venland. Bressinger was also naturally more muscular, and a better dresser – though that was not really a fair comparison, as Vonvalt was compelled to wear his formal Magistratum robes for most of the working day.

As for his comportment, Bressinger was a man of two parts. One day he might be irrepressible, flirting with the local women, verbally sparring with Vonvalt and boring us with his Grozodan songs and folk tales; the next day he could be profoundly melancholic, spending much of the time in sullen silence and picking fights in the local inns. I know that he had fought with Vonvalt in the Reichskrieg and was a talented swordsman, though I did not know at that stage precisely how they had come to be in one another's company, nor how Bressinger had come to be in Vonvalt's employ.

One thing was obvious though: Bressinger was fiercely protective of his master, and would not hesitate to intervene if he thought I was being rude or insolent.

I watched as he moved about the room as though driven by some magickal force rather than any will of his own. I did not know what he did in those long nights away. Certainly, bedding the local prostitutes was a part of it – but only a part of it. I know he drank heavily, and sometimes he returned with his eyes red, as though he had spent hours grieving. From the way he looked and from how he ignored me, I knew I would do well to avoid him for a while. I dressed and made my way downstairs, and then pulled on my cloak and stepped out into the crisp morning air and made off down the path. I could see the usual trinkets, candles and flowers piled up around the gate, along with the odd hastily scrawled message which Vonvalt would never read. Most were submerged under the snow, but others poked out like the fingerbones of a battlefield corpse. There were one or two loiterers too, standing at the far end of the street, but the bitter cold and presence of town guards would keep them away.

I stopped just as I reached the street. The town watchman, the lad who had escorted Vonvalt into Galen's Vale the day before, was walking across from me outside the mayor's gate. He, too, stopped mid-pace when he saw me.

"Good morrow," he said, his breath steaming in the bitter cold. Like me he wore a large cloak over his armour, and from his ruddy cheeks it was clear he had been out for some time.

My heart fluttered. He was comely for sure, with big square shoulders and a big square jaw containing a full set of decent teeth. Growing up an orphan on the streets and in the alms houses of Muldau, I had lived a rough, hand-to-mouth existence which had hardened my soul. But two years with Vonvalt's fastidious comportment and fatherly Imperial protection had softened me again, and recaptured some of my innocence. Had the lad approached me two years ago I would have given him short shrift – and some choice language to boot. Now I felt my cheeks reddening.

"Good morrow," I said.

"What is your name?"

"Helena Sedanka," I replied, unsure of what to do with my hands. I settled for clasping them in front of me. "And yours?"

"Matas," he said, adding, "Aker. Of the town watch," as though it were not obvious. Still, he sought to impress me, and manoeuvred slightly so that his weapon, an expensive-looking sword in a fine leather scabbard, was presented to me. I smile now to think that I actually *was* impressed by this. I was just a silly girl smitten with a soldier boy.

We stood in awkward silence. I, who frequently snapped and spat barbs at Bressinger and Vonvalt, two Reichskrieg veterans and Imperial agents, could find nothing to say to one provincial lad.

"Where are you going?" he asked. He must have been a year or two older than me.

"I am heading to the courthouse, and the watch house," I said. "I have official business."

"This is a pleasant coincidence," Matas said. "I am heading to the watch house myself. My patrol has just finished. Perhaps I shall walk with you?"

"Do as you please," I said. The words sounded harsh, which I had not intended.

We walked through the snow together. The streets were quiet, but those who did brave the early morning snowfall often went out of their way to make some very minor obeisance to Matas.

"You are well-known," I murmured.

He smiled. He had a beautiful smile. "We make our presence known," he said cheerfully. "The watch is well-funded in Galen's Vale. It allows us to mount regular street patrols. Lord Sauter believes that a safe town is a prosperous town."

"How long have you been in the watch?"

I could see the question had not pleased him. "Not that long," he said eventually. "Six months. You have to be a certain age to join up, see," he added quickly.

We turned down past the marketplace, where traders and journeymen were setting up stall for the day.

"What is it that you do, then?" he asked me. "I saw you yesterday. You work with the Justice?"

"I am his clerk," I said.

"You are not happy?"

My voice must have betrayed me. I looked up at him. "No, I am happy," I said. "It is a good job, and opens many doors for me. Sir Konrad would see me a Justice too."

"I have not heard of a woman working as a Justice."

"They are common enough," I said. "The Autun makes no distinction between a man and a woman in legal matters. 'All may be judged by the law, so all may uphold it'," I quoted from an old jurist. The line was one of Vonvalt's favourites.

"You are learned, then," Matas said, though whether he was intimidated by this or not was unclear from his tone. I found that people, particularly men, often were. "You have been? To Sova?"

"No," I said quickly. "Not yet, I mean. Our circuit will take us there eventually, but not for some months yet."

"How long have you been on the road?"

"Nearly two years," I said.

"Blessed Nema! That is no life."

I shrugged. I felt strangely compelled to defend it. "You get used to it. Besides, our function is an important one."

"I don't doubt it. But does it not weary you? Not to have a home to go to?"

I shifted, uncomfortable. I did not like sharing my past with strangers, particularly those I was attracted to. "I have not had a home for a long time," I said.

"That is a shame," Matas said.

"What about you?" I asked quickly. "Have you lived in Galen's Vale all your life?"

He nodded. "My mother died of a pox in my childhood, but I still live with my father. He was wounded fighting the Tolls in the Marches and now cannot use his legs."

"I am sorry to hear that," I said warily. I would not back down like I had with Sir Radomir. If Matas had an issue with my ancestry I would fight him on it, whether I liked him or not.

"You are a Toll, I take it?" he asked without malice. "Sedanka is a Marcher name."

"I am," I said. "Why? Does it bother you? I was not born when the Reichskrieg came to Muldau."

"It doesn't bother me," Matas said quickly. "I've no quarrel with them. We are all Autun now, anyway. Certainly it's all I've ever known."

I calmed down and offered him a sheepish, insincere smile. I was annoyed with myself; Matas was a pleasant lad. I was being awkward and poor company.

We turned on to the street which led directly to the Veldelin Gate. The courthouse was about a quarter of the way along, an ornate stone building bristling with turrets with conical roofs of grey slate and draped in damp Sovan pennants. The watch house was further down, next to the town gaol.

"What do you think about the murder of Lady Bauer?" I asked as we neared the courthouse, conscious that our time together was drawing to a close.

Matas shrugged. "'Tis a grave business for sure," he said. "Normally when there is a murder you cannot stop the commonfolk pointing the finger for love nor money, and we end up with a list of suspicious persons as long as your arm." He paused. "This is different. There is no one. Sir Radomir is adamant that Lord Bauer has not done it, as disagreeable a man as he is. No one else has seen or heard a thing. We raided the eastern closure and found no trace of fresh wealth, such as might point to a robbery gone awry. And there were no tongues wagging, even with persuasion, if you take the meaning. 'Tis as if the lady just vanished. Were it not for the crack to her skull—" He dinged the side of his helmet as he said it. "—anyone'd think she'd put a foot wrong on the banks of the Gale and drowned. 'Tis a deep river, with treacherous currents. Had it not been for the tree root, Tom Bevitt's boy would never have seen her."

I shivered at the thought of Lady Bauer's corpse tumbling deep underwater, spun around by the currents until there was nothing left to spin.

Matas sighed. "It's all foreign to me. Sir Radomir has his own theories, though."

"Does he suspect anyone in particular?" I pressed.

"I cannot say," Matas said. "Nema, I've said far too much as it is. We are not supposed to talk about it. Besides, I've not had much to do with it. Sir Radomir keeps a group of men who specialise in making enquiries, per the Sovan ordinances."

"I see," I said. We had reached the courthouse, and stopped outside its imposing iron gates. Above, a large stone statue of the two-headed wolf looked out ominously. The words *"De Jura Nietra Iznia"* were carved into the wall above it in High Saxan: *"No one is above the law"*.

"Did you say you were fetching records from the watch house, too?"

"Yes," I said.

"Perhaps I could assist you with that?"

I knew that if I dallied any further, I would miss Vonvalt's conversation with Lord Bauer, something he had scheduled for that morning. He did not want to waste any time on this case.

"There is no need, thank you," I said with regret. "It will be a short matter of collecting them."

He looked disappointed. "I would see you again, Helena." His forward manner secretly delighted me.

"And I you," I replied, for I was desperate to see him again too.

Immediately he brightened. "You are staying at Lord Sauter's residence?"

"I am, but I do not have much idle time," I said quickly. "I could send a message to the watch house when I am next free?"

He nodded. "That would work."

We stood awkwardly in the snow.

"Farewell, then," I said, embarrassed, toying with my cloak.

He touched the rim of his kettle helm. "And you," he said, and walked on. I don't know if he looked back; I had already hurried inside the courthouse.

෴

I could not take the records from the courthouse, for they were too voluminous, but I was able to get the ledger of criminal reports from the desk serjeant in the watch house. Then I hurried back the way I had come, passing through streets which grew busier with miserable-looking people by the minute. I passed through the marketplace and paused to check the time on the big temple clock, trying to ignore the corpses of frozen beggars clustered around the foot of the belfry. It was approaching nine.

I quickened my pace and reached the mayor's residence just in time to see Vonvalt and Bressinger walking down the pathway that led from the front door to the gate. Both were clad in impressive outfits that befitted their office as Imperial agents, including their formal, fur-trimmed overcloaks.

"Slow down, Helena, you'll slip on the ice," Bressinger called out irritably. I suspected he was nursing quite a severe headache.

"Sir Konrad," I said. He drew up short.

"Yes?"

I told him I'd been unable to retrieve the courthouse records. He looked decidedly unimpressed.

"I do not have time to deal with that now," he said. "I had

hoped you might show some initiative, Helena. You could have made a start on reviewing the records this morning in the vaults."

"Forgive me," I mumbled. "I was eager to accompany you to see Lord Bauer."

Vonvalt softened. He could hardly be angry that I was showing an interest in our work; but he also believed – rightly – that I was more interested in seeing lords squirm under interrogation than putting in the hard yards combing through records as he had had to do. Still, he did sometimes indulge me, and I was quick to take advantage of it.

Bressinger watched through narrowed eyes.

"Make yourself useful, then," Vonvalt muttered. "Put that ledger in my chamber and fetch your log of attendances. We will have a note of the interview after all," he added to Bressinger.

"Thank you," I said with a smile, and hurried off to do as he bade. I returned outside to find that neither of them had waited for me, and I had to ask a succession of day watchmen and local citizens the way to Lord Bauer's house until I caught up with Vonvalt and Bressinger by the front gate.

Lord Bauer lived in a large town house, similar in design to Lord Sauter's except that it was attached on both sides to other large merchant houses. There must have been twenty of them in all, a street or two away from the town harbour where a forest of ships' masts creaked and swayed in the breeze. Vonvalt pounded his large, gloved fist on the door and a short while later it was unlatched and opened. A servant girl with red-rimmed eyes and dressed for mourning greeted us. Fire-warmed air breezed out of the door.

"I am Justice Sir Konrad Vonvalt," he said gently. "I am here to see Lord Bauer. I do not have an appointment. Would you fetch him down, please, and show us into the reception room?"

The serving girl simply nodded, struck dumb as many were when faced with the embodiment of Imperial authority. We entered and were gestured, wordlessly, to a room to the right of the entrance hall. The decoration was similar to that of the mayor's, both expensive and fashionable.

We waited a while. My heart pounded with anticipation. I could hear muted voices, since sound carried even in these luxurious town houses. It was clear from the tone of what we could hear that Lord Bauer was not happy about this impromptu visit, but, like everyone else, he had no choice but to see us. After a while we heard his inevitable footsteps on the stairs.

"Sir Konrad," he said as he appeared in the doorway to the reception room.

"Lord Bauer," Vonvalt said, standing along with the rest of us. "Thank you for seeing me."

"Not at all," Bauer said. He was an average man in almost every respect – build, height, hair colour, features; there was little to distinguish him from a thousand other Sovan subjects. He had the healthy pink skin of the well-fed, and was fleshier than most, but he was not overweight. He wore a fashionably cropped black beard, which I'd heard the Emperor favoured. His clothes were clearly expensive.

He also had the haggard look of the recently bereaved.

"I was sorry to hear about the loss of your wife," Vonvalt said as we all sat down.

"Thank you," Bauer said. He cleared his throat. "I have not fully come to terms with it."

"No," Vonvalt said, "that is to be expected."

"Can I offer you anything at all?"

"Water, if you have it; ale if not," Vonvalt said.

"For the three of you?"

"Yes, thank you. This is Dubine Bressinger, my taskman; and this is Helena Sedanka, my clerk."

"That is a large volume," Bauer said, nodding at the ledger on my lap. It was a large volume, and one I still keep. It is from dusty old ledgers like these, and my private journals, which I am able to draw on to flesh out the details of these decades-old conversations.

"Helena will keep a note of our attendance," Vonvalt said.

There was an uncomfortable pause. "Justice, I have already spoken to the town sheriff."

"And now you shall speak to me," Vonvalt said.

"As you wish," Bauer said. The serving girl returned a short while later with three tankards of marsh ale.

"You do not drink, sir?" Vonvalt asked.

"I have not the stomach for it," Bauer replied. "May I ask why you have come, Sir Konrad? I thought a Justice's duty was to check town records and hear petty complaints from the commonfolk."

Vonvalt smiled thinly. "I am the Emperor's representative," he said. "My jurisdiction has no limits save the confines of the law itself. Murder falls very much within my purview."

Bauer looked uncomfortable. "I meant no offence, Sir Konrad."

"It is just as well."

Bauer cleared his throat. "You are investigating my wife's murder, then?"

Vonvalt nodded. "With Sir Radomir's assistance."

"That man suspects me," Bauer said with venom. "He's as crooked a lawman as they come."

Vonvalt frowned. "Why do you believe Sir Radomir suspects you?"

"That man has had it in for me for a long time. He has accused me of all manner of crimes in the past."

"Has Sir Radomir ever laid charges against you?"

"No," Bauer sulked. "Not for want of trying, though. Have you met him?"

"I have."

"Doubtless he has sought to poison you against me."

"He has done no such thing," Vonvalt said. "Sir Radomir is an officer of the law who is investigating the murder of your wife. You would do well to show the man some respect."

"I'll do no such thing," Bauer said, but then quickly retreated.

He seemed suddenly to deflate, like a water bladder pierced by a dagger. "I am sorry, Justice. I am not myself."

There was a pause. "It is no matter," Vonvalt said eventually.

Lord Bauer gave Vonvalt a sidelong glance. "I have heard it told that Justices have special abilities. Is it true you can make a man confess with sharp words alone?"

Vonvalt paused. "I have certain abilities, yes," he said. "I do not use them lightly."

"I have heard that you can speak to the dead," Lord Bauer said quietly. The air seemed to grow thicker and heavier. I shivered. Vonvalt had conducted necromancy a number of times in the past, but the process was a disturbing one that required a tremendous amount of skill and energy.

"Perhaps we should start from the beginning." Vonvalt said. "Tell me what happened with your wife."

"Yes," Lord Bauer said. "My dear wife." He paused. For a squeamish moment I thought the man was going to cry, but he comported himself. "Natalija went missing three nights ago. She had gone to Thread Street to inspect some new bolts of cloth from Grozoda. Some green velvets, I think. The colour is very much in fashion." He took a deep breath. I was grateful for his pauses; they gave my hand and wrist respite from my energetic quill scratching. "She never returned. The next thing I knew some local peasant lad had spotted her body in the Gale."

Vonvalt looked thoughtful. "Was she with anybody? Before her disappearance?"

"The serving girl, Hana." He gestured to the door, evidently indicating the girl who had let us in and brought us drinks. "They were close." He shrugged. "Closer than a mistress and servant should be," he added.

"I am to take it that Hana was separated from Lady Bauer at the crucial time?" Vonvalt asked.

Lord Bauer looked displeased. "The girl is of no use whatever," he said. "Natalija bade her return to the house to prepare for my arrival. I had been at the wharf for most of the afternoon – I've a dozen men who'll attest to that."

"Noted."

"Hana left my wife on Thread Street. She did not bear witness to anything. If she is to be believed."

"You suspect her?"

Lord Bauer shrugged. "I only have her word that Natalija sent her away. Perhaps it was part of a trap."

"You have questioned her, I take it?" Vonvalt asked, a note of distaste in his voice.

"Aye, that I have. Her story is unchanged, despite a thrashing."

I thought of the girl who had served us. She looked a few years younger than me. I felt sorry for her. A young serving girl like that would be very much trapped, a prisoner of her circumstances. I doubted she had much in the way of family. If Lord Bauer kept her in his service, he would almost certainly begin a sexual affair with her – assuming he had not already. When he eventually kicked her out, she would be left at the mercy of the town's alms houses. Even if those in Galen's Vale were better than most I'd come across, it was still a wretched existence.

"Do you know the name of the shop which Lady Bauer was last seen in?" Vonvalt asked.

"No. Sir Radomir will. He and his men were investigating yesterday morning – for all the good that will do."

Vonvalt paused. "Sir Radomir told me that you suspected a business rival, Mr Vogt, as being responsible for your wife's murder. What of that?"

Lord Bauer looked uncomfortable. "I have spoken hotly these past few days," he said carefully. "Mr Vogt and I are old business rivals. He once accused me of sabotaging some of his grain shipments."

"So I have heard."

"I was quick to accuse him. I fear I spoke in haste."

Vonvalt frowned. "Nevertheless, there must have been

something that made you accuse him so readily? Sir Radomir said you were quite convinced."

"In all honesty, Justice, he was all I could think of. In my grief I sought to latch on to anything at all which made sense. I have no enemies, not in the real sense. The competition here in the Vale is fierce, but not so fierce that we would resort to such appalling measures. We are businessmen, not animals."

"I still consider it very strange that you mentioned him at all if he is in no way connected."

"Justice, I swear … the ramblings of the bereaved. There is nothing there."

"I think we shall speak to Mr Vogt in any event," Vonvalt said.

"As you wish," Bauer said sullenly.

"And if we rule him and his agents out, for the moment," Vonvalt said, "then there is no one you can think of who would seek to do this?"

"No one at all," Lord Bauer said.

"You suspect something else then? Robbery?"

"How could I know? All I know is that she is gone."

Vonvalt emitted a small, incredulous laugh. "It is quite remarkable, my lord, that the wife of a prominent noble can be murdered in so brutal a fashion with nothing at all to be divined in its wake. I have seen nothing like it in all my years as an Imperial Magistrate."

Bauer shrugged helplessly. "I don't know what else to tell you, Justice."

"Hm," Vonvalt said. There was a long pause. "And elsewhere in your professional life? You are a trader, yes? A merchant?"

"That's right."

"What is the precise nature of your business?"

"I deal in shipping. I guarantee cargoes, in return for a payment."

"You guarantee them? How?" Vonvalt asked.

"I cover the cost of a shipment if it is lost."

"That seems like a venture fraught with risk."

Lord Bauer shook his head. "It is not, if you've a head for it."

"So I see," Vonvalt said drily, making a show of looking around the room. "And there has been no material change in your business? Are you in any man's debt?"

"I am not."

"All right," Vonvalt said. "Before I leave you, perhaps you could tell me about your business around the town? Sir Radomir said you had some responsibilities in the council?"

"I do," Lord Bauer said carefully. "They are rather limited."

"Such as?"

Lord Bauer shifted in his seat. "I have some official duties. I help organise certain charitable ventures from the town's tax income, as trustee. I also assist the temple with alms for the poor. Plus a few other minor duties."

"Nothing awry there?"

"Certainly nothing comes to mind."

"And what about your family? Is Lady Bauer survived by any children? I do not see any effects."

"I had a son, but he died of a pox a few years back. I also have a daughter. She took the death of her brother very badly, and fled to the kloster to take up religious orders. I have not seen her in a long time. No other children that made it past the cradle."

"I am sorry for your son," Vonvalt said earnestly. "It is a cruel fate to lose a child."

"'Tis a crueller fate to lose a child and a wife," Lord Bauer said, with such sudden and profound melancholy that I could not help but feel sorry for him. "Thank you for your kind words."

"Of course. Well I think we shall leave it there for now. If you can think of anything else, I am lodging with Lord Sauter. In the meantime, we will continue with our enquiries."

"I'm grateful for the assistance, Sir Konrad."

"Until our next meeting, then."

"Farewell."

On our way out, Vonvalt bade me speak to the girl, Hana. I slipped off while Vonvalt and Dubine were pulling on their cloaks and keeping Lord Bauer occupied. I found her loitering in the kitchen. My appearance startled her.

"Is it Hana?" I asked quietly.

"Yes, mistress," she said, dropping her head and curtseying.

"Never mind any of that," I said, hating how Imperial I sounded. "My master has a message for you. He is concerned for your welfare, alone in this house. Lord Bauer seems like a cruel man."

Hana said nothing, just twisted her dress in her hands.

"We will be in Galen's Vale for some weeks yet," I said. "Sir Konrad says that you must tell him if Lord Bauer makes any unwelcome advances, or otherwise mistreats you. 'Tis a crime, under Sovan law, to force a woman to carnality against her will."

She reddened, but said nothing. I doubted she would say anything.

"Well, I have passed on the message," I said. "One more thing. What was the last you saw of Lady Bauer? Lord Bauer says you were separated before she was taken."

Hana nodded. She began to well up again. "She sent me away to prepare the house," she said. "Light the hearths, begin preparing dinner and suchlike. I left her on Thread Street. That was the last time I saw her."

"You are sure? You saw nothing that made you suspicious? You were not followed, for example?"

"There was nothing, I swear by Nema," she said. Tears streamed down her cheeks. It was taking all of her self-control to keep her voice down. I reached out and gripped her shoulder, a simple sisterly gesture. I noticed she flinched, just a little.

"All right," I said. "It is all right. I must go now, but remember what I said, yes?"

She nodded, wiping her eyes furiously.

"All right," I said for want of anything else to say. I left her then, my heart heavy, and caught up with Vonvalt and Bressinger at the door.

"Come, then," Vonvalt said to me, as Bressinger opened the door and the cold air flooded in. "Let's go."

Outside, a couple of people dropped flowers at Bauer's front gate and darted off into the backstreets. In the distance, the temple bell tolled the hour.

"Bloody hell," Bressinger muttered once we were out of earshot. "Part of me hoped we'd have the business done this morning. I really thought he might have done it. You did not fancy just smashing him with the Voice?"

Vonvalt shook his head. "No," he said, with a hint of reproach. "Not yet, at any rate. You are more well-versed than most in its limitations. Lord Bauer may not have done it, but Sir Radomir is right: there is something suspicious about the man. To use the Voice on him now, without more and better information, would be very ill-advised. You heard him ask me about the power. Not only will his mind be guarded, but using the Voice now will make it doubly so in future."

"Hm," Bressinger grumbled. "I don't think I will ever understand."

"Patience, Dubine," Vonvalt said. "There will be time enough for it soon. Let us cast the net a little wider first."

V

Unwelcome News

"The law serves the vigilant."

SOVAN LEGAL MAXIM

It was late morning when we left Lord Bauer's, and we made for a nearby public house to have an early lunch. The place was reasonably clean, and, given the working day was in full swing, mostly empty. Still, our entrance turned what heads there were.

Much of the tavern was given over to wooden benches, but there were some private tables in the corner separated by partitions. It was into one of these booths that Vonvalt led us, away from prying ears. We sat, and within seconds had been approached by the barman.

"My lords," he said, only slightly uncertainly, since it was obvious that Vonvalt at least was ennobled. "It's a little early for lunch, though I can provide you with some cold cuts if you like? Two pence'll cover the three of you."

"Yes, thank you," Vonvalt said. "And some ale."

The barman bustled off.

Vonvalt sighed. "All right. Let us take a moment to see where we are. Lady Bauer was last seen perusing Grozodan velvets on Thread Street. The serving girl, Hana, can attest to her whereabouts of that evening at the very least. Did she say anything to contradict Lord Bauer, Helena?"

I shook my head.

"We should speak to the shopkeeper," Bressinger said.

"Yes, I was coming to that," Vonvalt said. "That is one order of business. I also want to look into Lord Bauer's activities. I don't know what you two made of him, but the man is clearly concealing something. This business with Zoran Vogt is very strange. He accuses the man and recants in the same breath."

"I've no idea what he meant by guaranteeing cargoes, either," Bressinger said.

"No," Vonvalt agreed. "It seemed to me akin to betting. Lord Bauer bets that the cargo will arrive safely and so keeps the money the shipmaster has paid. I want to understand more about that business model. It seems ripe for abuse. It may be that Lord Bauer has run afoul of someone, even if he does not know it."

"Helena and I can ask about the wharf. If Lord Bauer makes money out of it, you can be sure there will be others."

"Yes," Vonvalt said. "And did you note that he was reluctant to say what his duties were? As a councilman?"

"He said he assisted with alms and charitable ventures."

"But he said something else, too," Vonvalt replied, massaging his chin. "Helena, what was it?"

I pulled the ledger out of my satchel and found the page. I squinted at my rushed, scratchy script. "'Charitable ventures . . . trustee . . . temple alms . . . other minor duties'," I said, reading back my notes.

"That was it," Vonvalt said, nodding. "'Other minor duties'. What are those duties, I wonder?"

"Perhaps they were too trivial to mention?" I hazarded. It was difficult to gauge whether my comments were welcome in conversations like this. Sometimes Vonvalt actively encouraged both me and Bressinger to participate; other times he expected me to sit quietly and soak up all I could.

"Or he was caught off his guard, and did not want to let something slip."

"Lord Sauter will know," I said.

"Yes," Vonvalt said. "Of course he will. Good, Helena." I admit that small, earnest compliments like that made me swell with pride. "We shall ask the mayor this evening what he understands Lord Bauer's duties to be. I want to speak with him anyway."

We paused while the innkeeper returned with flagons of ale and plates of ham sprinkled with cinnamon. There was also some pickled cabbage, and a warm, spiced cheese sauce that could be found throughout the Empire. It was significantly more than he'd promised; the man had probably discovered who we were in the interim. We tucked greedily into the fare.

"Strange," Vonvalt said after a while, "that a lord's daughter should take up religious orders. It is a severe existence for one with a life of privilege ahead of them."

"Hm," Bressinger replied. "I had wondered about that."

"That kloster looked wealthy enough," I said, recalling its great fortress-like stone walls and towers built into the hillside overlooking Galen's Vale. "Perhaps it is less severe than some."

"Aye," Bressinger said, nodding. "The Neman Creed has bred a lot of fat monks."

"Keep your voice down, man," Vonvalt said. "You are a representative of the Crown."

Bressinger smiled, and winked at me. I had never been religious, and had no respect for the Creed. Bressinger certainly didn't. But since it was a state religion, and Vonvalt was an agent of that same state, he couldn't be seen or heard to disrespect it – and nor could we as his retainers.

"Lord Bauer said his son died," Bressinger said after a

half-minute's silent eating. "Taken by a pox, and that drove the girl to religious orders." He shrugged. "Grief does strange things to a person."

"Perhaps," Vonvalt agreed. "And perhaps there is another reason for her to do it, beside the death of the boy. Lord Bauer himself said it was her calling. And the young these days seem unnaturally devout – look at Claver. The man is barely twenty-five, and a priest to boot."

"A well-connected priest," Bressinger remarked.

Vonvalt waved him off. "I don't want to talk about that dolt. My mood is sour enough already." He looked troubled. "Though now you've turned my mind to it, it does seem more than a little strange. About the girl, I mean."

"It may be nothing," Bressinger said, shrugging.

"That it may," Vonvalt agreed, but his voice was thoughtful. He turned to me. "Perhaps you could ask that lad you were with this morning. The guard."

I reddened. "There was nothing untoward," I said hotly.

Vonvalt and Bressinger glanced at one another. Their knowing half-smirks made me feel like a foolish little girl. Immediately I felt myself retreating back to the old me, Helena the street urchin: defensive, choleric, pugnacious.

"I made no suggestion to the contrary," Vonvalt said.

I didn't trust myself to speak for a short while. Instead I toyed with the food on my plate like a child, waiting for my anger to subside. It had taken me a long time to learn to control my temper – a long time and endless patience from Vonvalt. "I don't know him very well," I said with forced calm. "Chances are our paths will not cross again."

"Well, we are on official business," Vonvalt said, "and a young lad like that, a member of the town watch, will have his ear to the ground. You would do well to bend it. See if he has heard any rumours about the Bauer girl. They must have been contemporaries."

"Is that a command?" I said sharply. I regretted it immediately. Bressinger looked irritated.

"I can make it one?" Vonvalt asked.

I poked and prodded at my ham. "No," I said. "I exist only to serve."

"Could have fooled me," Vonvalt muttered, chuckling at my prickliness. I saw him wink at Bressinger as he began to tuck back into his food – but then all of our attention was stolen by the door to the inn being thrown open.

"What's this, then," Bressinger murmured. The lad in the doorway was clearly a messenger, and from one of the liveried companies that had a preternatural ability to track people down. He saw us sitting in the corner and immediately walked over.

"Easy," Vonvalt said quietly as Bressinger made to get up. He turned to the lad. "You are looking for me?"

"Begging your pardon, milord Justice; sorry to interrupt your lunch. But there is an urgent letter for you." He held out an unmarked and sealed envelope. I could not make out the device pressed into the wax, but I could see from the colours and ribbon that it was from another Imperial official – perhaps another Justice.

Vonvalt frowned as he accepted the message. He was no stranger to urgent letters, but certainly he had not been expecting anything.

"Thank you," he said to the messenger, who left. He broke the seal and took in the letter's contents quickly.

"What is it?" I asked, unable to stop myself.

Vonvalt did not respond for a little while. He refolded the letter and pocketed it. He looked troubled. "It appears that matters have taken a turn for the worse."

"With the Bauer case?" Bressinger asked.

"No," Vonvalt said. "Matters of state." He checked about the place, but there was no one within earshot. Still, when he spoke again, it was in a low voice. "The letter was from Justice August. She is in Guelich, which is closer than I thought she'd be. It appears my ... treatment of Patria Claver in Rill has caused a greater upset than might reasonably have been anticipated."

"'Might reasonably have been anticipated'!" Bressinger said gruffly. "You knew what political ties the man had. Nema knows he told you enough times himself."

Vonvalt clenched his teeth as he endured a spasm of irritation. "Justice August says Claver has made an ally of Margrave Westenholtz. The two are apparently firm friends."

Westenholtz was a powerful man, the lord of Seaguard and a known political agitator. We had passed through Seaguard a number of weeks before, it having been the northernmost part of our circuit, but the margrave had not been in residence and our stay in the fortress had been brief.

"News travels quickly," I said. "Seaguard and Guelich aren't exactly close."

"August can commune with nature. It is one of her powers. I expect she has had a bird or two loitering about in the north for some time," Vonvalt said. He paused. "She takes an interest in the political health of the Order."

"As should you," Bressinger said.

I expected him to get a reprimand for that, but Vonvalt just shot him a look of irritation.

"What of it?" I asked eventually. "Let Westenholtz drink brine. You are a Justice."

"Westenholtz has sway with the Mlyanar Patricians in Sova," Vonvalt said, his voice grim. "The Mlyanar Patricians have sway with the Savaran Templars."

I recognised all of those names, and none of them were good news. The Mlyanar Patricians were a powerful faction of Sovan aristocrats who historically had opposed the Haugenate line, of which Emperor Kzosic IV's grandchildren were the most recent members. The Savaran Templars were a martial chapter of orthodox Nemans who expanded the southern boundaries of the Empire – the Frontier – through sporadic crusading. The two were linked by tradition, money and land holdings going back centuries, and together they were enjoying something of a resurgence as political operators.

"It seems as though Patria Claver has been busy propounding the cause of the Savarans for longer than he let on in Rill, beseeching various lords across the Empire to part with lands money, sons and daughters for another crusade south. August is worried that a crusade south could quite easily become a crusade north."

"What, she means to say that the Templars would move on Sova?" I asked. "Why?"

Vonvalt shrugged. "Sova is no stranger to armed rebellion. The Mlyanars are power-hungry agitators; and when power-hungry agitators form alliances with fanatical soldiers, one does not have to delve too deeply into Sova's history to see what the consequences are."

I sucked my teeth. "You have made more enemies than you bargained for."

Now Vonvalt shot me an irritated look. "Quite."

"*Nyiza*," Bressinger swore in Grozodan, and shrugged flippantly. "So what if Claver's pride has taken a knock? Nema knows it needed one. As Helena says, you are a Justice. What is he going to do, move against you in some way out of petty revenge? To move against you would be to move against the Emperor Himself."

"Except . . ." Vonvalt said, and I felt my stomach turn. Vonvalt's authority had always been a comfortable absolute. To hear from the man himself that it might have limits was deeply unsettling. "Except that it appears that the Magistratum may be falling out of favour with the Emperor. It is no secret that the Nemans have been bleating on about the repatriation of our powers for some years. Faith, even Claver would not shut up about it. Master Kadlec has been foolish enough to entertain the notion that in return the Order be left in peace. The Emperor has not taken Kadlec's capitulation well."

I sat in stunned silence for a few moments.

"The Emperor cannot make an enemy of the Mlyanars and the Order at the same time," Bressinger muttered. "That is two of the three Imperial Estates – and he is the third. He will run out of allies."

"Indeed," Vonvalt said. He sighed. "From her letter, it is clear that Justice August is concerned, and unsurprisingly. The Order's power has long been regarded with jealousy. I have always been of the opinion that a commingling of the right circumstances will curtail the Order's influence, and the primacy of the common law with it. The Emperor may be an unpleasant man, but he has long trusted his Magistrates to enforce the law. A man like Westenholtz in power, or heavens forbid, a Neman, will be the end of the Autun."

"But we are a way off that?" Bressinger asked hopefully.

"We shall see," Vonvalt replied, not entirely reassuringly. He sighed, and sat back up, for he had hunched forwards slightly during the conversation. When he spoke again, it was at a normal volume. "In any event, there is nothing to be done about it at the present moment. Come; let us be about our duties. The sooner we can finish our business here in the Vale, the sooner we can turn our attentions to matters of greater import."

VI

Merchant Assurance

*"Few things in this life can be guaranteed with greater
certainty than the incredible contrivances men will
go to to generate money from nothing at all."*

PHILOSOPHER AND JURIST FRANCIS GERECHT

We finished our lunch quickly and with a renewed sense of
urgency, and parted ways outside the inn. I was filled with insa-
tiable curiosity after August's letter, though I would have done
better to attempt to wring blood from a stone than to try to get
more out of Vonvalt. In the event, I needn't have worried myself;
it wouldn't be long before I would be begging gods I didn't believe
in for news of something – anything – else.

Vonvalt wanted to head for the courthouse and make himself
known before too much time had passed, since already he was
in danger of looking as though he was slighting the place. With
our master so engaged, Bressinger decided that he and I would
head to the wharf.

We picked our way through the frigid, slushy streets towards the forest of masts I had seen earlier. The air filled with the cries of sailors and dockworkers, and the streets thickened with merchant traffic. Watchmen and constables were aplenty here. They kept a careful eye on the town's crowning jewel.

We rounded a large timber-framed warehouse. Beyond lay the harbour. It wasn't the largest I'd seen – that honour belonged to the Imperial naval yard at Seaguard – but it was certainly the busiest. The water was jammed full of merchant cogs and the newer carracks, some as tall as a three-storey house. They creaked and groaned on the swell, ropes swollen and taut with water. Many of the ships bore the Autun colours, but there were plenty that didn't, instead flying the peculiar flags of exotic, non-Imperial lands that I had little knowledge of.

The waters of the Gale harbour were as brown and unpleasant as the river that fed it, and appeared to serve as the outflow of the town's sewers. Whereas the Seaguard harbour had smelled strongly of brine, here, despite the cold, the waters smelled like shit. We walked along the wharf's edge, careful to keep out of the way of the workers as they loaded and unloaded ships.

There were a couple of public houses that fronted the water a little further down the wharf, and we ducked into the first one we saw. It bore little resemblance to the tavern we had just eaten in. The floor was covered in rush matting that reeked of stale beer, and the single hall was filled with long trestle tables of cheap wood. The place was packed, and beleaguered women, enduring endless harassments both physical and verbal, moved among the punters with trays of marsh ale.

"Madam," Bressinger said to a passing barwoman, his Grozodan accent and features obvious among a sea of Hauners.

"Aye?" she asked, looking him up and down. She was probably working out how much she could feasibly overcharge him based on his smart clothes.

"I'm looking to speak to a merchant who deals in

guaranteeing cargoes," he said. He produced a groat from his purse. "Discreetly."

The woman made to reach for the coin, but Bressinger withdrew it with an impressive sleight of hand. "After I've spoken with him."

The woman looked put out. "Back table," she said. "That is where business is conducted." She squinted over to it, ignoring the punters calling out to her. She pointed to a man at the end of the trestle. "Mr Lorentz I know does something akin to what you mentioned. The specifics of it are lost on me."

"Thank you," Bressinger said, and handed her the coin despite what he had said.

We walked over to the man she had indicated. He was drinking alone, looking over some papers. Looking down the length of the table, I could see other merchants similarly sat, all on the same side. A couple were engaged in negotiations with ships' captains. Along the back wall, a few larger men loitered, armed. They watched us warily.

"Mr Lorentz?" Bressinger asked.

"Aye?" the man replied affably enough. He had the swarthy look of a Grozodan, and wore an expensive wool doublet of yellow and red. His cap had a large feather in it from an exotic bird I didn't recognise.

They spoke to one another in Grozodan for a minute or two, gabbling away and laughing as though they had known one another their entire lives, until eventually Bressinger produced his warrant of office. "I am an agent of the Crown," he said, now in Old Saxan for my benefit. "I would ask you some questions."

Lorentz studied the warrant. "Your master's reputation precedes you," he said, reciprocating in Saxan. "I can assure you my business is fully above board and all tax accounts are up to date. You may check the filings at the courthouse."

Bressinger and I sat. "I'm not here to ask about that," Bressinger said. "Nor am I here to conduct business. I want you to explain something to me, as though I were a simpleton."

Lorentz raised an eyebrow. "I will do my best. I am a loyal subject of His Majesty." I noticed that he subtly waved one of the big men off.

"You are not to speak of our conversation to anybody," Bressinger warned.

Lorentz inclined his head sagely.

"Earlier today we spoke to Lord Bauer," Bressinger said, his voice low. "The man spoke about the nature of his business. Guaranteeing cargoes in return for payment."

"'Tis common enough in other parts of the world," Lorentz said. "There is nothing unlawful in it."

"I'm not interested in the legality of the practice," Bressinger said impatiently. "I want to understand how it works."

"As you wish," Lorentz said. He looked about the table and collected a glass and a tankard, and arranged them in front of him. "Imagine that I am to ship a cargo of cloth from Leindau to Venland. How might I do it?"

"I'm not a merchant," Bressinger said gruffly. "The geography of the Empire is not my concern."

"So I see," Lorentz remarked dourly. I stifled a smile. "I might ship it east past Lothgar, between the Gvòrod Steppe, and then on to the Jade Sea. I might take the River Treba past Hasse and the duchy of Kòvosk. If I was particularly heavily laden I might have to go out past Denholtz, south past Grozoda, and then up through the Grall Sea. Three very different routes, and each route presents different risks. Northmen, pirates, foundering in rocky waters, the sea in storm, running aground in a shallow river . . . you take the point."

"Aye," Bressinger said.

"Many ships will sail without incident, but some will not. So each voyage a ship makes may be its last."

"Right."

"Let us take our cargo of cloth from Leindau. It has cost the merchant twenty crowns to purchase."

My eyes widened. Twenty crowns for a holdful of cloth! It was an extraordinary sum. It was no wonder the new merchant class had been able to construct their vast brick-and-timber town houses with glass windows and multiple hearths.

"If the ship sinks, the merchant has lost that sum," Bressinger said. "I understand that."

"Of course," Lorentz said. "So, in order to . . . *mitigate* that loss, the merchant will pay a man to guarantee the cargo."

"He will pay the man twenty crowns?" Bressinger asked.

"No!" Lorentz laughed. "Otherwise he would simply take the risk that the ship would sink. Either way, he has lost twenty crowns. No, he pays a *proportion* of the sum instead, which is calculated by taking into account all of the different risks: the season, the route, the cargo itself, the condition of the ship, whether it carries armed men, and so on."

"So Sir Konrad was right; it is akin to gambling."

"Aye, if that is what the Justice likened it to, then he is not far wrong. The guarantor is betting the ship will reach its destination intact, and therefore he keeps the sum paid. The merchant, provided he keeps to the terms of the contract – he must not, for example, deviate from the agreed route – has bought himself peace of mind, for if the ship is lost then he will claim its value from the guarantor. Some of the time the guarantor will actually send a man aboard the ship to act as his spy, to make sure the conditions of carriage are being met. I have known a fast chain of riders to do the job, too."

"I see," Bressinger said. "It seems like money for nothing to me."

Lorentz winked. "It seems like that, friend, because much of the time it is. But it is a commercial arrangement like any other, made between businessmen who have their ears and eyes open. As I said, there is nothing unlawful in it."

"And this is Lord Bauer's practice?"

"It is. He is not the only man to offer the service, but I am given to understand he has made a considerable fortune from it in a short space of time."

I noticed that one of the other merchants sitting at the table, within earshot despite our low conversation, was taking notice. I tapped Bressinger on the thigh.

"I know," he muttered to me, then turned back to Lorentz. "Thank you for your time, Mr Lorentz. I shall not keep you from your business any longer."

The merchant inclined his head. "I am pleased to assist the Emperor whenever I can."

We made our way back out of the inn. Even the cold air of the wharf, with its noxious humours, was more agreeable than the foul atmosphere of the tavern. We walked quickly back the way we had come, pausing only so that Bressinger could take directions to Thread Street from a passer-by.

"What did you make of that, then?" he asked me as we strode through the slush.

"I suppose it makes sense," I said. "Sir Konrad has spoken of complex banking schemes before, in Sova."

"Aye," Bressinger replied. "Seems like where there's money to be made, men will come up with just about anything." We passed a pair of liveried watchmen, and a wry look came over his face. "You must be looking forward to seeing your beau again?"

"He is not my beau!" I snapped, keenly aware that my reaction was precisely what he'd been aiming for.

"Aye, not yet," Bressinger said. "I saw the way you looked at him the other day. I told you such a lad is beneath your station. You are in the Emperor's service now."

"I wish I wasn't," I muttered.

Bressinger stopped suddenly and whirled to face me. "Watch how you speak!" he hissed. "Foolish girl." I was completely taken aback; Bressinger was often surly, but it was rare for his mood to turn so suddenly and sharply. I think he had surprised himself, for I could read quick regret in his features. He softened. "You cannot afford to have so loose a tongue," he said, somewhat hypocritically. "Not this close to Guelich."

"'Tis not a crime to criticise the Emperor," I said.

"Aye, but it might as well be," Bressinger said. "You have heard the man's reputation."

"Mm," I grunted.

Bressinger straightened up, looking around. "We are his representatives," he said. "You cannot say things like that, especially not in public. And besides, Helena, how would Sir Konrad feel to hear you say that?"

That, of course, was the real reason he had angered so quickly and so hotly. Bressinger did not care if I insulted the Emperor – Nema knew he did it himself often enough.

I sighed, my surliness cooling. "I know," I said. I felt wretched, and must have looked it, for Bressinger approached me and put his hands on my shoulders. "I know what you are thinking, girl," he said. "You are young and restless and you've had an upbringing Prince Kasivar of Hell would be proud of. But don't let your impulses be your undoing. With Sir Konrad's tutelage you have a future of wealth and privilege ahead of you."

"And what if I've no love for our work?" I said. The words spilled out of me, my emotions brimming over like the head on a poorly poured pint. I felt a sudden urge to cry, in anger, frustration, shame.

Bressinger couldn't conceal the alarm he felt. His face was too expressive. But given our close proximity over the course of the last two years, he would have had to have been blind, deaf and dumb not to notice that my mood had changed in the past few months.

"But you've taken to it like a duck to water," he said earnestly. "Think about where you started." He looked around, as though trying to conjure the right words out of the cold air around us. "I'm not meant to tell you this, but Sir Konrad sings your praises to me constantly. He is as proud of you as he would be a favourite daughter."

I didn't want to hear these words. He was not telling me anything I did not already know. I was well aware of how Vonvalt viewed me and how he felt about me. Those feelings – that pride, that patriarchal love, that urge to see me succeed and better myself – were the reason why I felt such anguish. I had already seen more of the Empire than most. I had seen the squalor most people lived in. Hell, I had lived it for years in Muldau, the cold, the uncertainty, the fear. Bressinger was right; all I had to do was keep doing what I was doing and I would be eventually sent to the Order to finish my training and become a Justice in my own right.

Yet I just could not see it in those terms. I found lawkeeping mostly drudge work. I was going to end up a stern figure like Vonvalt, haunted by his necromancy, dealing with men like Sir Radomir and Patria Claver, feared by the commonfolk. There was something sad about his itinerant life, devoid as it was of the love of a good woman and a house to call a home. The longer I was exposed to it, the more I wanted to be free of it. Vonvalt might have been wealthy and privileged, but neither seemed to bring him much joy.

"Come, Helena," Bressinger said, trying to gauge where the source of my unhappiness lay like a man casting a fishing line into a murky lake. "The men of Sova are not like the men of the provinces. The Autun may be many things, but they treat women as equals. You will find many a decent suitor there. A man who will challenge and respect you."

"Yes, Dubine," I said, feeling resentful and wretched and eager to close off the conversation.

"You've not taken a tumble with this lad, have you?" Bressinger asked suddenly.

"Nema!" I swore. "In what time? We've been in the Vale all of five minutes!" Bressinger remained inscrutable. I gritted my teeth. "No, I have not, and it would not be your business if I had!"

"Well, see that you don't," Bressinger said sternly, unfazed by my reaction. "If he gets you with child, Sir Konrad will be forced to find another clerk no matter whether you want to stay or go."

He turned and resumed walking towards Thread Street, and I was, with hindsight, grateful for that; if he had stayed, I would have said things that would have seen me out of Vonvalt's service as surely as getting pregnant.

We found the shop on Thread Street on the third attempt, since the place was lousy with tailors and dressmakers and all manner of cloth merchants. The shopkeeper was a fussy, bespectacled man who had clearly made a good bet on Grozodan velvets, for he was doing a roaring trade. The shop was as jammed with wealthy merchants' wives and their serving girls as the wharf-side tavern had been with punters.

The man was rushed off his feet and unimpressed with our Imperial credentials, and we spent far too long trying to get answers from him. The man had already been questioned by Sir Radomir's men, and was only able to confirm that Lady Bauer had been in the shop with Hana, that they had been perusing the velvets and that Lady Bauer had bidden Hana leave before she herself left.

It was mid-afternoon by the time we exited back on to Thread Street. The sun was low enough so as to be completely obscured by the Tolsburg Marches, and some of the slush on the streets was already re-freezing. To make matters worse, the clouds had drawn in again, and more snowflakes tumbled through the air, driven by the biting wind.

We hurried back to Lord Sauter's residence. Vonvalt was already inside. I had hoped that we could spend some time discussing the contents of Justice August's letter further, but I could hear his voice and another man's, which meant Lord Sauter was probably back. Bressinger and I decloaked and Bressinger removed his sword, and then we were led by one of the servants to the main reception chamber, a room of comfortable warmth and expensive furnishings.

"Ah," Vonvalt said as we appeared in the doorway. My face was tingling as the heat returned to my blood.

"Welcome to my house," a fat, bald man who could only have been the mayor said. "Sir Konrad has told me about you both. You must be Dubine and Helena."

We bowed. "Sire," Bressinger said.

"Come, sit," Sauter said. He seemed a pleasant man, and not the stern figure I had expected. I could see instantly why men like Sir Radomir disliked him. For all his good humour he had the mannerisms of the perennially nervous, and it was easy to imagine him besieged by forceful merchants and lords each trying to bend him to their will.

We sat. Food and drink were offered. I saw that Vonvalt had wine, and so Bressinger and I both gratefully accepted some, which was hot and mulled with spices. Protocol forced me to refuse the fare despite my growling stomach, since neither Sauter nor Vonvalt were eating.

"We were about to discuss the murder of Lady Bauer," Vonvalt said, and I realised that all Bressinger and I had missed were idle preliminaries.

"Yes, yes," Lord Sauter said, wringing his pudgy hands. "A terrible business. The whole of the Vale is shocked. And not a suspect in sight."

"You were right to bring it to my attention with such alacrity," Vonvalt said, taking a sip of wine. "Though I have been impressed by Sheriff Radomir's zeal for lawkeeping."

The corners of Lord Sauter's mouth turned downwards upon hearing the man's name. "Zeal is the right word," he said. He fidgeted for a moment. "Speaking candidly, Justice, I was pleased to hear of your arrival. Your reputation as a civilised and wise man precedes you. Sir Radomir has been ennobled by virtue of his position, but he is of a rough and unsavoury character."

"It is clear that the pair of you are not friends."

Lord Sauter sighed. "The truth of the matter is, Sir Radomir retains his position only by virtue of my patronage, not that he knows it. He is an effective lawman – too effective for some, if you'll take my meaning."

Vonvalt inclined his head.

"He is no friend of mine, that much is certain; but sometimes we must rise above such things for the common good. Criminal activity follows money like the tail on a dog, and Galen's Vale has a lot of money. Keeping order in a place like this requires men of a certain character."

Vonvalt was impressed. "To take such a selfless position is admirable," he said. "I have not come across many who have done the same. Vanity too often overwhelms common sense."

Sauter was pleased at the compliment, but he could only accept it with a weary shrug. "The Reichskrieg bred many villains, Sir Konrad, villains who have been since ennobled. But having a lordly title does not make one lordly."

Vonvalt smiled sadly. "I have heard of Galen's Vale before," he said, "but it has not always had a reputation as a major trading town."

"No, it has only been so for the last ten years or so, after the new wharf was constructed. It is to do with the depth of the Gale. The new seagoing carracks are a marvel, and can carry many tonnes of cargo, but they require deep water in which to sail. The Gale is deep enough to take them where other rivers are not. And it flows more or less to Sova itself. The volume of money it brings in is quite staggering. I had never seen a gold crown before I became mayor of the Vale; now the carracks deposit hundreds of crowns' worth of cargoes here every week. Even with a very low excise, the treasury is practically overflowing."

"You use the money for works?"

Sauter nodded. "We are able to keep the wall and all its forts in very good repair, and pay to armour and arm a large watch. You have seen the courthouse, too?"

"I have. A new building, and in the Sovan gothick style, too. It must have cost a small fortune."

"Aye, and it paid for itself. The practice of merchant law has thrived here."

"I am pleased to hear it. What I saw gave me no cause for concern at all – my colleagues here will attest to how little I say that."

"High praise indeed," Bressinger said, and we all shared a laugh.

"Without this business of Lady Bauer, I daresay there would have been little enough for me to do here," Vonvalt said, and the sombre mood quickly returned like a wet blanket thrown over a fire.

"Yes," Sauter said. "It was quite a shock. The Vale has its own share of murders, same as any town, but a lord's wife . . . It is unheard of."

"Indeed," Vonvalt said. "I have already spoken with Lord Bauer this morning, and we are making enquiries alongside Sir Radomir's team. These things must be investigated swiftly if there is any hope of bringing the matter to a just conclusion."

"Do you have any idea who may have done it?" Sauter asked hopefully.

"No," Vonvalt said simply. "But I am confident we are making progress. As you may appreciate, conducting a criminal investigation in a responsible manner requires me to keep certain matters to myself."

"Of course, of course," Sauter replied. "And your . . . abilities will help?"

"They will help," Vonvalt said, "should I have cause to use them."

Sauter's mouth worked for a moment. "Mr Maquerink said that you did not use your necromancy on her?"

"I did not," Vonvalt said patiently. "The circumstances were far from ideal. I am afraid that, as powerful a tool as it is, for it to work, many factors must be just so."

"S-such as?"

Vonvalt pursed his lips. "If the person was well-disposed to me, and if they were killed cleanly and recently, and are more or less intact about the head, then I can have a conversation with them much like you and I are having now."

Sauter was unable to suppress a shudder. "And if not?"

"Come now, Lord Sauter, we are having a pleasant evening. I would not want to spoil it," Vonvalt said gently.

"What of your other powers, then?" Sauter asked, irrepressible. It was unutterably vulgar, but Vonvalt sensed an ally in Sauter and was in the mood to indulge him.

"I have but two, the other being the Emperor's Voice. Most Justices have only the energy to sustain a couple. Even Master Kadlec only has three that I know of. Necromancy is the rarest and consequently has the fewest number of practitioners. But as I have said before, the power of the Emperor's authority and the weight of the common law is more than enough in the vast majority of cases."

"But not in this one?"

"We shall see."

Sauter shifted his weight uncomfortably. "It may be just a random slaying, of course," he said, grasping for reassurance. "A robbery gone awry."

"It may be," Vonvalt agreed. "Those are common enough. By the way, I'd be grateful if you could provide my clerk here with a list of council members and their official responsibilities, major and minor."

Sauter's eyes widened slightly. "Is a member of the town council under suspicion?"

Vonvalt waved him off. "No, I require it as an official myself, as part of my regular and ongoing duties."

Sauter accepted the lie with relief. "As you wish. Such records are kept in my office. I would be pleased to have a copy made for you."

"I'm grateful," Vonvalt said.

"My office is at your disposal, naturally," Sauter added.

"I know," Vonvalt replied. He looked out the window. The last of the light had faded, and once again the town was claimed by darkness. Snow pattered against the glass. "It is getting on. I have detained you long enough," he said to Sauter, and stood.

"'Tis no matter, Sir Konrad," the mayor said quickly, standing as well. "Are you comfortable? Do you have everything you need?"

"Certainly," Vonvalt replied. "If you will indulge me, sir, I will dine in my chamber tonight. I have duties to attend to which will take some hours yet. Will you have fresh candles sent up?"

"Of course."

"My clerk will require the same," Vonvalt added, and my heart sank, though I had been expecting it. Vonvalt would want me to go through the ledger I had taken from the watch house. I had hoped he might do it himself.

Sauter acquiesced with a nod.

"Very well then. I will say good night now," Vonvalt said.

"Good night," Sauter said, and we excused ourselves and tramped upstairs for a long night of reading.

VII

Midnight Run

*"An attempt on the life of a representative of the state is
an attempt on the life of the state itself. Anything that
interferes with the lawful and ordinary conduct of a
civilisation should be eradicated without hesitation."*

JUSTICE JOHANN KEITA

I was roused at some point in the night. My eyes were dry and
tired from the reading which I could only have concluded a few
hours before.

I looked about the chamber. It always took me a few seconds
to take my bearings. We had stayed in so many places in the past
two years that I had grown accustomed to a few moments of disorientation upon waking – insofar as one can become accustomed
to disorientation.

I had been in an unusually deep sleep, and it took me longer
than normal to recognise the expensive furnishings of Lord
Sauter's house. It was still dark outside. There was no way to

tell what time it was, but I could see the faint glow of moonlight illuminating the plaster around the curtains.

From the way the bed had shifted, and from the smell of an evening's debauchery wafting out from under the covers, I could tell that Bressinger had returned at some point earlier in the night. It was a small miracle that the man had not woken me. I turned to examine him – I made a habit of checking that he had not been sick, both for his sake and mine – and to my surprise, I saw that his eyes were open and staring at the ceiling.

"Dubine?" I whispered. His body was warm, and for all he looked as though he was carved out of stone, I instinctively knew he wasn't dead – though Nema knew he resembled a corpse closely enough. But he did not stir. After a few moments of my persistent staring, he shook his head subtly.

I did not take the hint. "Dubine?" I insisted. He shook his head again, slightly more vigorously. I had no idea what the man was driving at.

"Dubine!" I hissed. Now he stirred, ever so slightly.

"Shut up, girl, and be still for Nema's sake," he whispered through clenched teeth.

I practically recoiled with fury. I pushed myself up onto my side so that I was propped up on my elbow facing him.

"You don't speak to—" I started, when to my incredible surprise, Bressinger uncoiled like a startled cat and shoved me firmly with both hands.

I was pushed clean out the bed and hit the cold wooden floorboards of the chamber as gracelessly as a dropped sack of shit.

"What in Kasivar's name is the matter with you?" I shrieked, leaping to my feet. I was so angry I was about to physically attack him, when I saw that something had beaten me to it. Bressinger was thrashing about the bed as though he had been possessed. Something was clenched in the fist of his left hand, and for a good few moments I thought it was a belt. It was only when he rolled out of the other side of the bed and dashed the thing's head against the wall that I realised it was a snake.

A nauseating wave of revulsion rolled through my body. I shuddered with horror at the thought of even having been in the same room as the thing, let alone in the same bed. "Where the hell did that come from?" I asked breathlessly. My heart was pounding so hard it felt as though it were about to burst through my ribcage.

Bressinger ignored me. He snatched up his sword and threw open the chamber door so hard that the handle dented the wall.

"Dub— Where are you going?" I called after him, but he was already out the door and running through the hallway.

I dashed around the end of the bed and chased after him.

"Wait!" I called out, desperate not to be left alone in the room. Bressinger did not wait. He reached Vonvalt's chamber door, battered it open with his shoulder and brandished his sword – a Grozodan-style side-sword – so smartly that I heard it cut the air.

"There! By the chest!" I heard Vonvalt shout. I entered his bedchamber to see him up in the window box in his nightclothes, pressed against the lattice so firmly that he stood as much chance of forcing the window and falling to his death as he did of being killed by the snake. Half-coiled at the foot of a mahogany trunk, the creature itself was perhaps two feet long, and with drab markings that were almost imperceptible in the wan moonlight. If Bressinger had not acted with such frantic urgency I might even have considered it to be harmless.

Bressinger wasted no time in dispatching it; he threaded its skull with his side-sword and killed it instantly, though that did not stop him from hacking at the thing a few more times to make sure. Then he looked up at Vonvalt.

"Are you bitten?" Bressinger asked. He took a step forwards. "Tell me, quick!" His chest heaved from the sudden, explosive exertion, and his eyes were wide and frantic with concern. Bressinger was so rarely given to panic; now he looked half-demented.

"What's the matter?" I asked, looking between the two men and the serpent's corpse. "Is it poisonous? Did it get you?"

"No," Vonvalt said, stepping down from the window box. I could tell that he was slightly embarrassed by his reaction. "I'm fine." He walked forwards to where the dead snake lay and squatted down in front of it.

"A Grozodan asp," Bressinger said, his voice hoarse. He lifted the body up slightly with the tip of his side-sword, revealing subtle black stripes on its underside. The rest of its body was a drab, unremarkable brown. "A viper. There was one in our room, too."

"It is venomous, then?" I asked.

"'Tis lethal," Bressinger growled. He planted the tip of his side-sword into the floorboards and leant back against the wall. "Nema's blood, but a scratch from its fangs will kill a full-grown man inside the hour."

"And are they migratory?" Vonvalt asked. He threw open the chest and pulled out his own short-sword.

Bressinger looked confused. "What are you talking about?" he panted.

Vonvalt strode towards the door. "I do not consider it likely that two of them travelled here themselves." He nodded back towards the window in his chamber. "Come; if we are quick, we may still catch the handler."

We fell into step unthinkingly behind him and moved quickly through Lord Sauter's house. The commotion had roused the better part of the household, but Vonvalt bade them return to their rooms in his curt, imperious way. In moments we were out in the frigid air of Galen's Vale, our breath streaming away from our mouths in great clouds of vapour. In our haste, none of us had thought to put anything approaching appropriate clothing on, and only the intensity of the moment kept me from shivering violently.

"Shit," Bressinger said. "Look there." He pointed, and I followed the line of his finger to a dark shape lying in Sauter's front garden among an arrangement of plants. Even in the poor light, it was unmistakably a corpse. His armour and uniform marked him out as a town watchman, while a dark splash on the cobbles near the gate told of a violent end. I cast my mind back to the man who had met us when we had first arrived at the mayor's residence: a friendly everyman, polite and concerned with our welfare. That he had met his end for no other reason than he stood between his assailant and us filled me with a sudden sense of melancholy, in a way that many other deaths – even those of people considerably closer to me – had not.

"The blood is still smoking," Bressinger said.

"He cannot have been killed more than a few minutes ago," Vonvalt said.

"'Tis plenty of time to make off."

"No," Vonvalt murmured, shaking his head. "He will want to know if he has been successful."

I looked up about the houses that faced Lord Sauter's residence. Much like the building we had just exited, they were large and expensive-looking, brick-and-timber structures that reared up two, three and even four storeys into the night sky. They were foreboding in the darkness, like the hunched bodies of sleeping giants.

My time in Muldau had given me an escape artist's eye, and my attention was instinctively drawn to the mismatched heights of the roofs. Looking at the sturdy creepers that wound up the brick frontages and the extruding beams and drainpipes, it would not have taken much effort for anyone to mount the upper parts of the houses for a better vantage point, let alone a professional. It was only then that I realised how vulnerable the three of us were.

"We should move into cover," I said, both anxious and cold as my excitement drained away.

As usual, Vonvalt had pre-empted me. "I have him," he

murmured, his eyes flicking up to where two roofs, both thatched and misaligned by an entire storey, overlooked us perhaps fifty yards away. The faintest of silhouettes, what looked like a hooded head and part of a shoulder, jutted out from the gap. I imagined the man watching us, a bow clutched in his right hand.

"We've no hope of catching him," Bressinger said.

"He cannot stay up there for ever," Vonvalt replied.

"What is your plan?"

"I will run at him," Vonvalt said. "I will get close enough to bring him in range of my Voice."

"You mean to make him leap to his death?" Bressinger asked.

I looked at him, appalled. Even Vonvalt, who cut Bressinger a great deal of slack, looked reproachful.

"That would be murder," Vonvalt said.

"If you catch him you will hang him," Bressinger said, defensive.

"You are being facetious," Vonvalt said. "Make your quips later. I should like to bring him down intact. I want to know who sent him."

"What is your plan, then?" Bressinger pressed.

Vonvalt grimaced. "I shall try and compel him to flee. He has no hope of making any of the town gates; not with the curfew in place. My guess is he means to make for the Gale. We can expedite the process, on our own terms."

Bressinger sucked in a few deep breaths, as though he were motivating himself ahead of a game of handball in the Sovan arena. "Let us be about it, then," he said, "before we are frozen stiff."

"Helena," Vonvalt said, turning to me, "stay here. Crouch behind this pillar until it is safe to come out. There is no sense in all three of us being reckless with our lives."

I had half-hoped he was going to send me back inside, but not out of fear; as much as I wanted to be a part of the chase, I was indeed freezing stiff. Instead, I simply nodded.

"We must be quick," Vonvalt said, eyeing his quarry.

"Aye," Bressinger muttered impatiently.

"All right: let's move."

I watched as the two men leapt through the front gate and dashed down the street towards the silhouette like a pair of escaped prisoners. I expected at any moment one of them to fall with an arrow lodged in his chest, but the silhouette did not stir. I frowned at that. I gripped the cold, half-frosted brickwork of one of the gate pillars, and squinted to try and see better in the dull moonlight.

Then I heard Vonvalt use the Emperor's Voice.

Even from where I crouched, it was not without power. My skull seemed to vibrate subtly, and a faint ringing sang through my eardrums as though someone had tapped a tuning fork and held it next to my head. It was as powerful a blast of it as I had ever known Vonvalt to unleash – yet still the silhouette did not stir.

I whirled around. Off to the right, at the far end of the street, a hooded and cloaked figure unlocked from the shadows. A strange sense of paralysis overtook me; the person moved with such subtlety that for a few moments, in that dark street, I was not entirely sure that it was human. Then the spectre produced a very human weapon from inside his robes – a single-handed crossbow – and the illusion was broken.

"Sir Konrad!" I shrieked. Both he and Bressinger turned sharply. A quarrel whistled through the cold night air, but something – probably my scream – had thrown off the assassin's aim, and it holed nothing more than Vonvalt's nightclothes.

There was a brief moment in which no one did anything at all; then all four of us animated at once, as though we were all stringed to a common puppeteer. The assassin, his only opportunity now wasted, turned on his heel and fled. Vonvalt, Bressinger and I gave chase.

With hindsight, that reckless, headlong dash through the dark streets of Galen's Vale could have ended in disaster. None of us was intimately familiar with the town's layout, nor were any of us armoured, and had the assassin had his wits about him, he would have realised that the advantage still lay with him. Perhaps he was startled, or perhaps he did not want to put himself within the range of Vonvalt's Voice; whatever the reason, he ran like a madman, his wits dissolved like a block of butter in a hot pan.

The three of us cut absurd figures as we sprinted across the frost-slicked cobbles, our nightclothes flapping about us like rags. I admit that once the immediate danger had passed, I found the experience quite exhilarating; it reminded me of my childhood, evading Tollish guardsmen with a hot bun or coin purse clutched in my grubby hands.

Vonvalt, prescient as ever, had been right; his would-be murderer, so creative with his earlier misdirection, had run an unimaginative path to the Gale through the insalubrious eastern closure. Here, in spite of the cold, the very air was saturated with the smell of churned mud and offal, as well as that oily, fishlike stink that suffused everything with its greasy vapour. It put me in mind of the smell that sometimes radiated off Vonvalt after he had taken fish liver oil, a concoction which he swore by as a restorative, but was as antisocial a medicine as ever existed.

"Stop!" Vonvalt called, though he had neither the energy, the range nor the breath to bring the man to heel with the Emperor's Voice.

The man did not stop. In fact, he *could* not stop. In his blind haste, he had badly misjudged the bank of the Gale. Where it was not dusted with ice, the mud remained perilously slick, and he skidded down the steep slope and tipped headlong into the icy water.

"Shit," Bressinger muttered in dismay, no doubt assuming that Vonvalt was about to ask him to attempt a rescue. But once the three of us finally closed the gap, there was no sign of the man; just a few fractured plates of thin ice and a column of froth effervescing in the ink-black water.

"Where in Kasivar's name has he gone?" I wheezed, my breath agony in my throat thanks to the ice-cold air.

No one spoke for a few moments. We stood there, steam rising off us as though we were racehorses after three circuits in the arena, looking for any sign of the assassin. But it was clear that the Gale had claimed our prize.

"He could not swim?" I asked. It baffled me that someone could enter a body of water and simply disappear without resurfacing even once.

Vonvalt shook his head grimly, but it was Bressinger who spoke.

"The cold will have knocked all the air out of his lungs." He spat onto the mud, then arched his back and winced as his spine popped a few times. "Nema's tits, I did not need that."

"I don't understand," I said. "Could he not have just held his breath?"

Bressinger shook his head. "'Tis impossible," he said. "Think on it: how do you get into a cold bath?"

I shrugged. "With great reluctance?" I said.

"Aye," Bressinger said. "And even then, sometimes it makes you catch your breath." He nodded to the waters of the Gale again. They had enveloped the assassin as irreversibly as any peat bog. "When your whole body goes in like that, you cannot help but drink in a lungful. And with no air in your chest, you'll sink like a stone." He spat again, and then twisted his back from side to side. "The currents will have him now. By all accounts, 'tis a treacherous river."

"Blood of gods, man, will you shut up," Vonvalt muttered.

I looked up at him, but he did not meet my gaze. He stared at the hole in the ice, as though entranced by it.

"Sir Konrad?" I asked gently.

He sighed after a long silence. "Dubine has it," he said. He cleared his throat a few times. Like Bressinger and I, the cold air had savaged his throat, but unlike us, he had also employed the Emperor's Voice.

We stood there for a little while longer, but it was not long before we were feeling the cold once again. Behind us, night-watchmen approached, drawn to the clamour and no doubt dispatched in force by Lord Sauter. With the excitement over, my mood soured as I realised that a long and tedious night of explanation and official enquiries awaited.

Vonvalt took in a deep breath, and then let it out slowly. "Back to bed, the pair of you," he said. "I will deal with this."

⁂

Lord Sauter's residence was in a state of chaos when Bressinger and I got back, and though Vonvalt had been trying to do us a favour in releasing us, in fact we bore the brunt of the mayor's questioning. Sauter seemed to be annoyed by the turmoil, but I sensed that his irritation was really a façade, masking a profound sense of embarrassment at having come within a hair's breadth of hosting the assassination of an Imperial Justice. In fact, it was impossible not to suspect the man of having had a hand in it himself, though he did not seem like the type. He faced a flurry of difficult questions from Vonvalt in the morning, and so I could forgive his rudeness.

Bressinger insisted on keeping the snake corpses, telling me that they would fetch a handsome price at any apothecary's as they did in Grozoda. That something so venomous could have any healing qualities at all mystified me, but he assured me that not only was it an effective counter-venom when taken in minuscule doses, it also had a broad array of medicinal properties depending on how it was mixed and blended. He had a maid from the kitchens fetch a jar of vinegar and set the gruesome trophy on the chest next to our bed. I let him do it only on the condition that he exhaustively search the bedchamber for any further signs of snakes – but of course, there was nothing.

The clouds had drawn in again and snow began to fall by the time some semblance of peace and quiet reasserted itself over the household. Of Vonvalt there was still no sign, though I assumed someone had provided him with a cloak. As it would transpire, he had gone back to the watch house, and we would not see him again until the middle of the following morning.

In spite of the night's frantic labours, Bressinger was able to return to sleep absurdly quickly, and it was not long before he was snoring next to me. I, however, lay awake until dawn's first grey light began to suffuse the horizon. I could not help but turn the evening's events over in my mind again and again. Someone had tried to *kill* us. But for a few happy accidents, my life – or at least my life as I had known it – could have ended. It has happened to me so many times since that it is difficult to conjure up that initial crash of emotion; but I can recall, lying in the dark on that long, cold night, feeling profoundly unsettled. I did not know what devilry we had unearthed in Galen's Vale, but for someone to try and murder an Emperor's Justice meant that its roots probably ran deeper than the slaying of a local lord's wife. And of course, that was the real source of my fear – that anyone would try and kill an Emperor's Justice *at all*. It was – had been – unthinkable; even frantic, condemned men did not move against Vonvalt. Many things I had taken as absolutes were having their structure and limits tested. How could I possibly go to sleep when the very foundations of my worldview were being hacked away?

By the time sleep eventually found me, it was fitful and unsatisfactory. I thrashed about the bed as though I were in the grip of a fever dream, and despite Bressinger's increasingly irritated prodding, it took a long time to find anything approaching a deep slumber.

The town was rousing itself for another trading day when my body finally surrendered itself to unconsciousness.

I dreamt I was drowning.

The following day was a wretched one. Both Bressinger and I awoke to the sound of a tremendous clattering in the street outside, and still half asleep, we dashed to the window and threw open the curtains. Light, dull and grey though enough to burn the eyeballs, hit me with the force of a blow, and I realised we had been left to sleep in until the mid-morning. Standing in the street beyond Lord Sauter's front garden was a group of town watchmen; another pair of watchmen, stripped of their swords and armour, were standing atop the roof of the house where we had seen the silhouette the night before.

"Son of a bitch," Bressinger said, nodding towards the thing that had made the clattering noise. As the watchmen parted, I saw that it was a crude wooden construction not unlike a scarecrow, wrapped in a tatty cloak.

My eyes scanned the garden below, but of course the corpse of the guard had been removed, and now presumably occupied a slab in Mr Maquerink's mortuary. Physicians rarely wanted for business when Vonvalt came to town, but in Galen's Vale they would do a roaring trade.

I wondered how Sir Radomir had taken the news; his and Vonvalt's relationship was but one or two mishaps away from disintegration, and though the two had formed a bond of uneasy mutual respect, the sheriff did not strike me as the kind of man who would take the death of one of his own men well.

Bressinger and I dressed ourselves hastily. Vonvalt was not in his bedchamber, and we exited the mayor's residence to make enquiries of the men gathered outside. They informed us that though Vonvalt had spent the better part of the night with Sir Radomir, he was now back in the eastern closure. We retraced our steps from the night before, our cloaks pulled about us and heads bent into the cold wind, which carried a hint of sleet.

Vonvalt was standing on the bank of the Gale with another group of miserable-looking town watchmen, his hair wet and lank. He must have returned to the mayor's house at some point, for he was now clad in his Imperial best, though his boots and the hem of his cloak were befouled by the stinking mud. Even from a distance he looked haggard. His face was pale, and his features were drawn and tired-looking. Vonvalt did not function well without a good night's sleep, and I knew that I would be spending most of the day trying to avoid him.

As Bressinger and I approached, we observed a group of fishermen clad in waders and studded boots as they wrestled a small, single-man rowboat from the waters – evidently the method of our assassin's ingress. A town watchman did his best to try and usher back a crowd of onlookers which had gathered in spite of the weather, but rumours of a second murder were already spreading.

"I trust you are both restored?" Vonvalt asked us as we came within earshot. He did not take his eyes from the boat.

"Aye," Bressinger said. "We saw the decoy from the roof."

"Hm," Vonvalt grunted. "A shabby ruse."

"It nearly did for you," Bressinger remarked, nodding at Vonvalt's ribs where the quarrel had ripped through his nightgown.

"As though I needed reminding," Vonvalt said. His mood was even blacker than I had anticipated. He gestured to the rowboat. "Let us hope that this at least bears some fruit. I am told by local experts—" he wrinkled his nose, gesturing to the crowd of townsfolk "—that we have no hope of recovering the body."

"That the river produced the corpse of Lady Bauer was by all accounts a miracle," Bressinger said. I looked at him, surprised at how badly he continued to misjudge his master's temperament. Or perhaps he didn't care. Either way, Vonvalt was interrupted before he could respond.

"Milord," one of the men next to the boat called out uncertainly. Dealing with Vonvalt in his official capacity was an intimidating exercise at the very best of times, but it was clear to all Vonvalt was in a sour mood. "'Tis bare. You are welcome to inspect it."

Vonvalt regarded the boat as though the thing were cursed. "No," he muttered, and he turned on his heel and tramped back to the mayor's house.

≈

Bressinger and I were left to our own devices for the rest of the day. Vonvalt retired to bed for a few hours, and then returned to the watch house. Since nothing had been divined from the corpse of the guardsman, Vonvalt authorised the release of the body to his widow, and then attended the man's burial late in the afternoon. I felt at least partly responsible for the guard's death, and no small amount of guilt for missing the funeral in spite of the fact that Bressinger and I were not invited to attend, though Vonvalt would later tell me that it had been a fraught affair and he himself had not been welcome.

Bressinger went to the apothecary's to sell his prized snake corpses, and then on to a succession of public houses. For my own part, feeling adrift and suffering from a general sense of malaise, I took the time to have a long bath. I had hoped to relax, but I simply ended up ruminating on matters for several hours.

Vonvalt returned later in the evening, and we took dinner together in the dining room. He picked idly at the spread, lost in introspection, and would not be drawn into conversation – not that there was much to discuss about what had happened. There was nothing left in its wake by way of evidence, and we could only conjecture that it was related to the murder of Lady Bauer, though even that was not a given.

I think, like me, he had been shocked more by what the attempt represented than the attempt itself. I know that Vonvalt felt very strongly that his position as one of the Empire's foremost lawmen put him well above the risk of murder. It was not a matter of fear – his physical courage was beyond question – but thinking men are wont to dwell on things, and Vonvalt was a thinking man. He could not separate out the attempt on his life from an assault on the supremacy of the common law, and the latter was a difficult thing for him to countenance, particularly when one considers how Vonvalt had come to reach that belief. It was easy to forget, after all, that he had seen the civilising effects of the Sovan common law first-hand. His father had taken the Highmark and Vonvalt had been pressed into the Legions. He'd gone to war against his countrymen. Both he and his father had had to believe that Sovan citizenship, and what it represented, was an end in itself. How else could one have justified the horrors of the Reichskrieg? Vonvalt had embraced the ways of the Sovans with the zeal of the convert, and though he was no fool, I knew that as a consequence of his adolescence – for the man had only been fifteen years old when he had gone to war – the very kernel of his worldview was softer and more vulnerable than any would believe.

We had no choice but to put the matter to one side for the time being. It was an unsatisfactory conclusion to the business, and after a cursory meal, we retired to our bedchambers having barely exchanged more than a few words. I had hoped that Bressinger would provide a sympathetic ear on his return later that evening, but to my surprise, he was dismissive of my fears.

"Don't let it consume you, Helena," he said as we both settled down into bed. "He will have gathered his wits by the morning."

"You are not worried about him?"

"No, and he would not be happy to learn that you are. It takes more than a quarrel in the night to rattle our esteemed master." He snorted. "There is a joke in there, is there not? Quarrel? I have not the grip on Saxan that you have."

"You speak it well enough – at least when you are sober."

"Fighting talk," he scoffed. "Careful; I might let the viper get you next time."

"And just how much did you get for your snake corpses?"

Almost at once, the man's mood turned melancholy. "It matters not," he muttered. "'Tis all gambled and drunk up anyway."

I paused, trying to think of the right words to say. "Thank you, by the way," I settled on. "For saving my life."

He waved me off. "Do not think on it. You know I would not let anything happen to you, Helena. I would sooner die myself." He paused, and let out a great, shuddering sigh. "Nema knows I would sooner die myself," he repeated softly.

He rolled away from me and extinguished the lamp before I could say anything. I lay a hand on his shoulder for a few moments, unsure of what to do. Then, when he did not stir, I rolled over myself, and within minutes I had fallen into a deep, exhausted slumber.

VIII

Cold Air, Hot Words

"Act in haste, repent at leisure."

OLD SOVAN PROVERB

I awoke the following morning to the tolling of the temple bell. Despite the efforts of Lord Sauter's staff in stoking the residence's many fires, it still felt chilly, and I was reluctant to leave the warmth of the bed. Bressinger, however, rose with alacrity, and threw open the curtains to reveal another slate-grey sky and piles of fresh snow about the town.

"Come on, Helena," he said gruffly. I begrudged the man for the ease with which he was able to shake off sleep. It was something he attributed to his years as a soldier. There was no hint of the melancholy which had afflicted him so suddenly the night before. Indeed, the whole business with the snakes seemed already distant, like a half-remembered dream.

Bressinger gathered up his clothes and went next door to change, and I took the few moments of solitude to rouse myself more fully. Then I donned my hose, smock and kirtle, and a gown given the cold. Vonvalt had bought them all for me as part of my retainer, and as a consequence they were all made of high-quality, durable fabric. In our early months together I had simply been grateful to be off the streets, and was happy to take whatever Vonvalt had thrown my way. Now my tastes had refined. I took more of an interest in Imperial fashions, where clothes hugged the form and felt and looked more feminine than those of the provinces – scandalously so, depending on where you went. The Sovans had done away with headdresses for women, too, most of a century before, and the style of one's hair had itself become a fashion. Most women slavishly followed the hairstyles of the ladies of the day, though I rarely did anything with mine except tie it back.

I left the chamber and bumped into Bressinger in the hallway. He was clad in a shirt, doublet and hose, and his shoulder-length black hair was wet and had been tied up into a ponytail. We both went downstairs and met Vonvalt in the dining hall, where a hearty breakfast of bread, eggs and spiced ham had been set out as well as some steak-and-ale pie left over from the previous night. Vonvalt was drinking small beer and reading in silence from a thick tome on Sovan jurisprudence open next to him.

"Lord Sauter has not risen, then?" Bressinger asked as we sat.

"He has already left," Vonvalt said, not taking his eyes from the book. "He has duties at the kloster, to do with Wintertide." It was clear he was in some kind of bad mood, no doubt precipitated by the attempt on his life, or the recent letter from Justice August.

"When is it, this year?" I asked conversationally. Wintertide was the annual Neman festival that generally – but not rigidly – coincided with the solstice, and sat in a floating fortnight in one of two winter months.

"The second half of Rusen," Vonvalt said, and no more. He took a moment to eat some breakfast, and reopened his book. Then, after another brief spell of uncomfortable silence, he turned to me. "Tell me then, Helena: what did you make of the records from the watch house?"

We had not spoken about my findings last night. Vonvalt, consumed by the contents of Justice August's news and his own legal research, had bade me prepare notes for discussion this morning instead. Given that someone had tried to kill us, I'd thought that our discussions on procedure and record-keeping, though inevitable, would have been at least delayed. I should have known better.

"The records were good," I said, trying to focus on the task at hand. "Full and well kept. They provide the date of the complaint, Mr Vogt's details and a couple of paragraphs of narrative on the matter. Each entry was signed and dated by the constable who wrote it."

Bressinger made an impressed noise. Vonvalt grunted his agreement as he broke open a boiled egg and began smearing its contents on to a large wedge of tough buttered bread.

"It accorded largely with Sir Radomir's recollection," I continued. "Mr Vogt was shipping in a hundred tonnes of coarse grain to Kòvosk. It was to be animal feed for the Legions. There was a considerable amount of pressure to dispatch the grain quickly. Mr Vogt had purchased the grain on credit, using funds from a Guelan bank. He was to profit considerably from the sale of the grain, even with the payment due back to the bank. Apparently the grain shipment was held up by customs in Kzosic Principality and they found that Mr Vogt had not arranged for the correct import warrant from the Imperial customs house. Mr Vogt was adamant that he had arranged for such a warrant. But to complicate matters, it turned out the grain had spoiled along the way and was in any event unusable.

"When Vogt tried to claim on the guarantee for the spoiled grain, Bauer refused on account of the fact that Mr Vogt's failure to get the right import warrant had already voided the contract. Vogt was convinced that Bauer had somehow contrived for the customs officers to hold up the ship to swindle him out of his guarantee payment."

"But how could Bauer have known?" Vonvalt asked.

"The merchant we spoke to yesterday said that it was common practice for guarantors to use spies or networks of riders to keep an eye on the cargo they had guaranteed. Perhaps Bauer was tipped off about the grain going bad and had time to get word to accomplices in Kzosic Principality?"

Vonvalt sighed and massaged his chin. "This damnable practice," he said with his mouth full. He turned to Bressinger. "Your enquiries yesterday were successful?"

Bressinger inclined his head. "Aye."

"Tell me about how it works. I've a good idea, but give it to me in your own terms."

Bressinger recounted our conversation with the merchant, Lorentz, from the previous afternoon. When he was finished, Vonvalt nodded.

"It is akin to gambling then. And knowing merchant lawmen as I do, I can see plenty of scope for an unscrupulous man to weasel out of his obligations to settle the cost of a lost cargo." He mused for a moment. "I wonder why Vogt did not press the matter? The mercantile law here is well-developed. It would have been worth his time suing Lord Bauer." He thought for a moment. "We shall have to find a way to dig deeper into Bauer's practice. I want to arm myself with as much knowledge as I can before I use my Voice on him."

"You suspect him, then?" I asked.

Vonvalt shook his head. "I agree with Sir Radomir; Bauer hasn't the look of a man who has committed murder, especially not his wife. But he is hiding something. He was too quick to indict Vogt, and too quick to withdraw it. Whatever happens we shall need to speak to Vogt as well. Dubine, find out the man's whereabouts. If he is around then I would speak with him this afternoon. Let us hurry matters along."

"Sire," Bressinger said.

"Helena, was that all the ledger from the watch house said?"

"Most of it," I said.

"What else?"

"That Mr Vogt wanted the matter investigated."

"And was it? Did he instruct lawmen?"

"According to the ledger, the matter was signed off as closed two weeks later. Mr Vogt withdrew the complaint."

Vonvalt massaged his chin again. "Troubling," he said eventually. "And this complaint is two years old?"

"Thereabouts," I said.

"Come, Helena! What have I told you about the importance of precision in legal dealings?" Vonvalt suddenly snapped, making both me and Bressinger start.

"Nema's blood," Bressinger muttered, recovering the egg he'd dropped.

"Two years and three months," I said, sullen. "The exact date is written in the ledger."

Vonvalt clacked his tongue. "Very strange. I cannot think why the investigation would be willingly discontinued, particularly where materiel for the Reichskrieg was concerned. Is there any indication as to whether the shipment was sourced from elsewhere? Did Bauer himself, for example, go on to fulfil the contract?"

I shook my head. "There is nothing else recorded."

"Then we shall have to make further enquiries. I will speak to Sir Radomir again. Hopefully the constable who took down the complaint is still alive and available. Whatever is going on with the murder of Lady Bauer, I'm convinced her husband and Vogt have something to do with it."

"As you please," Bressinger said.

We ate quietly for five minutes, leaving Vonvalt to his thinking and reading. Bressinger and I both knew that it was rarely a good idea to break those periods of silence, particularly with idle conversation.

Eventually, Vonvalt turned to me.

"You will speak to the watchman today, the lad you know. What's his name?"

"Matas," I said with a surge in my gut. "Matas Aker." I tried not to show the petulance I felt. Vonvalt and Bressinger had enjoyed teasing me about it the past day or two, which put my hackles up.

"Ask him today about the Bauer girl in the kloster. If he is not on duty, find him at home. He will know about it, I am sure. They are of an age, and he is young enough to be well-versed in the town's gossip."

I felt my cheeks redden. I couldn't help myself. "I don't like doing it," I said, my voice lousy with resentment.

Vonvalt put his cutlery down, his features creased in irritation. "That's as may be, but I pay you the wage of a clerk of the Magistratum, which makes you an official of the Imperial Court – not that you act like it, with your complaining."

I recoiled from that, as though the man had raised a hand to me. "I am not a spy," I shot back.

I noticed Bressinger's eyes widen slightly. When Vonvalt spoke, it was with great restraint.

"You will do as I bid and make enquiries of the lad."

"'Tis a deceitful practice," I said. "You are taking advantage of me."

Vonvalt's hand clenched. "I care not a groat whether you are infatuated with him or not. Do as I bid, girl, and find out what he knows. You are being ridiculous."

I felt a hot wash of fury. The last few stretched sinews of my self-control snapped. "You are jealous of him!"

"Oh, Helena," Vonvalt said with a weary, disappointed anger. He pointed to the door. "Get out of my bloody sight, would you?"

"Sire—" Bressinger said, startled by the suddenness of the confrontation, but was himself cut off.

"Nema's blood, man," Vonvalt shouted, pounding the table

with his fist and then pointing to the door. "Go and make your-self useful!"

~

I left the room hot with anger. I stormed through the hallway and yanked on my boots, but in my haste I forgot my cloak. Instead I stomped out into the early morning, kicking through all of the trinkets and offerings left for Vonvalt, and made off down the street.

It feels so silly to write this now, but at the time I truly felt as though that was the end of it all. I had been balancing on the edge of a precipice for months and I had finally been tipped over the edge. I would stay in Galen's Vale for a little while and live off my accrued wages from my clerkship. After that, who knew? I could do anything I wanted. The world beckoned.

I quickly walked most of the way to the watch house, before I had to slow down to catch my breath. My carelessness in charging through the muddy slush meant that the hem of my kirtle was now dirty and would need to be cleaned. Slowing to a walk also meant I gradually began to feel the cold. I would need to buy a new cloak and pay for a launderer to wash my kirtle, two not inconsiderable expenses incurred in the space of a few minutes. The realities of a life without Vonvalt's patronage were already beginning to dawn on me. I furiously crushed them beneath an avalanche of righteous anger. I was a simple pawn to the man, to be used to leverage others' emotions. It was a line I had decided I would not cross.

Of course, I was being ridiculous. Vonvalt was right: my anger was born of my infatuation. I was embarrassed that I had fallen for a young man so quickly, and I was certainly in denial about my feelings. Besides, Sovan social mores, at least at the aristocratic level, decried such passions as vulgar and something to be kept private. At least both Vonvalt and Bressinger were not naturally born Imperials. They had known the merriment of provincial ways before adopting the stern comportment of the Autun.

It took me a long time to find Matas. I was directed by the desk serjeant to the Segamund gatehouse, the fortification which guarded the eastern closure. I remembered it as the gate by which Lady Bauer's body had been found, at the outermost extremity of the eastern closure. It was clearly a poor area. As I crossed the last cobbled street before the closure proper, I could see that the place was almost entirely given over to warehouses, poormen's accommodation and unsavoury or unsocial trades like tanneries and foundries. Here the Gale flowed wide and deep, its banks a hundred feet apart and crossable only by wherry. I began to feel the cold's bite in earnest. At least I'd had the presence of mind to don my boots; the ground was thick with half-frozen mud.

I followed the river. There was no embankment here, and the stinking slopes were strewn with rubbish and shit. Rats, pigs and foxes rootled freely through it all, untroubled by the human activity around them. There were few constables or watchmen in sight, and my good clothes marked me out as an outsider, ripe for robbery, as perhaps Lady Bauer's had. Despite this, I did not feel as vulnerable as I was. Growing up in Muldau had given me an edge that even two years as an Imperial agent could not blunt.

I caught sight of the Segamund gatehouse. It was formed of two formidable stone towers flanking the Gale. Between them I could see two large gates of cross-hatched iron bars, rusted and slimy with age. They were open, and looked as though they had been open for years. Atop the curtain wall, liveried watchmen in heavy overcloaks patrolled or huddled around braziers alive with orange flame.

I reached the Segamund Gate and asked to see Matas, and the guard led me up the steps to the wall. There, elevated above the buildings and warehouses, the cold wind sang freely through the crenellations and I began to shiver uncontrollably.

"Helena?" I heard a familiar voice call out. I looked over to see Matas standing by a brazier. He wore a large, fur-trimmed cloak that seemed to envelop him.

"Matas!" I called out eagerly. I heard his fellow watchmen muttering and joshing him. His angry glares seemed only to encourage them.

"Nema, you must be freezing," he said, unstrapping his cloak. I didn't resist as he wrapped it around me. It stank of smoke but I was too cold to care. Behind us the watchmen continued their jeering. "Come on," he said, rolling his eyes. He nodded towards the tower. "There's a fire in there. We won't be disturbed."

I followed him self-consciously. Our unguarded behaviour was unseemly by every social convention one would care to name; it was fortunate that our only audience was a group of watchmen who would not give a toss for whether it was seemly or not.

It was markedly warmer inside the tower. It was a square building, four floors high and partitioned into a number of rooms by cheap walls of timber-reinforced plaster. The first room we stepped into had a simple profile, home to little more than a few trestles and a large wooden shield bearing the markings of the Vale which was mounted on the wall.

"Is everything all right?" Matas asked, taking off his helmet and pulling the chainmail hood back. He mussed his hair about for a second, self-conscious that the armour had flattened it so much it was like it had been painted on to his scalp.

I fidgeted with the cloak. "I am pleased to see you again," I said.

He cleared his throat. "And I you."

I smiled. My heart thudded. "I have had a falling out with Sir Konrad," I said. It felt wrong to be confiding in someone in this way.

"What do you mean? Nema, you're not a fugitive, are you?" He sounded so suddenly and comically disappointed that I had to laugh.

"No!" I said.

"What's going on?" he asked, smiling confusedly.

I told him what had happened. I could feel myself getting upset as I recounted the heated words Vonvalt and I had exchanged, but it was Matas's look of concern that drove me, infuriatingly, to tears.

"Hey, come now," he said, putting a hand on my shoulder. Despite my crying, the physical contact sent a thrill through me. "There is no need for that. 'Tis an argument. I argue all the time with the serjeants." He shrugged. "The Justice seemed like a decent man to me. He won't hold a grudge."

"You don't understand," I said once I had regained myself. "I don't want to be a clerk. The pressure of it makes my brain boil. Sir Konrad has given me so much, I owe him everything, but . . . I am terrified I am not the person he wants me to be. He is the smartest and wisest man I have ever known. I am nothing, just a gutter rat from the streets of Muldau. I could barely read when he took me on. Now I can speak three languages. I wear fine clothes. Men of great rank and breeding are terrified of me when they learn that I am an officer of the Crown. I just . . . I feel like I don't know who I have become. I've transformed into a completely different person and it frightens me."

Matas had no idea what to say. Of course he didn't; who would, except Vonvalt himself? I hadn't meant to unburden myself so fully, but I hadn't been able to help it, despite how emotionally vulnerable it left me. Bressinger didn't want to hear of my woes. He already thought me ungrateful. I had no other friends to speak of, since we passed through every village and town like food through a gullet. Matas was the first person I had met who seemed interested in what I had to say no matter how foolish I looked.

And then he kissed me.

I was not expecting it. I had never been kissed before. Muldau had been a rough time, and romance had been as far from my mind as it was possible to be. And then I had spent two years with Vonvalt and Bressinger, every waking moment travelling, or dispensing the Emperor's justice, or learning. There had simply been no time for it, no opportunity.

I kissed him back, or what I thought was kissing back. I had very little idea of how it was supposed to go. I don't think Matas had much idea either. But it did not matter how inexpert it was; it was thrilling. My whole body felt as though it would combust.

We pulled away. I was glad my face was ruddy from the cold, for I was blushing furiously. Matas began to laugh, and then I laughed too. I think we would have kissed again, had we not been reminded of how close we were to being discovered by the sound of voices carrying in from the curtain wall.

"I have not been kissed before," I said.

"Nor have I," Matas admitted. "I did not think my first would be with one so beautiful."

I smiled. I could not stop. It was as though someone had distilled excitement into an essence and I had swallowed it.

But, as much as I wanted to enjoy and lose myself in that moment, already I could feel the unease growing in the back of my mind. It was like a splinter lodged under the skin. What was I doing? I could not simply leave Vonvalt. Did I really expect never to see him again? To avoid him and Bressinger for weeks while their business concluded and then just live out my life in the Vale? At the very least I needed to speak with him – and frankly – about how I felt. Now that the heat of the moment was well past, and I had more time to reflect, I began to regret my careless words and my storming off.

My unease must have been plain to see, for Matas asked me, "Is something wrong?" He looked suddenly downcast. "Are you not happy?"

"I am thrilled," I said, "truly." I sighed, looking about the plain chamber. "But I am *torn*, Matas, so torn. I do not know what to do. And I should tell you that I came here on a pretext – or rather, I was supposed to. Sir Konrad sent me to speak to you to ply you with questions about the Bauer case. I refused him. It was what led to our argument." I gestured to the room, laughing cynically. "And here I am anyway."

"What does Sir Konrad want to know from me?" Matas said, alarmed. "I had no hand in it!"

"No, no," I said, daring to touch him on the chest. His surcoat was cold where the chainmail had sapped all the heat from it. "It was about Lord Bauer's daughter, up at the kloster. He thinks you would know about it."

"Only what others know," he said, still confused. "I have no special knowledge on the subject."

"I think that is all he is after. Some local knowledge."

Matas shrugged. "I can tell you what I know, but ..." He frowned. "... Helena, I thought you wanted to leave the Justice's service?"

I sighed again. I did not know what I wanted. "I will have to speak with him no matter what I do," I said. "It might placate him if I return with something useful."

We stood in silence for a moment.

"There could be a place for you here," Matas said, toying with his gloves. "I know we have only just met, but I feel ..." He stopped, embarrassed.

"I feel it too," I said.

It sounds foolish and not a little dramatic, looking back on it now. It is funny to think how quickly we fell for one another. It is a thing that only the young seem capable of. But I think I would be doing both my younger self and Matas a disservice to simply dismiss my feelings as the wanton affection of a maid. Just because it was quick did not make it any less real. I sometimes have to force myself to remember that.

"Will you tell me what you know?" I asked. "I promise I will come and see you again soon. As soon as I can."

"Of course. But it is not much. Her name is Sanja Bauer. There was nothing special about her that I can recall. I have never spoken to her, though I used to see her around the town often enough. She is probably about our age."

"Lord Bauer said that she had a calling to take the cloth."

Matas shrugged. "I know she is up at the kloster. I've never really thought about it, but it did seem to happen very suddenly. And she has not left since, as far as I know."

I frowned. "But the kloster is less than a mile away," I said. "There is no ordinance in the Nema Creed that prevents people from leaving, is there?"

Matas shook his head. "No; they come down all the time. Most of the Nemans will be here for Wintertide, for one reason or another. You can see them fussing about the temple. And they bring gifts to the alms houses and orphanages as is traditional for the season. They are supposed to take in the beggars too, for the winter, but judging from the frozen corpses I have seen at the temple doors they have not," he added bitterly.

I nodded absently. I remembered being on the receiving end of similar charitable activities in Muldau. The monks and nuns used to come down from the klosters and distribute food and old clothes to us. Some of them were deeply virtuous, but there were plenty who preyed on the poor and young. I had no love for the Sovan religion, but I actively despised the hypocrisy which seemed to infect its more zealous adherents.

"But Sanja does not come?" I asked.

"I couldn't say with certainty, but I don't remember seeing her for a while now. Maybe . . . a couple of years?"

"How can anyone be certain she is still there?" I asked.

"Oh, I think Lord Bauer goes to visit her from time to time. I believe she is very devout. It is not unheard of for some to remain within the walls of the kloster for their whole lives, especially the old and crippled. For anyone else . . . Well, religion does funny things to your brain."

I was about to agree with him when a thought struck me. "You said she has not been seen for a couple of years?"

"Well, I have not seen her," Matas said. "That's not to say others have not."

"But you said a couple of years."

"Yes."

"Two years?"

He shrugged. "Could be about that."

"Two years three months?"

"Nema, I cannot be that specific!"

"Think!"

He looked surprised. He paused for a long moment. "Yes, I'd say so. I remember because I saw her at the Harvestide fair. And I do not remember seeing her since."

My mind raced. "I must speak with Sir Konrad," I said.

"Helena, is everything all right? What is it that I've said?"

"I'm sorry, I have to go." As I spoke, I heard a horse's hooves thumping in the mud outside, and someone from the tower above us hailing the rider. I recognised Bressinger's voice calling back.

"That is Dubine," I said. I planted a quick kiss on Matas's cheek. "I will see you again soon." With that, I hurried out the door.

"Ah," a serjeant said as he saw me. "There's a gentleman here to see you, miss."

"Helena!" Bressinger called up. He was sat atop Gaerwyn. He did not look angry, as I had expected; rather he bore a strange, urgent countenance. "I have been searching for you for the thick end of an hour."

"I must speak with Sir Konrad," I said, hurrying down the steps of the curtain wall.

"Nema's arse, you smell like a bonfire," Bressinger said as I approached. He had my cloak with him, and nodded to the one I was wearing. "You'd best give that back to the lad; he'll freeze without it."

I quickly removed it and hurried back up the steps, but the serjeant intercepted me. "I'll take it to him," he said with a wink. I muttered thanks and made my way back down to Bressinger.

"Come, quickly," he said as he pulled me up on Gaerwyn.

"What's the matter? I asked, pulling my own cloak about me. "I know I must speak with Sir Konrad."

"Aye, that you must," he said, kicking Gaerwyn to a canter. "But not about your spat. Events have overtaken it."

"Why? What's happened?"

"A rider has come, bearing another letter for Sir Konrad. It is from Sir Otmar Frost, up in Rill."

"What has he written?" I asked, shouting over the roar of the wind.

"The last words he'll ever write, Helena. The man has been murdered."

IX

Return to Rill

"Bad tidings and wise counsel are as
easily ignored as one another."

OLD MAGISTRATUM PROVERB

I can still remember vividly that journey back through the east-ern closure. My heart had not stopped pounding since mine and Matas's tryst; but whereas before it had fluttered with excitement, now it thumped with dread – and only part of it was to do with the death of Sir Otmar.

It was rare for Vonvalt and I to argue. We bickered and sniped, as people who spend too much time in one another's company are wont to do, but we seldom exchanged truly heated words. He was slow to anger, and in keeping with Sovan mores considered public displays of emotion to be vulgar. If I became angry, he tended simply to ignore or dismiss me until I calmed down.

To see Vonvalt genuinely angry was therefore a frightening

experience. Despite Bressinger's words to the contrary, I was anticipating a difficult confrontation.

Gaerwyn took us back through the closure at a faster pace than was permissible inside the town walls. It had not snowed yet, but clouds were piled high above the Vale, blotting out the weak winter light. I was in no hurry to see Vonvalt, and my mood sank to its lowest ebb as we closed on Lord Sauter's residence. Already some of the street lanterns in the town's central streets were lit, though the place was emptying by the minute, commonfolk and merchants alike driven away by the biting cold and the impending snowfall.

"I'll see to the horse," Bressinger said as we were admitted through the front gate by the guard and I dismounted. "Sir Konrad is in his chambers." He paused. "If you want my advice, you would do well to tell him the truth of your feelings. Sir Konrad needs his people present, their minds turned to the problems at hand. He cannot afford to have you distracted, now more than ever."

I approached the house like a girl approaching the gallows. I could see the flickering light emanating from Vonvalt's chambers at the top corner of the mayor's residence. I walked into the house and decloaked. There was no servant to greet me. I hung my cloak up and removed my boots, and walked up the stairs.

"Helena?" I heard Vonvalt call out. I tried to gauge his tone, but it was impossible.

"Yes," I called back. It almost came out as a whisper.

"I am in my room. Come."

I crossed the upstairs hallway and entered Vonvalt's chamber. He was sitting on the window seat again, once more stripped down to his shirt and breeches. The room was full of pipe smoke, and I could see and smell spiced wine on the little table next to the fire. The logs crackled and spat.

"Dubine has told you about Sir Otmar?" he asked.

"He has," I said.

"Then you know the situation is very serious."

"I do."

"Good. Then let us spare five minutes, and no more, to clear the air. I have more important things to worry about than whether my clerk likes me or not."

Despite his words, he did not look angry. Just grim.

"I owe you an apology," I said nervously.

"You do," Vonvalt said. "Sit."

I sat.

"Have some wine."

I poured some wine and took a long draw. That, and the fire next to me, thawed me out quickly.

We sat in silence for a moment. I waited for Vonvalt to speak, though much of my initial dread had evaporated.

"When I first saw you, Helena," he said, looking out of the window, "I pitied you. You were a maid, dressed in rags and temple cast-offs, subsisting on marsh ale and alms. Your parents were dead. You and hundreds more were simple wards of the state." He sighed, long and loud. "I was not an orphan, of course, but I lost my mother at a young age. I think you know this already. Disease accounts not for rank; it takes emperors as swiftly and easily as it takes paupers. Well, it took my mother, surely enough. My father paid a king's ransom to the apothecaries, but there was nothing they could do." He took a long draw of pipe smoke. "My point is, Helena, I know what it is like to lose a parent at a young age. And at an older one.

"I pitied you, but I saw promise in you. It rose off of you like an aura. You had sharp, intelligent eyes. I could see that the way you acted – like a street urchin, although you had temple make-work to keep you busy – was learned behaviour, not natural. You wore it like a cloak, to survive.

"I knew I could use you. Of all the beggars and whores and urchins and cutpurses in that wretched city, you were the only one with the temerity to try and rob me, an Imperial Justice.

I indentured you. I taught you the ways of Sova, of Imperial law and jurisprudence and the Magistratum. I taught you languages and manners. I gave you an education that many lords would kill for for their offspring. I paid you to boot."

"I know I have been ungr—" I tried, but he held up a hand to silence me.

"Helena, I am not a fool. I know that a maid such as yourself has no innate desire to become an Imperial Magistrate. I know that our lifestyle is not conducive to developing friendships, or relationships. I am not surprised that you are taken with this lad in the watch. To be frank with you, Helena, the only thing that surprises me is that this issue is only now rearing its head. You are, what, nineteen years old? 'Tis common enough to be three years married at your age."

He took a sip of wine, and a draw on his pipe. "I am very fond of you, Helena – though not in the way you intimated earlier," he added with his characteristic dourness, and I blushed furiously. "But I will not force you into a career and a life you've no interest in. It is no good for you and it is no good for me. So, I have a proposal for you."

I sat nervously. I had not expected any of this. I had expected harsh words and a frank dismissal. His reasonable treatment of me made me feel even worse. Already I was doubting myself, questioning whether I really wanted to stay in Galen's Vale. After all, would I not grow bored? Was I not better off staying with Vonvalt until we reached Sova? My thoughts were so clouded on the matter I felt as though I wanted to scream.

"Our business here is progressing quickly. We will either find out who murdered Lady Bauer in the next few days, or no one will ever find out. In that span of time, you will work dutifully and diligently. I will see that you are as involved in the matter as I can make possible. At the end of it, you can decide whether you want to remain employed as my clerk and apprentice, or whether you want to stay here. Does that sound fair to you?"

It was. It was so completely, objectively fair that I began to cry.

"I'm sorry," I said through my tears. "I am sorry for the way I have been recently. I cannot help my feelings. I am so torn on the matter." I did not cry often in front of Vonvalt, and he looked distinctly awkward.

"I am not trying to upset you Helena," he said. "I am trying to find a solution that works for both of us. The fact of the matter is, for all I want you to remain as my apprentice, if you resent me then your work will be poor and we will part on inevitably bad terms. And neither of us wants that, do we?"

"No," I said, wiping my eyes furiously. "No, I would hate that."

"Good." He extinguished his pipe and stood. He picked up a letter from next to him and passed it to me. I could see at the top an imprint of the device of Sir Otmar – the boar's head and broken lance – and from the shaky scrawl I could see that it had been written in a great hurry. Brown stains which could only have been old blood marked the parchment in great smears.

"What happened?" I asked, my hands trembling slightly.

"A lad from Kolst came across Sir Otmar at the Gabler's Mount watchtower. Sir Otmar had been wounded, gravely. He gave the boy his seal and enough money for the Imperial Relay and bade him find me." Vonvalt gestured to the letter. "Read it."

I looked at the letter again. It was barely three lines long, and I could only make out the following words:

sir konrd
all in Rill slain
the PRIEst

"Prince of Hell," I murmured. I looked up. "Claver."

"Come," Vonvalt said. "Lord Sauter and Sir Radomir are waiting. We've much more serious business to attend to."

The mayor, Sir Radomir and Bressinger were sitting in the reception chamber, the latter two still dressed for outdoors and warming themselves in front of the hearth. Sauter stood as we entered.

"You have received ill tidings, Justice," Sauter said, wringing his hands.

"Seldom a day goes by when I do not," Vonvalt said. "Sit, all. I must be brief."

Everyone sat. Vonvalt remained standing, as though he were addressing a courtroom. "At the very end of Vandahar, on the eve of Goss, we came across a small village in Tolsburg. Rill. There we discovered the widespread practice of Draedism."

Sir Radomir nodded. "'Tis common enough, in the north."

"Indeed," Vonvalt said. "The lord of the manor was Sir Otmar Frost. He was not a man of great means, but he struck me as decent, and a man with the welfare of his charges at heart. I fined him for turning a blind eye to the practice of Draedism and commanded that he erect a shrine to Nema somewhere prominent."

"A just outcome," Lord Sauter murmured uncertainly. Draedism had different reputations in different places, but somewhere like Galen's Vale probably had not had to deal with pagan rebels like those towns and wayforts on the Tollish border and up in north-west Haunersheim.

Vonvalt sighed. I could see he was angry. "At the time we were riding with a young and zealous Neman priest. He disagreed with me on how best to deal with the villagers – though certainly he had no basis on which to do so – and we parted on poor terms. I have heard separately from a colleague that this priest has made an ally of the Margrave of Seaguard. Now I have received a letter from Sir Otmar himself, telling me that he and all the villagers have been slain. I fear that since our parting ways, this priest has used this friendship with the margrave to take matters into his own hands."

"Is it not treason to countermand a Justice?" Sir Radomir asked.

"It is," Vonvalt said.

"What do you propose to do?" Sir Radomir asked eventually.

Vonvalt drew himself up. "I need to find out what has happened. My guess is that this priest, Claver, has probably taken a posse of Templar initiates south from Seaguard."

Sir Radomir nodded slowly. "The fortress has a reputation for cruelty."

"But it is an Imperial castle!" Lord Sauter said. "They are bound by the laws of Sova – by your decision as Justice! Are they not?"

Vonvalt shrugged. "The north is a wild and desolate place," he said. "In many places it is as rough as the Frontier. Seaguard is attacked frequently by northmen and pagans. The margrave will have taken his own view on how to deal with a place like Rill, particularly if he is a pious man."

"But it is not within his gift," Sir Radomir said.

"No," Vonvalt said. "It is not. Which is why I must undertake an urgent investigation."

"You mean to leave the Vale?" Sauter asked.

"Yes," Vonvalt said. "I expect I will be gone for balance of Rusen. In the circumstances, the timing is most inopportune; but I am sorry to say that these matters overtake the investigation of Lady Bauer's murder somewhat. Dubine will remain behind and act as my proxy. He will continue to assist Sir Radomir."

I looked immediately to Bressinger, who accepted this unwelcome news with a simple nod. I was sure he would protest later in private, but it would have been unseemly for him to do so at that time.

"There is no sense in delaying until the morning. I will make for Vasaya immediately," Vonvalt said. "Lord Sauter, you were going to provide me with a list of the town's council members and their duties. Please now see that you give it to Dubine."

"Of course," Lord Sauter said, confused and anxious. It was clear that neither he nor Sir Radomir wanted Vonvalt to leave.

"In which case, I will bid you all farewell – for the time being," Vonvalt said, forging ahead with single-minded determination. "Dubine, Helena, come with me."

There was no more discussion. Bressinger and I left the room and followed Vonvalt upstairs to his chamber. He closed the door behind us.

"Sire, you cannot—" Bressinger started with clockwork predictability, but Vonvalt silenced him.

"No, Dubine. You will not accompany me. I need you here. Despite Sir Radomir's best efforts, I fear this investigation will fail without Imperial intervention. Examine the list that Lord Sauter gives you, detailing Bauer's duties as a member of the town council. Once you know what they are, make enquiries – particularly of those duties he neglected to mention to us."

"Sire," Bressinger said, sullen. Vonvalt ignored his tone. He was too busy packing his things into a leather satchel. He would travel light.

"The next most important step is to track down Zoran Vogt. He is the key that unlocks the next door. It is a shame I cannot be there to use the Emperor's Voice on him; you must get as much from him – using legal means – as you can."

"Aye, sire," Bressinger said.

"Helena, what did you discover about the Bauer girl? Anything?" he asked.

The excitement I had felt after speaking to Matas had been so overtaken by events that when I spoke, it was more in awkwardness than enthusiasm.

"Sanja Bauer," I said. "That's her name. Matas told me that she was a normal girl. He did not know her well, but he did know her and saw her around the town. He could not remember her being particularly devout, and there wasn't anything obvious that seemed to cause her to go to the kloster." I paused, remembering my previous excitement. I could not conjure it again. "The thing I thought was most interesting was the timing of it. She seemed to abscond just over two years ago."

Vonvalt paused. "Around the time Zoran Vogt lodged his complaint against Lord Bauer."

"Exactly," I said.

Vonvalt rubbed his chin. "Nema, that is interesting."

"It may be coincidence," Bressinger said.

"I know that," Vonvalt said irritably. "Does the girl ever leave the kloster?"

I shook my head. "I don't think so. I don't think she's been seen since."

"It's not one of those klosters where they all shut themselves in for ever, is it?" Vonvalt asked.

"No, there are monks and nuns in town for Wintertide."

"I've seen them," Bressinger confirmed.

"Look into it, Dubine, but carefully. Find out more about that kloster, and ask around about Sanja Bauer. It is true that some people develop sudden piety, but the timing of this is likely to be more than coincidence."

Bressinger nodded. "Aye, I will investigate."

Vonvalt nodded. He reached out and he and Bressinger clasped forearms in the traditional Sovan way. "I'll be back by the end of Rusen at the latest. If I'm not then something has gone awry. I'll try to get word to you in any event."

"What am I to do?" I asked. Both men turned to me.

"Why, Helena," Vonvalt said, "you're coming with me."

※

We had had our fair share of cold nights travelling through the northern stretches of the Empire, but the ride from Galen's Vale to Vasaya was something else. The wind was an icy blast that sliced across the open countryside like a reaper's blade. Vincento's hooves pounded the Hauner road and covered us in muddy spray.

Insidious snow settled on our old waxed cloaks and worked its way into the fibres so that the cold was like a dead weight draped over our shoulders.

Still, we rode on, recklessly and unsustainably fast. The cords of my fingers ached where I clung to Vonvalt. My face went from painful to completely numb. The wind and wet caused me to shiver uncontrollably. I knew that I would not be able to continue travelling in this way for long, but Vincento cantered on, heedless of the dark, empty Hauner road and its dangers. He was an old warhorse, after all.

We reached Vasaya after a few hours, though it felt as though we had been travelling all night. It was a small walled town, less than half the size of Galen's Vale. We pulled up to the main gate-house and dismounted.

"Ho there," the gatemaster called from atop the wall. He was clad in mail, and I could see by the firelight that he was wearing Imperial colours. The town behind was quiet and still in the dead of night.

"I have need of the Relay," Vonvalt called out. "Two horses, ready to leave now."

"Of course, sire," the gatemaster said. Vonvalt proffered his seal, and the man squinted at it. "Hold on," he said. "I'll come down."

We waited, our breath steaming in the air, as snow tumbled down around us. I shivered, eyeing the braziers flanking the gate with longing.

A small flap opened in the main gate. Vonvalt approached and once more proffered his seal.

"A Justice – Sir Konrad," the gatemaster said, suddenly flustered. He touched the rim of his helmet in salute, then motioned to someone we couldn't see. A few moments later, the heavy iron gate rumbled open.

We stepped through. Just beyond the gate I could see a long stable block, housing twenty, perhaps thirty coursers, each fit, well-fed and well-tended to, all paid for out of the royal purse. Taken together, I was looking at one link in a very long chain: the Imperial Relay, running from Seaguard at the top of the Hauner road to the southernmost tip of Grozoda. It was the fastest way to get a message from the fringes of the Empire to the throne room in Sova itself.

The idea was beautifully simple. Rather than have one horse carry a messenger a thousand miles, why not have a hundred horses carry the messenger ten miles each? The Sovans had had some form of relay system in place for centuries; all they had done was extend it across the Empire. The distances had increased but the principle remained the same.

We walked quickly across the muddy path and into the stable block. Bleary-eyed stable boys on night watch were roused to remove Vincento's baggage and transfer it to the two new horses that Vonvalt and I were to take north. It was a brisk, efficient operation and few words were traded. The gatemaster delivered us to the duty stablemaster, who checked that Vonvalt knew the route north. It was easy enough; we would simply follow the Hauner road to the next Relay station at Espa ten miles away.

Within minutes we had said our farewells to the gate and stablemasters and were nudging our horses back out on to the road. The animals did not require much in the way of instruction; I almost fell off the back of mine as it broke into a hard canter, and we charged headlong into the snowy dark.

⚘

The journey quickly became very tiresome. We would ride hard for ten miles until the horses were foaming at the mouth and their flanks were slathered in sweat. That would take most of an hour. Then we would find the next Relay station, switch our baggage over to a fresh pair of animals and repeat the whole exhausting process. There was little to do except hold on and try to not think about the cold. The horses were well-trained and knew the route. We did not have to guide them much; the Hauner road was wide and well-kept. Its strategic importance meant that heavy obligations had been placed on those lords who owned the land it cut through to keep it in a constant state of good repair. Still, the punishing northern winter meant that, despite the lavish sums spent on its upkeep, sections of it had been given over to mud and flooding, and ice had caused much of the paving to fracture.

Dawn came, and with it an increase in traffic. Those who frequented the Hauner road knew to listen out for the thundering of hooves and move out of the way; those who did not often found themselves, and their belongings, in the muddy sumps on either side. Vonvalt and I were not the only people using the Relay, and occasionally we would shoot past a messenger, dignitary or even another Justice heading in the opposite direction. These were brief flashes of excitement in an otherwise monotonous and draining journey. The thrill of being on official business, of the looks of excitement and bewilderment as we thundered past with cries of "make way!", faded quickly. The insides of my thighs became badly chapped and my pelvis felt as though it would break under the sustained pounding from the horse's back. The wind caught my cloak like a sail and every muscle in my body began to ache badly simply with the effort of staying on the animal. After a few days and nights of multiple changes of horse and cramped, cold, functional accommodation at the small wayforts which made up the majority of the Relay stations, it finally dawned on Vonvalt that we needed to take a break.

We stopped at a small, unwalled town called Josko. We had covered nearly two hundred miles in half a week, and I felt like Kasivar himself had had his way with me by the time our horses plodded through the mud to the Relay station on the town's outskirts. For once there was no snow cloud, and the dark blue evening sky soared overhead, glittering with stars. Ours and our horses' breath fogged the twilight air. My body felt numb with cold and as stiff as a corpse.

"We're making better time than I thought we would," Vonvalt said gruffly. His beard was long and scruffy, and the scarf he had pulled up to his nose was crusted with ice where the cold air had crystallised the moisture of his breath.

I could barely respond. I mumbled something back, but my horse chose that moment to whinny.

"You'll have to speak up, Helena," Vonvalt said. I could hear the smile in his voice. "You sound a little . . . *hoarse*."

In the depths of my misery I could not help but laugh. In fact my laughter became somewhat hysterical, and soon I found that I was crying and the cold was threatening to freeze the tears to my face. The guardsman who approached us looked baffled that two travellers, coated head-to-toe in freezing mud, could be engaged in such raucous mirth.

"I said my clerk sounds hoarse," Vonvalt explained once he'd managed to comport himself.

The guardsman simply rolled his eyes as he took the lead rein. "I've heard that one before," he said, and we followed him into Josko.

❧

We followed the Relay for another day and night, then turned our horses in at the Imperial station at Baquir on the Tolsburg border. From there we leased a pair of palfreys from a local stable, turned off the Hauner road and made across the countryside for Rill.

We were approaching the village this time from the east, riding towards the Tolsburg Marches, whose grey slopes and jags loomed on the distant horizon like gigantic splintered teeth. The land here was covered in a brilliant carpet of snow, which had the effect of making it seem even more bleak and featureless than before. We plodded through the fields of unbroken white, past skeletal trees and buried stone waymarkers. Our only navigational aid was the sun's wan light as it struggled to penetrate the cloud cover. The snow had the effect of damping all sound, too; after our thunderous race up the Imperial Relay, progress now felt slow and eerily muted.

We spent a full day riding across the countryside. The horses left deep furrows in their wake and were clearly unhappy about wading through drifts up to their calves. The air itself was bitterly cold and danced with snowflakes. Ours and the animals' breath came out in great clouds of mist. Despite my layers, the wind seemed to find gaps in my waxed cloak like knives made of ice.

It was mid-afternoon before we saw a familiar landmark – the old abandoned watchtower at Gabler's Mount. Since the watchtower itself was a quarter day's ride from Rill, and Vonvalt did not want to reach the village in the dark, we made for the old stone tower itself.

"Besides," Vonvalt said, his voice strangely muffled by the snow. "Sir Otmar's body may still be there."

We rode for the tower at a trot. It was a single column of grey stone, maybe twenty yards in cross section. It was easy to pick out in the desolate landscape as the only thing fashioned by human hands. It stood like a monolith, haunting in its isolation, and I felt a growing sense of dread as we approached. But we needed shelter for the night, and the watchtower was the only thing in sight capable of providing it.

We reached its lichenous base after an hour of riding. I looked back the way we had come, tracing the channels of our progress through the snow with my eyes. I had a sudden fear that someone would be able follow us, despite there being no sign of another soul for tens of miles. I prayed that the snow would grow heavier and erase the tracks.

I wished Dubine was with us.

"Yes, his corpse is inside," Vonvalt said grimly as he re-emerged from the tower's entrance. He saw my look of horror and added, "It is nothing too ghastly to look at. The cold has frozen him stiff. Were it not for the blood you would think he were asleep."

"I don't want to go in," I said. I don't know why I was so het up about it; I had seen plenty of bodies before. But for some reason I could not shake a profound sense of foreboding.

"We must," Vonvalt said. He looked up at the sky. "We are losing the light, and we will need wood for a fire. Come, Helena, it is a corpse; Nema knows you have seen enough of them."

I kicked the snow in frustration. "Can't you move him?" I asked plaintively.

Vonvalt looked at me with a curious expression. "Of course," he said. "Did you think I wanted to spend the night in there with him?"

I wanted to cry I felt so relieved. "I can gather wood," I said hurriedly. The same forest in which Lady Frost had preached her pagan sermons lay barely a mile away, and though the woods looked dark and forbidding, it was better than watching Vonvalt wrestle a corpse out into the snow.

Vonvalt nodded, looking up at the sky again. "But be quick. You remember what to look for?"

"Yes," I said, irritated. "And I will bring enough for the whole night."

"Good," he said. "I am going to examine the body. Call out to me before you come back in. It is important."

"All right," I said, assuming he meant something about making his toilet.

It took longer to reach the woods than I had anticipated. The horse was cold and uncooperative and wanted to stand in the lee of the tower, and did not take kindly to my heels in its flanks. But the animal had not reckoned with my own fear of being in the woods after dark – an idea that frightened me even more than being in the tower – and eventually surrendered to my urgings.

I dismounted at the edge of the forest. It was a dark and silent tangle of trees that seemed to stretch away endlessly and made me feel as though I were standing on the edge of the known world. Quickly, and talking to the horse to steady my nerves, I gathered up a few armfuls of sticks from under the snow and lashed them together, then hooked them on to the saddle and remounted. By the time I was on my way back, it was dusk and the wind was picking up.

I reached the tower and was ready to head inside to get out of the cold, but I stopped short. I cocked my head and frowned, trying to hear. There was a voice, and it wasn't Vonvalt's – but there was no sign of anyone else having joined us. The tracks we had left in our long slog across the country had faded under the snow.

I strained to listen, thinking that perhaps I had mistaken the voice for the wind moaning through the decrepit crenellations of the watchtower. But no, I had definitely heard a voice – and it was not Vonvalt's.

I dismounted the horse and approached the watchtower entrance slowly, my footfalls creaking in the fresh powder. That same sense of foreboding I had felt when we first approached the tower returned. My footsteps became leaden. When the wind died down again I could clearly make out Vonvalt's voice, though not his words.

The second voice belonged to Sir Otmar Frost.

I felt such a violent chill that my eyes briefly lost focus. A profound feeling of horror overcame me. I rocked in situ, unable to take another step forwards. It was as though my feet had suddenly been bolted to the ground.

Vonvalt did not exercise his necromancy often. As I have said before, it took a heavy toll, normally leaving him shaken and exhausted. But just because he did not perform it often did not mean he did not perform it at all. It was a powerful investigative tool, and the right words or a name drawn from a victim's lips could immediately solve a case. But I had not yet borne witness to it directly, and that only fed the horrors of my imagination.

I could hear Sir Otmar's voice clearly now. He sounded slightly unhinged, but his words were clear and conversational. Occasionally he would let out a sudden burst of nonsense as old memories surfaced or his damaged mind railed against what was happening to it. But for the most part, he seemed to be quite lucid.

It was also utterly unbearable. There was something so dark and unnatural about it that I couldn't stand to hear it. Instead, I jammed my hands over my ears and began to scream.

❧

I have little recollection of what followed; the next thing I can call to mind is waking up next to a crackling fire in the watch-tower. There was no sign of Sir Otmar. Vonvalt sat nearby and smoked his pipe.

"I am sorry," I said, breaking him from his trance. He looked at me, but his expression remained far away and melancholic. I hated seeing it. I hated seeing him look so . . . *haunted*. So fallible. It is an expression I shall never forget.

"Sir Konrad?" I asked. His look was beginning to frighten me.

"Yes," he said, shaking his head as though trying to shake the memories clear from his mind. "Yes. Sorry. I should be the one to apologise. I should have told you of my intentions. I thought you would be longer gathering the wood. I did not want to . . . distress you. But with the body frozen as it was, near perfectly preserved – the opportunity was too good to pass up."

I said nothing. Despite the fire's warmth and the shelter from the wind, I could not get the sound of Sir Otmar's voice from my mind.

"It was Claver, as he wrote in his letter," Vonvalt said quietly. I did not reply, and Vonvalt did not take his eyes off the fire. "They were burned. All of them. Eventually."

"Gods," I muttered, feeling sick.

Vonvalt took another long draw on his pipe. "Try and get some sleep, Helena," he said. "I will watch the fire."

Although sleep was the furthest thing from my mind at that point, I must have achieved unconsciousness at some point in that long and cold night, for I awoke the following morning to find Vonvalt toasting some bread. True to his word, he had kept the fire going all night, which explained how I had managed to sleep at all. Too many times on our travels I had awoken just before dawn next to the smouldering remains of a fire, shivering violently, the cold having seeped deep into my bones.

Vonvalt looked as though he had not slept at all.

"Here," he said, holding the toast out to me. "There is some meat in the satchel behind you."

We ate in silence, then cleared our things away. Vonvalt told me to wait inside while he went out, ostensibly to perform his ablutions, though in reality to conceal the corpse of Sir Otmar, which I had suspected was not far from the watchtower. He returned a while later, bade me in his circumspect way to "make myself comfortable" – no happy prospect in such vile cold – and then, once we were ready, we set out on our horses to Rill.

The sun made a brief appearance that morning, but it was soon concealed by cloud, and after an hour of travel we found ourselves riding under a low ceiling of slate grey. The horror of the evening before already seemed a distant memory, and in fact there was some good to come out of it; for one thing, it was not a terrible surprise to find Rill a circle of charred beams and broken foundations.

We surveyed the scene with a sense of detachment. Given that it had been burned a couple of weeks before, the snow had buried much of the remains – including the charred bones of the unfortunate Draedists who had inhabited it. Vonvalt spent an hour kicking through the snow until he had found the place where Claver and his posse had set the stakes where the villagers had been immolated, and grimly picked through the skeletons. I saw among them the ribcage of what had obviously been a young child, and found myself weeping quietly on the back of my horse.

"They were burned here," he said, indicating the ground where he stood. He sounded tired. With gloved hands he poked through a pile of bones. "There are some sword cuts, too. See these notches?"

I nodded, looking to where he was pointing. I still had not dismounted. My horse was idly cropping the frosty grass where Vonvalt had kicked the snow aside.

"Soldiers carry swords," Vonvalt said, standing up. He looked to the north-east, squinting as if he might see Seaguard from where we stood. "These people did not stand a chance."

Vonvalt moved among the ruins wearily. Sir Otmar's manor, slightly more robust than the other houses, had fared a little better, though the roof had been completely consumed by flame. I watched Vonvalt go in and then come back out a few minutes later. He looked up at me.

"Don't go in there," he said.

All I could do was nod.

Vonvalt was angrier than I had seen him in a long time. The ruins of Rill represented more than just the violent and needless death of a peaceful village. They represented the beginnings of the decline in the primacy of the common law. Once it would have been unthinkable, even for a zealot like Claver, to oppose the judgment of a Justice. Now we were walking among the charred evidence of his defiance. Despite everything, the letter from Justice August, the attempt on his life, the letter from Sir Otmar – the séance with Sir Otmar – I still think that Vonvalt did not quite believe that the authority of Magistratum could be so brazenly challenged. His mind railed against it. The supremacy of the law to him was incontrovertible fact.

Eventually, he returned to his horse. It was past noon, and I assumed that, given the time, we would be making our camp in the watchtower again. I was surprised, then, when an hour later we rode straight past the old fortification and into the snowy fields beyond.

I cleared my throat, conscious of the winter twilight. "Where are we going?"

"Directly to Seaguard," Vonvalt said through gritted teeth. "I care not a jot for the rank of the man. Margrave Westenholtz will hang for this."

X

Seaguard

*"All lords should be anxious when a Justice appears,
obsequious during his stay and relieved by his departure."*

OLD MAGISTRATUM PROVERB

We had already visited Seaguard once, since it had formed the zenith of our large loop away from distant Sova. But that did not make a second approach any less breathtaking. It was the last bastion of the Empire, the Autun's outstretched claw. Beyond lay the North Sea, roiling, frigid and grey, and all that separated the mainland from the kingdoms of the hardy northmen. As with the Frontier to the south, the north held its own mystique, a frightening and desolate land of cold, miserable steppe and cold, miserable people.

Seaguard was a huge fortress, once the seat of the old Hauner kings before Haunersheim had been subsumed into the Empire half a century before. Its walls, towers and keep were all fashioned from the same local black stone, and I had heard it described by many as Kasivar's house. It was an apt description. The place had been designed to inspire terror, and looking at those huge, obsidian-dark walls rearing up from the cliffs, I could say with confidence that the designers had succeeded in their goal.

Given how often the northmen raided the coastal towns and ports of Haunersheim, in spite of the rangings undertaken by the garrison, many had decided to up sticks and live in the shadow of the fortress itself – defying Imperial ordinances in doing so, since most Imperial fortresses liked to keep a good half-mile of ground clear around the outermost curtain wall. It was therefore through a burgeoning town that we travelled on our approach to the main gate. Here people barely stopped to look at us; they were used to seeing Sovan officials coming and going to Seaguard. Instead they carried on with the dreary stiffness of the perennially cold, haggard from cruel winters and the constant fear of attack. The snow here had been trampled into muddy slush, and the air was redolent of cookfire smoke and seawater.

The walls loomed as we drew up to the gatehouse. The fortress was sheer, a cliff face of thick stone wall forty feet high, and I watched as cloaked soldiers in the red, yellow and blue livery of the Empire patrolled it above. They must have been able to see thirty miles on a clear day. Seabirds trilled above them, searching for scraps of fish among the township below.

We were accosted by guards at the gate, who recognised us from our previous visit and who allowed us entry without undue delay. Stable boys were quick to relieve us of our horses, and the duty serjeant ducked out of his station at the foot of the gatehouse to provide the first layer of official greeting.

"Justice," he said, bowing. He was a big man, undoubtedly strong but with a hint of fatness that came from living off a castle larder. The margrave was a stern man – such was his reputation – but he treated his men well. It was an unpleasant duty, garrisoning Seaguard and patrolling the coast, but ironically it tended to attract some of the better military lords of the Empire. It was a prestigious posting, after all, from an aristocratic point of view; the castle was vast and well-provisioned, and there was guaranteed combat to be had. Many in the aristocracy jostled for the position of Margrave of Seaguard, as they did for the larger Templar forts on the southern Frontier and the eastern boundary of the River Kova.

"Serjeant," Vonvalt replied. "I want to see the margrave immediately."

The serjeant bowed nervously. "I can take you to the keep, sire, but I can't guarantee an immediate audience with the margrave."

We followed the serjeant through the outer bailey, which, thanks to a liberal distribution of straw, had mostly avoided being trampled to stinking mud by the comings and goings of dozens of armed men and their horses, and then through a smaller, secondary gatehouse into the inner bailey. The ground was paved here, and overlooked by a wide wooden mezzanine with retractable steps which provided the only access into the keep. The ostentation which I had seen at other Imperial strongholds and wayforts – some little more than large country mansions with the odd bit of crenellation – was absent here.

The serjeant led us up the stairs to the main entrance, a small arched door enclosed by multiple iron lattices. After some back-and-forth with another guard, we entered a low, dingy passageway that took us to the disarming room. Here Vonvalt surrendered his sword and dagger to an apologetic guard, and then we proceeded into the main entrance hall.

And there we remained.

We must have been waiting for almost half an hour before one of the margrave's retainers appeared, a young man clad in expensive-looking clothes of fine wool. "Sir Konrad, forgive me," he said, bowing disingenuously low. "Lord Westenholtz is occupied with pressing matters of a military nature at this time. He bids you welcome and asks if you would accept his hospitality. I have been instructed to show you to private quarters and provide you with victuals – should it please you?"

Vonvalt ground his teeth. As the Emperor's representative his authority was extensive. He was the embodiment of Imperial justice. I had seen him stride into delicate meetings between highly ranked Sovan nobles, interrupt important court proceedings and even bring a wedding to a grinding halt. But he was always careful to avoid interrupting military matters. Notwithstanding the fact that his warrant of authority would happily take him into the heart of the most sensitive martial briefings between the highest-ranking generals in the land, he rightly considered it imprudent. The Imperial Magistratum had long ago found that to interfere with the Emperor's armies was to walk headlong into the curtain wall of His office's executive power.

The margrave was clearly a savvy operator and knew that Vonvalt, unless he was feeling particularly reckless, would have no choice but to wait. It was a power move, and it offended Vonvalt to his core to be stung in such a way.

"I see," Vonvalt said eventually. He said it mainly to discomfit the messenger, who, in fairness, needed more discomfort in his life.

We stood in silence for a few moments. Eventually, the retainer said, "Would the Justice like me to show him to his quarters?"

Another silence. The retainer squirmed.

"I suppose that you shall have to," Vonvalt said eventually.

We made awkward progress through the castle. The retainer moved hesitantly, as though Vonvalt might strike him from behind at any moment. The keep was well-appointed with tapestries and rugs and hearths, and, despite the odd frigid draught from an embrasure, was pleasantly warm. More modern Sovan fortresses, most of which bordered the provinces of the Kova Confederation to the east, had ducts underneath their wooden flooring to direct and circulate the hot air more efficiently. For the Autun's many and extensive faults, ingenuity was not among them.

The rooms we were shown to were luxurious state apartments

which did not, unlike the castle's exterior, want for ostentation. As with much of the rest of the keep, the walls and floors were smothered in tapestries and rugs, and decent-sized windows of lead-latticed glass provided outstanding views of the North Sea. It was about as far as it was possible to get from our meagre quarters in the Gabler's Mount watchtower.

"Have some food and ale brought to my room," Vonvalt said. "Enough for two of us. My clerk will dine with me. I have no wish to make a common mess this evening."

The retainer bowed, eager to be shot of this prickly customer. "Certainly, sire."

"And inform the margrave that he is summoned to me the instant his military matters are dispensed with. Be sure to use that precise wording."

The retainer, facing an impossible situation, could only nod weakly.

"Good," Vonvalt said. "We'll have our baggage brought here too. And arrange to have our clothes washed."

"Sire."

"You are dismissed," Vonvalt said to the man. "And see that you carry out my instructions with alacrity, or I'll have you whipped along with your master."

❧

No messenger came. Vonvalt was exercised into a quiet fury over the course of the evening, and was abysmal company. When it eventually became clear that the margrave was not going to speak with us, we retired to our beds.

That night I dreamt of a solitary watchtower standing on an infinite white plain. I could not help but approach it, though it filled me with dread. The instant I stepped over the threshold I woke up in a blind panic, convinced I had heard Sir Otmar's voice in my ear; but there was nothing, just the knocks and thumps of a castle that never knew a moment's peace.

I slept the rest of the night fitfully, as though suffering in the throes of a fever dream, and awoke before dawn, red-eyed and exhausted, waiting for the winter sun's wan glow to fill the room.

∽

In the morning we readied ourselves and ate breakfast in the common hall. By virtue of Vonvalt's position, we were able – indeed, expected – to dine at the top table, and did so surrounded by a small array of the margrave's knightly retainers. Some were cold, damp and muddy, having spent the night patrolling the coast as far as Enos, the nearest town to the west. Others were fresh and clean, preparing to disembark on the day range.

"Are you here on official business, Justice?" one of the knights opposite Vonvalt asked. His surcoat was a blue so dark it was nearly black, with the white gull device of Margrave Westenholtz displayed across his chest. He smelled of saltwater and his face was speckled with mud.

"After a fashion," Vonvalt replied humourlessly.

"If one of my men has done something to warrant your attentions, sire, I'll hang the man myself, mark my words. This is a place of law and justice."

"Aye," another knight chipped in. I could see that he had a Savaran cross on a chain around his neck. "We are a godly company. We have already sent two dozen men south these past few weeks, to join the host marshalling at Vasaya. And the margrave has seen fit to spare thirty more."

Vonvalt grunted. "I saw no such host. And we came up the Relay directly."

Of course, we had but passed through Vasaya in the dead of night; it was no surprise we hadn't seen anything.

"'Tis there, Justice," the knight said earnestly. "A few hundred men from the Northmark, by now. Patria Claver has promised the Patricians he will push the Frontier out by a hundred miles."

Vonvalt smiled thinly. I was keenly aware that one of the

knights who had put the torch to Rill might have been sat at the table with us.

"Let us hope that they meet with success," he said eventually. He came off as sour and stand-offish, and despite the efforts of a few other knights, he could not be drawn into further conversation. He and I ate in silence while the soldiers ate rambunctiously, the night patrol trading banter with those about to undertake the daylight range. In spite of the many protections I had both spoken and unspoken, I felt uncomfortable. Soldiers, Imperial or otherwise, lordly or lowborn, were often little better than brigands, and only separated from such by a uniform.

We finished our breakfast and made to leave. At that moment, a man whom I had seen loitering in the wings suddenly stepped into our path. For a brief, wild moment I thought it was another assassin.

"Sir Konrad?" he asked.

"Yes?"

"Lord Westenholtz awaits your pleasure, milord."

"You'd better take me to him then, hadn't you?" Vonvalt said.

The messenger bowed, wrong-footed by Vonvalt's tone, and led us out of the mess hall and back through the castle. We were taken to the same floor that our quarters had been on, but now to the other corner of the keep, where the margrave's private apartment was.

Ordinarily we would have seen the margrave in the audience chamber on the ground floor. It was where the man would hold court, hear local petitions and administer the lands which Seaguard was responsible for managing on behalf of the Emperor. The very fact that we were being ushered to the man's private quarters was telling. He clearly did not want to see his authority questioned in front of his men. It was a problem with this type of lord, presiding over massive fortresses right on the fringes of the Empire. With Sova many hundreds of miles away, the margrave would enjoy unchecked authority over his dominion. Vonvalt was very much an unwelcome guest for a man who had grown accustomed to being his own liege lord.

We were shown into a solar. Here the light streamed in from two large windows, which looked out over the naval yards below. A forest of masts, each attached to a seagoing carrack, swayed in the winds. Imperial colours fluttered and snapped. Beyond, tossing on the rolling waves, I could see one such ship making sail across the straits, insect-sized against the roiling grey water.

The margrave was standing behind a desk, facing us as we entered. He was a tall, plain-looking man, with a shorn, stern face and dark hair. He had the muscular frame of the exercised and the lifeless grey eyes of a man well-accustomed to death in all its forms. He exuded no warmth or welcome; a mere functional nod was the only acknowledgement of our presence – unutterably rude in the circumstances. He wore a coat of brown leather over his doublet and his breeches were concealed to the knee by a pair of military-style riding boots. He wore gloves, too, and a heavy waxed cloak was draped over the back of his chair.

"I see you are about to head out," Vonvalt remarked.

"Indeed," Westenholtz replied. "I like to lead the ranges every now and then. It is an easy way to win the respect of the men."

"They would not respect you otherwise?" Vonvalt asked. I knew that the meeting would be caustic, but Vonvalt did not normally give in to such petty vindictiveness.

The margrave took the barb in his stride. "They respect me well enough," he said mildly. "You are a military man yourself. Your reputation precedes you. I know of your heroics in the Reichskrieg."

"I do not trouble myself to remember those days very often."

"Aye. Some men are more suited to books than the battlefield."

My gaze shifted between the two men. I was not particularly impressed with this exchange, but I also hated the margrave. If they insisted on trading trivial barbs, I wanted Vonvalt to win.

"Empires are built and maintained with words. Swords are a mere precedent to the quill."

"I am not a learned man, Justice," the margrave said, shrugging. "'Tis no use quoting your withered old jurists at me. Tell me what brings you to Seaguard – again. I'm told you were here not long ago."

"I have heard a disturbing report," Vonvalt said.

"Oh?" the margrave asked. "Concerning this fortress?"

"Yes."

"I have heard nothing which gives me cause for concern. As the lord and master of this castle, I—"

"*You have razed the village of Rill and immolated its occupants!*"

The Emperor's Voice. It hit the room like a thunderclap. Candles were extinguished. I felt it forcefully, something simultaneously intangible and a hard physical blow. It was stunning, like someone slapping a pot helm with the flat of a sword. It would have crushed a weak-minded man and sent a strong one reeling.

The margrave of Seaguard remained standing, unfazed.

"You need not waste your parlour tricks on me, Justice; I've no hesitation in admitting it," he said simply.

Something was wrong. Vonvalt, the epitome of self-control, was visibly confused. The Emperor's Voice was not infallible, but we had no reason to think the margrave would be able to withstand it. Only those trained by the Magistratum should be capable of such a thing.

"Shall I allow you some time to gather your thoughts, Justice?" Westenholtz asked. "You seem to be somewhat unsteady."

"On whose authority did you burn the village?" Vonvalt demanded.

"My own, of course. Rill is a village which falls within my remit. Its people are my villeins and Sir Otmar is my retainer. Was," he added.

Vonvalt's hands closed to fists. "You do not deny countermanding my judgment?"

The margrave shrugged. "It appeared to me, Justice, that you had erred somewhat in your judgment. Patria Bartholomew

Claver was good enough to inform me of your mistake. Trouble yourself not, Justice; even a member of the Magistratum is not infallible."

"You have exceeded your authority by a damn sight," Vonvalt snapped. "Countermanding the judgment of a Justice is treason. Explain yourself before I indict you here and now!"

Westenholtz smirked. "You have been gone too long from Sova, Sir Konrad. Your authority, such as it is, may not be as unshakeable as you believe it to be."

Vonvalt took this admirably in his stride, but it had a profound effect on me. What the margrave had said, especially in the light of Justice August's letter, was undoubtedly true. It had been at least two years since Vonvalt had been back to Sova. His only direct connexion with the Magistratum was with the clerks who brought him his stipend and who ferried his ledgers back to the Law Library for cross-referencing. In the seat of the Empire, two years was an age. Entire provinces had been subsumed in less time.

"What nonsense you utter," Vonvalt spat. "And what did Claver tell you anyway? Pray tell me the nature of the 'mistake' I made that he was so decent to bring to your attention?"

"That you released avowed heretics on a mere fine. The law is clear: those who practise Draedism should be burned."

"There was no avowal. I accused none of heresy. I was not bound by the canon law and dealt with the matter entirely appropriately." He snorted angrily. "Seaguard has a reputation for cruelty, but I did not know it to have a reputation for stupidity. Tell me: what was it about the insane ramblings of that young upstart Claver that was able to command you so? I did not realise the most powerful margrave of the north dispatched armed men to raze his own villages on the hearsay of a pious boy!"

That hit the mark. Westenholtz drew himself up in a sudden fury. "Such impudence in the face of your betters! One whose father took the Highmark should know better than to lecture an

Imperial margrave. You dare come here and question my actions and threaten *me* with indictment? I should have you flogged! Get out of Seaguard and return to your weakling masters in Sova! You will find the world a much-changed place, mark my words. The Empire has little need for your crusty old hermits any more!"

A deadly silence descended. By this stage I had shrunk back so far I was almost at the door. I was so unimportant I wasn't sure if the margrave had even noticed my presence. I considered it fortunate that this was a functioning castle and visitors were relieved of their weapons in the disarming room. Otherwise I was certain Vonvalt would have sought to cut the margrave down. He probably would have succeeded, too. For all his bookishness, Vonvalt had spent his formative years as a soldier, and Westenholtz had been right about one thing: Vonvalt's reputation as an accomplished swordsman often preceded him. I had also seen Vonvalt frequently keep his hand in with Bressinger, and as inexperienced as I was in matters military, I knew that I would not want to be the drafted peasant standing in the way of Vonvalt's whirling steel.

"This matter is far from over," Vonvalt said.

"Oh, I consider it very much closed," the margrave countered, but Vonvalt had already turned on his heel and was storming out. I followed in a daze.

Once we were out of earshot of Westenholtz's apartment, I said, "What are you going to do? He confessed to breaking the law."

"Don't you trouble yourself, Helena; I am going to see that man hanged," Vonvalt snapped.

We made straight for our private quarters. Our clothes were laid out for us, having been laundered and dried overnight.

"At least they can get something bloody right here," Vonvalt snapped, and began to stuff his effects roughly into his bags.

"Will you arrest him?" I asked, my heart pounding. I had never seen such an argument before. In a battle of words Vonvalt normally crushed his opponents. It was hard for me to see the man bested.

"Yes, but not now. These bloody mutterings about the Magistratum in Sova. Power struggles are nothing new in the Order, but for a man, even one as powerful as Westenholtz, to speak to a Justice in that manner – to have the *temerity* – means something is wrong. I must apprise myself of the latest developments, and quickly. And I cannot do that while we are stuck out here in the arse-end of nowhere."

"'The wise man arms himself with knowledge before a sword,'" I quoted.

Vonvalt looked at me, and smiled briefly. "Kane. Never a truer word was spoken. Come: get yourself ready. Then prepare an indictment for me with a delay of execution."

"For the margrave?" I asked, my mouth suddenly dry.

"Yes," Vonvalt replied.

My hands shook as I pulled out a roll of parchment. "What's the charge?"

Vonvalt looked grim. "Murder."

XI

The Investigation Resumes

"Even the eyes of the owl do not catch everything."

OLD SOVAN PROVERB

There was not much time. Vonvalt and I discussed the wording of the indictment. I knew that some of the information he was giving me had been gleaned from Sir Otmar's corpse, and I shuddered at the notion, unable to conceal my horror.

I drafted it quickly, but not recklessly. An indictment was not necessarily a long document, but it had to be proper and accurate and meet the formalities required. That was true of all indictments, but particularly so where the charge was for such a serious crime – and being levelled against a powerful Imperial lord to boot. The Sovan system of justice was said to be the greatest leveller since death, but as with so many other things, the reality often gave the lie to the principle.

I had drafted dozens of indictments in the two years I had spent with Vonvalt, but I had to concentrate as hard as I could to stop my hand from shaking. My heart thumped in my chest and my blood sang with anxiety as I scratched the words on to the paper:

His Most Excellent Majesty the Emperor Lothar Kzosic IV, by his Justice Sir Konrad Vonvalt of the Order of the Imperial Magistratum, hereby indicts Margrave Waldemar Westenholtz with the murder, or its incitement or authorisation thereof, of Sir Otmar Frost, Lady Karol Frost and the other inhabitants of the village of Rill, located in the province of Tolsburg, on a date to be determined but nonetheless falling within the Month of Goss.

On this charge and pending execution of this indictment, Margrave Waldemar Westenholtz shall stand to be tried, on which date and by which manner to be determined, and if found guilty of the charge shall have no recourse but the Emperor's mercy.

Does it not seem odd, reader, that we went to the trouble of penning an indictment at all? Given the lawless and bloody times that were to come, the notion of following due legal process seems risible. Indeed, even back then Vonvalt technically had the authority to simply execute Westenholtz; the man had confessed, after all. But there were a number of reasons why he could not. Westenholtz was a powerful noble, with the patronage of the Mlyanar Patricians and the loyalty of the Savarans. The Order was an increasingly political body, and Vonvalt may have been zealous, but he was no fool. Simply because he did not like the fact that the Magistratum was becoming entangled with Imperial statecraft did not mean that he could ignore it. To kill Westenholtz would have been akin to taking a match to a barrel of oil.

There were other reasons aside from practicality. Common-law convention generally demanded that lords were to be tried by juries. Indeed, as the Empire expanded and more and more people came to be within a day's ride of a courthouse, it was expected that eventually all would be tried by jury, and the role of the Imperial Magistrate as the dispenser of summary justice would fade. It was already happening; our two-year circuit had been spent almost entirely in the hinterlands dealing with peasant disputes while the burgeoning legal trade filled the towns and cities.

"Good," Vonvalt said, reading the indictment. It was a document that was imbued with arcane power, exuding a near-tangible authority. I wondered what magic permeated the parchment. "Very good, Helena. Your handwriting is excellent, clear and legible." He applied wax to it and then impressed it with his seal, then rolled it up and stored it carefully away.

We packed up the rest of our things, donned our travelling clothes and hurried out of our quarters. We picked our way back to the disarming room, where Vonvalt was reunited with his sword, and then we were back outside in the courtyard, into the crisp winter air. There our attention was drawn by a large gathering of soldiers, each wearing a distinctive black surcoat embroidered with a white Savaran star. In their midst was a Neman priest wearing a tatty purple habit. The priest was delivering a sermon and the men were listening, rapt.

Vonvalt motioned for me to keep walking, and it was not until a few minutes later, when we had reached the stables and were mounting our horses, that he spoke to me.

"Those'll be the Templar initiates that that knight alluded to at breakfast," he said sourly. "Claver's handiwork."

In a matter of minutes we were mounted up and urging the beasts out of the castle gates.

"What are you going to do with the indictment?" I asked as we moved through the township and left the vast edifice of Seaguard to fade into the morning mist behind us.

"I will have it dispatched from Baquir," Vonvalt said. "I want to be out of the range of the margrave's men – and those Templars – before we post the notice back to him."

"You think he would send men after us?" I asked, a chill running through me. It was as though for my entire life I had been looking at the world through a thin veil, and now it had been pulled away. It is amazing how fragile even great institutions of state can be; how quickly the world order can descend into chaos.

Vonvalt's face was grim set. "What happened here goes beyond mere insolence," he said. "Margrave or no, he would never have spoken to me like that without being assured of his position. If the patricians and the Templars are both behind him, we need to be careful."

"Is it not dangerous to issue the indictment, then?" I asked. I spoke more loudly now that we were out of earshot of the villagers. "Will it not enrage him?"

"It is, and it will," Vonvalt replied. "Hence the delay. An indictment with a delay of execution is merely a piece of paper until I say otherwise. But I do not want the man to put me from his mind merely because he has put me from his sight."

"Could he not just tear it up? Or burn it?"

"Of course. But I have still issued it. The indictment is a mere formality. My word as Justice is enough."

"What about Claver? Will you indict him too?"

Vonvalt all but spat. "We will find Claver, mark my words," he said darkly. "An indictment will be the least of his troubles."

We reached Baquir the following morning, where Vonvalt had the indictment dispatched by a liveried company of messengers. Then we returned our horses and went back to the Imperial Relay.

The journey back down the Hauner road was as fast and frantic as the journey up, but mercifully uneventful. This time, as we reached Vasaya and we were reunited with Vonvalt's destrier Vincento, we could see the large Templar encampment that the knights in Seaguard had told us about. Hundreds of tents were pitched perhaps half a mile from the town, and the air was redolent of cook fires and filled with the distant ringing of military drills.

Vonvalt eyed the mass with contempt, as though he could set the tents alight with his glaring alone. The business in Rill had stung him badly and seemed to have knocked his mind out of joint. In the two years I had known him personally, I had seen Vonvalt get angry fewer times than I have fingers. Now he seemed to exist in a semi-permanent state of it.

We pulled away from our vantage point and carried on down the road. It took us most of the afternoon to reach Galen's Vale, and we approached the Veldelin Gate as night was falling. I could see that the Wintertide decorations had been removed, and it was only at that point that I realised that we had passed into the month of Ebbe and the Imperial New Year. It meant we had been gone for thirteen days, and it was clear that Vonvalt was eager to have the Bauer case disposed with so we could conclude our business in the Vale. Of course, by that time, the gulf between what Vonvalt wanted to happen and what actually came to pass had grown very wide indeed, and would remain misaligned for the rest of his life.

Although I did not say anything to Vonvalt, I took great comfort from seeing the wet, mossy walls of the town again. It felt something like a homecoming. It speaks volumes of my naïveté at that time that my thoughts were now preoccupied with seeing Matas again, as though our courtship could resume uninterrupted by greater events.

We passed through the gate to find the town slowly bedding down for the night. I was bone-tired, but to my immense disappointment, instead of heading for Lord Sauter's residence and to the soft, comfortable beds therein, we made straight for the watch house and up to the sheriff's office. To our great surprise, we saw that Bressinger and Sir Radomir had, by coincidence, just themselves returned from somewhere, having arrived as little as a few minutes before us. Both were still armed and cloaked, their faces ruddy from the cold.

"Justice," Sir Radomir said, surprised, as Vonvalt pushed the door open. "You are back."

"I'll have some of that," Vonvalt said, nodding to the wine in the sheriff's hand. "And for Helena, too."

"What happened?" Bressinger asked.

"By the look of you both, you did not achieve the satisfaction you sought," the sheriff said, pouring out two over-generous measures of hot wine. I accepted my goblet gratefully, and we spent a moment decloaking and arranging ourselves into the chairs in front of Sir Radomir's desk.

"No," Vonvalt said, and relayed to them what had happened in Rill.

"Nema," Bressinger swore. "The situation gets worse by the day."

"Indeed," Vonvalt said tiredly. He'd finished his wine and Sir Radomir obliged him with some more. "Westenholtz cared not the least that he'd acted against the Emperor. If anything he seemed to delight in his own insolence. What troubles me the most was his immunity to the Emperor's Voice."

"What *exactly* is the Voice?" Sir Radomir asked, his eyes flicking between the two men. "A trick? Or some kind of magick?"

"It is magick, be in no doubt," Vonvalt said. "It is the power to compel a man to reveal his mind. As I have said before, it does not work in every circumstance, nor on all men; but it should have worked on him. Lord Westenholtz has had no training from the Order as far as I know – though having read Justice August's letter, I am not so sure any more," he added warily.

"It would take a man of special character to resist it," Sir Radomir said. "I'm no lamb, and by Nema I thought I'd been hit by a charging bull."

"And you are certain that Westenholtz ordered the deaths of the villagers?" Bressinger asked. I had to concentrate to understand him; his Grozodan accent thickened when he was tired.

"He told me himself."

"Seaguard has always been a severe place," Sir Radomir said grimly. "But 'tis still a rare thing to take the sword to one's own villeins. The margrave must be a very pious man."

"To a fault," Vonvalt said. "I'll warrant Claver needed little honey in his ear before he was dispatching armed men south." He sighed. "Speaking of which, we saw men for the Templars, too. Thirty or so, wearing the white star. And more encamped at Vasaya. Hundreds, there."

"Bloody Fate," Sir Radomir muttered. "We had the same here, last week. Neman priests up from Guelich asking for fighting men for the Frontier. Sauter said he would release anyone in the town's service who wanted to go. Perhaps a hundred went, all told. 'Tis an easy sell for the poor."

"They'll be waiting for the margrave's men, then," Vonvalt said. "Vasaya will be a staging area for them all."

"Actually, I think they're waiting for Claver," Sir Radomir said. "Last piece of news I heard was that he was ranging as far east as Roundstone to beseech Baron Naumov. He's another one of your lords with a reputation for piety. But that news is hardly fresh."

"If Claver is planning on heading south with those Templars, I'll bring the whole company to a halt until he is turfed out of it, mark my words," Vonvalt said. "By Nema, it is a foolish enterprise."

The conversation had started to pass me by. My heart was pounding. Had Matas gone? I had left in the dead of night nearly two weeks ago without a word. Did he think I had lost interest and absconded?

"We've had no news of anything like what you have mentioned here in the Vale," Sir Radomir said. He looked troubled. "About the Mlyanars and that lot making moves in the Senate."

"No," Vonvalt said. "But we are still hundreds of miles from the capital. News can travel slowly, particularly if those at its source want it to." He was quiet for a moment while he lit his pipe. Soon the familiar haze and smell of smoke filled the room. "What progress have you made here?" He gestured around him at the stacks of old leather-bound ledgers that had appeared in the office since we had last been in. They were dusty and worn and smelled of damp. "This is new."

"We have made great strides in the past week," Sir Radomir said. There was not so much pleasure in his voice as grim professional satisfaction. I imagined that when all was said and done, even if the crime was solved, Sir Radomir was the type of man to consider that they had failed as lawkeepers the moment Lady Bauer was struck dead.

"Aye?"

"The roster of councilmen you asked for," Bressinger said. "Mayor Sauter provided it to us."

"Eventually," Sir Radomir growled.

"Hm," Bressinger agreed. "It transpires that Lord Bauer may be more involved with the running of the Vale than he has let on."

"The 'minor duties' to which he alluded?" Vonvalt asked.

"Oh yes," Sir Radomir answered with relish. "The man is responsible for the town's bookkeeping. All of the Vale's treasury accounts for money leaving the coffers."

Vonvalt's eyes widened. "Faith," he said.

"Aye," Sir Radomir said. "He has help, too. A slimy man by the name of Fenland Graves."

"That's an odd name," Vonvalt remarked.

"He's not from the Vale," Sir Radomir said.

"I'm to take it Graves does the legwork on the accounts?" Vonvalt asked, smoking his pipe.

"Right," Bressinger said. "Under the supervision—"

"—and direction—"

"—of Lord Bauer."

"Lord Bauer controls where the town's money goes?" Vonvalt asked, his eyebrow arched.

"Aye," Sir Radomir said. "But it gets better than that."

"You recall that Bauer said he dealt with the town's charitable ventures?" Bressinger said.

"From the tax income, yes," Vonvalt said.

"Well," Sir Radomir said, gesturing to the stack of ledgers. "We have found evidence of regular—"

"—and significant—"

"—sums being paid to the kloster," Sir Radomir finished. "Nema, but it took some late nights and sore eyes to pry out that gem."

Vonvalt sucked on his pipe for a moment, then took it out of his mouth and let a vast cloud of smoke fill the room. "There is a connexion?" Vonvalt said. He of course had seen it immediately, but he was not about to steal the wind from the sheriff's sails.

"Aye," Sir Radomir said. "The connexions are ten a penny now, thanks to Helena's legwork." I felt a flush of pride despite my exhaustion. "'Tis to do with the timings. Zoran Vogt made his complaint against Leberecht Bauer just over two years ago. Then he withdrew it. A little while later, Bauer's daughter went to the kloster and hasn't been seen in the town since. Lord Bauer said she did it out of grief for her dead brother, though even taking that into account, it appeared to be somewhat sudden and unexpected." He gestured to the dozens of ledgers stacked up about the place. "Since that time, we have seen large sums of money being regularly diverted to the kloster. Do you see?"

Since Sir Radomir was looking at me as he finished, I was the one to answer. "Sanja Bauer is a hostage," I said. "Lord Bauer is being blackmailed to keep her alive by someone in the kloster."

Sir Radomir nodded, a look of grim triumph on his face. "We paid the kloster a visit not three days ago, but they fed us some shit about the girl being taken ill, knowing the town ordinances are strict when it comes to contagious pox. We have promised to return when she is better. It only adds fuel to the fire of suspicion."

"That also explains why Bauer withdrew the complaint so hastily," Vonvalt said.

"And why he recanted so quickly after blaming Vogt for the murder of his wife."

"He spoke hotly, without thinking, and then remembered that his daughter's life was at stake."

"'Tis the only explanation that fits. His wife is murdered, he blames Vogt – and I tell you, Justice, the man was adamant – then in all but the same breath he withdraws the accusation. A few sharp words from an intermediary, I'll warrant, and he was put back in his place."

Vonvalt took all this in. "This is excellent work," he said. "Both of you. This is exactly what I had hoped for."

"We could not have done it without your direction, sire," Sir Radomir said, in what I imagined was an exceptionally rare concession.

"There's one thing that bothers me," I said, drawing all of the attention in the room. "Why mark it down in the official accounts? The ransom payments, I mean. Why leave a record at all?"

"'Tis the nature of your Sovan bookkeeping," Sir Radomir said. "Money coming in and money going out must tally. He runs the accounts but any lord you care to name has the right to inspect them. He cannot fail to record it; he can only conceal it and hope that no one has a need to check the numbers too closely. And gold flows as plentifully as water in this place. I'll warrant few have bothered to check the records while their pockets are heavy."

Vonvalt rose, a look of fierce pleasure on his face. "This is more than enough to wield the Emperor's Voice to maximum effect. I'll have the truth out of Bauer and Vogt tonight, and more likely than not their brains through their noses. Where are they?"

At this, both Sir Radomir and Bressinger's features fell.

"That is the bad news," Sir Radomir said sourly.

"We've just got back ourselves from a two-day journey west, to the Imperial wayfort at Gormogon," Bressinger said tiredly. He performed a little Grozodan flourish, blowing into his fingers and then splaying them as though his hand were the head of a dandelion. "Bauer has gone. Absconded."

"And Vogt was never here," Sir Radomir added bitterly. "According to the Merchants' Guild the man is on a trade mission and has been for some time. Probably fucked off the moment you arrived. That little titbit of news is a few weeks ripe now and it still angers me."

Vonvalt sighed, deflated. He sat back down. "That is ... a shame," he said, trying to control his irritation. "I had hoped to be done with this business tonight."

"As had we all, Justice," Sir Radomir said, reproachfully.

Vonvalt looked up. "Do not take offence, Sir Radomir. It is not a criticism of your office. We must play the hand as it is dealt."

"Bauer's man Graves is recently returned from a trip himself, possibly from Roundstone," Bressinger said. "We have not had the time to question him yet, but he may provide some information."

"That is better than nothing," Vonvalt agreed. "Though if Bauer and Vogt are both gone, we will have to be careful about how we approach him. He is likely to have been warned."

"And his mind hardened in anticipation of the Voice," Bressinger cautioned.

"Aye," Vonvalt murmured. He thought for a moment, his mind whirring over with this fresh information like the cogs in the temple clock. "Let us assume, then, that the Bauer girl is a hostage. That tells us two things: that Zoran Vogt is certainly connected to the death of Lady Bauer, however tangentially, and that someone up there—" he pointed to the kloster "—is as well. Tell me, Sheriff: are there any unsavoury characters operating within its confines?"

Sir Radomir shrugged. "None that I personally am aware of. We get the usual complaints, of course."

"Aye?"

"Abuses of one sort or another. Being a mixed house of men and women and children leads to lecherous behaviour. We hanged a man a few years back for molesting. Cut his cock off to boot. Not in that order."

"But nothing that gives you a sense of any financial impropriety?"

Sir Radomir shrugged. "The Vale is swimming in money, Justice. There is a great deal of legitimate extravagance. It makes the illegitimate extravagance the harder to spot. As I say, it was only after Bressinger noticed the regular payments to the kloster that I turned my mind to it. And even then it did not faze me that much, not straight away. Lord Sauter is generous with his charitable spending. Had Helena not made the connexion as regards the timing of it all, I might have thought nothing more of it."

Vonvalt rubbed his chin. "What does the tax money for the kloster get spent on?"

"Alms for the poor. Repairs to the temple and the kloster itself. There is a well-staffed infirmary and hospice up there. Funding missionaries to the Frontier. Arming all those new Templars, the poor sods. I believe they also maintain emergency food stores in the vaults under the kloster, if there is a poor harvest."

"I fear we may have to engage in some mathematical calculations," Vonvalt said. "To see just how much is being sent up there. It is unlikely that there are but two men involved in this, given the large sums."

Sir Radomir took a long draw of wine. "By Nema," he growled, "this is the last thing I need. A bloody great conspiracy."

"But as with a wedge of cavalry, Sheriff, there will be but one man at the head of it," Vonvalt said. "Certainly Lord Bauer remains suspect, though it sounds like his involvement is very much against his will. And now we can be certain about Vogt. But there must be someone else, someone operating out of that kloster. Who did you speak to when you went?"

"No one of importance. A strange old bastard called Walter. Obenpatria Fischer is the head of the place, but he gave us short shrift. The canon law makes them full of themselves," he added. "They think they are above dealing with the likes of me."

Vonvalt clacked his tongue. "They are certainly not above

dealing with me. But ..." he sighed angrily "... we shall have to consider how we approach that thorny issue too. It is true that the canon law gives them some immunity to aspects of my office. Circumspection may be required. I shall see how I get on with Graves."

There was a pause. We all sat in silence for a moment. Never had the answers seemed so close and yet so beyond our reach.

"Wait," I said, suddenly. Everyone looked at me inquisitively. I had been lost in my own thoughts, working through the timings of everything again. "The story goes that Sanja Bauer took the cloth because her brother died. Lord Bauer said when we spoke to him that the boy died of a pox."

"Aye," Sir Radomir said.

"Well, what if he didn't? What if the boy died of something else?"

"You mean the boy may have been murdered?" Vonvalt asked.

"If he was, it would give the lie to Lord Bauer's account of the manner of his death," I said.

"And prove him to have lied," Vonvalt said thoughtfully.

"And add another murder to the tally," Sir Radomir said. "It could provide useful leverage."

"Nema, Helena, that is a good thought," Vonvalt said. "The boy may have been slain. A pox will have died with his flesh, but like Lady Bauer's corpse, the bones will tell us whether he died of a blow. It would be another pillar to bolster our theorising."

Bressinger was clearly not pleased. "That is an unhappy prospect," he said. "'Tis nothing we need to concern ourselves with now, surely? Let the lad rest, whatever the manner of his death."

But Vonvalt was too focused now to pay either of us much attention.

"We have a path forwards," he said, as if Bressinger hadn't spoken at all. "Find and question Graves, and send out riders to track down Vogt and Bauer."

"They will be long gone by now," Sir Radomir said bitterly.

He added a long and loud yawn to this. "Nema, I am tired. Gods know how the two of you are faring."

I hardly needed reminding of how exhausted I was. Sir Radomir's own yawn set me off – and Bressinger with him.

"I will think about how to approach the kloster," Vonvalt said, irritated by this collective display of fatigue. "That is clearly the seat of the conspiracy. In order to maximise our impact, some . . . subterfuge may be required." He glanced at me as he said it. "Is this man Graves likely to abscond, too?"

Sir Radomir shook his head. "I've a few guards keeping an eye on his house." He stifled another yawn. "We are about to close the gates for the curfew in any event. The man'll keep 'til morning."

Vonvalt rose, and we all stood with him.

"All right," he said. "To bed with you all, then. Tomorrow, we'll see what Graves has to say for himself."

XII

Confrontation on the Hauner Road

*"A Justice should never lose control of a situation;
he should never enter a place where he does not
know the exit and he should never ask a question
to which he does not know the answer."*

MASTER KARL ROTHSINGER

❦

Vonvalt roused us unceremoniously at dawn with a pounding on the bedchamber door.

"Up, both of you. We've no time to waste," he called, and we heard his footsteps retreat down the corridor and then down the stairs.

"Nema," Bressinger grunted as he pressed himself out of bed. "I'm getting too old for this."

He threw back the curtains. Grey light slanted into the room. The sun was barely over the horizon and cold drizzle filled the streets. Another miserable day in the Vale, but one charged with anticipation. If the questioning of Graves proved productive, the whole matter could be put to bed by nightfall.

I pressed myself painfully out of bed. My legs and back were in agony after the week's hard riding in the cold. Bressinger snatched up his clothes and left to change next door, and I pulled on my own and ran a brush through my hair.

We met Vonvalt in the dining room. Lord Sauter's servants had once again gone out of their way to put on a profligate breakfast spread, and I poured out a measure of marsh ale and helped myself to a slice of piping-hot meat pie.

"I'll not beat about the bush with this man Graves," Vonvalt said through a mouthful of food. "We'll go there straight after breakfast."

"What of the kloster?" Bressinger asked. "Have you settled on a course of action?"

Vonvalt inclined his head. He was about to say something when a hammering at the front door stole everyone's attention. After the usual muffled words and slamming of doors and boots, the door to the dining hall was flung open and Sir Radomir entered, looking flustered.

"Your man, Claver," he said, out of breath. "He's back and moving south on the Hauner road, with the Templar host from Vasaya."

Vonvalt immediately pushed himself to his feet. "How far?" he demanded.

"Ten, maybe fifteen miles south. They must have passed us in the night."

"Our horses!"

"I have already given orders for them to be made ready," Sir Radomir said, but he was talking to Vonvalt's back as the man swept out of the room.

My heart pounded as the rest of us scrambled after him out of Lord Sauter's residence, pausing only to don our cloaks. In minutes we were atop our horses and roaring through the streets of the Vale, Vonvalt bellowing commands to the bewildered towns-folk to make way. Behind us, Sir Radomir and a party of town watchmen followed.

We thundered through the Veldelin Gate and made straight for the Hauner road south. Our horses kicked up great tufts of mud and grass as their hooves pounded the rain-softened turf. The morning weather showed no signs of improvement, and it did not take long for our clothes to become sodden. After a few minutes we had to bring the horses down to a moderate canter. It felt slow and counterintuitive, but the horses could only gallop for a few miles before they were spent.

We caught up with the tail-end of Claver's train after a couple of hours of hard riding. It was a slow-moving caravan of hundreds of men, horses and carts. All were wearing the black livery of the Savaran Templars with the prominent white star over the chest. Some were clearly lords, who sat atop expensive war horses and had teams of retainers leading more horses and carts full of strongboxes. The rest were knights of varying means. Some were mounted and carried lances and shields; more still were dis-mounted and trudged along the road with nothing more than a pack and sword. Interspersed among them were purple-cassocked Neman priests, holding aloft copies of the Nema Creed on poles festooned with pennants or braziers.

We rode parallel to the Hauner road. The going was tougher, particularly given the side of the road had been turned to claggy mud by the rain and the foot traffic seeking to avoid the Templars. But it was still quicker than trying to thread through the vast quantity of men and materiel.

The caravan was spread out over most of a mile. As we rode past we began to attract a significant amount of attention. Heads turned and voices faltered. Whispers and muttering chased us like the cold breeze. After our experience with Westenholtz, and the fact that at least some of these men were his retainers, I took little comfort from the protection Vonvalt's status was supposed to afford us.

Claver travelled with affected humility, and looked a far cry from how he had when we had travelled with him all those weeks before. He walked shaven-headed and barefoot like a penitent and his purple robes looked threadbare. He did not read the Creed or exhort or sing; he simply strode on in silence while lords jostled obsequiously to be near him. I wondered what had happened to his horse.

"Patria," Vonvalt called out as we pulled alongside the man. "You have amassed quite the retinue."

Claver smiled thinly, as though he had expected us to catch up with him. I wondered if they had deliberately travelled past Galen's Vale at night, to avoid just such a confrontation. The men around him eyed us warily.

"Sir Konrad," Claver said. He managed to freight the two words with condescension. Though it had not been long since we had last seen the man, he looked older and more imperious. He did not have the agitated, excitable air of before. This was a man who had that intangible quality that only comes with having the protection of very powerful men.

"Tell me, Patria; are the men who murdered the inhabitants of Rill among this host? It would save me a great deal of time if I could hang them all in one sitting."

I had to stop my mouth falling open. I looked over to Bressinger, who remained admirably impassive. Sir Radomir, however, was unable to conceal a flash of surprise.

Claver smiled another condescending smile while the men around him enthusiastically gave voice to their outrage. Vonvalt weathered it like a cliff might weather the pounding tide. The Templars did no more than put on a display of affront, and it was clear that whatever political upheaval was going on in Sova, the idea of going further and drawing a blade against a Justice still remained taboo.

If only it could have remained so.

"This host is making its way south to the land of the

unbeliever, to wage righteous crusade there," Claver said once the hubbub had died down. He spoke as though Vonvalt was a child that he was tolerating with avuncular gentleness. He gestured to the newly initiated Templars. "You can see for yourself they are marked with the white star of Savare, the God Father. Their subservience to the common law is gone. Their bodies are chattels of the Church. You have no authority here, Sir Konrad."

"No man is above the law," Vonvalt said. "If your lackeys are so confident they are beyond the reach of my blade, have them confess. By your own words they cannot be harmed. Call it a test of faith."

No one spoke. By now the caravan had ground to a halt in step with Claver, and was slowly bunching up behind us. Never before had I felt so keenly such a weight of attention.

Vonvalt turned to the host and raised his voice. "Who here has come from Seaguard? Which of you put Rill to the torch? In the name of Emperor Kzosic IV, I accuse you of murder. If you confess I will behead you here and now." He turned and pointed to Claver. "Patria Claver asserts that you are above the common law and that I can do no such thing. If you trust the priest's words over mine, then speak! Confess! You have nothing to lose."

I did not think it was possible for the Hauner road, one of the largest roads in the Empire and trafficked by thousands every day, to be silent. But at that moment we might as well have been standing in a graveyard. In front of us an armed host of hundreds of men, full of righteous zeal and no doubt feeling the invincibility that comes with being part of a mob, had been brought to a stop by a single Justice. Not even the haughty lords with their expensive armour and swords could bring themselves to speak. They might have been Westenholtz's men, but they did not share their liege lord's careless arrogance.

"These men have given themselves to the cause of the God Father," Claver said loudly. His mask had slipped. I could see the anger behind his words, and fear. "They are disciplined. They will not engage with these foolish games."

Vonvalt ignored him. "I'll warrant there is a man here who did it. I say it again! In the name of the Emperor, I accuse anyone here who burned the people of Rill of murder! Let any man who denies the charge defend himself!"

"'Tis not murder if they are heathens," someone called back. My heart leapt. I had hoped that no one would be foolish enough to answer. Vonvalt certainly believed that no man was above the law, but even I knew that Claver was right; the canon law held sway here. These men *were* chattels of the Church, one of those rare carve-outs that placed a man beyond the reach of the Emperor's long arm. Such immunity often came with burdensome obligations, however, such as signing up to one of the Neman martial orders for a considerable term of years, and was not lightly conveyed.

"Who said that?" Vonvalt called out. I could see the fury in his face. His nostrils were flared and he sucked down air in deep, trembling breaths. "Who said it?!"

A little further back the host parted slightly. A dismounted knight stepped forwards. He was heavy-set and had an ugly, cruel face. Of all the types of people who joined the Savaran Templars, he appeared to me to fall into the category of those who simply wanted to kill and could find no better lawful way of doing it.

"Sir Konrad, let this farce end," Claver called out impatiently. "You cannot harm this man. He is subject to the canon law."

"*What crimes did you commit in Rill?*" Vonvalt asked the man. The Emperor's Voice. It was as though thunder had split the sky. The idiot reeled as though he had taken a punch to the nose. I could see instantly that he was particularly susceptible to the Voice, having neither the training nor the natural wit to resist it even slightly.

"I raped one woman and then burned her alive! I t-*tried to kill her children but they escaped!*" the man shrieked.

A ripple of dismay washed through the assembled men. It had been easy to assume that they were all of the same outlook as Claver himself, a host of mostly bad people looking to kill and maim under the pretext of righteousness. But of course many of the Templars were pious and decent, if misguided, and did not want to keep company with a confessed rapist and murderer any more than the next person.

His peers shrank back from him as Vonvalt and Bressinger dismounted, the former with rage in his heart, the latter with a reluctant sense of obligation.

"Sir Konrad!" Claver shouted. "I have warned you."

"Shut the fuck up!" Sir Radomir spat.

Vonvalt pulled his sword free of its scabbard. He did not break his stride. The knight ahead of him was still reeling from the Voice, but yanked his own blade out nonetheless.

"You have confessed to the crimes of rape and murder," Vonvalt said, implacable. "By His Most Excellent Majesty the Emperor Kzosic IV, I, Justice Sir Konrad Vonvalt, adjudge you guilty and sentence you to die by beheading."

Bressinger followed Vonvalt at a fast walk, hand on the hilt of his sword. The knight ahead staggered backwards, slipping slightly on the muddy paving of the Hauner road.

"Help!" he shouted to his associates, but they shuffled back, as though Vonvalt stood at the centre of some invisible circular barrier. Some must have believed he deserved to die, even if they did not believe in Vonvalt's authority. Others were simply afraid to be wounded or killed themselves if they intervened. More still simply did not believe that Claver was right about their immunity. In one way or another, however, they were all frightened. I wish I could convey with my quill and ink the awesome figure Vonvalt cut at that moment. He was power incarnate, a wrathful god, as unstoppable as the rising of the sun.

"Wait!" the knight shouted. "Just wait!"

Vonvalt did not. The knight lunged forwards. Vonvalt parried the man's blade with startling ease and stepped to the side. He moved his sword three times: the first took the knight's sword hand off at the wrist; the next gave Vonvalt a clean angle on the man's neck; and the third chopped his head off in one powerful, brutal stroke. A groan went up from the Templars. The knight's body remained upright for a few seconds before crashing unceremoniously to the ground, spurting hot blood onto the flagstones.

I watched, astonished. I looked to Sir Radomir, who mirrored my surprise. The watchmen behind were actually enjoying the spectacle. With hindsight, it was to be expected. In their minds, this was what an Imperial Magistrate *was*: death incarnate, swift, decisive, just. But they had not seen the Justice I knew; the nuance, the patience, the slow, rigorous application of the law. They saw the Sir Konrad of the stories and legends. For me, it was a frightening display of recklessness.

Vonvalt wiped and then sheathed his blade. "Is there anyone else who wishes to confess?" He turned and walked back towards the head of the caravan. "Patria; perhaps you would like to confess to incitement to murder? It was you, after all, who had Westenholtz dispatch these villains south?"

Claver was pale with fury.

"You," he said, pointing a trembling finger at Vonvalt. He laughed a sudden and brittle laugh, as though he had surprised himself. "I wonder if you realise quite how foolish you have been here today. How foolish you have been this past month. What unyielding forces are at work in Sova to dislodge you and your old pagan order."

"Say the words, priest," Vonvalt spat. "Confess. See if your gods or your canon law protect you from the Emperor's Justice."

Claver sneered. He gave Vonvalt a long, appraising look. "As someone who is so eager to hand out death warrants, I suppose it is only fitting that you sign your own."

Now it was Vonvalt who smiled thinly. "No one is above the law," he said. "No one. Not you, not Westenholtz, not anyone.

I do not care for your silly tricks. I do not care if these men are Templars. I do not care if they have sworn oaths to the God Father. If they have committed murder, I will have their heads."

Claver took a step forwards. Bressinger moved to meet him, but Vonvalt held out his hand.

"Use your Voice on me," Claver hissed. "Do it, here and now. See what happens."

Vonvalt shook his head. "You would have me embarrass you further? Are you so keen to die?"

"Do it!" Claver roared.

Vonvalt knew that Claver had probably the same resistance as Westenholtz, so he did something no one – including myself – expected.

"Sir Radomir?" he called over his shoulder. "Take Patria Claver into custody."

Claver and every Templar in hearing range was about to bellow their protestations in what I have no doubt would have been an awesome spectacle of outrage, when a powerful voice cut through it all in an instant.

"Sir Konrad!"

All turned. A woman was approaching from the direction of a nearby coppice which lay off to the side of the road, a tall, powerful-looking woman clad in a heavy waxed cloak and leading a white palfrey. She had greying dark hair and her features were creased with age and responsibility. About her person were tokens of office, faded from wear but unmistakable.

"Justice Lady August," Vonvalt replied, bowing. If he had been startled by the interruption, he hid it well.

"I have already questioned Patria Claver," she said. Claver frowned at this, but said nothing. "You had no way to know, of course."

"I see," Vonvalt said after a pregnant pause.

"Come; we have much to discuss," she said quietly, nodding in the direction of Galen's Vale. She looked over to the head of the war host. "Patria Claver, God Father speed you and your Templars on your way."

"Hm," Claver grunted. He shot Vonvalt one last venomous look, then resumed his trudging down the Hauner road. The man was more eager to take advantage of August's convenient falsehood than to press this particular bout with Vonvalt.

Behind him, the Templar host roused itself to action like a gigantic beast slowly awakening from a long slumber, and marched its way south.

XIII

Deaf Ears

*"It is impossible to impress upon a man the severity
of a situation until the point of its remedy is long
past. 'Tis something to do with the nature of a
human being, that ingrained idiocy. The gods
must shake their heads at us in disbelief."*

JUSTICE SOPHIA JURAS

❦

"You received my letter?"

"I did."

"Then you are aware that what you just did was very
ill-advised."

"You have, of course, not questioned Claver."

"Of course I haven't."

We were in a tavern just off the Hauner road, a few miles north
from where Vonvalt had confronted Claver. It was a pokey little
establishment, dim and full of low beams and alcoves where
private business might be conducted in peace. The innkeeper, a

small and discreet old man, seemed to know Justice August well enough to bring her what was evidently her preferred drink, as well as a small tray of morsels. Sir Radomir and his men had repaired to the Vale, eager to be shot of these matters of state.

"That knight confessed to murder," Vonvalt said. I could tell he was beginning to regret his actions. There was enough grey area and overlap between the common and canon law that he could have argued his way out of an official reprimand – had there been one. But he had crossed a line, and he knew it.

"I'm not talking about that dolt," August said. She was a force of nature, beautiful and powerful. I found myself immediately in her thrall. "I mean threatening Claver with arrest. If you did see my letter then it should be obvious to you why that was a bad idea."

"With respect, Justice—"

"Piss on that. Do we not know one another well enough? Or is it for the girl's sake?" She nodded at me, but didn't take her eyes from Vonvalt. I guessed – correctly, as it would later transpire – that the two had had a romantic history.

Vonvalt cleared his throat. "Resi, then. Your letter was somewhat oblique."

"Prince Kasivar of Hell," August said, rolling her eyes. "That letter sent a warning as bright as the Kormondolt Bay beacons. I told you Claver had made an ally of Westenholtz."

"Westenholtz is but a man."

August stared. "He is the most powerful man in the Empire except perhaps the Emperor himself."

"Don't be ridiculous," Vonvalt snorted. "The Emperor's sons govern entire principalities. Westenholtz has but a castle and a few leagues of marsh to his name."

"Konrad," August said. Her tone was all the more alarming for its sudden and genuine concern. "When were you last in Sova?"

Vonvalt waved a hand. "At least two years."

"But you have been keeping abreast of the news?"

"What little there is that makes its way to the north, aye."

August reached out and put a hand on Vonvalt's. "Konrad, there is turmoil in the Order. Perhaps my letter did not convey the severity of the situation. Master Kadlec is perilously close to ceding the secrets of our powers to the Mlyanars. I have good reason to think that he has already been trading away some of the arts of the Order for the sake of a quiet life." She all but spat those last words. "I have heard rumours out of Roundstone that a growing company of men are immune to the Voice of the Emperor – Claver and Westenholtz included."

My heart sank. I could see Vonvalt deflate with dismay. "It is true," he muttered. "At least with Westenholtz. I tried it on him myself. The man barely blinked."

August sat back, her face a mask of worry. "Then the situation is even worse than I thought – and I considered it to be very bad indeed. There is no doubt, then, that Claver is immune as well?"

"I dared not find out," Vonvalt said. "But I should imagine so."

"Bloody faith," August swore. Vonvalt lit his pipe. August pulled out her own pipe and lit that too. In seconds the small nook which the four of us were occupying was filled with a haze of smoke.

"Tell me you exaggerate," Vonvalt said, "if even a little. The Emperor cannot be sitting on his hands while Westenholtz and the Mlyanars foment rebellion. It seems like madness for him to go against the Order as well."

"The Emperor and his Haugenate supporters in the Senate have always been more than a match for the Patricians. But now there are the Templars to consider. Historically they have been tied to the Mlyanars, but – well, you know their reputation."

"I know that they leave the Empire with great fanfare and then lose a lot of men, land and prestige in a very short space of time," Vonvalt said with contempt. "If that is what you mean."

"Indeed," August said dourly. "But they are not the same force they were a hundred years ago. It has become fashionable for lords to send a second or third child to the Templars now. Moneyed knights with plate armour and good horses. They are more prudent with their conquests, and they garrison their takings with vast castles funded with money from the Mlyanars. The fortresses in Südenberg, Keraq and Zetland are apparently a marvel to behold."

"All in the name of Nema?"

"Ostensibly."

Vonvalt rubbed his face. "Are the Templars not engaged in crusading? How can they pose a threat to Sova if they're tangled up waging warfare?"

"This is where your man Claver comes in," August said, nodding to Vonvalt. "He has spent many months touring the Empire, rabble-rousing and prying more sons and lands from lords who have taken the Highmark and still fear for their positions. Claver has been selling it as a demonstration of faith and loyalty to Sova, and men have been falling over themselves to sign up. Now there is a glut of Templars; more than enough to garrison their fortresses and create a ranging army."

Vonvalt wrinkled his nose. "Come now, Resi. The Legions are tens of thousands strong, hardened from years of campaigning. They would trounce a mob of Templar initiates ten times their number."

"The Legions are scattered to the four winds," August said. "Faith, Konrad, listen to the words I am telling you. At least half of them are stuck out east along the River Kova, fighting the Confederation. The rest of them are all over the Empire, garrisoning, keeping the peace, even campaigning still." She waved her hand. "But that is all beside the point."

Vonvalt sighed. "Go on, then," he said. I watched Bressinger give him a sidelong look. Obstinacy was not one of Vonvalt's faults, but that afternoon he could have fooled everyone at the table.

August gritted her teeth. "Claver belongs to a group of

orthodox Nemans who believe that the powers of the Order should be restored to the Church. They have been lobbying the Emperor for years to allow priests to attend the Grand Lodge and learn our ways. Claver has gone a step further though; he says that the Templars should be given the powers to be used as weapons. Think, Konrad; it does not take a great deal of effort to twist the Emperor's Voice, to use it to make a man disarm himself, for example. And there are other, older powers in the codices in the Master's vaults which even the Order does not employ. The use of such powers for a soldier is beyond measure. For a politician it is unthinkable. The Emperor Himself does not even wield the Voice. People have never fully trusted the Order, but they have at least always trusted us to use our powers as a force for good. To uphold the common law for the benefit of all. Claver means to take these powers and use them to conquer the known world in the name of Nema. And Westenholtz and the rest of the Mlyanar Patricians are ready to help him."

There was silence. It was difficult to process what August was saying. I had seen first-hand the Voice fail against Westenholtz, seen Claver and his Templars marching down the Hauner road, seen a dozen other things which all verified August's concerns. But even then it was hard to believe that something so potentially momentous was in motion. August, for all her sincerity, did sound a little mad. It makes me ache, now, to think that we did not heed her warning with enough alacrity; that we did not simply abandon the Bauer case to Sir Radomir and his men and charge south to the capital. There was still a little time on our side, even then, to make a difference.

"I do not know what it is you expect me to do," Vonvalt said eventually. "The law is the law. As an order we are apolitical. In theory at least."

August waved her pipe animatedly. "Unless we intervene, the Order will be destroyed, subsumed by the Church and our powers with it. We have become complacent over time, assuming that all simply accept the primacy of the common law. Justices have become soft. We are a collection of philosophers and jurists, more interested in writing and selling books than practising the law. Some of these towns I have been through have not seen a Justice for years."

Vonvalt drew himself up. "I have business to attend to in the Vale. I will not leave here now. Not until it is concluded."

It was clear that Vonvalt did not fully buy August's tale of impending doom, and he would confess as much to me a long time later. He had his reasons, which only sound flimsy with the benefit of hindsight. The man was a Reichskrieg veteran, after all. He had seen first-hand what the Legions were capable of. He knew, as we all did, that Westenholtz and Claver were dangerous men who were clearly involved in political manoeuvrings of one sort or another. But he never seriously considered that anyone in their right mind would move against the Emperor and succeed. Kzosic IV was a ruthless man and a brilliant strategist. One needed to look no further than the table we were sat at to see the evidence of his success: a Jägelander, a Grozodan and a Toll, all of us Imperial subjects – more than that, *officials* – our kings dead and our countries mere provinces, all in the last fifty years. Only August was a native Sovan.

"Irrespective of all of this," Vonvalt said, gesturing rudely to August's face as though all the words she had spoken hung in a cloud in front of her, "all the Patricians and Templars and church-men in the world cannot take the Order's powers forcibly. It takes years of patient study to become proficient. I am not concerned that a few people have learned to withstand the Emperor's Voice. It is the weakest of our powers and the easiest to learn to resist. Anyone with a decent education and a good presence of mind can all but frustrate it without any training at all. The power to converse with the dead, with animals, to read minds . . . these are things that must be instilled in someone through careful tutelage over many months. All Master Kadlec needs to do is refuse. If the masters are killed, the knowledge dies with them."

"It only takes years because it is couched in lengthy terms of academia. Strip away all the jurisprudence, and a focused individual could make a good go of many of our powers in not much time at all." She pressed on before Vonvalt could offer a rejoinder. "And anyway, the threat of torture might change the master's minds. Or perhaps the lures of fabulous wealth and a harem of docile adolescents? Come, Konrad; they are lawmen, certainly, but not all share our zeal for it. They are not above bribery when the stakes are so high. Master Kadlec himself has already started breathing our secrets to the Nemans, yet one word in the Emperor's ear would have put a stop to the Patricians' overtures in an instant. These are not warriors, Konrad. Their days of ranging the fringes of the Empire are long past. They will not defend the common law at all costs."

There was a long silence, the longest yet. Vonvalt's eyes were closed. He chewed absently on the end of his pipe. Then, he took a deep breath. "After my business here is done I will return to Sova with all haste. You have my word on that. And to the extent I can do anything to reassert the supremacy of the common law and the position of Master Kadlec and the Order, I will do that too."

"You would do better to turf Kadlec out on his ear and take up the position yourself," August muttered, but after Vonvalt pursed his lips, she inclined her head. "Thank you, Konrad. I pray, then, that you conclude your business here soon."

"It's all but done. A few more moves and I shall have the culprits."

"And then you ride south?"

"After I have tried the men."

August's hand clenched into a fist. "That could take weeks!"

Vonvalt shrugged. "It is not within my gift to take any other course. You know as well as I do that the Order requires it now, wherever there is a courthouse to be found within a day's ride. It is expected that one day trials will supplant our work altogether, when the rest of the Empire has been tamed and civilised. And it will not take 'weeks'; you are being ridiculous."

August fixed Vonvalt in the eye. "Konrad, every day you dally here is a day our enemies can use to plot."

"Resi, you discredit yourself with this raving," Vonvalt said sharply. "I have heard what you have said and I have told you what I will do. Let that be the end of the matter!"

I could tell that he had wounded August, not only professionally, but personally too. She took a long draw of wine, then extinguished her pipe and stood.

"You know you are being intransigent, Konrad," she said. "I pray that it is only you who has to suffer the consequences of it." And with no further ceremony, she left the tavern.

Vonvalt rolled his eyes and finished off the last of his ale. "She speaks as if the sky were falling down on our heads," he muttered.

"She is no fool," Bressinger said. "You do not think that perhaps your history with her is clouding your judgement?"

"The Empire suffers a half-dozen rebellions a year," Vonvalt snapped. "This one will wither on the vine like the rest of them. It only seems to be more important because we have become personally embroiled. We have important work to finish here. Only then will I indulge this. It is more likely than not that in half a month, Westenholtz and Claver's heads will be on spikes outside the Imperial palace and the Templars' corpses will be drying in the wildflower meadows outside Keraq."

Bressinger grunted. "I hope you're right," was all he said.

But Vonvalt wasn't right. He was as wrong as it was possible to be.

XIV

One Last
Evening of Peace

*"No man was an effective Justice who
did not have a heart of stone."*

FROM CATERHAUSER'S THE SOVAN CRIMINAL
CODE: ADVICE TO PRACTITIONERS

◆◆◆

The horses hadn't another hard ride in them, and it took most of
the afternoon to get back to the Vale. We spent the journey in
miserable silence. By the time we passed under the Veldelin Gate,
darkness was falling and the drizzle was turning into sleet.

Vonvalt turned to Bressinger, his black beard looking unkempt
and glistening with rainwater.

"You come with me," he said. "There is a matter I want to
attend to tonight. Graves will have to keep another day now," he
added, irritated. "Helena, you may do what you will. I will see
you at dawn."

I did not question it. I was pleased to be out of Vonvalt's

company. The man might have been in denial about events happening around him, but I was frightened. An evening's distraction was most welcome – and I knew exactly where I was going to go for it.

I stabled the horse back at the watch house block, then hurried through the cold streets in the fading light as the wardmen lit the lanterns and tried to round up the beggars. Matas and his father lived in the western closure, according to the watch house serjeant, where a large portion of the town's population of middling wealth lived. The houses here were not like those slumped shacks in the eastern closure, where Lady Bauer's body had been fished out of the Gale, but they were also a far cry from those of the town's wealthy merchants and ruling classes which I had quickly grown used to. Instead they were tall, simple constructions, timber-framed and daub-walled, crammed in so tightly that little light seemed to make it through the gaps between the roofs above.

Matas lived in an apartment at the top of one of the blocks, and I surmounted the rickety stairs and knocked on the door.

"Helena?" Matas said, looking confused as he opened the door. It seemed strange to see him in simple, homespun clothes. "How . . . why are you here?"

I laughed at his confusion and pulled him into an embrace. It was improperly familiar, but after the day's sorry events I was in sore need of comfort. I think even he was slightly taken aback by such an inappropriate display of affection, but his arms closed around me and pulled me tight nevertheless.

"Kasivar's tail, where have you been?" he asked. "I was afraid you and the Justice had moved on. I saw your taskman rattling about the place, but he was not interested in speaking with me."

"Oh, never mind, Dubine," I said off-handedly, actually quite annoyed that Bressinger had not told Matas where I'd gone. "I have been to Seaguard up the Imperial Relay."

Matas's eyes widened. "The Relay! By the God Mother! I would kill to use the Relay. Is it as exciting as they say? Thundering up the Hauner road at the speed of an eagle. I've heard one can reach the coast in a week in good weather."

"It is exactly as you describe," I said. "Though I must say, my rear did not thank me by the end of it."

Matas was about to say something vulgar, then stopped himself, a prisoner of social convention. He blushed, and my mouth fell open in surprise once I realised what was going on.

"You beast!" I said, shoving him, though I wore a smile. "You ... are in the presence of a lady." I put on false airs and he laughed.

"I would be happy to give it a rub down?" he said, taking the plunge. By Sovan standards it was exceptionally improper – though I had heard much worse in Muldau. In any event, it was nice to have a break from the stuffy comportment I was used to and just be bawdy with a lad I was attracted to.

I shoved him again. "You will do no such thing, sir," I said. "An Imperial agent such as myself cannot allow her ... rear ... to be—" I couldn't finish. I burst out laughing, and he laughed too, and then we were kissing. Oh, how my heart aches as I recall these stolen moments. It drives me mad to think of the choices I made. How things could have been so different.

"Here, come in," Matas said, leading me inside. "My father will be delighted to meet you."

"And I him," I said with warmth.

Inside was a small living space that contained a table and chairs, and a cooking area with an iron kettle and spit. There was a fire burning in a small hearth which was mercifully not filling the space with smoke, though the effect was a stifling heat which was compounded by the fact that there were two more apartments below us with their own fires burning. Other than those things, there was little to ornament the place.

"Matas? Who is it?" a voice called from the room next door.

"Someone with me I'd like you to meet."

"If it's that bloody Tivec boy again—"

"Father!" Matas hastily interjected with an apologetic smile. "'Tis a girl. Mind your tongue. I'd like you to meet her, and she is keen to meet you, though I cannot think why."

"Kasivar," I heard the man grunt. There was the sound of more grunting, heaving and straining, then some clattering, and finally a man appeared in the doorway in a rough-looking wheeled chair.

"My, you're a pretty one," he said gruffly. "Forgive me, miss, for not standing. As you have probably guessed, I cannot."

I admit I was a little taken aback by the man. He had the look of Matas about him, naturally, and though far from elderly, his injury had clearly sucked the youth out of him. He was dressed in many layers and it was clear that he felt the cold keenly – certainly it explained the near unbearable heat of the apartment. His legs were covered in blankets and he wore simple but otherwise good-quality clothing. A close-cropped white beard covered the lower half of his face, and his hair, shoulder-length, was shot through with grey. He wore herbs about his person and this was to cover up what was quite a powerful odour, but I could forgive him that given that he was probably only able to leave the place a couple of times a week.

I bowed to him in the Imperial fashion. "I'm pleased to meet you," I said. "Helena Sedanka."

"Hm," the man replied. "You have the voice and mannerisms of an Imperial, but the surname of a Toll." He made the remark not unkindly, but it did not set me at my ease either. I remembered that Matas had told me his father had sustained his injury fighting in the Marches, so, like Sir Radomir, he probably harboured a deep dislike for everyone from Tolsburg.

"Helena had nothing to do with the Reichskrieg," Matas said quickly. "I'll not brook any unpleasantness."

"Bah," the old man said, dismissing his son with a wave. When he looked back at me, there was a slight twinkle in his eye. "I don't care for any of that any more," he grumbled, though I did not entirely believe him. "My name is Vartan. I am pleased to meet you too, Miss Sedanka. You'll join us for supper?"

"I'd be glad to," I said.

"Matas, Doroteja is supposed to be bringing us something tonight. Tell her we have a guest; she may have a little kenna in her."

Kenna was the unofficial national dish of Sova, and consisted of pork in a spiced cheese sauce. Looking about the place, it seemed like an extravagance the Akers could ill-afford.

"There is no need to go to such lengths on my account," I said hastily. "Really, I'll have anything. In my work I am used to eating whatever is left at the end of the night. 'Tis the hazard of the trade."

"Don't you mind us, miss," Vartan said, as Matas left. "Doroteja is happy to look after us. What is your work, anyway? 'Tis odd to see a girl of your age and looks being put to work."

"I am a law clerk," I said. "I work for Sir Konrad. He is an Imperial Justice."

Vartan looked visibly taken aback. "You are a Sovan official? You work for a Justice?" The change in his mood was pronounced. He went from being haughty and gruff to suddenly respectful and, it appeared to me, ever-so-slightly alarmed. "Is it true what they say about a Justice's powers? Do you have them as well?"

I smiled in what I hoped was a reassuring way. "Sir Konrad certainly does have powers – and I certainly don't."

Vartan's reaction to me and my profession was one which I had always encountered but was becoming increasingly cognisant of. Until the Bauer case and our time in Galen's Vale, I had been naïve. Now I was finally realising: the common-folk, even my elders and betters, were *frightened* of us. They were scared not just because of Vonvalt's powers; they were scared simply by virtue of our being Imperial agents. For most the Sovans remained conquerors, even if they were now ubiquitous. And although I always considered myself a Toll first and a Sovan second – indeed, I've never considered myself an Imperial, not really – that was certainly not how others saw me. I might as well have been wearing the Imperial colours and device. We were the embodiment of the Emperor's authority itself, as though he were hovering a few feet above us and commanding our limbs with lengths of string. And although we frequently heard mutterings of the Emperor's reputation for cruelty, it took me a lot longer to piece together that the commonfolk thought we might be as cruel and wanton as he. If only I could have explained to them the zeal with which Vonvalt beheld and applied the common law. He cherished it above all else.

"I've heard it told they can speak with the dead," Vartan said uneasily. He fussed about with his blankets, suddenly unable to meet my eye. "It seems mightily unnatural to me," he grumbled.

It seemed mightily unnatural to *me*. I did not want to think about Sir Otmar again.

"Much of what people hear is rumour," I said, glad that, at that moment, we were interrupted by Matas returning.

"She did have a little kenna," he said as the distinctive scent of spiced cheese filled the small room. "It'll want warming though."

Vartan's face brightened. He looked to me for my approval, and I smiled encouragingly. His general demeanour was strange, a mixture of gruff and obsequious, and it dawned on me that his injury, and his being confined to a wheeled chair, had robbed him of much of his former character. I imagined he had once been rough and unsavoury; now he was completely at the mercy of his son and this Doroteja woman.

We chatted idly while Matas moved about the kitchen area preparing the kenna and the other bits and pieces that Doroteja had prepared. They were simple, staple foods plentiful in the local area: root vegetables, potatoes, bread and cheese.

"He must be such a help," I said quietly, though Matas was sure to have heard.

"The boy is a saint," Vartan said. "I would have died long ago without his care. However," he added, more loudly now, "I am fitter than I have been in a long time. And I have Doroteja to care for me. I keep trying to kick the boy out. He needs to make his own way in the world, not stay cooped up with me. Don't I lad? Eh? Keep trying to kick you out?"

"Aye, that you do," Matas said, grinning as he ladled the kenna into wooden bowls.

"If you don't mind my asking—"

"A Toll a head taller than me," Vartan said, cutting me off. Matas sat down with a loud sigh and a roll of his eyes.

"The man gets bigger every time."

"A bloody great Toll," Vartan continued, warming to his theme. "Big black beard he had, and long black hair down to the base of his back."

"And fingers like sausages and arms like boughs of oak," Matas said.

"Do you want to tell the story?" Vartan demanded, brandishing his knife at Matas. "I can put you in a wheeled chair of your own, eh? Think of the pair we'd make then! Wheeling around the Vale!"

"I'd outpace you," Matas said. They were both laughing now, and me with them.

"Aye, but I've had a lot more practice." He slapped the wooden wheels. "I'd attach a couple of blades here, spin 'em right through your spokes."

Matas looked at me, checking to see that I was all right, but I was perfectly happy to just listen to the banter. It was so lovely, honest and refreshing.

"Anyway," Vartan said through a mouthful of kenna. "So, I'm in the Marches and it's the Reichskrieg, right? Like every other stupid Hauner lad in the province, I've been drafted into the Legions. We're marching under the banner of Margrave Neumann – perhaps you've heard of him?"

I shook my head as Matas said, "Of course she hasn't!"

"Well, he wasn't a very good commander, see. Well, that's not fair; he was all right on open ground. But the Marches are different. 'Tis the weather, you see? Changeable. One minute it's hot sunlight, the next the God Mother is taking a great big spray of cold piss on you."

I burst out laughing at this, a shocked, high-pitched squawk that pleased Vartan no end but left Matas red with appalled humour.

"So it's a foggy day and Neumann says that we've got to take this hill; I can't even remember the name of the bloody thing, just a big lump of earth. Supposedly there's a wooden fort at the top, but I never made it that far. We're moving up the hill, slow as you like through the mud, when suddenly these Tolls appear out of the fog itself. By Nema, I was terrified. I didn't even have a sword or armour like some of the lords did, just a club and a raggedy little gambeson I'd purchased for a song.

"So these great big Tolls appear, and they're stripped to the waist and all painted up like. They used red paint to make it look like blood. Some of the lads just turned tail and ran. There was no force between heaven and earth that could have made them stay. But I thought, 'fuck it all to Kasivar', pardon my Sovan, and I ran at the nearest one and tried to hit him with my club."

He fell silent for a moment. He had told the story jovially enough, but I could see from the way his face fell that the moment of the blow, the instant paralysis, the realisation that he would probably die, still lived with him as clearly as if it were the day itself.

"You must have been tremendously brave," I said, filling the brief silence. I reached out and rubbed the back of his hand, and he smiled at me.

"Bless you, girl," he said softly. Then, suddenly, he brightened up. "So, you yourself are a Toll, not that you'd know it from the way you speak. What is your background? How did you come to be in the Justice's service?"

It was not something I liked talking about, particularly with strangers. But Vartan had allowed himself to be vulnerable with me, and so I obliged him with the same courtesy.

"I was born in Muldau," I said. "Tolsburg had been a Sovan province for about five or six years, but there was still plenty of fighting going on around the Marches. Then there was a general uprising when I was about three. My father was killed. My mother kept me safe for another few years, but she herself was killed when Muldau was sacked – again. After that it was the town orphanage, and then the workhouse when I was old enough." I shrugged, but in truth the story still brought me a great deal of pain. "I lived a hand-to-mouth existence for over a decade before Sir Konrad visited Muldau on his circuit. I tried to rob him, but rather than indict me, he apprenticed me."

"Nema, what a stroke of luck that was! You're fortunate he didn't have your hand off!"

"Yes," I said dourly. "That is almost word-for-word what he told me."

Vartan laughed, and Matas managed a chuckle. Even I smiled. But I had left out a great deal. Years of poverty, of alms and indenture, of violence and attempts on my maidenhood. The story of my youth is not a pleasant one, and its telling was sure to dampen the mood of even the liveliest of parties.

"Apologies, I didn't mean to spoil the evening," I said. "'Tis not a pleasant tale."

Vartan pointed the knife at me. "I'll not have that. Not at my table. Look at where you were, and look at what you've become. I'd never in a thousand years have believed that tale if I'd not heard it from your mouth. You've made something of yourself. You'll go very far in life as an agent of the Crown. Good on you."

I'll admit that Vartan's words warmed my soul. I offered him my heartfelt thanks, and finally set about my kenna, which was cooling rapidly but no less delicious.

We talked long into the night. It was a wonderful evening spent in good, honest company. We laughed and joked in a pure and unguarded way. I even felt my affected Sovan accent and mannerisms slipping, and my native Tollish tones coming through. By the end of the evening my cheeks and belly ached from the merriment, and I was utterly intoxicated with the idea of being Matas's wife and Vartan's daughter-in-law. It was hardly surprising, given all I had heard that lunchtime from August, that I craved such simple, hearty comforts.

"Well, I'll be retiring," Vartan said. Matas and I were openly holding hands at the dinner table, and it was clear that the evening was reaching a critical juncture. Vartan was not a stuffy chaperone. He was a simple man who had long ago dispensed with needless formality.

"Good night," Matas said.

"Good night, Vartan," I said with a heartfelt smile. "Thank you for hosting me. I've had a wonderful evening."

Vartan waved me off with a humble smile of his own, and wheeled himself back into his room without ceremony.

I was nervous as we went to Matas's bedchamber. Although I'd a headful of ale, I was very much inexperienced.

"I don't ..." Matas said softly. He said no more, but I knew what he meant. He didn't know what he was doing either.

"Between us I'm sure we can make it work," I said, and we fell into the bed, giggling at ourselves and our mutual inexperience.

I'll not forget that night. The initial pain, and then the pleasure of it. After the first go we had several more. It was inexpert and unadventurous, but executed with the enthusiasm of adolescents. We sweated, bounced, groaned and giggled our way through three bouts, before we finished, exhausted, lying naked and tangled in each other's warmth until the cold morning sunlight filtered through the clouds.

"Will the Justice not have missed you?" Matas asked, his fingers lightly caressing my hip.

"I don't know," I said. I had been thinking about Vonvalt for some time. He had entered my thoughts at the same time Matas had entered me, and I was feeling confused and not a little annoyed with myself.

"What is the nature of your relationship?" Matas asked.

"What do you mean?" I asked, audibly and visibly irritated by the question. "You have seen for yourself that I was intact."

"God Mother no," Matas said quickly. "Not that. Nothing like that. I just wonder, you know. You have spent years together on the road. He is a man of . . . power. And means."

"The man is twice my age," I said, though that in itself was a personal preference more than anything that would be considered peculiar in the provinces. Even in Sova large age gaps were common, particularly with the nobles. Sometimes children would be betrothed effectively from birth to ensure the right bloodlines were maintained and alliances were forged. "He has never said or done anything untoward. I am his employee, not his lover."

I could feel myself getting angry and defensive. I had never talked about my relationship with Vonvalt before. There had been no one to discuss it with. When he had first taken me into his service, I'd assumed he'd have expected some kind of sexual favour in due course, given that he was a wealthy agent of the Crown. I was not happy about it, but I'd resigned myself to it for a better life, sick as I was of scratching a living off the alms houses of Muldau. Then weeks had passed, and whole months, and he had expected nothing from me but hard work. I was seventeen when he had apprenticed me, a woman by most standards, and past nineteen now, overripe for marriage and childbearing by all accounts, and still he had made no pass at me. We had been alone in one another's company dozens, hundreds of times, both sober and drunk. On the odd occasion we'd even been forced to share a bed, but he'd simply turn away from me and go to sleep. Sometimes I'd even wondered if Vonvalt had been homosexual, but Bressinger had let slip one night after we'd both had a skinful of wine that Vonvalt visited his fair share of brothels. The only difference was that Vonvalt was much pickier and subtle about his entertainment, whereas Bressinger would chase down anything that moved.

For my part, I had experienced a range of conflicting and confusing emotions for Vonvalt, as young girls are wont to for older men. Vonvalt was comely, powerful and mysterious, with each of those qualities accentuating the other. He was many a maid's dream; though I had been naïve about the power I wielded as an agent of the Crown, I could pick up the jealousy radiating off the girls of Galen's Vale as easily as if it were heat from a bonfire. But as time had gone on, I had become acquainted with his faults – his hypochondria, his fastidiousness. He was melancholic and untalkative, and whenever an opportunity for solitude presented itself he would seize it.

There were other things to complicate the mix, too. He was my employer but he was also my protector. I know he had killed men, both in the Reichskrieg and in the course of his duties as a Justice. He would kill without hesitation to protect me. He was a source of both fear and comfort in this regard. Our relationship was therefore complex. It was characterised by aspects of just about every male relationship going: father, uncle, brother, husband – everything except lover, which is perhaps why, on reflection, I was so quick to allow Matas to fulfil that role in my life.

I realised that I had been silent and contemplative for several long moments. I could tell that Matas was seeking some form of comfort, and that I was not providing it. I turned to him and spoke earnestly.

"I am in love with you," I said, "and I do want to build a life together. But I have other duties, too. Sir Konrad and I have a deal.

I will work with him until the end of the Bauer case and then I will let him have my decision."

"And you will stay?" Matas asked.

Despite the whirlwind of thoughts and emotions crashing around my head, I felt sure enough to nod. "I will stay," I said.

XV

Graves

*"To join the Order of the Imperial Magistratum
is to embrace a severe life of honour and duty. No
initiate should be under any illusion whatever:
it is a rough time filled with rough deeds."*

JUSTICE REGINALD DE BERENGAR

They had exhumed the boy. They had done it overnight, under the cover of darkness. Vonvalt, Bressinger, Sir Radomir and a few watchmen had gone to the town's graveyard and, acting on the Justice's authority, dug up the boy's bones. Then they had taken them to Mr Maquerink's, the physician who had performed the autopsy on Lady Bauer's corpse, and had them examined.

"The boy was slain," Bressinger told me over a mug of marsh ale later that morning. We were sitting in a public house just off Apothecary Street. Vonvalt was still speaking to Mr Maquerink. Bressinger had lost his appetite for the investigation for the time being and had sought solace in the nearest tavern. "He had a blow to the head, same as his mother."

"What a wretched business," I said. I felt rotten about the whole thing. It had been my idea, and it had seemed like a good one at the time; but now that the deed had been done, I was overcome with a profound sense of melancholy. The thought of a group of surly men pulling up the little bones of a long-dead child made me want to weep. I wished I'd kept my mouth shut.

Bressinger took a long draw of ale. "Aye." The man looked as though he were about to cry.

We sat in silence for a moment, drinking and listening to the hustle and bustle of the tavern's patrons around us.

"How was your night? You spent it with the Aker boy."

I didn't blush this time. I simply nodded. "I did. We are in love."

Bressinger shrugged. I admit I was taken aback by his nonchalance. "I guessed as much." He accepted another tankard of marsh ale and saw half of it away in a few large gulps. "You will stay, then? Bear his children here in the Vale? Live out your life as a housewife?"

I did not care for his tone, and the slight glassiness in his eyes told me the ale was getting the better of him. But I felt compelled to engage with the man. After all, I had made up my mind to leave Vonvalt's service. If I wasn't sure enough of the decision to defend it, then it was not the right decision.

"Our life will be what we make of it," I said brusquely. "But I will not sit idle and watch our children all day."

"You are not in Sova, Helena. Women are treated differently in the provinces. The lad is smitten with you because you are pretty and you stretch his mind. But he is a product of his upbringing as much as anyone else. No matter what he might say now, he will expect you to settle soon enough."

"You do not know him," I said, getting angry.

"I know lads like him," Bressinger said, unfazed by my tone. "You are young and you have fallen hard for each other. But you will not be able to bear the monotony of it, living in the same town for the rest of your days. The novelty of it will wear off quickly, and when it does Sir Konrad will be long gone."

"We will travel," I said, defiant.

"With what money? You do not appreciate how much Sir Konrad is paid. Even his humble lifestyle takes a lot of coin to maintain. Paying for every lodging, every meal, stabling, storage. Paying for new clothes and laundry. Travel is expensive, girl. The stipend Sir Konrad receives would keep a family in the western closure in victuals for a year."

"I know how much Sir Konrad is paid," I said. "I am his clerk."

"Aye, for now."

"You would not see me happy?" I asked. It sounded almost plaintive. Despite how sure I had felt the night before, I could feel Bressinger's arguments working on me, digging up my private doubts like an expert grave robber.

"Wake up, girl!" Bressinger snapped, drawing looks from the nearby patrons. "Look at the hand most are dealt. You do not know how lucky you are. Your wage alone would draw the eye of most provincial manor barons. Sir Konrad has taught you languages, law, philosophy, jurisprudence . . . you have the education of a noble. And you are *good* at it, Helena. Nema, you have talent as raw as coal in a seam." He had spoken with the passion of the mildly inebriated; but now he took on a more sombre look. "You have his eye, too. The means to succeed. The bones of the boy . . . it is a cold thing, to have thought of that."

"I *hate* that I thought of that!" I snarled.

"But look what you have done! Look what it has achieved! In a stroke you have proved Bauer a liar. *Proved* it. The man looked Sir Konrad in the face and told him the boy died of a pox and the girl took the cloth out of grief. Before it had the veneer of believability. Now we *know* it to be a falsehood. Even Sir Konrad didn't think to dig up the boy's bones." Bressinger regarded me with a strange mixture of contempt and respect. "You are like him in more ways than you'd care to admit."

"I am nothing like him," I lied, sulking.

Bressinger drained the last of his marsh ale and regarded me for a long moment. I was getting the uncomfortable feeling that, for the first time, the dynamic of mine and Bressinger's relationship was shifting. He was losing power and I was gaining it. He could see me absorbing Vonvalt's lessons, his ways, his mind. He could see a Justice in the making, and the more learned I became, the more adult I became. I wasn't the urchin from Muldau that he had known, the rough orphan girl, the daughter and niece and sister all rolled into one. I was a woman, and a powerful, intelligent woman at that. I think he felt threatened by me.

"Sir Konrad will never tell you this," Bressinger said soberly. "But he will be heartbroken if you leave us."

"Stop," I said, shaking my head. I didn't want to hear it. It was so deeply, frustratingly unfair. "How dare you lecture me like this. It is my life and I will do with it what I will."

"Yes, I have come to expect that attitude from you."

"Arsehole," I snapped, flushing with sudden anger. Bressinger snorted, but beyond that he did not react; he just seemed to slump slightly, like a pillow with half its stuffing removed.

I stood up and strode towards the door, propelled by my anger. I turned only once. Bressinger stared at the trestle, and slowly raised his hand for another ale. Disgusted, I left the tavern.

❧

I made my way to Mr Maquerink's around the corner, past the slack-jawed gaggle of Vonvalt's followers and their stupid trinkets and offerings, and walked through the ground floor entrance. Once more I could hear Vonvalt's voice rising up from the cellar. I felt like an intruder as I walked down the stairs. At the bottom, a familiar scene confronted me: Vonvalt and the physician, leaning over a table, studying a corpse.

"Helena," Vonvalt said with jarring joviality. "You should be proud of yourself. You have the incisive mind of an investigator."

I bit my tongue. The bones on the table affected me less than I had expected. Just a miserable little pile, scarcely distinguishable from one another. In fact, I was a little surprised at how little there was left. Bodies buried in coffins took many years to fully decompose, and I did not imagine that Lord Bauer had put his son straight into the soil.

I had almost been ready to tell Vonvalt that I would be cutting our agreement short, but intrigue filled me, as unstoppable as the tide.

"That body has been limed," I said out of a sudden urge to be clever and perceptive.

"That is precisely what we were just talking about," Vonvalt said.

"A most impressive deduction, miss," Mr Maquerink said. "You have had training in this area?"

"Not formally," I said, quickly warming to my theme despite a hot feeling of self-loathing. "As you say, it was a deduction. Lord Bauer almost certainly buried the boy in a coffin. If that was the case, then there should be more to the corpse's bones than that sorry pile."

It is difficult to put into words how I was feeling. I have alluded to Vonvalt's praise before as something that I cherished, but I put it higher than this; it was *addictive*. It was a sweet elixir. And now, thanks to Matas's unwelcome questions, I found myself looking at Vonvalt in a new light, too, an altogether unhealthy light. He *was* comely, and imperious, and erudite. Back in his presence, Matas became a boy in my mind, immature and silly with his notions of love. I felt a strange and sudden urge to distance myself from him.

I hated myself for thinking these thoughts, particularly in plain view of a corpse. It speaks volumes about the intensity of the confusion that I felt, the thicket of emotion, that I can still remember the feelings so clearly to this day. It is frankly a miracle that any person makes it out of their adolescence even vaguely sane. I am still not sure that I did.

"There is no doubt in my mind that there was foul play here – and that Lord Bauer knew of it." Vonvalt added the last sentence with a sneer of distaste. "I've arranged with Sir Radomir to have armed constables sent after the man. Hopefully we can run him down soon."

"What will you do now?" the physician asked.

"I am going to speak to Bauer's assistant." He turned to me. "Has Dubine gone to the tavern?"

"Aye. He was not in the best frame of mind," I said. I didn't feel bad about reporting on him. I wanted to wound him as he had me.

To my surprise and irritation, Vonvalt did not seem annoyed. "No, I suppose not," he said absently. "This past night has been rough on him." He turned back to Mr Maquerink. "Thank you for your time, again. And sorry to have kept you up most of the night."

"I am always happy to assist where I can," the old, tired physician said magnanimously, though I had no doubt he would be closing his shop the minute we were gone. Once he was out of earshot, I turned to Vonvalt.

"What happened to Dubine?" I asked bluntly.

"What do you mean?" Vonvalt asked.

"You know what I mean," I said. "It is something to do with children, that much is clear. Whenever we discuss the death of a child, or it forms part of our work for whatever reason, he becomes melancholic and combative. He is in a black mood now, drinking himself to a stupor—" I caught myself, as the obviousness of the situation struck me, as it should have done a long time ago. "Sir Konrad," I asked, my anger forgotten in an instant. "Did he lose a child?"

Vonvalt looked at me sidelong, and continued to do so for a long while, weighing me in his gaze. When he spoke, it was with complete solemnity. "You are not to tell him that I spoke to you. Do not let on that you know, even if it is to offer sympathy. If you do, you will see just how black a mood Dubine is capable of."

"All right," I said uncertainly. "I won't mention it."

"I'm serious, Helena. You mustn't bring it up."

"I won't," I said, now feeling somewhat melancholic myself.

Vonvalt sighed. In that moment, he seemed to age ten years. "Dubine didn't lose one child," he said softly. "He lost two."

My hand went involuntarily to my mouth. My immediate reaction was one of shame. How could I not know this crucial piece of information, which explained so much of Bressinger's mercurial temperament?

"How?" I asked. It came out in a whisper. That Bressinger had endured such heartbreak brought me immediately to the verge of tears.

"In the Reichskrieg," Vonvalt said, and for a moment I thought he was going to end there. "We were nineteen – the same age you are now. He and I were in the same company. The specifics of it matter not. We were fighting in the Southmark of Denholtz, a wild place which still sporadically erupts in rebellion to this day. While we were engaged there, a small army of Venlanders moved west into Grozoda and overwhelmed the Imperial garrison in Annholt. They put the town to the sword, including Dubine's wife and twin baby sons." Vonvalt paused for a moment. "Well, it does not take much to imagine what that does to a man."

"Nema," I said. The tears were rolling freely down my cheeks. "I didn't know."

"No, and that is by design. Dubine is a hard man, but he carries this burden every day. It has taken many years of friendship and patience to get him to where he is now, but the pain can only be dulled – never eradicated. You must excuse his occasional outbursts."

"Of course," I said, feeling absolutely wretched.

Vonvalt shook his head, and straightened up. "There. You wanted to know, and now you know. Do not let Dubine carry the weight of your grief as well. Comport yourself. We have work to do."

I wiped the tears away from my cheeks and eyes. "Yes," I said. "Yes, of course I will."

"Come then," Vonvalt said, "let us be about it."

༄

We made our way to the town's treasury, a two-storey timber-framed building sandwiched between the town hall and a temple. The square that these buildings fronted, a wide, flagstoned space, was normally kept clear of stalls by town ordinances; today, however, a travelling market all the way from Venland was selling goods from the Jade Sea, and the place was jammed with merchants and punters.

We pushed our way through the press of people and up to the treasury building. For obvious reasons the place was not open to strangers, and we were stopped at the door by a guard.

"You are Sir Radomir's man?" Vonvalt asked.

The watchman tipped his helmet. "Aye, sire," he said. He was a lank-haired man of maybe thirty years, his face ruined with pox scarring from some childhood illness. Like Sir Radomir, he was unfazed by Vonvalt and the authority which he represented.

"I'm here to speak with Fenland Graves. Is he inside?" Vonvalt asked.

The guard nodded and pushed open the door. Almost immediately beyond was a wooden staircase. "He is. Here, I'll take you up. I'll have to take your sword, though, sire; 'tis not permitted in the treasury."

Vonvalt sighed. "I am afraid you will have to make an exception with me." He gestured up the stairs. "Come on. I've pressing business to attend."

The guard paused, wrong-footed. "Suit yourself," he said eventually, and started walking up to the first floor.

"You have been watching him?" Vonvalt asked.

"Aye," the man said quietly without breaking his stride.

"And he has not done anything untoward?"

"Nothing I've seen, sire. Just the ordinary comings and goings."

"I should like to question you later on where he has been. You have kept a record per Sir Radomir's instructions?"

"Aye," the man said, a little testily.

We reached the top of the stairs. Here was a wide, square-shaped landing space covered over with an ornately patterned red rug.

"Mister Graves carries on his business in there. Here, I shall accompany you. He believes me to be guarding him."

"There is no need, thank you," Vonvalt said. "You may return to the watch house and resume your normal duties."

The man again paused, seemingly unsure what to do; then he grunted and turned to leave.

"Odd fellow," Vonvalt muttered to me once the guard was out of earshot. He rapped sharply on the door. "Mister Graves? Open the door please. It is Justice Sir Konrad Vonvalt."

"Enter," came the simple reply.

Vonvalt and I exchanged a look. Vonvalt pushed open the door – and was nearly yanked off his feet as someone on the other side pulled it suddenly and sharply.

"Look out!" I screamed. A man in watch house livery and armed with a sword was standing to the right, about to take Vonvalt's head off. Unthinkingly, I lurched forwards and pushed the man in his ribs. Caught off balance, he staggered to the side and his sword lodged in the dark, solid wood of Graves's desk.

"What is the meaning of this?" Vonvalt roared, righting himself. There were three men in the chamber, all armed and armoured, each wearing the yellow-and-blue surcoats of the Galen's Vale watch. Each had a sword in his hand. The meaning of it was inescapable.

"Helena, go," Vonvalt called to me, his face grim. He pulled his short-sword from the scabbard at his waist. I admit I did not rate his chances.

"Sir Konrad!" I shouted.

"Go! Fetch Sir Radomir!"

But as I turned to leave, the guard who had led us up blocked the stairs.

"What are you waiting for, you dolts!" he shouted to the three men in the room. "Kill him!"

I watched, helpless, as the three men advanced on Vonvalt. The man who had already taken a swing at Vonvalt moved in again, bringing his sword up in a sharp, inexpert side-swipe. Vonvalt knocked it aside almost casually, and then with a deft stroke caught the man's jaw and split it in half. He staggered backwards, wide-eyed, blood pouring from the disgusting wound. His hands automatically went up to clutch his face and Vonvalt quickly stabbed him through the heart.

"Nema's fucking tits," the guard behind me snarled. He yanked his own sword out.

"No!" I shouted. By the gods, I was no shrinking violet, but moving against a soldier half my height again took all of my courage.

"*Drop your weapons!*" Vonvalt bellowed. The Emperor's Voice. The glass panes in the window behind the desk cracked. Both men in the room reeled. Blood exploded from their noses. They both watched in horror as their hands suddenly discarded their swords. Even I was dazed, my strange, hopeless charge at the guard checked.

Vonvalt advanced on both the remaining men. They were like newborn pups, helpless and dazed. They lifted their hands uselessly to try and fend off Vonvalt's furious blows, but it didn't do them any good. Vonvalt dispatched one with a revolting stab that went directly through the man's mouth and out the back of his neck; the other, weeping, sank to his knees and had his kettle helm knocked off with a tap from Vonvalt's sword, and then his head split down the middle from crown to chin. I watched with revulsion as brains slipped out of the man's cracked headcase like an oyster from its shell.

"Behind you," I tried to shout, breathless from the effects of the Voice and from the gory spectacle I had just witnessed. The guard on the landing space had avoided the worst of the effects of the Voice, and was moving to cut down Vonvalt from the rear.

I leapt forwards to block his path. "Sir Konrad!" I shouted again, and was dimly aware of Vonvalt whirling around before the man, caught at an odd angle in the doorway, jabbed me clumsily in the side of the skull with the pommel of his sword. I can remember the feeling of it to this day: the sudden, sharp pain, the soundless explosion through my brain, the swimming vision. I sank to the floor, only dimly aware of Vonvalt's shouts. I think he shouted my name.

Then he used the Emperor's Voice again, and I was knocked clean into unconsciousness as surely as if I'd taken a second blow.

I came round to see an anxious-looking and blood-flecked Vonvalt standing over me, next to a much more serene-looking Mr Maquerink.

"Slowly, girl," the wizened old physician said, sensing my disorientation. "You are safe."

I struggled to get upright. In my dazed state I was convinced that the guard was nearby, about to finish the deed.

"*Calm down,*" Vonvalt said. I felt the force of it hit me. In his concern he had accidentally employed the Emperor's Voice. It did not so much calm me as snap me out of my malaise in the same way a sharp slap might have.

Mr Maquerink gave Vonvalt a chiding look, but Vonvalt did not care for the physician's censure.

"Graves," I croaked.

"She needs to drink," Vonvalt said with the same urgent concern as the father of a sick child.

"Here, take this," Mr Maquerink said. He pressed a tankard into my hands, and I took a long draught of what turned out to be marsh ale.

"I daren't give you anything stronger," Maquerink said, seeing my nose wrinkle at the ale-flavoured water. "It is unwise to cloud a head that has suffered a blow."

"He tried to—" I started, but Maquerink shushed me.

"Take a few moments to gather your wits," he said.

"Dubine has gone after Graves," Vonvalt said in order to sate my immediate need for information.

I leant back against the bed – for it was a bed in Mr Maquerink's house, thankfully, and not the horrible corpse slabs in the cellar – and exhaled. It was only at that point that I became aware of a dull, throbbing pain in my head which seem to increase in severity with each passing second. I reached up to touch the side of my head, but Maquerink stopped me.

"Don't touch it for the moment," he said. "There is a salve upon it. I have washed the wound, and in a little while I will dress it."

"Is it bad?" I asked.

"It will heal," Maquerink said. "I have knitted it with gut. It will scar, but your hair will cover it, when it grows back."

Immediately I reached up to feel the wound, and discovered, to my horror, that the right side of my head had been clipped back to fuzz. Bizarrely, it was that trivial fact which tipped me over the edge. Suddenly overwhelmed, I began to cry with deep heaving sobs.

Vonvalt looked about as awkward as I would have expected him to, but Mr Maquerink gave me a look of pained sympathy.

"I am sorry, Miss Sedanka," he said. "I would not have done it if it had not been necessary in order for me to inspect and clean the wound. The hair will not take long to grow back to an acceptable length."

It took me a while to calm down. The physician offered me more to drink, stronger and more palatable small beer, but he had been right to withhold it from me initially. The alcohol made my head swim in spite of the minute quantities, and I handed the tankard back after just a few gulps. He took it out of the room; Vonvalt obviously wanted to speak to me in private.

"Where is Graves now?" I asked.

"Dubine and Sir Radomir are pursuing him with a handful of men. He has made east, for Roundstone. I do not know what headway he hopes to make there, if that is his ultimate destination. Either way, he will not get far. He has only been gone half a day."

I didn't have time to respond. Feeling suddenly nauseous, I reached for a bowl next to my bed and brought up all of the small beer and marsh ale which I had just drunk.

"Physician!" Vonvalt thundered, and Mr Maquerink was back in the room in a flash as I emptied the last of my stomach's contents into the pot and collapsed back into the bed.

"What is the matter with her?" Vonvalt asked.

The physician ignored him as he pressed a hand to my forehead and inspected the wound.

"Stay awake, girl," he said. "You must not fall asleep after a blow to the head. The brain is fighting to close down. If you sleep now, you may not regain consciousness. The next few hours will be critical to your recovery."

Even with this terrifying news, the urge to close my eyes and drift off was overpowering. I was exhausted, mentally and physically.

"Helena! Listen to the man," Vonvalt said. I could see the fear in his eyes.

". . . Tired," I managed.

Mr Maquerink moved quickly to the window and threw it open. Cold winter air rushed in, a soothing balm to my perspiring forehead.

"We must make her uncomfortable. The body craves unconsciousness, but it will be fatal for her," Mr Maquerink went on. He turned back to me. "Helena you must stand, or at the very least sit up. Here, come over to the window."

I allowed them to manhandle me over to the open window. The cold air gushed in like a waterfall.

"Here, remove these outer layers," the old physician continued. I felt the robes being tugged away from me until I was clad in no more than a thin slip of fabric. I soon began to shiver uncontrollably.

"This is good," Mr Maquerink said. Both he and Vonvalt were taking great pains to avoid looking at me. We were committing all sorts of sins in the eyes of both Sovan and provincial mores. A single stiff gust and all would be revealed. Even in the clutches of this sudden and terrifying malaise, I felt a hot kernel of embarrassment somewhere at the back of my mind.

This sorry practice of keeping me awake continued for some time, and involved cold air, cold water and forced marching around the apothecary's ward. It was torture in its purest form, and my body protested every step of the way. I felt like a shuffling corpse, barely reacting to Maquerink's ministrations. By the time darkness fell and snowflakes began tumbling through the open windows, however, I did feel somewhat more alert, though that was about the only good thing to come out of it.

Both Vonvalt and the physician led me back to the bed and bade me sit. I felt frozen to my core, and as exhausted from the constant shivering as from the knock to my skull.

Mr Maquerink examined me carefully, comparing my condition to different star and zodiac charts he kept and performing mathematical calculations based on a large number of factors. He also took a long gulp of my urine, which he pronounced to be fine, albeit far too concentrated, and gave me more marsh ale, this time to sip. Then he offered me a protracted explanation as to why he had done all he had done – with Vonvalt, an inveterate hypochondriac, nodding along knowingly – before finally allowing me to rest. The only thought that struck me was how much it was going to cost Vonvalt to keep me there. Physicians of Mr Maquerink's calibre did not come cheap.

"The cost," I mumbled, but Vonvalt was quick to shush me.

"Rest now, Helena. Do not trouble yourself. I'll come back to see you first thing in the morning."

I relaxed, elated to finally give in to the unconsciousness I craved. I looked forward to a long, restful night of sleep, to perhaps be aroused in the middle of the following morning to a lavish breakfast.

Instead, it would turn out to be one of the most terrifying nights of my life.

XVI

Speaker to the Dead

*"To drag words from the lips of the dead is a vile
and irreligious practice, sure to poison the soul of
any man who partakes in it irredeemably."*

SIR KRISTOPHER MAYER

❧

I awoke to the sound of a tremendous calamity. Slamming doors, slamming bootsteps, men shouting. I pressed myself up in the bed, dazed and disorientated. My head wound pounded with every heartbeat. It was still the middle of the night; it was dark outside the window, the only light produced by the town's wan and smoky street lanterns.

For a horrible moment I thought the physician's house was being raided by brigands, but even in my confusion I was able to pick out the familiar voices of Bressinger and Vonvalt among the din.

The door to the ward was kicked open by a heavy boot. Four men struggled with a thrashing fifth: Bressinger, Vonvalt, Sir

Radomir and another armed and armoured man I did not recognise, but who wore the town's colours. I could not make out who the fifth was until he was shoved roughly down in the cot next to mine.

It could only have been Graves.

"Light, quickly!" Vonvalt snapped. A sixth figure appeared in the doorway: Mr Maquerink.

All of them moved as though I were not there. For a moment I wondered if I had perished in the night and it was my ghost watching them, transparent and unnoticeable. But the town watchman spared me a brief, grim glance, and I knew that I wasn't unnoticed. I was being ignored.

I watched proceedings with a horrified fascination, trying to piece together what was happening in spite of the pain in my head. It was only when a lantern was brought in and candles were lit that I could see the long trail of blood leading into the room, and the crimson wetness staining the front of Graves's clothing and that of most of the men holding him.

"Hold his leg!" Bressinger grunted at Sir Radomir. Graves was thrashing like a rabid dog. I could hear his breath rattling and sucking in his chest. The man had been run through; that much became obvious. I could see the wound, in the ribs on the right. Blood frothed out of it like pink sea foam.

The four of them continued to wrestle the stricken Graves. In the madness and panic, I realised Vonvalt was trying to ask him questions. As Sir Radomir, the watchman and Bressinger struggled to contain the man's flailing, Vonvalt was examining him as though in the court room. At the time I thought he had lost his mind; quite what he hoped to achieve was beyond me. Graves was in no fit state to do anything except thrash his way into oblivion. But after what came next, I can see now why Vonvalt was keen to try and get something – anything – out of him before he perished.

It was hopeless. I don't know how long it took Graves to die. I am certain it felt like longer than it was. Most men would drop dead in an instant from a wound like that. With Graves, it felt as though we all had to wait until the last of his blood drained from his body.

And then, after a deep, rattling breath, there was silence. Graves sagged and pulled against those who, seconds before, had strained to contain him. I fancied that his skin took on a waxy pallor.

Vonvalt turned to Bressinger with a mournful expression. "Fetch my things, as quickly as you can," he said quietly.

Bressinger walked smartly out of the room.

"What happens now?" Sir Radomir asked.

"I am going to try and speak with him," Vonvalt said.

For a moment the sheriff looked completely baffled. Then realisation dawned on him. "Nema," he muttered.

"I'll have no part in this," the watchman I did not recognise said in a local accent. He backed away from the corpse, shooting Vonvalt a look that was half fear and half disgust.

"Get you gone, then!" Sir Radomir spat.

"You would do best to leave, too," Vonvalt said once the other watchman was out of earshot. "To say this will be unpleasant would be to understate the matter significantly." I started as his eyes suddenly locked with mine. I had thought myself invisible in the commotion.

"You too, Helena. You are not ready."

"No," I said, surprising myself. I do not know what possessed me to want to witness the spectacle. Certainly I regret doing so. At the time, I think I fooled myself into thinking that it was my duty to watch. Necromancy was a practice that was integral to the Order of the Magistratum. Every Justice had to try to learn it, even if only a minority were able to successfully channel the power. If, despite my constant vacillation, I was to become one, then I would have to start somewhere. Reflecting on the matter now, however, I think in fact it was almost entirely morbid fascination.

Whatever the reason, one thing is certainly true: if I could erase all knowledge of it and purge it from my memories entirely, I would. I did not think for a moment that I would eventually become a practitioner myself.

Vonvalt shrugged. "Suit yourselves," he said. "Help me move the beds."

Sir Radomir, Mr Maquerink and I dragged the beds away from Graves, and then Vonvalt and Sir Radomir manhandled Graves's corpse on to the floor. Blood still leaked from the wound, but it was slow now, brown in the wan candlelight and lacking in all vitality.

"Get back, please," Vonvalt said. We watched as he fussed over the corpse, until Bressinger reappeared, carrying a black strongbox which I had come to associate with a deep-seated sense of dread.

"Thanks," Vonvalt muttered.

"Come, Helena," Bressinger said, moving to take me away.

"No," Vonvalt said as he opened the box. He pulled out its contents: a number of trinkets, and then the *Grimoire Necromantia*, a stout tome enclosed by two black leather covers and locked with a clasp.

"You cannot expect her to watch?" Bressinger said, incredulity straining his voice.

"I told her to leave," Vonvalt said. "She wishes to stay."

"Helena," Bressinger said, turning to me. Fear for himself and concern for me battled for control of his features. "You are not ready."

Before I could answer, Vonvalt clapped a hand on Bressinger's shoulder, drawing his attention. "Quickly now. We don't have time for this."

Bressinger sighed. I watched as Vonvalt donned a silver medallion in the shape of what I initially thought was the deer of the God Mother, Nema. In fact it was the Draedist god Oleni, whom the Sovans had co-opted.

Bressinger and Vonvalt then faced one another. Bressinger put his hand on Vonvalt's shoulder, and they spoke in High Saxan: "*Azshtre stovakato bratnya to zi chovekna eyrsvet linata. Kogata govoria dumitenta boga maĭka, toĭmoz daesevŭrne vyr zemyatra nazivite.*"

The candles flickered. I was dimly aware of Mr Maquerink leaving at this point, having had his fill of the arcane, but Sir Radomir remained, though he had backed into the corner. The air was saturated with a nervous energy. I have never known a silence like it.

Vonvalt turned away from Bressinger and unlocked and opened the *Grimoire Necromantia*. He flicked to the right page, and, satisfied, positioned himself at Graves's feet.

"When I begin," he said, "no one is to leave the room. All of you must remain perfectly still and silent. No matter what happens and what you see, do not move. Above all, do not touch me."

"Wait," Sir Radomir said from the corner. He was blanched, and his voice was thin and difficult to hear above the raging silence. "I have changed my mind."

"Out then, and quickly," Vonvalt said. The sheriff left.

"Do not scream," Vonvalt said to me. "You will want to, but you must not."

"All right," was all I managed. It was a whisper.

Vonvalt nodded to Bressinger, who nodded back. Then he turned to the *Grimoire Necromantia* and spoke a short invocation which I must not repeat here. Once he had finished, he closed the book and handed it to Bressinger, who locked it and returned it to the strongbox. Then Bressinger took several decent steps backwards.

And waited.

I watched the corpse of Graves. Blood pounded in my ears. The silence was so profound it was deafening. It took me a few minutes to realise that Vonvalt was speaking. It was very low and very soft, and it was in a language I did not understand.

Then Graves's eyes opened.

It is difficult to express in words the feeling of shock, revulsion and horror that overcame me. I remember my eyes swimming out of focus and my stomach dropping. The feeling was reminiscent of standing at the top of the Tower of Saint Velurian at the Temple of Savare in Sova, the tallest building in the Empire. Looking down at the distant ground, one is overwhelmed with a sense of profound unease; it is dizzying and terrifying and leaves the mind feeling unhinged.

My brain was railing against what I was seeing. It was so deeply disturbing that I began to weep uncontrollably. I wanted to stop watching but the sheer impossibility of it compelled me. Graves's eyes were black, deep, infinite pools of ink that seemed to suck the light out of the room. His lips twitched. Vonvalt's words, spoken quietly but urgently in that arcane tongue, seemed to be tugging the man's mouth open like someone gently pulling on a length of gut.

Graves's entire body started to crick and crack now, twitching and jerking like a puppet. It was a grotesque sight. His contortions forced more dead blood out of the wound. The sound of popping bones filled the small room and made me want to vomit. Eventually the man's mouth opened and started to move, opening and closing like that of someone drowning. In the same moment, I felt another presence in the room. I felt it with absolute conviction. My skin broke out in gooseflesh. The candles guttered and faded. I hoped to all the gods I could think of that they would not go out. They remained lit, but the light they provided was different, somehow. It was as though the light itself was black.

Vonvalt stopped his muttering. I looked over to him. His eyes had taken on a glassy expression.

"You work for Lord Bauer," Vonvalt said.

The corpse twitched and stirred.

"Lord Bauer," Graves said. It sounded like someone speaking with a mouthful of soil, or marsh water. It was gravelly and bubbly and deep.

"In the town treasury," Vonvalt said.

"Jade . . . and cotton on a fair breeze," Graves choked and mumbled. "Summer lark . . . a fine bolt of cloth. The sea. I see the sea."

"Who killed you?" Vonvalt asked.

"Who killed me?" Graves responded.

"Who killed you?" Vonvalt pressed.

"Bloody great Grozodan man, I see him now," Graves said in a moment of jarring lucidity. I briefly met Bressinger's eye. He shared my expression of muted horror. I wondered how many séances he had been a part of. I knew from Vonvalt's conversation with Sir Otmar's corpse in the watchtower on Gabler's Mount that he could perform the necessary rites by himself. I found myself wondering what Bressinger's role in this particular séance was.

"You work for Lord Bauer," Vonvalt repeated.

There was a long pause. Eventually, Graves said, "Of the things I have done, never in all my life."

"You helped with the town's treasury accounts."

"The Father of Time is a stern patron."

"Hearken to me!" Vonvalt snapped suddenly, making me flinch.

"The Trickster has me," Graves said. I saw black goo drool from his mouth as he said it. I could feel myself weeping. Mindful of Vonvalt's warning, I tried to stifle the sound.

"You worked for Lord Bauer."

"In the town's treasury," Graves drooled.

"You paid money to the kloster."

"That is a dark place," Graves said.

"Is Lord Bauer's daughter a hostage in the kloster?"

"They are all hostages in that place."

Vonvalt repeated the question three more times before he received a vaguely intelligible answer.

"She is the guest of a dangerous man," Graves said. It came out as a sigh. "I am in great pain, Justice. Release me and begone."

"What is the name of the man in the kloster? Who has Sanja Bauer?"

"The kloster . . . it is a dark place," Graves said. Now his voice sounded like a young maid's. "Mine is a black future."

"Tell me the name of the man."

Graves's mouth opened and closed like a suffocating fish. "The Trickster has me," he mumbled eventually. "The name of the man you seek is the water hunter."

"Tell me the name of your employer in the kloster."

"That is a dark place."

"The name!"

"A dark place for dark deeds. Father of Death, take me. I have told you the name. I see the White Deer."

"You see nothing but marsh."

"I see the girl in the room. Who is she?"

I started at this. My skin crawled. A small moan escaped my lips.

"Silence!" Vonvalt snapped. It was unclear whether it was directed at me or Graves.

"I hear her, too." Graves's voice had taken on a different quality. Someone – something – else was speaking through him. "It has been a while since we last spoke. Who have you brought to meet me, Justice?"

"You've lost him," Bressinger said out of the side of his mouth. "Come back."

"No, he is still before me," Vonvalt said, his eyes still glassy and vacant. I was losing the thread of the exchange rapidly.

"Give this man to me," Graves said.

"He has not answered my questions," Vonvalt said.

"You heard him. Your investigation ends in the kloster. But you already knew that. Release him."

"I want the name."

"You have had close enough. A name for a name; the girl, in the room. I see her."

Bressinger looked over to me. He nodded his head towards the door. He was gesturing for me to leave, but Vonvalt had told me to remain still and silent. He had told Bressinger the same thing, for that matter, but the situation appeared to have evolved.

"You see nothing. Answer my question."

"It matters not. I will meet her soon . . . The threads of time converge. I see it." Graves chortled and more black goo frothed from his mouth and trickled down his lips. "Your taskman is right. You should leave. Go back."

"Out," Bressinger whispered to me.

I got up to leave. I moved quickly and quietly past Vonvalt. My robe clung coldly to my legs, and it was only at that moment that I realised I had wet myself in fear.

"Girl!" Graves snapped with the sound of a bough struck by lightning. I shrieked and flinched so violently that I came into contact with Vonvalt.

I was no longer in Mr Maquerink's house. I was standing in a marshland of black water and bone-pale grass. A random scattering of dead trees as jagged as lightning and black as obsidian thrust upwards about the landscape. The sky above was a roiling sea of white which sat beneath a kaleidoscopic array of stars and swirls of cosmic cloud. I saw that every time they broke, a vast funnel-like portal seemed to hang over the world, like the eye of an enormous storm.

I was standing next to Vonvalt. Opposite him was Graves, calf-deep in marsh water. There were other things, other presences I felt as keenly as if they were human men standing in front of me.

"You shouldn't be here," Vonvalt said. I turned to him, to see his eyes were as white as balls of marble. "Dubine!" he shouted. I turned back to see Graves reaching for me. I opened my mouth to scream—

And then we were back in the room. I sat, reeling. During the process of being pulled away from whatever place I had just been in, a strange, almost violent succession of visions had cut through my mind like a scythe through rye: Lady Karol Frost;

a two-headed wolf cub; a solitary rook in an orchard; and a man tied to a stake in a wildflower meadow, flames licking at his feet.

I blinked as the visions faded from my mind and looked around the room. The candles were brighter. Graves was still, his eyes blank and staring at the ceiling. A thin wisp of smoke was rising from the amulet at Vonvalt's neck. Bressinger was crouched on the floor, moaning. Vonvalt took a few steps back and sat down heavily on the wooden floor.

"Faith," he said. His face was pallid and drawn.

"I'm sorry," I stammered. "It was an accident. I'm sorry." I was crying again. The tears came freely. My skin crawled. My mind felt injured. I wished I hadn't seen any of it. I still wish it to this day.

Vonvalt looked up at me. I had never seen him looking so exhausted. "The two-headed wolf," he said. "The Autun. Did you see it?"

I had seen it. I nodded.

"Lady Frost too?"

Again, I nodded dumbly.

"What does it mean?" I asked hoarsely.

"I don't know," Vonvalt said, almost breathless with the strain of it. "I must rest."

"I am sorry," I said again. "Did I ruin it?"

Vonvalt shook his head. "I had lost him already. I should have left earlier."

"Left where? What was that place?"

Vonvalt waved a visibly shaking hand at me. "Later, later. I need rest. And something strong to drink. Dubine?"

"Yes," Bressinger mumbled. He straightened up. He looked pale and drawn too. He walked out the room. I heard some distant, muffled conversation with Mr Maquerink, and then a few minutes later Bressinger returned with a flagon and some cups. He pressed one into my hands and then handed one to Vonvalt, and kept one for himself. He poured a generous measure in all three and then drained his in a few large swallows.

I did the same. Vonvalt sipped his.

"We will speak in the morning," he said. He sounded exhausted, utterly drained of life.

"I don't want to be in this room," I said suddenly. "Please don't make me stay here."

"Come," Bressinger said. "We'll head back to Lord Sauter's."

I let Bressinger lead me out of the room. Mr Maquerink was in the hallway. It was disturbing to see a man of learning look so deeply troubled. He led us downstairs wordlessly and gave me a cloak to wear. Then Bressinger took me outside into the cold, snowy air of Galen's Vale and we began the walk back to the mayor's house.

❧

I awoke in the morning after a dreamless sleep to find a woman sitting at the end of my bed.

"Hello?" I asked.

"Good morning, miss," the woman said. "Beg pardon for the intrusion. The Justice requested I attend you. There is a bath prepared for you downstairs, and breakfast is waiting in the dining hall."

"Right," I said, feeling thoroughly disorientated, as though I were in some liminal space. The events of the night before already felt unreal and distant in the cold light of the morning.

"Come then," the woman said. I did not recognise her, but she was likely a member of Lord Sauter's household. She had that motherly, matronly quality that all older female servants seemed to possess. I felt myself responding to it immediately. She exuded calmness and unflappability at a horrifying and tumultuous time.

She took me downstairs where a steaming, lavender-scented bath awaited. Without a word passing between us she stripped me of my clothes and helped me in. In my state I was as docile as a lamb. The water was slightly too hot for comfort, but I was in no mood to turn down a good bath. There was even scented soap, which the woman proceeded to work into a lather with a sponge and vigorously scrub my back.

"Have you spoken to the Justice this morning?" I asked.

"I have," the woman said. She applied the sponge quite roughly and I winced.

"Was he all right?" I asked.

"What do you mean?" the woman asked. The house seemed very quiet. Normally in the morning the street outside bustled with people. Instead, the whole town seemed still.

"Did he seem . . . Did anything seem the matter?"

"You mean, after his trespass?"

I frowned at the strange answer, but my attention was drawn by the water. I realised I couldn't see anything from my navel down; the water was so murky it was almost black. I lifted my hands up through the water and brought up twigs and roots and old bones with them.

I looked sharply up at the woman. It was Lady Karol Frost. Her skin was black and charred. Under her arm was a two-headed wolf pup. She was strangling it.

"The mark of the Trickster is upon you now, girl," she said through heat-split teeth, and she laughed as I screamed.

XVII

A Dangerous Undertaking

*"'Tis a better fate to die in the service of the law
than serve a regime which does not uphold it."*

SIR RUDOLF BLIX

"Now you see why I do not like to do it."

I pressed myself up in bed, heaving in deep lungfuls of air. Sweat sheened my brow and soaked my robe. I was trembling badly; my teeth rattled in my skull like dice in a cup.

The nightmare faded away, like a stone dropped into a murky lake.

Vonvalt was sitting at the end of the bed, smoking his pipe. His cheeks were wine-blushed in the candlelight. Outside it was still dark. Snow tumbled through the air, pattering gently against the window lattice.

"How long has it been?" I asked. "Since . . ."

"About an hour," Vonvalt said. "Here: take some wine."

He poured me some and I accepted it. I took the whole cupful down in one long draught.

"Am I awake now?" I asked shakily. "Please tell me this is real."

"This is real," Vonvalt obliged.

"What happened? How did Graves come to be stabbed?"

"Bressinger chased him down on the east road. His flight was short and unimaginative, much like the man himself. Instead of surrendering himself, he came at Dubine – and paid for it with his life, as men tend to when they come at Dubine." He smoked for a few moments. "Describe your nightmare to me, now, while it is fresh."

I didn't want to, but I told him anyway. He didn't move as I recounted exactly what I had seen.

"What does it mean?" I asked.

Vonvalt was silent for a moment. He smoked for a little while, then said, "I do not know. I have some ideas which are too ill-formed to share."

"What was that place? The marshland?"

"That is the afterlife, Helena, or at least some part of it. There are men within the Order who know all of the old lore, but their knowledge is not widely shared. That is in part what Claver and his church are after."

"There is an afterlife?" I stammered.

Vonvalt shrugged. "There is something," he said. He sounded tired and drained. "I do not understand the precise nature of it. But afterlife seems an apt word."

"And you travel there to question the dead? Like a lawman at a trial?"

He nodded once. "In a sense."

"Did something go wrong? What did he keep saying about the Trickster? I thought you said the Imperial gods were all nonsense?"

"It is not as simple as that," Vonvalt said. He took in a deep breath and let it out slowly in a great sigh. "There are entities which exist in that realm. Spirits, demons, old souls . . . many have conjectured what they might be. Some are harmless. Some are malevolent. Sometimes when questioning the deceased, one of those beings interrupts the process and makes mischief. It is frightening, but there is never any danger. They cannot hurt us – in a physical sense, at least. The Trickster is the Imperial name for an old Draedist demon called Aegraxes. He is known to play games with those who dabble in necromancy. It is not the first time our paths have crossed."

"You speak as if all of this is real!" I said tearfully, desperate for comfort.

"It *is* real, Helena. Perhaps not in the sense of you and I, and the affairs of the Empire. But it is there, playing out on another stage, another dimension where earthly laws do not apply."

I shivered uncontrollably. "And that's what happened with Graves?" I asked, my voice hoarse with wretchedness. "This entity hooked on to him like a parasite?"

"Aye. That is a good way of putting it."

"A lot of what he said didn't make sense."

"No. But it was never going to, not with the amount of fear and hatred he took with him."

I sat, thinking for a moment, recounting the séance in my mind. "He said he could see me in the room. It seemed to unsettle you."

"Hm," Vonvalt said.

"What did it mean? Was it bad?"

Vonvalt smoked for a little while longer. "I do not know. He should not have been able to. The summoning only works one way, and I did not mis-incant. I travel to their land; they do not travel here."

"Why did he ask for my name?"

"There is power in a name." He extinguished his pipe. Outside, the first of dawn's weak grey light began to suffuse the sky, and I realised that Vonvalt had deliberately stayed with me until daylight.

"What did you say to Dubine, at the end? Before we were pulled out?" I asked, hungry for information, desperate for anything to rationalise what I had seen. "What was his role? You did not need him when you spoke to Sir Otmar."

"No, I did not. You remember what I explained to Lord Sauter. Sir Otmar was . . . a friend, of sorts. He had sent me a message in his dying moments. There was less risk in seeking him out. He was yearning for help, for justice. Graves was hostile. At the time of his death his mind was in disarray, a miasma of negative emotions. Such a mind is vulnerable to the eldritch forces within the afterlife. Dubine's role was to provide something like a beacon that I could follow if something went wrong – not that there was any chance of that."

I got the strong sense that he was lying, but given how desperately I wanted to believe it, I latched on to the idea like a limpet on a rock.

"I am going to try and sleep," Vonvalt said. "I will be next door. You should rest, too, doubly so because of your injury. I assure you there is no danger at all. You will be frightened, that is natural – but know that there is nothing that can harm you."

I doubted I would ever be able to sleep again, but the fact that it was no longer night-time did seem to alleviate much of the more immediate fear.

"I will try," I said with an insincere smile. He nodded, and I watched him leave the room.

Despite my fear I collapsed back into the bed. My skin was rough with gooseflesh, but the wine was starting to take hold and dim my fear as much as the receding night.

Eventually I did fall asleep. Mercifully, that time, I dreamt of nothing.

I was roused at noon by a member of Lord Sauter's household staff. I could hear the temple bell chiming in the distance. Cold rain drummed against the window.

Tired, in pain and still frightened, I dressed myself and went downstairs to see Vonvalt taking lunch in the dining hall. There was no one else around.

"I am sorry to have woken you," Vonvalt said. "Unfortunately, we have no time to spare. I hope you are at least somewhat restored."

I sat down in a sour mood and began to load a plate with some of the greasy meat and bread laid out in front of me.

"What's going on?" I asked, frightened that this could be yet another nightmare. "It's very quiet."

"Sir Radomir and Dubine are attending to the executions," Vonvalt said. Then, when he caught my bemused expression, he added: "I have been interrogating every member of the town's watch. We turfed out two more who were loyal to the kloster – or at least, to its coin. I have only just come back from questioning them. Their executions will be kept as quiet as possible. We do not want the town to lose faith in its watch."

"Did they reveal anything?" I asked.

Vonvalt shook his head. "The conspirators have been careful with their information. These men had only one point of contact: Fenland Graves. The two I have just spoken to told me that Graves paid them to report on Sir Radomir's investigation into the Bauer murder – and, as you of course are aware, to murder us in turn. In a perverse sort of way, it is a good sign; it means we are cutting to the bone of the issue. Desperate men are forced to desperate deeds."

I shook my head. "I can scarcely believe it."

"No," Vonvalt said. "Nor can I. But with Graves's corpse thrown on a convict's pyre and his fellows in the kloster no doubt tipped off, we can ill afford to dwell on it. There will be time enough for unravelling all of that at the end of this sorry business." He sighed.

"A part of me is still tempted to take a host of armed constables into that kloster and just smoke out the wrongdoers. But those old fortresses . . . who knows what manner of secret tunnels and exits there are running into the mountains? I am worried that a heavy-handed approach will net us perhaps a few junior conspirators and see the rest scurry off and bed in somewhere else like ticks. One does not take a hammer to a wasps' nest, after all."

I had long guessed what his alternative was.

"You propose for me to enter the kloster," I said. "As some wounded fawn."

Vonvalt nodded. "You have the kernel of it, aye," he said. "Helena, you know I would never willingly put you in harm's way. But you are an official of the Crown, and, if I have my way, you will be a Justice in your own right one day. It is time for you to grapple with the sharp end of my work."

After the séance, I was feeling somewhat numb and reckless, and I gave my assent to this dangerous course far too readily. "I will do it," I said, though it had never really been a choice. If I wanted to continue on in Vonvalt's service – at least until the end of the Bauer matter, and the conclusion of our bargain – I would have to get used to this sort of clandestine work.

"Bressinger will remain in Galen's Vale," Vonvalt continued, "incognito. I will have to leave. There will be a ruse. I'm thinking a pretend falling-out." He nodded to the wounded, shorn side of my head. "Your injury makes a convincing pretext. The séance, too, might be considered a final straw. You would tell the gateman that you have had your fill of Imperial service and demand sanctuary. They are obliged to give you a month's worth under the canon law, and to be honest they would probably like the opportunity to thumb their noses at the Order."

"If there is a man within the kloster who is running a conspiracy with Vogt and Bauer, then he may suspect this for what it is," I said.

Vonvalt nodded slowly without breaking his gaze with me.

"They may. It is a risk I am afraid that we are going to have to take, for there is no one else I will bring into my confidence on this."

"You wish me to go tonight?"

"Yes," Vonvalt said. "We must strike while the iron is hot. I have already begun to hint at an imminent departure. Lord Sauter will be a victim of the ruse; Sir Radomir, however, will be informed, for your safety."

"What is my specific goal? To locate Sanja Bauer?"

"Indeed," Vonvalt said. "That will be the cornerstone of the strategy. Find her and find out what has happened to her. Get her to give you the names of those who have taken her hostage – if that is indeed what has happened. Then get you gone."

I considered this for a moment. "It will take some time," I said. "Days, perhaps weeks. I cannot just go in acting like a wounded fawn and then start poking around. Even assuming I am not suspected, there will be protocols. They will have me doing menial jobs with restricted access to much of the kloster. It is a severe lifestyle. All must pay their dues."

"I know," Vonvalt said. "While you are there I am going to search for Vogt and Bauer. I will make for the Imperial wayfort at Gresch in the first instance. If I am able to find either of them, then I will use my Voice and compel them to speak. I have more than enough to pry a full confession out of them, whether they are expecting it or not. If I am able to do this, I will pass word to Dubine and he will come and remove you, under armed guard if necessary. But if they have gone for good, then this may represent our very last chance to get to the bottom of this matter before we leave the Vale. And we must leave the Vale soon, Helena. We *must* return to Sova. You must do your very best. Do not be reckless, but act with all haste. I am counting on you."

There was another silence. Despite myself I was beginning to feel the first tugs of trepidation.

"I want to speak to Matas before I go in," I said.

Vonvalt looked slightly disappointed by this, but nodded his assent. "You had better go now, then," he said. "I want you knocking on that kloster gate tonight."

≈

I finished my breakfast quickly and left Lord Sauter's house. Outside the cold, wet streets were bustling with lunchtime crowds seeking shelter from the rain. I made straight for the watch house, and found Matas upstairs in the common room. He was the only one in there; the rest of them had gone out drinking with Sir Radomir, no doubt recovering from the double blow of Vonvalt's questioning and the unearthing of treachery in their midst.

Had I had more time to calm myself, perhaps rest further and eat more, I might have made better company for Matas that afternoon. But I was in a strange, foul mood. With Vonvalt becoming increasingly reckless, the whisperings of rebellion, and indeed, having had a disturbing glimpse of the afterlife itself, I was beginning to feel like I had in Muldau: lost, anxious and melancholic.

Matas made a great deal of the injury to my head and my shorn hair, and the attempt on my life. He had known and been friendly with the men who had tried to kill Vonvalt and me, which naturally fuelled his sense of guilt and frustration. He paced the room like a caged animal, exercising himself into a fury, the target of his emotion vacillating between the would-be murderers and me myself for having the temerity to be a Justice's clerk in the first place – as though it had somehow been my fault.

His anger sharply contrasted with my own sense of detachment, and I did not handle him well. Although we had fallen for each other, and fallen hard, we had also not spent that much time in one another's company. I did not know how to deal with his impotent anger at all; and, if I am honest, I found this outward display of emotion, which came from a place of care and a desire to protect me, deeply irritating. Being back with Matas after having spent the previous days with Vonvalt, Bressinger and Sir

Radomir made Matas seem childish and naïve. I had seen considerably more of the world than he had, and I had been exposed to real, mortal danger. Galen's Vale had not been attacked since the Reichskrieg had subsumed Haunersheim fifty years ago. For all I could see he spent his days traipsing around in expensive armour doing very little. By what right did he presume to lecture me on safety? It felt condescending, and did nothing but breathe fresh life into my fears for our future.

Ultimately, when the time came to inform Matas of Vonvalt's plan, I did so dispassionately, as though he were a mere acquaintance. I further told him that he was under no circumstances to attempt to contact me. And then I watched him struggle to find the words to express his feelings.

"I feel like you've changed," he said eventually, quietly. "I feel like you do not want to be with me any more."

"What do you mean?" I asked. I tried to sound understanding, but in truth I found his tone irritating. After Bressinger's drunken words with me in the inn the day before I felt as though I was beginning to resent Matas for something that hadn't even come to pass. Being with him now felt instinctively like the wrong choice, despite the love I felt. Could I really give up the path of a Justice after all I had seen in the past few months? Knowing what I knew about the Mlyanars and the Templars and the complex Imperial politics happening behind the scenes? If I wanted constancy in my life, then surely the best thing to do would be to engineer it myself, using the powers at my disposal – not hide away in some provincial town while the civilised world collapsed around me.

Ultimately, Bressinger's words, drunk and emotional as they had been, had resonated with me. They had struck on my own private fears like a hammer on a red-hot sword. Could I be sure that Matas would not expect me to stay put and while away my days child-rearing?

Our meeting ended up being a crushing disappointment, and it was my fault that it was. I was stand-offish and insufferable.

"The way you are with me. It's like you don't enjoy my company any more. Since our night together you seem like a different person."

I waved him off. "It is a coincidence. I have a great deal on my plate. Working for the Justice takes up all of my time."

"You said you would leave his service."

"I know what I said."

"Do you still mean to?"

"Matas!" I said, exasperated. "I have told you that this very afternoon I am going to enter the kloster as a spy. Why are you burdening me with this now?"

He fell silent, wounded. Eventually, he said, "What is it you want of me? You make me feel like a maid who has been taken advantage of."

"I want you to realise that I have obligations. At present. There are things I have to do—"

"But you don't!"

"Fine then! Things that I *want* to do. Because I feel I must."

"Flame of Savare, Helena, you were nearly murdered!" Matas shouted, gesturing roughly to the shorn side of my head and the contusion there.

"'Tis the nature of the practice," I said, though it sounded ridiculous.

"I know watchmen three times your age who have not come as close to being killed!"

I let out an angry sigh. "Matas! You are asking me to give up a lot. I need time to consider it."

"I am not asking you to give up anything!" Matas shouted. "I would not have you spend one more minute with me if resentment is all I can expect from it!"

Now I fell silent. I knew he was right, of course, but I was feeling stubborn and resentful, and I was in no mood to concede anything. How foolish and unkind I was, and how I hated myself afterwards.

There was nothing more either of us was going to say, and so we parted ways just as the light was beginning to fade. We embraced, and I kissed him, but it was perfunctory and I could tell that I had hurt him deeply, perhaps irrevocably.

I should have treasured those stolen moments. I should have taken his hands in mine, held him tightly, and I should have refused to go into the kloster and left Vonvalt's service then and there.

Instead, I left Matas, wounded and confused, and made back to Lord Sauter's residence.

XVIII

Gloom Keep

*"One cannot uphold the law if one does not follow it. He
who comes before the bench must do so with clean hands."*

FROM CATERHAUSER'S PILLARS
OF SOVAN CIVIL LAW

I left just after darkness had cloaked the Vale. Vonvalt and I
agreed that the ruse would work best if I turned up at the kloster
looking as though I had fled in the night. I gathered up a few
effects which I knew I would have to surrender on arrival and
gave Vonvalt the rest of my things to be added to the Duke of
Brondsey's cart.

To reach the kloster I had to leave Galen's Vale by the north, via
a poorly tended gatehouse that was a far cry from those guarding
the River Gale and the Hauner road. No one said anything to
me as I left. Like many towns it was much easier to leave than
it was to get in. The rain had abated and the night was clear and
crisp. The stars shone brightly above. Had I a physician's mind

for astronomy, I might have been able to name some of them; as it was, only one larger object drew my attention, a bright dot distinguishable by its red tint.

The path to the kloster was well-worn, given the significant amount of foot traffic that passed between it and the town below. There were all manner of religious orders within the Empire. Some, like the Savaran Templars, had only one purpose – to violently stake claims to shrines and parcels of land many hundreds of miles away which the Autun had contrived to make holy. Others' purpose seemed to be to simply while away their lives in silent contemplation, unable to leave their klosters or even speak to one another.

The kloster above Galen's Vale was home to one of the orders of Saint Jadranko. Jadranko was one of Creus's canonised apostles, a popular subject of worship in most temples since Jadranko advocated the bare minimum of obeisance. He was a stout follower of the Fool, one of Nema and Savare's many demigod children, whose role was to speak plainly to all irrespective of their rank and position.

The Jadrans were not severe. They allowed mixed klosters of men and women, though all were expected to remain celibate. They were also allowed to leave fairly frequently, mostly to purchase provisions, distribute alms and run the town's temple below. I did not know at that stage much about them beyond this vague reputation, but it did help alleviate some of the trepidation I felt as I approached the gatehouse, a fortification significantly more imposing than its counterpart at the northern closure of the Vale behind me.

"Who goes there?" the nightwatchman cried through the vision slit.

"One who would seek sanctuary," I said, the time-honoured invocation.

I heard the gatekeeper mutter a curse, as though this were a common occurrence. In fact, it might well have been; the temptation would be strong for many to try their luck with bed and board for a whole month. A bit of silent contemplation and godly boredom would be a small price to pay. I imagined that the kloster would seek to discourage such naked opportunism by making that first month a hard one to endure.

"What do you seek sanctuary from?" he asked me in the voice of a mummer who has been trapped in the same hated role for two decades.

"My employer," I said in a frail voice. "He is a Justice."

The gate was unlocked and yanked open.

"You're the Justice's clerk," the man said. He was a wizened old creature dressed in several layers of overcloaks. Somewhere underneath it all was a threadbare habit. "You came down the Hauner road?"

"Yes," I said. It did not occur to me to question how he knew this. News of the presence of a Justice spread fast.

The man squinted at me through old, watery eyes. "You are injured?" he asked.

"I was injured in his service."

"You look haunted, girl. Did he raise a hand to you?"

"No, I ... He made me party to his witchcraft. We spoke to the dead."

The old man gasped theatrically. Immediately he turned to one side and motioned me over the threshold. "Come in, child, come in. The Magistrates are a wicked order. They meddle in powers that were long ago those of the Church. No layman has the right to speak to the dead. Come, come, I shall take you to the obenpatria at once."

I knew that mentioning the séance would get me quick access. I also knew that being a comely young woman would also help. There was absolutely no doubt in my mind that an old, stinking beggar would have been given short shrift. Indeed, I sensed from the man's reaction that my presence here was something of a prize for the order.

Feeling bolder than before, I crossed over the threshold and followed the nightwatchman inside. We hurried down a covered walkway which enclosed a pleasant square lawn bordered by snowdrops and other winter flowers. In other circumstances I would have paused to admire the flowers and enjoy the tranquillity of the simple garden, but I was being hustled into the kloster proper, a complex of buildings in a medley of architectural styles ranging from basic Draedan to modern Neman gothick.

"In here, come," he said, gesturing to a stout wooden door.

The gatekeeper led me hurriedly through a warren of warm, dimly lit stone passageways, until eventually we reached the obenpatria's apartments. We stopped outside the entrance.

"You must be respectful," the nightwatchman said sharply.

"Of course," I said.

The nightwatchman rapped on the door. A moment later the obenpatria bade us enter in a loud, commanding voice.

The nightwatchman opened the door and ushered me inside. The reception chamber was sparse, home to little more than a desk and several shelves of books. A hearth, well-stoked, was the only concession to comfort.

The obenpatria himself reminded me of Lord Bauer, being a plain-looking, unremarkable man, grey-haired and -bearded, his stomach given over to fat. He sat behind the desk, attending to some papers by the wan candlelight. In my heightened state I fancied he regarded me as a predator regarded its prey, but in reality it was probably simple curiosity. He wore a habit of deep purple cloth fastened at the waist by a sash of white silk.

"Who is this you have brought to me, Brother Walter?" he asked mildly.

"This is the Justice's clerk, Excellency," the nightwatchman, whose name was evidently Walter, said. "She has abandoned him because of his devilry, and seeks sanctuary."

The obenpatria regarded me. His eyes seemed to narrow slightly, but it might have been my imagination.

"Has she now?" he asked. "What is your name, girl?"

"H-Helena," I said, affecting a stammer.

"Helena?"

"Sedanka."

"Helena Sedanka," the obenpatria said. He turned back to the gatekeeper. "Thank you, Brother Walter. You may leave her with me."

The gatekeeper bowed and scraped his way back out of the room. The heavy wooden door closed with a thud. My heart pounded. I tried to convince myself that the obenpatria would not suspect my motives so quickly, but my body would not be assuaged. I began to sweat.

"You look frightened, girl," the obenpatria said. "There is no need to be. This is a place of worship and prayer. There is nowhere safer in the whole of the Empire. Come, sit."

He gestured to a wooden chair in front of his desk. I recognised it for what it was; Vonvalt called them "piss off chairs" because they were so uncomfortable the sitter would not want to stay long. I walked forwards, now very hot in my cloak, and sat.

"Have you sought sanctuary with us?" the obenpatria asked.

I nodded.

"You are aware of the canon law?"

"I – don't know," I said, catching myself. I did not want to make it look as though this had been a prepared move.

The obenpatria looked at me for a few quiet moments. "The canon law dictates that any who claim sanctuary should be offered it for a period of a month. The rule is not infallible, of course. Tell me, Helena: have you committed treason?"

I shook my head emphatically.

"Murder?"

Again, I shook my head.

"Have you renounced the Creed of Nema?"

One last shake. It seemed astonishing that anyone who was guilty of any of those crimes would admit to it in the circumstances, but I would learn later that the penalty under the canon law for claiming false sanctuary was death.

We sat in silence for another few moments.

"What brings you to the Order of Saint Jadranko?"

His manner was mild now, closer to that of a monk than a ruler. Within the kloster walls, he was second only to the Emperor – and an Emperor's Justice, though our experience with Waldemar Westenholtz had shown me that even that apparently limitless power did indeed have limits.

I told him the fiction that Vonvalt and I had agreed: that the injuries I had suffered, both physical and mental, during the recent days in his service had been the final straw after months of doubt. Vonvalt's departure south marked a convenient point to flee. He nodded and winced sympathetically as I recounted my story, and made a show of inspecting the scarred, shorn side of my head. But it was the tale of the séance that he was most interested in. He could not keep the hungry look from his eyes as I mentioned it.

"Tell me more about this power," he said. "I have heard tell of it, of course, everything from folk tales to official reports, though I have never witnessed the practice. Did you know that it was once a holy power, rather than a civil one?"

He posed the question innocently, as one with a mere scholarly interest in the subject. But, like so many Nemans, he was keenly aware of the historical transfer of power that had taken place between the forces of religion and the forces of law – and was bitter despite being a half-dozen generations removed from it.

"I do not know much about it," I said. It was only a half-lie. Vonvalt had lectured me on the history of the powers of the Order of the Magistratum, but I had found it as dull as many other things he lectured me on, and the knowledge had failed to take. The fact that I was about to hear it again was clearly some form of cosmic revenge.

"You will of course know better than most how the Sovans pride themselves on their system of common law."

I nodded.

"Did you know that of the two heads of the Autun, one represents the canon law, and the other the common?"

"I do," I said. Children of three knew that.

"Once it was the case that it was temple priests who spoke to the dead. It was a ritual that was reserved for only the most holy and learned men of the cloth. The rituals were complex and lengthy. Those who undertook them sought to understand the mysteries of the afterlife and so better minister to the masses. It was a . . . profoundly respectful process."

"You do not think it respectful now?"

The obenpatria snorted, instantly offended. "These so-called *Justices*. They swan around the provinces and conjure up the spirits of the departed as though it were a game. They haven't the skill to do it properly, either. Half the time they obtain nothing but nonsense."

I stiffened slightly at that. I thought of the incredible reluctance with which Vonvalt exercised the power of necromancy; the haunted and drawn look that he wore for days afterwards; the exhaustion and horror that followed each use. To suggest that he engaged in the practice lightly was as far from the truth as it was possible to be. As for the remark about skill, it was true enough that Graves's words had been little better than gibberish. But could the men and women of the Church really do better?

"It is a ghastly thing to behold," I said quietly.

The obenpatria turned back to me, as though he had forgotten I was there.

"I do not doubt it. Questioning the dead as though they were a witness in a trial; is it any wonder that they rail against it? That the spirits of the afterlife claw into the breach between worlds and voice their displeasure? Tell me, did it go to plan, this séance?"

I shook my head.

"No. I'd lay bets it was commandeered by some malign entity?"

I shivered. How could the man possibly know?

"Yes," he said, eyeing me. "You need not answer. I can see the effect it has had on you. Necromancy is not supposed to be thus. It is not supposed to be frightening and disturbing. Done correctly it is a wonderful thing. Our Neman elders used to revel in the process and the wisdom it yielded. Justices are like grave robbers, smashing their way into the holy dimensions and stealing what information they can."

He lapsed to silence, stifled by his own nostalgic anger. Eventually, he said, "You disapprove of your former master's misuse of the power, I take it?"

I nodded vigorously.

"Hm," he said. "Rightly so. Well, fear not, my child; there are still godly men about, powerful men, who I hope will soon see these powers restored to the Church."

"You mean Patria Claver?" I asked.

The obenpatria nodded. "Aye. The man is a living saint. He has honoured us with his presence on more than one occasion. He would see the Neman Church restored."

I did well to hide my alarm at this. If the kloster had thrown its hand in with Claver, then the Bauer matter, already tangled and complex, was about to take a turn for the worse.

"Well," the obenpatria said, in a tone of voice that made it clear our talk was drawing to its end. "We shall do what we can to wash away the sin of it." It took me a moment to realise he was talking again about the séance. "It clings to you, even now, like a black cloak. I sense it."

I shuddered. "Help me," I said, and it was not entirely part of the act. The last thing I wanted was to somehow be tainted by my contact with the afterlife.

"I will, child, I will. My name is Obenpatria Fischer. You will refer to me as 'Your Excellency'." He stood up and, wearing a grim countenance, walked past me to the door. He opened it and called out into the corridor of stone beyond. I heard a muffled response, and then hurried footsteps. Fischer turned back into the room, this time trailed by another young girl dressed in a white frock and wimple.

"Emilia, this is Helena," he said, introducing us. Emilia looked at me briefly, before returning her eyes to the floor.

"Hello," she said in a Hauner accent, bobbing briefly.

"Hello," I replied.

"Emilia will show you around and teach you our ways. She is not so far out of the Trials herself." Fischer watched me for a little while longer – long enough for it to be uncomfortable. Then, eventually, he nodded. "All right. Nema be with you," he said, and I was dismissed.

※

Emilia showed me to my quarters. It was more like a cell than anything else, a small stone room, illuminated during the day by a single small window, furnished with nothing except a cot and a desk. Atop the desk was a leather-bound and illuminated codex of the Nema Creed, and I had to remind myself that, despite the severity of my surroundings, the kloster was a wealthy place.

"'Tis too late for you to do or attend to anything now," Emilia said. She seemed a sullen sort. "You'd just as well stay in here now and start the day tomorrow."

"What is the routine?" I asked.

Emilia sighed.

"I know I am an imposition," I snapped, my anxiety suddenly getting the better of me. "You do not need to remind me with such theatrics."

The girl looked at me with wide eyes. I realised immediately that at least part of her surliness was born of fear of me. It was easy to forget my own imposing presence. One did not spend two years shadowing a Justice and not take on some of his countenance. I may have seemed like small beer to someone like Obenpatria Fischer, but to many of those my own age and younger, I was as imperious as Vonvalt was to me.

"Bathing is at sun-up," she said in a slightly more conversational tone of voice. "I will fetch you."

"And then?"

"Prayers, then tasks before lunch."

"What will my tasks be?"

Emilia shrugged. "I do not know. You should expect it to be menial."

I paused for a second. "Did you seek sanctuary here?" I asked.

She looked embarrassed for a moment, then defiant. "It matters not how I came to be here. I am here."

"All right," I said. "I wouldn't think less of you either way."

"It matters not to me what you think."

We stood in awkward silence for a few moments until it was clear our interaction was over.

"Well, thank you again for your kind assistance." I said. "I appreciate that I am a burden on your time."

She softened at my supplication, but only slightly. "Good night, then," she said.

"Good night," I replied, and then she was gone.

I lay on the cot and stared at the blank ceiling.

"Nema's tits, what have I got myself into?" I asked the air.

❧

The lifestyle turned out to be so regimented that it took only a few days to become accustomed to it. We would rise at daybreak, undertake the *kupaiyanne*, which was the ritual bathing, attend temple for the two-hour morning sermon, undertake our tasks – which for me, given my position, were indeed menial in nature, including cleaning the latrines, cleaning out the stables, tending to the sick livestock and scrubbing the floors – then came lunch, another round of tasks, dinner, private prayer and bed. Private prayer turned out to be something of a misnomer, for while it was expected that the kloster's occupants would spend some of that time in the temples or smaller chapels in the kloster complex, in reality it was an hour or so of free time. It was also the only time that the members mixed, men with women, and therefore inevitably when the greatest amount of forbidden behaviour took place.

After my initial anxieties faded, a process which was accelerated by the comfortable monotony of the daily routine, I slipped into my role with a little more confidence. I was quizzed plenty of times by both nuns and monks – mainly during *kupaiyanne*, but also at mealtimes and evening prayers – on my history with Vonvalt. While it did pain me slightly to lie about how he had mistreated me, I found it easy to exaggerate. After all, I *had* grown weary of our time together, and I *had* wanted to leave his service. Given that all the best lies are formed around a kernel of truth, I found it very easy to convince everyone of the tough life I had led. The unsightly scar on the shaved side of my head also did much of the talking for me.

I was constantly aware of the urgency of my mission, which made me come across as anxious and easily exercised. I was also constantly torn between further ingratiating myself so as to assuage all suspicion, and the need to start investigating the conspiracy. This tension caused me a great deal of stress, and I ate and slept poorly.

Brother Walter, the old monk who had been on gate duty the night I had arrived, watched me ceaselessly. Of all the people within the kloster, he was the least friendly. He continually pulled me up on what he considered to be poor work, or made me repeat trivial tasks for no other reason than it pleased him to be difficult. When he was not staring at me, hawk-like, from across the dining hall, he was secreting himself in doorways and alcoves under the pretence of oversight and leering at me. Not since Muldau had I felt such a weight of unwanted attention, but as much as I wanted to write his behaviour off as a ghastly old man's lechery, I could not help but feel that there was something else to it – particularly since he had recognised me at the gate on my first night there. It was difficult to shake the constant feeling of paranoia; but I felt as though my instincts as regarded Brother Walter at least were right, and resolved to avoid him as much as humanly possible.

Eventually I realised I could not waste any more time gilding my subterfuge, for the temptation simply to carry on in the kloster's comfortable, quiet routine was becoming overwhelming. So, just over a week after I had entered the kloster, a few days before Ebbe would start to wane, during the morning round of tasks, I decided I would start to make discreet enquiries of Emilia. She and I had become closer, but I still sensed she was wary of me, and that she – unlike most of the other monks and nuns I had spoken to – did not quite believe me and my reasons for being there.

"Does something special happen for Ebbe?" I asked. We were in the garden in front of one of the cloisters, weeding the bank of flowers.

"There is a service in temple tonight, but it is not mandatory," she replied, ripping out a large clump of stringwort and dumping it in a wicker basket between us.

"Perhaps I will go," I said.

"Suit yourself."

I pretended to take an interest in the weeds in front of me.

"What do you make of Brother Walter?" I asked. In spite of the man's utterly repugnant behaviour, I tried to turn the point into something approaching sisterly banter.

Emilia looked at me, briefly and blankly.

"What do you mean?"

"I mean . . . you know." I paused, flummoxed. I knew that she knew what I was talking about. She *had* to have known. She wasn't an automaton. No one could have mistaken the man's general manner, and while I had no doubt that a good portion of the men in the kloster would be turning a blind eye to it, some-one like Brother Walter was certain to have a reputation among the women.

"No, Helena, I do not know what you mean."

"I fear he does not like me. He is constantly disparaging my work."

"Perhaps your work is not very good?"

I was surprised at how much that offended me. It took a great deal of effort not to snap at the girl.

"What are his duties?" I asked. "Is he close to Obenpatria Fischer?" I realised as I said it that it was a treacherous line of questioning. It was not a natural thing to be interested in, especially for someone who was new to the kloster and apparently seeking to make a life there.

Once again, Emilia looked at me. Her face was completely inscrutable.

"Brother Walter is one of the most senior men in the kloster; of course he is close to Obenpatria Fischer. I'm surprised you do not know what his duties are by now."

There followed another uncomfortable pause, as there so often was with our conversations. This time, however, I was resolved to cut to the heart of the problem.

"Emilia, do I offend you?"

She did not like that. I could tell immediately that the confrontation had embarrassed her. Her cheeks flushed.

"You do not offend me. I have no issue with you," she replied tightly.

"Emilia, stop your infernal weeding for a moment and look at me." I said it gently, but with an undercurrent of firmness, like a mother trying to tease something out of a sullen child.

Emilia looked at me.

"I want us to be friends," I said.

"You do not want me as your friend," she replied. She spoke quietly.

I leant in closer. "I do," I said. "I really do. I want to know why you are so distant with me. It is not a requirement of – *our* faith," I said, catching myself. "We are allowed to fraternise. I have seen people do much more than that," I added, wriggling my eyebrows. I had hoped to make her smile, but to my horror she burst into tears.

"Bloody Nema," I said, looking round to see if there was anyone loitering. Fortunately, we were alone; it was a sunny morning, if a little chilly, and the only sound was the distant bustle of the Vale below us. "What is the matter now?"

She said nothing, just wiped her eyes furiously. I reached out to put a hand on her shoulder, but she recoiled suddenly and sharply.

"Sorry!" I said, drawing back. There was nothing to do but let her cry it out. It was like watching a small fire slowly extinguish itself. She could not go anywhere. Tasks were mandatory, and if either of us were seen leaving the gardens we would be punished.

After a short while she subsided. To my amazement she then went back to weeding as if nothing had passed between us.

"You're not serious," I said, looking at her with incredulity. "You're not going to tell me what that was about?"

"It's better if you don't know," she said without emotion.

"Emilia," I said quietly. "What is going on? What's happened to you? Has someone—"

"Flame of Savare, would you stop talking!" she snapped.

Now it was my turn to recoil. I watched her for a while, but she ignored me so resolutely that I had no choice but to eventually go back to my own patch of soil. We finished the rest of the session in silence, and after the bell tolled us to lunch she launched to her feet and raced off to the dining hall before I had a chance to ask her anything else.

XIX

Deeper Down the Rabbit Hole

*"The Sovans have spent centuries trying to unpick
the secrets of the creatures which roam the holy
dimensions; but, like the deep black waters of
the sea, only those which lie closest to the surface
can be in any way examined. Who knows what
leviathans lurk in the depths of the afterlife?"*

PROGNOSTICATOR GAVRO JURIĆ

Life in the kloster continued. Emilia actively avoided me. While
I was confident that, given enough time, I could crack her, I did
not *have* enough time. The rope had been played out. I had no
doubt that both Vonvalt and Bressinger were being watched; the
moment Vonvalt turned around and made his way back to the
Vale was the moment the hourglass was upended. Nothing was
going to happen while I scrubbed the floors, sang hymns and
drank the kloster's wine. I did not have the weeks and months

required to slowly gain Emilia's trust and draw her out. I was going to have to undertake a more drastic course of action.

I spent a few days planning, though really I was delaying the inevitable. I knew what I had to do: follow the documents. Vonvalt had taught me long before that contemporaneous documents were the gold standard of evidence. Human beings obstructed and lied – particularly when their lives were at stake. Even well-meaning witnesses could drastically misremember events. I did not have time to put my faith in people; like the ledgers in the town's treasury, I needed documents. It was just that the documents in question – Obenpatria Fischer's private correspondence – would be secreted away in his apartment.

Which meant breaking into that apartment.

The Fool's Day fell on the fourteenth of Ebbe, and the Fool was the Jadrans' patron saint. Such an important day necessitated plenty of ceremony and observance, and Fischer, as the obenpatria, would be engaged all evening in a vigil to take place in the kloster's main temple. With everyone expected to attend, and with my time running out, I knew that I would not have a better opportunity. In spite of this, the plan still filled me with a keen sense of dread. In normal circumstances, breaking into Fischer's private rooms and searching through his correspondence would be grounds for severe punishment; but if Fischer was indeed part of a criminal conspiracy, and I were caught, even my lofty Imperial credentials would not save me.

The night before the Fool's Day I sat at the desk in my chamber and leafed through my copy of the Neman Creed, trying in vain to settle my nerves. As I turned the pages of the gorgeously illuminated codex, I could see that the whole thing was set out with infamous Sovan pragmatism. The first half of the book was dedicated to all their gods, demigods and saints, and which one to pray to and why – almost like a set of instructions – while the latter half, clearly aimed at the less practically minded Sovan, was given over to various parables and histories.

I knew that the lion's share of the text came originally from Saint Creus, who according to Sovan mythology had been the earthly conduit between the gods and mankind. Over time, further volumes had been added, including the Book of Lorn, which had tried and failed to supplant the pagan Draedist practices of northern Haunersheim, Tolsburg and Jägeland. Against the original Sovan religious orthodoxy, however, these further books were ignored by everyone more than a bow-shot from Sova, and even Vonvalt, who was not a religious man, referred to them as "marsh ale for the soul".

At the beginning of the book and at the head of the pyramid was Nema, the God Mother, who in most iconography took the form of a white deer. Her godly husband was Savare, the God Father. Between them they had ten demigod children known collectively as the Deti, ranging from the Fool, whom the Jadrans followed, to the Trickster, demigod of misfortune – and, as it transpired, horrifying elemental demon from the afterlife.

The Deti of course coupled with other astral beings (and sometimes one another), and spawned an entire pantheon of further demigods and saints, to the point where you could find one for almost any aspect of life on earth – gods of death and destruction, healing and music, love, luck, war, wisdom, strength, protection, time, trade, knowledge, travel, magic . . . It was easy to see how the Neman Creed was able to swallow other religions so entirely and pretend that they had always been lost offshoots of the main branch.

I spent much longer flicking through the codex than I had intended to. I decided that, despite my lack of belief, a prayer in the circumstances could hardly go amiss – and then the pages fell open at the entry for the Trickster.

I can distinctly remember the feeling to this day, the way my vision seemed to lose focus and every last inch of my skin broke – almost burst – out in gooseflesh. The image there of Aegraxes, a two-headed snake rendered as a black-and-white etching, was forever burned into my mind's eye. For a brief moment I thought my morbid curiosity might compel me to read the words written, but I became so filled with a profound sense of dread that I used a few dabs of melted candle wax to glue the pages shut.

Robbed of all enthusiasm, I settled on a prayer to Kultaar, demigod of luck, a cheerful-looking mouse-like creature whose recorded interventions included saving the Emperor's grandfather at the Battle of Sanque by placing an unfortunate charioteer between him and a ballista. I had not said prayers with any regularity since I was a child, when too often charitable handouts had been conditional on religious obeisance. Fortunately, Kultaar did not seem like the overly prescriptive type, and to the extent that he existed in anything approaching the description and image contained within the Creed, rather than as some malign interdimensional being, I was sure that he would forgive my fractured, rambling entreaties.

Eventually, I closed the codex and climbed into the bed. The last thing in the world I wanted to do was snuff out the candle, for reading the Creed had given me a sudden and healthy fear of the dark. But, knowing that it would burn down eventually, I blew it out, and wished for all the world that a drunken, snoring Bressinger was in the bed next to me.

☙

I had no idea what time it was when I finally drifted off, but by the time I was roused in the morning, it felt as though I had barely slept at all. I had resolved to feign illness throughout the course of the day so that I would be excused from the vigil that evening, but as I headed into the ritual bathing, I did not have to lay much in the way of groundwork. By then I was so nervous and so exhausted from a night of fitful sleep that I barely had to pretend at all. A number of my fellow nuns commented on my pale, waxen appearance, the faint sheen of perspiration on my face, my withdrawn and sullen comportment, and by the time the service came around I was being practically ushered back to my room. This was not entirely born of altruism; a communicable disease would ravage the kloster to the last man.

I waited in my room for as long as I dared, hoping that everyone had indeed reported to the vigil as required. But despite my nerve-fraying anxiety, my journey through corridors was uneventful, and I reached the obenpatria's apartments – which sat across from the office in which I had first met him – without incident.

I pressed my ear to the door, but I heard nothing through the old slabs of oak. Then I took the handle in my sweating hand. It only then occurred to me that the door might be locked. I half-hoped it was. With a deep, shaky breath, I twisted it and pushed, and was amazed when it swung open obligingly on well-oiled hinges. Perhaps by Kultaar's intervention Fischer had simply forgot to lock it; or worse, he simply didn't bother to because there was nothing incriminating inside. Either way, I wasn't going to stand on the threshold thinking about it. I darted through and closed the door behind me.

Beyond was a chamber of breathtaking luxury. It was more akin to the solar of a senior aristocrat. Plush rugs of rich royal blue ensured that the obenpatria's feet would never be discomfited by the cold flagstones of the floor, while a well-stoked hearth, hanging tapestries and thick curtains suggested that the flagstones had never been particularly cold in the first place. Beyond the first chamber, which acted as a sort of reception room, I could see Fischer's bedchamber, where a large four-poster bed dominated much of the available space, with the rest given over to other ostentatious furniture. Gilt-framed paintings hung on the walls, while plinths held up marble busts of the kloster's previous obenpatrias. There was even a private bathroom, where I could see gold-plated taps and expensive mirrors. I caught my reflection in one of them and I barely recognised the young woman staring back at me, with my head half-shaved and my features gaunt from stress.

I quickly set about searching the place. I looked for stashes of documents and correspondence. There was nothing in the reception room, but there was a desk in Fischer's bedchamber. I rifled through the drawers, pulling out bundles of opened letters with trembling hands and leafing through them, trying to digest their contents as quickly as possible. It was just as well that Vonvalt had taught me High Saxan, for most of the letters were written in it.

None of it was interesting. I scoured the bedchamber, increasingly frantic, overcome with a gambler's recklessness – except I was betting with time, rather than money. I might well have been gambling with my life. How long did the vigil last? Were people already dispersing back to their chambers? Would Fischer take some wine afterwards with other senior members of the kloster, or would he come straight back to his apartment and to bed? And would I hear any of it? Would I have any warning?

What brief confidence I had felt upon entry evaporated. Suddenly it seemed as though I had taken an insane risk.

I decided that I had done enough. I would be able to look Vonvalt in the eye when I informed him of my failure, knowing that I had done all I could. I turned to leave, relieved, when I noticed a small corner of paper protruding from the bottom of one of the drawers in a chest in the corner of the room.

I took two steps towards the apartment door, then stopped. With a profound sense of self-hatred, I turned back, dashed over to the drawer and yanked it open.

My brow wrinkled in confusion. I could not see anything inside that could account for the corner of paper, just underwear. Then, as I reached in, I realised that there was a hidden compartment at the bottom of the drawer. It was hardly ingenious, just enough to deter all but the determined searcher. I pulled away the thin board and could barely stifle a gasp as I saw the slim bundle of letters underneath.

I snatched up the first one and clutched it, my fingers staining the parchment with sweat. It read:

Excellency,

I was so thrilled to hear of your donation to the Order of the Temple of Savare; the Jadrans have always been a pious and godly company, and though I was unsurprised by your willingness to fund our cause, I was thrilled by the depth of your generosity.

On my return I will be sure to introduce you to Baron Naumov. I have spent some time with him this past year. Roundstone has been something of a second home during my tour of the South- and Eastmark of Haunersheim, and I have found a close ally in the baron. Like many other old Sovan Hauners, he is a devout man. He will be most interested in your scheme.

I will write to you again when my time permits. As matters stand I intend to catch up with one of the Imperial Magistrates moving up the Hauner road. You will recall our discussion about the Order of the Magistratum and their diabolical chokehold on the old Neman magicks. I expect it will be an educational experience!

From there, and for the purposes of any further correspondence, my destination remains Seaguard; like Baron Naumov, I hear good things about the margrave. After that, I shall return south, though I have not settled on a final route yet. The steady hand of the God Father will guide me.

Yours in faith,

Bartholomew Claver

My heart thumped in my chest. The letter had clearly been sent in the weeks before Claver had caught up with us at the Jägeland border. The man had a talent for deception, for none of us had suspected his motives. I tried to think of whether any of us had let anything sensitive slip, for his questions had been incessant – something which had seemed merely irritating at the time, but which now filled me with a dark sense of foreboding. But there would be time enough to ruminate on it later. For now, two things had become abundantly clear: the first was that Claver had designs on the Order of the Magistratum itself. The second was that a healthy fraction of the funds from the Galen's Vale treasury had ultimately made its way to the Savaran Templars. The only outstanding question was whether Lady Bauer's death had anything to do with it.

I snatched up another letter and opened it. From its contents, it must have come a number of weeks later, and in response to a letter from Obenpatria Fischer. It read:

> *Excellency,*
>
> *Thank you for taking the time to write to me again. Your eagerness to continue to assist fills my heart with joy. I will see that the CoP receives word of your piety; the Neman patriarchs in Sova are always keen to hear of and meet men of special character.*
>
> *I and my fellows in the Order of the Temple are most buoyed by your ready access to further funds and your kindly disposition towards our cause. There is no need for further correspondence; the more we keep in our heads and hearts and the less committed to paper the better.*
>
> *I will see you soon.*
>
> *Yours in faith*
>
> *Bartholomew Claver*

"CoP" had to mean the College of Prognosticators, one of the governing bodies of the Neman Church. I wondered if Claver really did have the ear of such a senior and august institution, or whether this was empty bragging. Regardless, the meaning of "eagerness to continue to assist" clearly suggested that Fischer had volunteered more money for the Templars' coffers, no doubt to gain exactly the kind of favour that Claver had promised in return. If the funds flowing into the Treasury from the mercantile excise were anything like as high as the records suggested, even a small cut of the money being quietly stolen and funnelled into the kloster would be irresistible to a man like Claver and his Templar army. After all, huge sums of money were what armies required. Not only did soldiers need swords, spears, arrows, shields and armour, but they required vast quantities of food – as did their horses – and an endless procession of skilled tradesmen and women to construct their fortifications, cook their meals, shoe their horses, fix their siege engines, tend to the sick and injured, sate their lusts, minister to the masses, and so on. Nothing on earth is as expensive as warfare, but fortunately for Claver, this ready line of credit would take some of the edge off.

I refolded the letter, placed it back where it had been, replaced the board and covered it back over with underwear. I dared not spend any more time in the bedchamber. What was clear was that there was a link between Fischer and Claver, and that would be enough for Vonvalt to prise the truth from Fischer's lips with the Emperor's Voice, like a bar between a hinge and a doorjamb.

I pushed the drawer closed, relieved that this dangerous enterprise was over, turned to leave—

—and then froze in horror as I heard the apartment door open.

I looked about frantically. The only sensible place to hide was under the bed. In moments I was down on the floor and out of sight, fists clenched, teeth gritted, my heart pounding so hard that I was sure it could be heard.

I wanted to cry. I had been so sure that I would hear the vigil coming to an end; I did not think that the kloster's entire population could disperse without making a huge deal of noise. Perhaps they had, and I had been so consumed by the correspondence that I simply hadn't noticed – or perhaps the thick stone walls of the kloster had simply masked the noise. It hardly mattered.

The bed was high enough that I could see out from under it, while being low enough that I could not be seen. I tried to calm myself with some deep, quiet breaths. There was nothing under the bed, no reason for anybody to check. All I needed to do was hold my nerve; an opportunity to leave would present itself.

I heard Fischer bustling around the reception chamber; then, not five minutes after he had come in, there was a knock at the outer door. Fischer sighed, and then came the sound of the door being pulled open.

"Brother Walter," Fischer said. The sound of people bustling through the corridors filtered through into the bedchamber – footsteps on warm stone, pleasant conversation, the trill of an unguarded laugh. I was so desperate to be out there among them it was agony. What a wretched corner I had painted myself into. I could not help but blame Vonvalt entirely.

"Something troubles you?" Fischer asked wearily.

"'Tis the Tollish girl. The sanctuary-seeker."

"Yes," Fischer said impatiently. "I am tired, Brother. What is the matter?"

"She is not in her chamber."

I bit my hand to stop myself crying out. I felt like a fox trapped in a cage. Animal fear, urgent and primal, overcame me. I began to debate insane notions in my mind: perhaps I could dash past both of them and out of the apartment door, navigate my way through the warren of corridors, burst out of the main entrance, sprint past the gate guard ... And then what? Further, darker images took hold, welling up in my mind like oil through sand. I thought of being ridden down on that cold, treacherous path back to the town, of being run through and left for dead on the side of the road, or worse – having my head smashed in like Lady Bauer and thrown, gasping and insensible, into the frigid Gale.

"Is she not ill?" Fischer asked. "That is what I had been told."

"Ostensibly."

"Well then, perhaps she has gone off to void her guts."

"There is no sign of her in the women's latrines."

"What have I told you about that?" Fischer said sharply. "You remember our discussion."

"This is different." Walter was close to exasperation; only the confines of hierarchy kept his anger in check. "I suspect her."

"Suspect her of what?"

"Of seeking sanctuary falsely."

Fischer sighed with an air of theatricality. "We have trodden this path before."

"I told you, this is different. Sister Klein was a liar. You know the Venlanders cannot exhale without spewing mistruths about the place. She—"

In my mind's eye I pictured Fischer holding up a hand for silence. "My forbearance sags under the weight of your sin, Brother," he said.

"I only do what I think is best for the kloster," Walter mumbled. "For the order. You do not think it strange that she is here? The Justice's clerk, in the kloster? No doubt poking around."

"And what is it that she might find?" Fischer asked.

Another silence. I imagined Brother Walter squirming uncomfortably under his master's gaze. What was the man hiding? The two men were not talking as conspirators would; when I thought about it, had there really been anything that incriminating in the letters? Was there anything in there that couldn't be explained? Was Fischer simply transferring what he considered to be legitimate money to the Templars? Was it in fact Brother Walter who was operating in league with Vogt and Bauer? I felt like I was the closest I had come to unlocking the secrets of the kloster, and yet the furthest I could be from being able to do anything about it.

"Eject her," Brother Walter urged, ignoring his master's question. "You would not even have to give a reason. It is the best thing for the order."

I heard Fischer draw himself up. "I decide what is the best thing for the order," he said. "Begone now, Brother, and leave the girl be. You are not to follow her again."

There was another silence in which I fancied Walter stared venomously at Fischer; then his shuffling, retreating footsteps sounded through the reception chamber, and shortly after that, I heard the door close.

I heard Fischer groan, and there followed the sound of two hands being rubbed against a bristly face. Then he called out in a clear voice:

"You can come out now; he is gone."

XX

Kultaar's Gifts

*"Few people will thank you for being cleverer than
them. A man will prefer the ravings of his neighbour
over the word of the most learned scholar in Sova."*

SIR WILLIAM THE HONEST

A small, involuntary moan escaped my lips. It was the helpless, hapless wail of the doomed. Unless you, reader, have been somewhere you are not supposed to be – and your very life is at stake, or at least you believe it to be – then I cannot convey to you effectively the terror of such a situation. In my experience, it is worse than the mortal combat of the battlefield. The latter is a horror in itself, but it is a physical horror, and if you are armed then your fate is at least partly in your hands. Here, I was helpless. Even in the best possible case, if it really was Brother Walter who was the criminal mastermind, and Fischer was just a well-meaning if misguided benefactor to the Savaran Templars, the obenpatria was hardly about to take kindly to me infiltrating his private quarters and rifling through his correspondence.

"Come on; I don't have all evening," Fischer said impatiently. "Out with you; the man is gone."

With sweating, trembling hands, I began to shift out from under the bed. I felt like a girl approaching the gallows, though if the situation were really as bad as I deemed it to be, then I could do worse than a brisk hanging.

I was about halfway out from under the bed when I heard a second voice cut through the air:

"Excellency; forgive my hesitation. I did not hear the door close."

With teeth clenched so firmly it felt as though they were about to buckle, and barely daring to breathe, I quickly and carefully pressed my way back under the bed. I imagined the Deti standing around a table, rolling dice and manipulating figurines, my reprieve no more than a stroke of cosmic luck. Perhaps my prayer to Kultaar had worked. Either way, I could not take much more stress. I felt as though my heart were about to give out.

"Come," Fischer said, "to the bedchamber. Nema knows I am weary."

"Who was that with you?" the mystery woman asked. I could not place the voice, but she sounded like one of the older nuns. "I could not hear from where I was concealed."

"Brother Walter," Fischer said wearily. His voice was louder now as he approached the bedchamber. "The man has been a thorn in my side for years. He has some project going on in the kloster, some scheme which I have yet to fully uncover. He seeks out reasons to suspect people like a boar seeking out truffles. I am sure the man is half mad."

"I've never liked him. Few of the women do. He is a lecherous sort."

They were both in the room now. My eyes were screwed shut. I heard at least one of them sit down on the bed.

"Leave it. It is spoiling my mood."

"Your *mood*," the woman said, her voice playful. "You are feeling somewhat lecherous yourself."

Too late I realised what was about to happen. I pressed my hands over my ears, but to no avail. The sound of kissing and moaning and undressing wended its way through to me like thread through the eye of a needle. It was not long before the bed was shaking with the unmistakable slap of flesh against flesh. Fischer had many faults, but unfortunately for me, lack of stamina was not one of them. In some ways I wished I had been caught; enduring this horror, becoming an unwitting and unwilling pervert, was one of the most disagreeable episodes of my time in Galen's Vale.

Eventually the man spent himself inside his unlucky lover – I never learned her identity. Though their coupling had taken an age, I had to console myself with the fact that I had not been caught. I waited as she redressed and left, and Fischer washed and prepared for bed. This brief time was marked by fresh horror as I waited for the man to inadvertently drop something under the bed and bend down to gather it; but, as before, Kultaar had evidently heard my prayers, and my hiding place remained undisturbed.

The man extinguished the lamps next to his bed, bathing the chamber in darkness. Absurdly, the greatest danger now was falling asleep myself. The incredible mental strains of the last hour or so had left me profoundly exhausted, and the rug underneath the bed was comfortable, the chamber warm and dark. Nonetheless I forced myself to remain awake, digging my nails into my thigh whenever I sensed that fatigue was about overwhelm me.

Fischer of course eventually fell asleep. I waited probably another hour until I was sure; then I snuck out through the apartment. Every step seemed to echo like the tolling of the temple bell; every creak and crack of my bones seemed to resonate like the earthy rumblings of a landslide. I pictured Fischer lying awake in the darkness, watching my retreating form, the slow breathing of his apparent sleep a mere pretence. I became increasingly het up as I waited for his voice to penetrate the still like a knife, and it took all my self-control not to dash for the door, yank it open and flee. But, drawing on some deep reserve, I tiptoed out, opened and closed the door, and after a brisk trot through the warren-like corridors of the kloster, I was back in my chamber.

I lay on my front on my bed and broke into hysterical laughter. It seemed to go on for ages, as though someone had unstoppered me and could not get the cork back in. I had to put my pillow over my face, for although the walls were thick stone and effectively prevented sound from travelling, I dared not risk being heard.

Eventually I calmed down enough to turn in. As I lay in the dark, my nerves still far too highly strung for sleep to come, I thought about what I would do next. The greatest temptation was simply to leave, for the kloster was not a prison, nor was I a prisoner, and I was free to go at any time. But I felt compelled to stay. With hindsight, it seems insanely reckless that I would do anything other than slip out the gate, but at the time I had this inexplicable desire to double down whenever I encountered the slightest success. It was why I had had such difficulty in walking away from Vonvalt's employment – every time I thought about it, some achievement or word of praise from him would stoke my pride and convince me of the error of my ways.

I resolved to try and find out more about Brother Walter. It did not seem like as difficult a task as the one I had just undertaken; Brother Walter was less subtle, and he had few friends about the kloster. I gave myself until the end of the week to see what the man was about. If I hadn't found out anything useful by then, I would leave.

At least, that was the plan.

❧

The following day was a tedious one. I realised that an illness lasting a single day would do nothing but raise suspicion, especially one that had seen me escape the many uninteresting Fool's Day services, and so I maintained the pretence. As before, the other nuns were keen to keep me confined to my chamber, and so I passed an extraordinarily boring day leafing through the Neman Creed, staring out the window and pacing my room like an animal in a cage. I half-expected Brother Walter to come and poke his nose through the door, but he seemed to have taken Fischer's advice to heart. The man's position at the kloster was evidently more precarious than anyone knew.

The hours passed. The sun set and darkness claimed the Vale. I willed it to be bedtime so that I could at least pass the remainder of my confinement in unconsciousness. But then, during the hour or so of private prayer after dinner, there was a knock at my door.

"Come in," I said with a dry mouth, realising that they were the first words I had spoken all day.

It was Emilia. She opened my door, slipped inside, closed the door behind her and waved me quiet while she listened out for any footsteps in the corridor. It seemed strange to see her in little more than her night robes, without a wimple on. Her hair was fairer than I would have guessed from the colour of her eyebrows.

"What in Kasivar's name is going on?" I asked, my heart pounding and my blood singing in my veins. "You'll get us both a whipping."

She crossed the several steps it took to reach the bed and sat down. I could see she was upset.

"About the other day," she said.

"Yes?"

She opened her mouth and closed it again. I waited patiently. I knew from experience that no form of hard or soft questioning would draw her out.

"This kloster ... it is a dark place," she said. Her voice was mournful. "Mine is a black future."

It was all I could do not to scream. My head swam and my body broke out so suddenly in gooseflesh that it was almost a violent experience.

"Faith, are you all right?" Emilia asked me, startled out of her low mood by my reaction. I didn't answer. I felt sick with horror. Graves had said those exact words during the séance. The exact words. I could see his eyes – the Trickster's eyes – boring into me as he spoke them.

"Helena?" Emilia asked.

"Where have you heard those words?" I gasped. I was sweating and trembling and on the verge of tears. The whole thing came rushing back in a flood of emotion – the séance, the nightmares, the terror of the experience.

"Helena, you're frightening me," Emilia said. "What's the matter? What did I say?"

I focused my mind and controlled my breathing using relaxation techniques that Vonvalt had taught me for calming one's nerves. It felt like a long time until I was ready to speak again.

"I have heard those words you said, those exact words, spoken by . . . another. It startled me."

"I don't understand," Emilia said. "I didn't hear them from anyone. I didn't think anything of it. I just said what I felt."

My heart was still pounding, but some sense of calm was reasserting itself. I used my sleeve to wipe the sweat from my brow. I realised that Emilia had no idea what I was talking about. To press her on the matter was just going to confuse her, and she had only just decided to open up to me.

"I'm sorry," I said, shaking my head. I offered an apologetic smile. "A moment of madness. Please." I motioned for her to keep talking. She looked at me warily.

"I was a maid," she said. "My master was a kind man, but he died suddenly and with debts, and I was turfed out onto the street. I had nowhere else to go, and they were kind here, for a while. Obenpatria Fischer is a good man, a pious man. He does not know what goes on in the deep places of the kloster."

I frowned. "What do you mean?" I asked. I had to stop myself from asking about Brother Walter.

Emilia looked around. The silence enveloped us like a blanket. Nothing stirred.

"There are bad men here," she whispered. "I don't know what exactly it is that they are doing. But there is more than one. They use the old dungeons. They are like bees in a hive."

"Who are they?" I asked, equally quietly.

"They do not attend the services like the rest of us. It is like they have some kind of special dispensation. I only know of one. I see him occasionally. They wear the purple habit like the rest of us; it makes them harder to spot. And my eyesight is not the best."

"What dungeons?" I asked. "I see that this is an old building. It is halfway to being a castle."

"Exactly," Emilia said. "It was not always a kloster. It is very old; the tunnels cut deep into the bedrock."

"How do you know this? Surely it is all out of bounds?"

She went quiet for a moment.

"One of them tried to force himself on me," she said quietly. My heart sank. There were plenty of vile men out there eager to take advantage of desperate young girls. I had had my fair share of unwanted attention in Muldau. But I was tough, or I certainly had been back then. Emilia did not look as though she had much in the way of street nous about her. For a man to have attempted to force himself on her, particularly in a place that was supposed to be a safe haven, must have permanently fractured the girl's trust in the powers of good.

"What happened?" I asked. "You need not tell me the details. 'Tis common enough in my line of work."

"He did not succeed," she said sharply, suddenly fierce. Her temper died quickly, though, like an ember in a bucket of water. "I kicked him . . . down there."

I smiled at that. "Good girl," I said.

"We were in the store houses. You know that the kloster has food stocks for the Vale in case there is ever a shortage."

I nodded. Given the volume of merchant shipping that passed through the town, and the stability that the Sovan hegemony had brought to the provinces, the practice of stockpiling struck me as somewhat obsolete.

"I ran from the man. I ran blindly, I was so scared. I must have taken a wrong turning or two, because I ended up finding some sort of tunnel or passageway. I didn't recognise it but before I knew what was going on, I had come across the old dungeons. I don't know if Obenpatria Fischer even knows about them. They are a damp and miserable place."

I said nothing. I had learnt from Vonvalt that sometimes it is best to let a person talk with the occasional prompt rather than to bombard them with questions, as may be tempting.

"Well, there were some people being kept in those cells. At least one. I saw light coming from one, under the door. I was so frightened, I didn't know what to do. Then I heard voices coming from one of the doors. I couldn't help myself. I went over to look through a crack."

"What did you see?" I asked.

"There were men dressed as monks but I had not seen them before. They were counting money, huge piles of coin. They were making notes in ledgers and using scales to weigh the coin. Then they were putting them in sacks of grain. One of them said that 'Tanner' was taking a long time. It was only afterwards I realised they were talking about the man who attacked me. I didn't dare wait any longer; I ran back the way I had come. I did not see the man, Tanner. I was fortunate. I made my way back to the store house and then from there back up to the kloster."

"When did this all happen?"

"Not two weeks ago."

"Have you told anyone?"

"No. No one. I have been terrified."

"Why are you telling me?"

"Because you work for the Justice," she said.

"Not any more," I said.

"I don't believe you," she said. "The others, they talk about you, you know. They say that your Justice's man is still in the town. They say there is an investigation going on still, into Lady Bauer's death. There are rumours that you did a séance. Is it true that Justices can speak to the dead?"

I ignored her last question. "Why do you think I still work for him?" I pointed to the scar on my head. "I have left his service. I have suffered too much—"

"I do not believe you," she said again. "Your stories ring false. Others are convinced, perhaps even Obenpatria Fischer, but not I. You are clearly irreligious. You pay lip service to it all. You are distracted, like you are looking for something else. And I think the thing you are looking for is the thing that I have just told you about."

"No," I said. "You are wrong."

"You have to stop them," Emilia said, suddenly grasping my sleeve. "I will never find peace while they continue here. I want a quiet life. I want to just . . . live out my days here in comfort. I have no other options. No other household would take me as a maid. But I am going mad here. I jump at shadows. I am terrified of being alone." She began crying again.

I watched her for a while. The timing of this seemed a little too serendipitous. She had said that Fischer didn't know about the dungeons, which struck me as very odd. I was also conscious that Fischer was the one who had bade her look after me during this first month of sanctuary. Could it all have been a ruse? She was a very good actress if it was, and her reasoning was sound. If she thought I could help her, then it made sense that she would tell me of her problems and not someone else.

If it was all some kind of test, to see whether I really was a spy, then I realised I had to tell her that I could not help her; that

I really had left Vonvalt's service, and I was keen to forget all about that part of my life; that what she should do was speak to Obenpatria Fischer and tell him of her concerns. To feign ignorance and apologise.

Instead, I looked at the poor wretch and saw a young girl who could have been me in other circumstances; who had been attacked and who desperately wanted to be free of it all.

So I said, "I can help you. You are right; this is why I am here."

And to my immediate relief, she cried a little harder and moved in to hug me tight. It was quite the performance, and I bought it completely.

The men came for me a few hours later, in the dead of night.

XXI

Prisoners

I had been duped. Emilia was precisely what I had suspected her
to be: bait, skimming across the surface of the pond. She had
played her part well. The fact that *she* had been the one to refuse
to speak to *me* had been a nice touch.

They had a key. They were as silent and quick as assassins.
I was barely awake before I felt rough hands grab me and gag
me. I thrashed and screamed, but it was no good. They were
well-practised. A bag of rough, scratchy cloth was pulled down
over my head so I had no idea where I was being taken, though
after a little while I could sense downwards motion. Eventually,
I stopped thrashing. It was fruitless and exhausting.

They carried me down into the bowels of the kloster. Despite
the rancid hood they had shoved over my head, I could smell the

damp and hear the dripping of groundwater. It was cold, too; clad only in a light nightgown, I began to shiver.

After a long while I heard sounds that spoke of some sort of habitation – voices, the thumping and scraping of doors and furniture and, most jarringly, the laughter of women. Then we stopped, and I heard the hard pounding of a fat fist on a heavy wooden door.

"Yes," came the muffled response from inside. The door opened. "Ah," continued the same voice. I had expected Walter or Fischer, but it was a different voice, lower and smoother, filling the chamber like a spilt beaker of oil. "Set her down on the chair."

I was sat down and the hood was pulled from my head. I found myself in a comfortable-looking candlelit office. The place had clearly once been a cell, albeit a large one. Now bookshelves lined the walls and the floor was covered in rugs and rushes. The man who had bade us enter sat behind a desk stacked with ledgers and adorned with various trinkets and ornaments.

"Do you know who I am?" he asked. He was a plump man, clad in an expensive-looking doublet and hose. He had what Vonvalt called "merchant fingers", fat fingers encrusted with rings. He had a hard, cruel face, dark hair and a bushy auburn beard.

"Zoran Vogt," I guessed.

"Very good!" he replied, affecting delight. "Have you seen me before? Or are you just a clever maid?"

I said nothing. I had not seen him before, but I felt like I had, for all he had become part of our lives in the last few months. My heart sank as I realised that Vonvalt, who was currently pursuing Vogt and Bauer to the Imperial wayfort at Gresch and beyond, was on a wild goose chase.

"You may leave us," Vogt said to the men who had brought me down. "I think I will be all right. You have searched her?"

"She wears nothing beyond this slip," one of the guards said.

"Begone, then," Vogt said, and the guards left. He fixed me in the eye for a long while. "So. The Justice thought to infiltrate the kloster. Tell me what he knows."

I said nothing.

"I do not have time for silly games, girl. Tell me what you know, now."

I shook my head. I wanted to cry, more out of frustration than anything else. It had been a long time since I had felt this utterly helpless.

Vogt took in a great deep breath, then let it out. He grabbed a goblet of wine that was on the edge of the table and took a long draw. "Your man has caused us no end of trouble," he muttered, setting the glass back down heavily. "Everyone running scared." He waved his hands in the air and made a "wooo" sound, as though impersonating a ghost. "You'd think the Emperor Himself was here in the Vale, strutting among all the shit-ditches and frozen beggars."

I sat in silence. I had no idea what to say. Of course, I wouldn't tell him anything voluntarily, but the urge to reveal all, to show off and be clever, was greater than I had imagined it would be.

He snatched the glass back up and drained it. By the ruddy hue of his cheeks, I could see he was slightly drunk. "My men tell me that the Justice has collared some of the sheriff's retainers and ranged south looking for me," he said, "but his taskman is still loitering around the town's inns and brothels. He's got half a drive on him, that Bressinger. I daresay there'll be a clutch of black-haired Grozodans running around the place in a year." He smirked. "What's he doing here? Keeping an eye on you, is that it?"

"Who told you about me?" I asked with venom. "Was it Walter?" I had a sudden urge to out the ghastly old wretch.

Vogt looked briefly baffled. "What, the old pervert who keeps drawing gate duty? What's he got to do with anything?"

"He is part of your scheme," I declared. "You are not so clever that I haven't noticed. He is about as subtle as a horse put out to stud."

Vogt's bafflement slowly turned into humour. He laughed throatily. "You do not mean the illegal still he keeps? The man is making brandy in one of the old vaults! The man is a fucking idiot – literally." Vogt laughed again. "Did you think we'd sent that dolt to spy on you? I do fear for the Justice's cause if you are all he can scrape together."

I felt anger seep through every fibre of my being as Vogt mocked me. "If you hurt me . . . " I said. I had meant to threaten him, but in truth, it sounded feeble.

Vogt rolled his eyes. "The full weight of the Emperor's justice will come crashing down on us, I imagine," he sneered. "Come, girl, tell me what he knows. And don't make the mistake of thinking that because you work for a Justice you are somehow immune to my special attentions."

This time I kept silent. I had heard all kinds of threats and insults in my time. I knew I was stronger than my fear would have me believe. I made a promise to myself that whatever happened, I would not yield anything unless forced to. I would not be able to face Vonvalt or Bressinger again if I did not at least attempt to keep the details of our investigation secret. The irony was, Vonvalt had told me in the past that if I was ever faced with torture, I was to simply tell my captors everything I knew, that they'd have it out of me anyway.

Vogt looked irritated. "You test me, girl." He stood up and walked towards me. I shrank back instinctively into the seat, turning away – for all the good it did me. A stunning blow caught me across the face. Pain exploded through my head. One of his rings had cut a gash into my cheek, and blood immediately flowed from the wound and pattered onto my nightgown.

I had seen it coming, and had already resolved not to react. A small, involuntary cry did escape my lips, but otherwise I simply sat there, staring at the floor catatonically while the blood flowed. Vogt sighed heavily again and walked back to his chair behind the desk.

"Tell me what he knows. Tell me why you are here. You may yet live if you answer my questions."

There was a knock at the door. Vogt gritted his teeth. *"What?"*

The door opened. I sensed hesitation.

"Spit it out, man," Vogt said.

"The Obenpatria wants to see you—"

"Gods alive," Vogt said, launching to his feet. "Shut your fucking mouth, you dolt!"

Well: that confirmed Fischer's involvement.

"Get her to the cells," Vogt snapped, gesturing to me angrily.

"Come on, girl," the man said roughly. I saw he was wearing a purple habit like the rest of the monks. He took me by the arm and led me out of the room and into a dank hallway. I could see that the place we were in had once been – and remained, at least in part – a dungeon. But, like Vogt's, many of the cells had been converted. Where once they had had stout iron bars, now there were wooden partitions and doors. Despite the late hour, I could see that some were lit, judging by the candlelight that shone through the gaps in the door frames. I could hear noises, too, including heavy grunting and the dramatic, false moaning of a practised courtesan.

These rooms of course were not for me. I was taken to the part of the dungeon which remained a dungeon, a damp, stinking place. There was one larger cell with two lumps I could see underneath the straw, one in each of the corners furthest from the gate. I was thrown inside and landed on the cold flagstones with a yelp. Then the gate was locked behind me and the guard left without saying another word.

There wasn't much light, only that from the braziers round the corner. Once I was confident that the guard was out of earshot and neither of the straw-covered shapes was going to move, I crept towards one corner to inspect my cellmates.

I was arrested by a sharp, hissed, *"Don't!"*

I whirled around. The other lump in the far corner had resolved itself into a young woman, probably the same age as me. She was gaunt and filthy, and a horrible stink emanated from her.

"What?" I asked, aghast.

"Dead," she said, nodding to the other lump under the straw.

I shrank back from the corpse in the corner. "Who are you?" I asked her, but I could see who it was. Despite two years of mistreatment, her features were unmistakable. "You're Sanja Bauer," I said dumbly.

"How did you know?" she asked.

"We've been looking for you," I said.

"Well," she gestured to the cell. "You've found me."

Her composure was remarkable. Despite enduring many months as a hostage, she still retained that air of dogged nobility.

"Are you the Justice's clerk?" she asked.

My face folded in confusion. "How . . . ?"

She nodded in the direction of the door. "The guards. They tell me what goes on." She shrugged off my look of surprise. "It is not as though there is anything I can do with the information."

I shook my head. "I'm . . . I did not expect . . . You seem so calm."

She shrugged again. "I have been here for years. This is my life now. I have adapted. I do not spend all of my time in the dungeons; a week here, a fortnight there, depending my 'behaviour' and the whims of my captors. I have only been back in this cell for a few weeks. Before then I was in one of their rooms, with books to read. They treat me well enough, on occasion, given I am a prisoner."

I looked over the dirty, reeking girl in front of me, and strongly suspected her of lying. Perhaps she thought me some kind of agent of Vogt's, sent to test her. "You do not have the look of one who has been well treated," I said.

She laughed bitterly, gesturing to her filthy clothes. "This . . . this is for my own protection. The men gamble and whore down here. They drink a skinful and then come looking for something to stick their little pricks into. But even a drunk man will not come near me in this state."

I had to admire this resourcefulness. For someone who had at one time been used to expensive clothes and perfumes and a life of privilege, it must have wounded her pride to debase herself so utterly. But the fact that she had done so spoke of an exceptionally tenacious spirit.

"What is this place?" I asked. I whispered, but Sanja spoke normally.

"This is where they run their little empire from," she said. "Fischer, Vogt, my father."

"Nema," I breathed. "We were right."

"Right about what?"

"About . . . everything. We have been investigating the murder of your mother," I added. I said it unthinkingly. I assumed she knew. She seemed to know everything else. But her face fell suddenly, like a drawbridge with its chains severed.

"What?" she asked in a trembling voice.

I cursed myself a thousand times; but I could not un-say the words.

"Kasivar, I'm sorry," I said. It sounded so pathetic. "I . . . thought you knew."

The news stole her spirit with the swiftness of a practised cut-purse. It took a long time to console her. At one point one of the guards came to investigate, and I felt my whole body stiffen in terror; but he saw Sanja crying and seemed unmoved, as though it were a regular occurrence. It struck me that she might not have weathered her time in captivity as well as she had let on.

After what seemed like an hour or maybe longer, she seemed ready to talk again. She had spent most of the time lying face-down in the filthy straw and whimpering inconsolably, but eventually she ran out of tears. When she looked at me again, she had changed markedly. I didn't see a defiant, devil-may-care prisoner who had long since made her peace with her lot. I saw a frightened young girl, her soul crushed to a fine powder, the last of her reserves of morale exhausted.

"I'm so sorry," I said, for what must have been the hundredth time.

She waved me quiet. "I had wondered," she said. Her voice was quiet now, barely above a whisper. "There was a time, perhaps a month or two ago. Everything was a little . . . frantic. The guards started treating me differently. Lots of hushed conversations and angry words. And . . . you will think me mad, but I just had a *feeling*, too. This horrible feeling that she had gone. That a little part of me had gone, like someone . . ." she made a pinching motion with her fingers ". . . snuffing out a candle."

"She cannot have known you were here," I said.

Sanja shook her head. "She knew. I do not know what combination of lies and threats my father used to keep her from saying anything. But he broke her spirit a long time ago. And she was not a strong-willed person to begin with."

I imagined that Bauer had told his wife that Fischer and Vogt had murdered her son, and if she said or did anything they would murder her daughter too.

We fell to silence again. In spite of my many questions I did not want to press her. I had given her some of the worst news a person can receive, and in an offhand, unthinking way.

"You said the Justice had been investigating it?" she asked eventually. "As painful as it is for me, 'tis hardly a great crime of state."

"We deal with a great many crimes," I said, aware that I sounded like Vonvalt, "anything from larceny to treason."

Sanja grunted. "His arrival has certainly set the hares running here. How go your investigations?"

I gestured to the cell around me. In spite of everything, she barked out a laugh, but it was quickly extinguished by guilt and grief. I had seen, and would come to see, many recipients of the same news – that a cherished loved one had been killed – and there are as many different ways of dealing with it as there are people. Some collapsed; others could not stop laughing from the sudden shock. Sanja, though, seemed to conform to what I would consider to be the most common: initial grief, followed by a period of some lucidity. She would enter her most melancholy phase in the days ahead.

"How did my mother come to be killed?"

"She was struck on the head," I said. "We do not know by who, specifically," I added, heading off her next question. "We do not think it was your father, though."

Sanja snorted. She looked bitter. "Why?"

I fiddled with the hem of my slip. "We do not know that either, beyond conjecture."

"You do not know much," Sanja said, a hint of irritation in her voice.

"We know a great deal," I said, slightly testily myself. "I am here, am I not?"

"Where is the Justice?"

"Further away than I would like," I murmured. "Do you know a man called Fenland Graves?"

"I have seen him here before. He works in the treasury, one of my father's most trusted men."

I nodded. "We have been questioning different people around Galen's Vale. The trail led us to him."

"What did he have to say for himself?"

"Not much," I said. "He's dead."

"Good," Sanja snapped. "How?"

"Our taskman killed him."

"The Grozodan?"

I paused. "You *are* well-informed," I said. I spoke cautiously, and her expression changed. I realised that I had already been duped once by a girl in this kloster. Could this be another elaborate hoax? The girl was certainly Sanja Bauer; one could easily see her father's features in her face. But perhaps she had been turned in some way? Vonvalt had told me stories of victims of abduction who had gone on to fall in love with their captors – going so far as to defend them at trial.

"You suspect me," she said with dismay. She grabbed her

disgusting clothes. "Look at me. *Smell* me, for Nema's sake, if by some chance you haven't yet. You think I would inflict this on myself if I did not have to?"

"Hm," I said. I ignored her anguished look. I was suddenly feeling very unfriendly indeed.

"Please," she implored. "Listen, do you think if they wanted information out of you they would waste time with this ruse? Using me as some kind of bait? They would put hot irons up you. They know the circle is closing. There is too much attention on them and the kloster. They don't have the time or patience for an elaborate subterfuge."

"No," I said. "No, I don't think so. They would not torture me. They dare not. Not while the Justice is out there. He knows I am here, and he knows who they key players are. If they harm me, or kill me, they lose the only leverage they have over him." The realisation of this hit me at the same time that I said it. I was imprisoned, but that was all I was. Vogt might have landed me a sharp slap across the cheek, but I doubted he would go further. I probed at it; the wound stung, and in these conditions would turn sour quickly. It needed washing with wine.

"Listen," Sanja said, growing desperate. "I told you, the guards tell me things. You arrived before Wintertide, no? They said that a Justice had arrived with his retainers, a Grozodan swordsman and a pretty young clerk. They wouldn't tell me much more than that, just that the Justice had been making enquiries around the town. I could see it had them scared though."

"Uh-huh," I said.

"I'm not a spy!" she said, suddenly fierce. She threw her hands up. "I don't care one jot if you speak to me. By the sound of it you don't know a thing of use anyway."

She turned away from me and lay down. I looked at her for a long time. "Tell me how you came to be here," I asked eventually.

"Oh, you can drink brine if you think I'm speaking to you," she said.

I took in a deep breath and nodded to myself. "All right," I said. I lay down myself and closed my eyes. I felt a few pangs of guilt, but I had to be prudent. I knew first-hand of the subtlety of Fischer and Vogt. The information flow between Sanja and me from that point on could only go one way – to me.

❧

I did drift off in spite of everything, for I was awoken by a guard bringing us food. Nothing had visibly changed. Our surroundings were still poorly lit by the same brazier round the corner. There was no natural light.

We took up the food and ate. It was much better than I had expected it would be. The bread was a little stale, but there was no mould, and they had even provided us with some sausage and cheese.

After an uncomfortable ten minutes or so, Sanja started speaking as though no time had passed since our last conversation.

"It happened a few years ago," she said. "My brother had died suddenly of a pox." I managed to hold my tongue on that one. "I was obviously . . . distraught. Maybe even hysterical. My brother and I were close." She paused, and for a moment I thought she was going to break down all over again. But she retained her composure. "My father suggested I spend some time up here, praying in the temples. The commonfolk are permitted to; it is not a closed kloster like some."

"I know."

"I didn't really want to. I do not hold much to the Imperial gods, or any gods for that matter. But I came anyway. They came and took me the night I arrived. Vogt's men. Fischer's men. Whosever men they were. My father had had a dispute with Vogt, and Vogt had reported him to the sheriff. I thought it was revenge. It took me a long time to realise I was a hostage. I do not think my father was working with Vogt at the time. I think that only happened after they took me. And while I am alive, he will do their bidding to keep me so."

"Do you have any idea what it was your father was doing? The record indicated a dispute over a shipment of grain, but Vogt withdrew the complaint and it was never investigated."

"I have no idea," Sanja said wretchedly. "I have never been told any details of it. I just know they have their hands in a lot of different things – most of it to do with shipping. I am so sick of being here. I fear I am losing my mind. I will get a pox from all the wretches they leave in here with me. They used to let my father visit to see that I was still alive. Now I do not even get that any more, though gods know I hate the man. By Nema I *hate* him. Look at what he has reduced me to!"

"The Justice will come back and save us," I said uneasily.

Sanja probed me for more information. I drip fed her some of the less sensitive details. I was still slightly wary, but I could not see the harm in telling her a few titbits. Besides, as she rightly said, if my captors wanted the information out of me, they didn't have to be particularly imaginative about how they got it.

The time passed. Sanja reminisced about her life and her mother and became melancholic. I tried to steer the conversation between areas that would upset her, like a captain steering a ship through icebergs, but I generally failed, and much of my time was spent comforting the girl who had lost so much.

I do not know how long I was in that dungeon for. The guards would not speak to us and the only way to vaguely keep track of time was by how frequently they brought us meals. It was not long before my sleeping patterns themselves fell into an odd routine as I lost all track time.

And then, roused from another fitful sleep, I saw a guard standing at the gate. My cheek pulsed painfully.

"Come on," the guard said. Sanja was asleep – or more likely pretending to be – in the corner.

There felt little point in resisting. I allowed him to grip my arm and I was taken out of the cell and around the corner. He did not cover my head this time. Instead he led me down a narrow, ill-lit spiral staircase. I wondered just how deep the foundations of the kloster ran.

"My cheek needs bathing," I said. It felt hot to the touch. "I will catch a pox if it is not."

"Shut it," the guard said.

We reached the bottom of the stairs. There the passageway opened out into a broad, low-ceilinged rib vault, lit by braziers. The floor was flagstoned, mouldy and damp. In fact, as we approached the bottom of the stairs, I could see by the firelight that the space continued for some tens and perhaps even hundreds of yards.

There were four men standing in an open space. One was Vogt. There were two others, armed and dressed in light armour, whom I did not recognise.

And then I screamed.

The fourth, bloodied and bruised, was Matas.

XXII

A Stolen Life

"The wolf with two heads sees in both directions."

OLD SOVAN PROVERB

"No!" I shrieked. I tried desperately to yank my arm out of the guard's grip, but I could not. Instead he pulled me into him from behind and half-crushed me in a bear-hug.

Matas wasn't wearing his town watch livery. Instead he wore simple, dark-coloured garments. One of his eyes was sealed closed and was rapidly bruising. His mouth had taken a knock, too, judging by his split lip. He looked dazed and woozy, but I could see that he saw and recognised me.

"Let him go!" I shrieked.

"Shut up!" Vogt snapped. He seemed agitated, like he was not fully in control of the situation.

"Helena," Matas mumbled. He smiled at me. Oh, that smile. My heart aches to remember it.

One of the men struck him. "Shut up, you little prick," he snapped.

"Stop it!" I screamed. "Please!"

"You shut up!" the man who had struck Matas now shouted at me.

"Nema, will all of you shut up!" Vogt snapped. He turned to me. "We found him sneaking into places he shouldn't have been," he said. "Your beau, is he?"

"He is nothing to do with any of this," I said. Tears streamed down my face. "Please—"

"Stop," Vogt said, holding up a hand. "Stop it. He's not going anywhere, so stop begging. Now listen. This is a happy accident. I can get the information I want out of you and I don't have to lay a hand on you – again." He added the last comment with a smirk. "So: tell me what the Justice knows. Tell me everything about his investigations. If you tell me, your boy here will live. If you don't, he will die. 'Tis as simple as that."

"Tell them nothing!" Matas shouted with the last of his energy, and earned a kicking for it.

"Bloody Nema, these two," Vogt said to the guards. They laughed obsequiously. "Last chance, girl."

"We don't know!" I shouted. My voice was strangled with grief. "We don't know anything about what you're doing here."

"That's what Emilia said," one of the guards piped up.

"Kasivar's fucking arsehole, Broderick, shut your mouth before I have your tongue out," Vogt shouted. He turned back to me. "You are investigating Lady Bauer's death."

"Yes," I said.

"You have discovered nothing at all?"

"We know that money has been coming into the kloster from the town's treasury," I said. "More than can be lawfully accounted for."

"And?"

I tried to think. Tried to think of what I could tell him that would be enough without giving away everything we had discovered.

"We thought Fenland Graves was responsible," I blurted out.

Vogt looked at me. Then he laughed. "Nema, you lawmen are useless aren't you? You thought that hopeless dungheap was responsible?" He laughed, and the two men holding Matas – and the man holding me – joined in.

"Well he's dead now," I snapped.

Vogt's face immediately fell. "Yes," he said. "Dead by your master's hand, was he?"

I bit my tongue so hard I could taste blood. What a fool I had been to gall the man!

"So," Vogt sneered. "Murdered by a Justice. There's irony in that, is there not?" When I did not reply, he snapped, "Speak, girl!"

"He attacked our taskman," I said. The explanation seemed like reason at the time. "He was killed as an act of defence."

"Well, we've only your word for that, don't we?" Vogt said.

"I swear that's what happened," I said.

"An act of defence?" Vogt asked. His demeanour had changed. He quirked the corner of his mouth, as though he were mulling it over. "I imagine that's probably right. Graves always was a fool. Well, here's another act of defence for you."

I didn't realise, didn't acknowledge what was happening until it was already over. Vogt pulled his short-sword from the scabbard at his waist, took a few quick strides over to where Matas was and thrust the sword into his gut.

"No!" I screamed. My legs gave out. The guard holding me let me go as I became a dead weight in his arms.

"Matas!" I wailed, crawling towards him. I heard the men laughing. That people are capable of such cruelty never fails to shock me, even to this day.

They had let Matas drop to the floor, and he lay there in a growing pool of blood, his breath bubbling from his lips. Vogt was shouting at me, but I could not have made out the words even if I had wanted to. Everything had dissolved into a miasma of anguish. I might as well have been stabbed in my own gut.

I reached Matas. Nobody stopped me. I took his head into my hands and pulled his body into mine, weeping inconsolably. I have thought about that moment many hundreds of times over the course of my life. Such visceral grief tends to brand itself indelibly on to one's mind. It still has the power to make me weep all these years later. Matas was such a good lad, truly genuine and kind-hearted. I would have been honoured to be his wife. How things might have been different.

His breath came out in a horrible rasping sound, and it took me a moment to realise he was trying to whisper something in my ear.

"There is . . . a passage behind you," he said haltingly, every word fresh agony. "It is how I got in. It leads out . . . into the foot-hills. You must flee, Helena. Leave me. I am done for . . . but there is hope for you still."

"Don't say that," I said. "Don't you say that. My place is here with you. Don't make me leave you now – I should never have left you."

I kissed him over and over again on the side of his face and head, as if in doing so I could restore his health.

"Helena, please . . . For me . . . You must leave. Fetch the Grozodan – and Sir Radomir. Bring a physician. If you get here quickly enough with help, I may yet be saved."

I didn't realise at the time that Matas was simply trying to get me to run away, and had realised that suggesting he might be saved was the best way to do it. He knew full well that he could not survive a wound in his gut like that. It is strange; for the long-est time afterwards I resented him deeply for making me leave his side, when I was so sure that I should have stayed with him. But of course, he was right. Vogt would simply have killed me too – and while I might have welcomed death in that moment, it would have been completely senseless.

"I love you," I whispered frantically into his ear. I needed him to know. He had to know that it wasn't all in vain. "I love you."

"I . . . love you, Helena. Now please, go. Run to the end of the vault. There is a – *ack!* – doorway that leads to a spiral stair. Run for me, Helena."

I kissed him again. The men around us were beginning to close, perhaps realising that something other than parting words were being exchanged.

"That's enough, girl," one of them said roughly, and reached out to grab my arm. Before he could touch me, I pressed myself up off the floor, turned and ran as fast as I was able to the end of the vault.

Grunts, and then shouts of surprise chased me down the vault. It was not long before I heard swearing and running footsteps behind me, but I dared not turn around. I had learnt many years before never to turn around. If someone was going to catch me, they were going to catch me. A stolen glance rarely helped.

The light quickly faded to dull gloom as I ran deeper into the long, ill-lit section of the vault. I saw a black door-shaped hole in the wall ahead, which could only have been the exit Matas had referred to. By the time I reached it, there was no light to see by at all.

The men continued to give chase, but they were probably slightly drunk, unfit and unenthusiastic – despite the furious exhortations from Vogt. Thanks to my fleetness of foot, it was not long before their huffing and puffing faded into insignificance. Another lesson I had learned in Muldau was to keep running long after the danger was assumed to be past. I ran through that black hole – which looked for all the world like the open mouth of a gigantic snake – and took the spiral staircase downwards as quickly as I dared.

The staircase ended in a long flat corridor of stone, but I only discovered this after I had walked its length, stumbling and staggering like a blind girl. I could not hear any pursuers at all now, nor see the tell-tale flicker of orange torchlight, and so I took this section at a slow, trembling walk. It felt like an unforgivable delay, and I wept openly the entire time, but I could not risk putting a foot wrong and breaking a leg. If that happened, I might as well have stayed with Matas.

Eventually I reached a low doorway of stone, which led to another steep spiral staircase. Now I could feel the cold air of the night gusting up the tunnel like breath, and the merest hint of moonlight suggested that I was close to making good my escape.

After what felt like an age, I exited into the frigid dark. Disorientated, it took me a moment to realise that I had come out at the base of the foothills just as Matas had said I would. I whirled back around to see the entrance to the tunnel. It was skilfully concealed among the rocks and would only be visible to a careful observer.

Galen's Vale lay below me, a little way down the hill but not far. I ran across the cold, hard earth to the northern gate. The gates were locked and guarded at this hour, though given the state of it neither of those things would have stopped a determined infiltrator.

"Who goes there?" the gateman called as I hammered on the heavy reinforced wood.

"Helena Sedanka!" I shouted. "I am Sir Konrad's clerk! I must speak with Sir Radomir at once! There has been a murder!"

"Bloody hell," the man grunted, and in less than a minute we were charging through the streets on a grey palfrey.

"Make way! Watch there!" the guard shouted a few times as other watchmen jumped out of the way. It did not take long to reach the watch house. I took great comfort from the fact that I could see the windows aglow with firelight. It was like a beacon of justice in an otherwise lawless world.

I leapt off the back of the horse and burst through the front door.

"Nema's teeth, what's the matter?" the duty serjeant asked.

"I must speak with Sir Radomir at once!" I shouted.

"He'll be asleep," the serjeant said, frowning. "Tell me what the matter is. Someone been bothering you?"

"There's been a murder up at the kloster and there'll be more to come if you don't get me Sir Radomir this instant!" I thundered.

"Kasivar, what is this bleeding racket?" another watchman said as he entered. "Ah, Miss Sedanka. Jorge, 'tis the Justice's clerk. What's the matter, miss?"

I was about to tear my hair out.

"Helena." I recognised Sir Radomir's voice from the top of the stairs. He tramped down them in his heavy boots. He was wearing his watchman's uniform from his feet to his waist, and a simple white sleeping shirt. "Gods, what ails you?"

"The kloster!" I shouted. I could barely speak I was so breathless with frustration. "They've stabbed Matas. It's Vogt! And Fischer is there too! You must come quickly!"

"Nema!" Sir Radomir grunted. He turned to the serjeant. "Sound the alarm. I want ten men, armed and armoured, ready to move off in two minutes. Horses, quick, and swords! And rouse Maquerink and the Justice's taskman. Now, move it!"

I stood, mute, as all around me descended into organised chaos. A bell started ringing, crashing loudly in an otherwise silent night. Men rushed about, retrieving weapons, breastplates and helmets from the armoury. Outside I heard the clatter of horses' hooves on the cobblestones. It did not take long for a small host of watchmen to gather and mount up outside the watch house. Several carried torches, and the orange flames flickered and danced in the cold night. Sir Radomir gestured me to join him on his horse, and he pulled me up with a strong grip. I hugged his cold cuirass and he kicked his spurs into the horse's flanks. Once more I was tearing through Galen's Vale, this time in the opposite direction.

"Tell me what has happened?" he called over his shoulder.

I explained as much as I could. I was so caught up it was hard to get all my thoughts out at once. But Sir Radomir pieced it together quickly.

"Nema. If only Sir Konrad were here. Gods know how far south the man is now. At least Bressinger is to hand."

We thundered through the northern closure and out of the gate. Our progress up the dark, winding path which led to the kloster above was slower, but the horses were sure-footed and knew the route well enough, and we surmounted the road in a handful of minutes.

"There it is," I said, pointing to the concealed entrance I had come out of. The kloster itself loomed a few hundred yards' worth of track above. "Quickly!"

"You men with me," Sir Radomir said, pointing at the nearest three watchmen; then he pointed to another. "You wait for the physician and Bressinger and follow me in when he arrives." Lastly he turned to the serjeant. "Serjeant, take the rest up to the main gate. Arrest Obenpatria Fischer the moment you clap eyes on him. No one else is to leave. Understood?"

"Sire," the serjeant replied.

We dismounted and I led Sir Radomir to the entrance, scrabbling over the rocks so quickly that I chafed my hands badly on the rough ground.

"Nema, I don't like the look of it," Sir Radomir said, and snatched a torch from one of the men. "Come on then. You stay behind me, Helena. Tell me the way."

We moved, me, Sir Radomir and three watchmen, armour clattering and mouths puffing, up the stairs and back into the bowels of the kloster. Soon we were back in the low, dimly lit vaults.

Matas was lying where he had been stabbed. His face looked ash-grey, and his eyes were closed. Standing next to him, frozen in place and aghast at our arrival, was Vogt.

"What the fuck?" was all he managed.

"Bind him!" Sir Radomir snarled. Vogt started like a hare, but in seconds Sir Radomir's men were on him, driving him to the floor with knees and boots to the back of his legs and binding him roughly.

I ran over to Matas and collapsed on the hard stone floor next to him. He was unconscious, and his skin was sheened with perspiration. I clutched his hand and squeezed it, sobbing. I watched as my tears fell from my eyes and pattered down on to his face.

"Matas," I said, my voice hoarse and strained. In that moment, his eyes fluttered open and focused on me for a fleeting moment.

"My Helena," he said, and smiled. Then his eyes closed again.

For a strange moment I felt nothing at all, as though there was simply too much grief for my mind to accommodate in one sitting. Then, as I felt the anguish building inside of me, ready to burst out in an animalistic wail, I saw men entering the vaults – the same ones who had dragged me down here. They must have been drawn by their master's cries, but for all their great bravado in murdering a helpless lad and smacking about a maid, they baulked when squaring off against Sir Radomir and his town watchmen.

"Here," one of the watchmen close to me said, shoving his pike into my hands and drawing his short-sword. He nodded to Vogt's prostrate form. "Best watch him, Miss."

Then, before I knew what was happening, he, Sir Radomir and the rest of them rushed forwards to engage with the newcomers in a bloody, chaotic melee.

I looked down at Vogt, who looked up at me. My grip on the haft of the pike tightened. It was a heavy length of wood, eight feet long. Its tip caught the light of the nearest brazier.

A flash of panic widened his eyes.

"Don't even think about it, girl," he said.

I looked over to my left. Several men were lying on the floor; two of Vogt's henchmen and one watchman. Their groans and cries filled the small, low space as their lifeblood drained away. I watched as Sir Radomir took the life of another, smashing his sword into the man's face and neck like it was a chopping block. The sheriff wielded his sword like a hatchet, his style brutal and functional, honed in the Reichskrieg and then on the streets of

Perry Ford and Galen's Vale. It had none of the lethal grace and flair of Bressinger's swordplay, but it did the job, much like the man himself.

I turned back to Vogt and levelled the pike at him. Even then, though, I doubted I could do it. With as just a cause as I was ever like to get, and with hate and anguish permeating my every fibre, I still couldn't bring myself to plunge the tip of the pike into the man's flesh. The act of killing, after all, is so offensive to one's nature, especially when the victim is as helpless as a kitten – even if not as innocent. I wondered what Vonvalt would think if he could have seen me in that moment. Would he have had sympathy, or would he have had me arrested for murder? That I had any confusion about it at all was telling.

I was broken from my reverie by movement. A glimmer of motion in the false darkness on the other side of the brazier. I brought the pike up instinctively, but nonetheless with difficulty. I felt my bloodlust melt away, to be replaced with an overwhelming sense of exposure and fear. The pike was unwieldy; it would not take an agile man to outmanoeuvre me.

"Put it down, lass," a voice called out. "You're going to get yourself hurt."

A man wearing a Jadran habit stepped out into the firelight. He carried no more than a dirk, but it was more than enough to best me with.

I kept the pike between us, the tip trained on his heart.

"Get back," I said, but my voice was quiet and hoarse. Fear closed my throat up. I knew I had only one thrust – which had to at least incapacitate him – before he closed the gap and killed me.

"I'm not interested in you," he said. "Just Mr Vogt here."

He knelt down furtively next to Vogt and started sawing through the cords that bound him.

"Stop it!" I tried to shout, but it was barely a whisper. The pike felt heavy in my hands. My grief and fear were overwhelming me, as though someone had draped heavy chains across my shoulders.

The cords around Vogt's wrists snapped, and both men started scrabbling frantically at those around his ankles. I was watching Matas's murderer escape, and there was nothing I could do about it. Worse – I could hear fresh clashes from where more of Vogt's men were entering the fray at the other end of the vault.

Vogt and his man stood up. "Here, give me that," Vogt snapped, taking the dagger. He pointed it at me. "Right; now you listen to me, girl," he said, seconds before the head of the man next to him was split from his crown to the top of his nose. Vogt cried out and flinched violently as blood sprayed the side of his face. The man in the habit collapsed to the floor, and his assailant pulled his sword free with a squeal of steel on bone.

It was Bressinger. Behind him were four more watchmen. They must have followed us up through the sally port after the initial rush. Lurking at the back, clutching a medical case and looking distinctly uneasy, was Mr Maquerink.

"Don't kill him!" I shouted as Bressinger lifted his sword to dispatch Vogt. "He is a witness!"

Bressinger's arm halted mid-stroke. Vogt shrieked and dropped to the floor. The watchmen looked at him in disgust.

"Bind him," Bressinger said to a pair of the men behind him, and then, to the other two, "You, come with me." Then I watched as they ran off to join the fight and rebalance the numbers.

I dropped the pike again, glad to be rid of its burdensome weight. I watched dispassionately as Vogt was pressed into the stone floor, his hands and ankles rebound with such tightness that he cried like a little boy. Mr Maquerink stepped out from the shadows and moved past me, kneeling beside Matas.

And then there was nothing for me to do but wait out the rest of that long night.

⚮

It took three days for Matas to die. Vonvalt returned on the second. I was sitting in the ward in Mr Maquerink's house when I heard the Justice arrive downstairs.

Matas did not stir when the cold gust from the open door found its way upstairs, nor when the sounds of Vonvalt and Bressinger talking quietly echoed through the house. Vonvalt had actually been on his way back for most of a week. Bauer had been found, but not by him; rather, Justice August had found him. Doubtless to speed the conclusion of our business in the Vale, she had taken it upon herself to track the man down, using her powers to enlist the local wild-life to the task. She had discovered him in Estre – one of the three principalities surrounding Sova – was governed by Luka Kzosic, the Emperor's second son. Bauer was being transported back to Galen's Vale by August herself and a small troop of Imperial soldiers from the wayfort at Gresch. The caravan was expected imminently.

Mr Maquerink had done all he could for Matas – he had cleaned and bandaged the wound and lain him down on one of the beds in the ward. But Matas had taken a sword through the gut. Only his youthful strength, and perhaps a fortunate angle on the thrust, kept him in this suspended half-life. I held his hand and wiped the sweat from his brow, but he varied between deep unconscious-ness and brief spasms of delirium, and I knew, in my heart, that he would not recover.

"I am sorry, Helena," I heard Vonvalt say.

I turned to see him standing in the doorway, ruddy-faced from the chill, a tall, imposing figure in his stately clothes and heavy cloak. He radiated cold and he was spattered with mud.

I turned back to Matas. I admit that I found it hard not to blame Vonvalt.

"I have been told the boy came looking for you," Vonvalt said quietly. "Driven by love and worry, no doubt." Vonvalt's words, spoken with soft contrition, brought fresh tears to my eyes. "There is to be a trial," he said. "I will have confessions from Bauer and Vogt today—"

"Do you think I care about that at all?" I snapped. Anger filled me. I felt my skin flush and I felt suddenly lightheaded. "Do you think any of that matters to me now?"

Vonvalt stood there. He looked at me apologetically, but it was clear he was not going to say anything. He was either too awkward, or felt that Matas had been acceptable collateral damage to his mission, or a mixture of the two. Either way, I wanted to be rid of him.

"Get out," I snarled. "I don't want to see you."

Vonvalt nodded. "As you wish," he said, and left.

I cried then until my throat was raw and I had no more tears left to shed.

⟡

People came and went. I heard snatches of news: that the kloster had been dissolved, that all the monks and nuns were being rounded up for questioning, that Lord Sauter had been arrested, that the Legions were coming to secure the town and the treasury.

They were all either wrong or hugely exaggerated. It was true that, as I stood vigil over Matas, Sir Radomir's men were questioning every member of the kloster. Emilia was arrested and put in the town gaol, and there were other arrests as well as a few dramatic but short fights in which Vogt's henchmen were killed or detained and then summarily executed as the law permitted.

The kloster was not dissolved but most of its activities, save those which were necessary for the functioning of the town, were suspended. Most of the monks and nuns were confined to their quarters, allowed out only to eat together. I think the town authorities were afraid of them all massing together, but I knew that the majority of them were completely harmless.

Bauer arrived in an armoured cart flanked by Imperial soldiers from the wayfort at Gresch. Rumours of his complicity in the murder of his wife spread throughout the town like wildfire, and

I heard that he was booed and pelted as he was led into the town gaol. Whatever the ultimate legal outcome of the case, his status as a social pariah was cast in stone.

Sanja Bauer was freed from the kloster dungeons and repaired to the family home. Sir Radomir had her placed under guard for her own protection, and to keep an eye on her.

❧

Matas died without ever regaining full consciousness on the morning of the third day. The words still hurt to write them. I still feel keenly the pain of his death. He was my first love and he was snatched cruelly from me. I did not just mourn him; I mourned the life I could have had. That *we* could have had. It would have been quieter and less eventful, certainly, but it would have been mine, and we would have been together. That the choice of whether to stay or go was taken from me made it all the more difficult to endure. Life was a little bleaker, a little less colourful after that.

To his credit, Vonvalt did briefly halt his work for the morning. The town watch had its own plot in the temple burial ground, and we had a short service in which a number of people, including Sir Radomir and Vonvalt, said a few words. Vonvalt also arranged for Matas's father to receive an allowance from Imperial funds. Vartan attended the funeral, but his son's death brought old, buried prejudices and resentments to the fore, and he would not speak with me. That, too, was a difficult thing to have to deal with.

There is not a great deal more to say about it. Although I am an old woman now, some wounds never fully heal. The pain of it all is something I have tried to repress over the years, sometimes successfully, more often not. But I know how I felt about him and how I felt – feel – about his death. Spilling ink offers me no catharsis, only more pain. For that reason, I will not dwell on the matter any longer than I must.

Indeed, I did not have much time to dwell on it in any event. The end of the investigation was merely the beginning of wider events, and there was a great deal more bloodshed and heartache to come before we could close this miserable chapter in Galen's Vale.

XXIII

Trial Preparation

"It is imperative that a Justice take the time to fully familiarise himself with the facts and nuances of a matter, and particularly when dealing with an infamous or widely disliked accused. The wider populace is easily exercised and given to pass immediate judgment on the barest of evidence."

FROM CATERHAUSER'S THE SOVAN CRIMINAL
CODE: ADVICE TO PRACTITIONERS

It was Sir Radomir who came to find me. I had holed myself up in an inn. I had plenty of money which I rarely had any need to spend. Staying there for at least the medium term did not pose a problem. I wanted my own space for a while, to grieve, and then to spend time thinking about what I wanted to do with my life.

I had no doubt that Vonvalt knew where I was. I had not been particularly secretive about it, though he would have ensured that I was somewhere safe. Sometimes I found that a comfort. Other times I found it stifling. Had Vonvalt been a different sort of man, it would have been frightening, though knowing him as I did, I knew that it came from a place of concern rather than control.

The trouble was, sometimes I didn't want his concern.

I had expected Bressinger, rather than Sir Radomir, to come and speak to me. The sheriff knocked softly on the door two days after Matas had died.

"Sir – Radomir," I said, faltering as I opened the door. Immediately I was appalled. I had barely bathed and I was clad in my nightclothes. My hair looked like a bird's nest. I cared not one jot if Bressinger saw me like that, but I was not close to Sir Radomir, and the man was a town official to boot.

"Miss Sedanka," Sir Radomir said, affecting not to notice my poor state. "Justice August—"

"Just give me a moment," I said, flustered.

"Of cour—" he began, but I had already closed the door in his face.

I bustled round the room, changing into something more appropriate and combing my hair. The room did have a rudimentary mirror, but I could stand to look at myself only briefly. My face looked pale and drawn from days of anguish and poor appetite, and having lived on the road for two years, I did not have a great deal of meat on my bones from which to draw reserve strength. The cut which Vogt had left on my cheek was unsightly, and my hair to one side was still fuzzy and short and revealed the scar which Graves's man had left me with.

When I felt some semblance of seemliness, I reopened the door. Sir Radomir was standing in the hallway, leaning against the wall. He pressed himself away with a clank of armour.

"Justice August would speak with you," he said. "She is in the courthouse with Sir Konrad. 'Tis a matter of great importance, so I'm told, and not a little urgency."

I stiffened. I did not want to see Vonvalt, but I could hardly refuse two Imperial Magistrates.

"All right," I said, and followed the sheriff out of the inn.

We walked through the streets at a brisk pace. It was a sunny morning, and a mild breeze carried with it the smell of effluent and offal.

"You and Sir Konrad have had a falling out," he remarked.

"Is it any wonder?" I snapped.

Sir Radomir shook his head. "No, not to me. You forget that Matas was one of my lads, too."

I had forgotten that, and I felt a flash of guilt. "You are right. I am sorry."

Sir Radomir waved me off. "I'll not pretend it is worse for me than you. But – Helena – however you feel about it, you cannot hold Sir Konrad responsible for the death of the boy. I feel the lad's loss keenly, believe me, but he made his own decision."

"Hm," I grunted. I was in no mood to hear this.

"You must make amends. The Justice is not himself. I have not known him for long, but that is enough to see. He is distracted. He is having to work twice as hard, but he has half the help. Bressinger does what he can, but he is a blunt tool, not suited to detailed think-work. He is more acclimated to removing heads than using his own. I have given Sir Konrad the men I can spare, but they hardly meet his requirements. He needs you, Helena. His head is elsewhere. He needs you by his side, working with him. I do not think you appreciate how much he depends on you."

I shook my head. "He does not."

"He does!" Sir Radomir said emphatically. "It is not just your labours he misses; it is your company, too. You are many things to him. He will never ask you to come back. He respects you and your decision too much, and he would prefer your happiness over his own. But I know that he greatly fears that his relationship with you has soured too much to be repaired. And if I may add, I think the world of lawkeeping will be the lesser if you decide to leave it behind."

I didn't want to hear Sir Radomir's words, but I couldn't ignore them. And, as with Bressinger's words before, they resonated with me in a way that I wished they hadn't.

"I will think on it," I said.

"That is all I ask," Sir Radomir replied, as we reached the courthouse. "Come," he said, "they are in the vaults."

≈

Vonvalt and August were huddled in a dark, ill-lit corner of the cavernous record vaults of the courthouse. There was no one else down there, just shelves stacked with scrolls and codices, and reading benches for lawmen to use as they searched for precedents.

"Helena," August said as Sir Radomir left me with them. "I have heard of your exploits, and of your loss. Your bravery and your commitment to the cause of justice is to be highly commended."

"Thank you," I said, put off guard by this charm offensive.

August smiled sadly. "It is a cruel fate to lose a lover. I know your heart must ache. You can take some succour that his murderers will die."

"We have had full confessions from the three of them, as of this morning," Vonvalt said grimly. "Fischer, Bauer and Vogt. It will take but a little time to draw up the indictments. The trial will be nothing but a formality."

"Helena," August said seriously, cutting across me before I could probe further. "I want to discuss the séance you had with Fenland Graves."

I shivered. The vault seemed to darken. "I had hoped to forget about it," I said.

August nodded. "I understand that," she said, "but ..." She paused, looking for the right words. "The visions you had. The dreams. I fear they may be important."

"I have told Resi about the sequence," interjected Vonvalt. "About Lady Karol Frost strangling the two-headed wolf pup. And of Aegraxes' intervention."

"Did you see anything else?" August asked. She spoke softly, but there was an intensity in her eyes that made me feel frightened.

"No, just the marshland, and the funnel in the sky," I said, and I told her everything I had seen in as much detail as I could. Once I was finished, she looked grim. She sat back, thinking for a moment.

"Many years ago, I was undertaking some research into the afterlife in the Law Library in Sova," she said. "I was reading specifically about Kane, and the Great Gvòrod Plague. Do you know of what I speak?"

"I have heard of Kane," I said. "Not the plague."

"Then you have not been paying attention in my lessons," Vonvalt said sternly. Both August and I ignored him.

"You'll know then that he was a Justice and one of our wisest and most learned jurists," August said. "He died about a century ago, but his works form something of an orthodoxy which under-pin much of the Order's practices to this day. Justice Kane was also one of the Order's best necromancers. Legend has it that he could commune with the dead as easily and casually as you and I are speaking now."

"I can think of nothing worse," I said.

Vonvalt and August exchanged a brief look. "It is not always so upsetting," she said. "Graves was a rare case."

"The Great Plague of Gvòrod was a famine that ravaged the Gvòrod Steppe," Vonvalt said, eager to press on. "A cloud of locusts so thick they blotted out the sky consumed every acre of crop for five hundred miles. Thousands perished. It changed the nature and course of the Gvòrod Empire for ever, ending the Gevennah Dynasty and leaving its western city states to be subsumed by the Kova Confederation."

"I don't—" I started, but August interrupted me.

"Justice Kane had conducted a séance about a year before with Princess Bayarma at the behest of her husband. The woman had perished in childbirth. During the séance, Aegraxes – the

Trickster, if you hold to the Neman gods – spoke to Kane in the same way he spoke to Sir Konrad a few weeks ago. He gave Kane a glimpse of the future, a . . . sequence of visions, if you will, each rife with symbolism. The significance of these visions was only apparent many months later, after the plague itself had come to pass, and Kane spent much of the rest of his life theorising about the spirit dimension and the practice of divination."

"Divination?" I asked.

August waved her hand like she might conjure up an explanation from thin air. "Looking at visions and symbols and deconstructing them so as to understand what the future might hold. Kane realised – too late – that he had been afforded a glimpse of the future. The death of Princess Bayarma had, through some extremely significant but unthinkably tangential way, led to the destruction of the Gvòrod Empire; and in conducting a séance with her, by crossing the bridge into the afterlife, Kane had become privy to great, world-shaping events. He called his theory that of *Entanglement* – the means by which necromancers can see the future because they have become entangled with the spirit of a historically significant person."

"And Graves is one such person?" I asked.

"Graves, Bauer, Fischer, Lady Frost – any one of these people could be historically significant," August said. "We are talking about chains of causation that have their roots in the beginning of time, with each new branch throwing the entire future into a different direction."

"But why Lady Frost? There is no connexion between what happened in Rill and the criminal conspiracy in the Vale," Vonvalt said to August.

"There is at least one," I said.

Vonvalt looked at me sharply. "What?" he asked.

"Claver was corresponding with Fischer. I found letters in Fischer's undergarments drawer, concealed. 'Tis clear from at least those letters that Fischer was diverting the illicit funds sent to the kloster by Bauer to Claver and his Templars." I shrugged. "Fischer told me himself on the first night I was there that Claver had been visiting the kloster. And Claver's catching up with us on the Jägeland border was no accident. He was seeking you out. Fischer knew this."

"So, Claver and Fischer corresponded. Claver was probably corresponding with most obenpatrias in Haunersheim," Vonvalt said.

"But most obenpatrias in Haunersheim are unlikely to be operating large criminal enterprises in which noblewomen are murdered," August remarked. "If Fischer is close to Claver, and Claver is close to your enemies, they are not likely to abandon him to his fate."

"I think it perfectly likely that they will abandon him to his fate. Though I do admit that I am troubled that Claver was seeking me out," Vonvalt said. "Was it clear from the correspondence whether he was seeking me out personally, or did he just want to meet a Justice?"

"I don't know," I said. "It just said an Imperial Magistrate. But I got the sense that his goal was to learn more about the Order."

"Nema knows he asked us enough questions. And I, like a fool, obliged him."

"You could not have known his reasons for probing were nefarious," August said.

Vonvalt sighed. "No. Not that it particularly matters anyway; it sounds as though Kadlec is doing that job for us already – though I do feel as if we are drawing conclusions where none lie to be drawn."

"The connexion is *you*," August said. "You are the thing that links Rill with Galen's Vale."

"I link a thousand settlements across the Empire, if my presence is the only measure of the linkage."

"Think on it, Konrad," August said. "However you cut it, it all began in Rill, did it not? The disruption of the Draedist ritual;

Claver's anger that the peasants were not burned. It all stems from that. Had you not met Claver, or Sir Otmar, or if you had bypassed Rill entirely, either by accident or design, the place might never have been razed. Whether there is a connexion or not to the Bauer case is in many ways immaterial."

"There was one more thing," I said, "though I am loath to dredge my memory for it."

"What is it?" August asked sympathetically.

"Emilia," I said. "A girl in the kloster – Obenpatria Fischer's spy. She spoke the same words as Graves." I shuddered as I recalled it. It was as though my mind were fighting against me, trying to dislodge the memory and cast it away like a fox with a thorn in its paw. "Graves said . . . 'the kloster is a dark place – mine is a black future'."

Vonvalt's eyes widened slightly. "I recall that," he said. "I remember Graves saying those words. In fact, now that I think about it, he sounded like a maid when he said it."

"This girl," August said. "She said the exact same words or similar words?"

"The exact same words," I said. I felt like crying.

August sat back. "It is in keeping with what I have been saying. You are at the centre of something," she murmured to Vonvalt.

"Faith," Vonvalt muttered, drawing a hand down from his forehead to his chin.

"The image of Lady Frost strangling the two-headed wolf-cub – the Autun – is a stark warning that her death will lead to some harm to the Empire," August said. She turned back to me. "Perhaps even its destruction. When you communed with Graves, you were shown the future – or at least, a possible future. As Kane would theorise, you and Sir Konrad have become entangled."

I cleared my throat. "But surely it is all open to interpretation," I said, floundering for an explanation that was at least passably rational. "The strangling could mean . . . I don't know, *economic* strangulation. Perhaps there will be a blockade along the Gale, or the Kova, or even the mouth of the Jade Sea."

"Aye, it might mean that," August conceded.

"One thing is certain, Helena," Vonvalt said. "Whatever is happening, it would appear that our actions here in the Vale may have some future significance."

"Which is why I have been urging you to return to Sova," August said. "You *must* speak with Master Kadlec and the Emperor."

"I said, did I not?" Vonvalt replied testily. "We will be here another two or three days at most. A vast criminal enterprise has been operating out of that kloster for years. It is not a trifling matter that I can simply turn my back on." He gestured to me. "We know from Helena that Claver has spent at least some time with Obenpatria Fischer before leaving off on his proselytising, and that Fischer has been diverting money to the Savaran Templars. We would do well not to try and second guess every one of our actions from here on out. This connexion between Fischer and Claver may mean that foreclosing the investigation here in favour of tearing south to the capital may be as much the 'wrong' course of action as it may be the 'right' one. All we can do is what we have always done: ensure the supremacy of the common law. Everything else – justice, order, civilised society – stems from that one absolute."

"Just use the Voice on Fischer again and have it out now," August said. "If there is a deeper connexion between him and Claver you can find out the long and short of it today."

"If I use the Voice on any of them again their hearts will give out," Vonvalt said irritably. "They are half-dead as it is. They need time to recover for the trial."

August sighed mightily. She started shuffling together her effects. "I have changed my plans. I will remain here in the Vale until your business is concluded; then I shall accompany you south. Our voices in conjunction will be better than one alone."

"Do as you please," Vonvalt said.

August gave me an encouraging smile as she stood to leave. "I look forward to spending more time with you, Helena," she said. "You have a gift for our work. 'Tis no wonder Sir Konrad has given you his patronage."

"Thank you," I said, taken aback by such praise; but she was already leaving. A few moments later, it was just Vonvalt and me, sitting in uncomfortable silence.

"Why can Justice August not just return to Sova herself?" I asked eventually. "Why does she need you at all?"

Vonvalt wrinkled his lip. "Lady August does not enjoy the same status that I do," he said. "Although we are of the same seniority, she is seen by some as a little . . . eccentric."

"I see," I said.

"She can commune with animals," Vonvalt said. "She has a talent for it, more so than any other Justice. But it has affected her mind. She was not always this intense. She used to have a much straighter head on her shoulders." I thought he was going to say more about it, perhaps give some insight into their feelings for one another – for it was clear that August's concerns about the Order were not the only reasons she was hanging around – but after a few moments of thought, it was clear that he was finished.

Another silence seized the vaults. There was so much to be said, so much air to clear – and so little time.

Vonvalt took a deep breath. I braced myself. "I know you blame me for the death of Matas. That is underst—"

"I don't," I interrupted. My heart ached as I said it. I shook my head. "I don't blame you."

"There is a chain of causation here," Vonvalt said. "If I had not asked you to go to the kloster, he would not have come looking for you."

"I did not have to go to the kloster at all," I said. "I could have refused. I told Matas where I was going and I told him not to follow me. I . . ." I bit back tears. Emotion threatened to overwhelm me. "I was hard on him. We parted on bad terms."

Vonvalt looked at me through a sympathetic grimace. "That must be difficult," he said. "I'm sure he did not begrudge you that, at the end."

I nodded, not trusting myself to speak. "I just want him back," I said after a little while, and then broke down.

"Come, Helena," Vonvalt said, standing. He walked round the desk and crouched next to my chair. Then he did something I did not expect at all: he pulled me into an embrace.

In all our two years together, we had never been in contact like this. It felt odd and awkward, but at the same time comforting. He smelled like smoke and wine. I sobbed into his chest and he shushed me with a tenderness I did not think he was capable of.

Eventually, he pulled away. I could have held on to him for another hour. He poured me a large goblet of wine and pressed it into my hands.

"Here," he said. "Drink this. Wine helps. Sir Radomir will tell you that."

I could not help but laugh. I took a long draw of wine. Then I drained the goblet. Vonvalt was about to admonish me, but he could see I had fresh tears in my eyes.

"Will you hold me again?" I asked. My voice was barely a whisper.

Vonvalt nodded, and pulled me into an embrace. This time he did not let go.

❧

Vonvalt had taken over an empty chamber on the top floor of the courthouse, and it was there that I found myself half an hour later, eating a lunch of roasted duck on a trencher. The room was well-appointed with expensive furnishings, though the desk in the centre was piled high with books and scrolls, which gave the place a messy, disorganised feel. Several empty goblets and tankards lay scattered about the place, along with a plate of left-overs from the night before.

"It is a shame that the Order expects me to try these men," Vonvalt said. Once again his pipe was in his hand, and whorls of grey smoke filled the room as he gesticulated. I think the leaf calmed his nerves. "It is not like it was ten years ago, when I could simply have had them hanged on my word alone. The times are changing. But, I have signed confessions from them all, which is why I am confident the matter can be disposed within a day or two." He looked out of the window for a moment, watching the hustle and bustle in the street. "It is just as well," he added after a while. "Sanja Bauer will not speak."

I looked up from my plate. "What?"

"She will not speak against her father," Vonvalt said. "She has no interest in the trial. She wants only to be left alone."

"How can she not give evidence?" I asked, incredulous. My mind immediately returned to that cell she had been kept in, the filthy conditions, the years of darkness and squalor and poor meals, the threat of assault . . . "The man is responsible for the death of her family!"

"It is not as uncommon as you might think," Vonvalt said. "She is a young girl and has been treated about as badly as it is possible to be treated. Now she cannot cope with life outside her cell. I am told by Sir Radomir that she sits in her room all day in silence and will not engage with a soul. He thinks that she has spent so long acclimating to her bondage that being rescued has unravelled her mind. I think he is right."

"Sweet faith," I whispered. "The poor girl." She had seemed so robust, at least before I had given the news about her mother. "Still, I can't believe that she would not want justice done. After what her father has done to her."

Vonvalt shrugged. A long career of dealing with these sorts of incidents had left him unemotional and detached. "The girl is more likely to harm our case than to help it. Her testimony would be confused, fractured ... perhaps even hostile. The defending lawmen would take it apart as surely as a physician dissecting a cadaver. In any event, I will not put her through it. The girl has endured enough."

I paused. "Defending lawmen?" I asked. "You mean they have representation?"

Vonvalt nodded. "Two purebred silvertongues, so I am informed. I have been asking around the mercantile courts for gossip. Pavlé Garb and Hendrik Beyers. Old stalwarts of the circuit with an impressive list of victories to their names. Decent and honest lawmen, I'm told, and powerful advocates. I think they relish the challenge of squaring off to an Imperial Justice too much to let their personal feelings towards their clients get in the way."

"But with the confessions, surely that poses no obstacle?"

"You know I do not like to tempt fate with these things," Vonvalt said, and I did – the man's only concession to superstition was the power of the jinx. "The signed confessions, obtained by my Voice and witnessed by Sir Radomir, should be the end of it. Were we fifty miles north, the men would have already hanged by now, for better or worse. But ... " He shrugged. "Now we are at the mercy of the court. It is not over until the jury convicts them and the warden passes sentence."

"Even so—"

"Yes, Helena," Vonvalt said, annoyed at my fate-tempting. "I expect them all to die very soon. But the men have nothing to gain by entering guilty pleas except the hangman's noose. They might as well gamble everything on a hearing, no matter how desperate it is. Procedure, if nothing else at all, is on their side."

"You will take the role of the Crown's lawman, then?" I asked. Even with the Sovan system of roving Justices, the majority of criminal trials still took place without them. Instead, lawmen representing both the Crown and the accused would present different versions of the case to a group of empanelled laypersons – a jury – and it was this panel who would decide on the matter of guilt. A local lord or professional warden would sit as an adjudicator and ensure that the matter was conducted in line with Sovan procedure, and pass the sentence if the accused were found guilty.

The presence of a Justice, who had the functions of lawman, juror and warden all rolled into one, butted awkwardly up against this structure and also, given their powers, rendered it somewhat unnecessary. It was why Justices tended to stick to the Imperial hinterlands, where the legal infrastructure was poor or non-existent and where they could deal with matters summarily.

Still, it was perfectly open to Vonvalt to take up the role of prosecuting lawman under the Law of Precedence, and here he had exercised that right. At least it meant the trial would be very short. It just vexed me that the three defendants were bothering to contest the proceedings at all in the face of such overwhelming evidence.

Vonvalt nodded. "The jury will decide whether the three are guilty or not, and so I must make sure I get a good run at them. Hammer it all home, make it watertight. Worry not, Helena; we will be on our way to Sova very soon."

"What did they say?" I asked. It occurred to me that despite the knowledge being within my grasp, I did not actually know what it was the men had confessed to doing. My curiosity suddenly overflowed. "What is it that they have been up to? Vogt, Bauer and Fischer?"

Vonvalt smiled at me. "You can hear all of that in my opening remarks the day after tomorrow," he said. He handed me a piece of parchment that had a list of precedents on it. "The law library in the vaults is well-stocked. It is mostly mercantile law, but they have some relatively recent volumes of criminal precedent. Fetch these for me, will you, and start drawing up the relevant parts. Quickly, now, Helena; there is a great deal of work to be done."

We worked all afternoon and well into the late evening. By the time we broke off to take some dinner in a nearby inn, the gates had closed for the night and the town was cold and quiet.

We sat in the inn's common room. Bressinger joined us for dinner, and Sir Radomir came afterwards to have a drink. After a few hours the barkeep left to go to bed in a huff, tired and resentful that we had kept him up; now the fire burned low in the grate and all four of us nursed mugs of cheap marsh ale.

"By Nema," Bressinger said as I finished summing up the indictments for each man and what it meant for them. "You are as sharp as a blade. These past few months have been like a whetstone to your mind."

I smiled and drank, trying to appear modest, but I knew he was right. It suited me. I had never done a trial like this before, involving serious crimes and a vast weight of evidence. It was also the talk of the town. It was an event. All trials were public under Sovan law, unless they involved secrets of state, and from the talk in the taverns it sounded like this one was going to be a carnival. I'd even heard that some merchants were delaying their departure so that they could catch a glimpse of a Justice in action.

"How do you feel about giving evidence?" I asked him. Given that all three of us were witnesses, Sovan procedure dictated that we all give our version of events in front of the jury.

"Bah," Bressinger said, waving me off. "I've done it a dozen times in Sir Konrad's service. 'Tis nothing to me but the job. Let the fancy men try and poke holes in my story."

I clenched and unclenched my hands. "I am nervous," I admitted. "I am tempted to take some wine beforehand."

"Don't," Vonvalt said sharply. "Do not do that. It is ammunition to the defending lawmen. You must keep a clear head. And take your time in answering questions. You will be surprised at how easily you are caught out. It is one thing to watch it being done, the examination of a witness; it is another entirely to be on the sharp end of it."

We all looked over as the door was flung open. Justice August stood in the doorway. A cool gust blew into the common room. She pulled the door closed and removed her cloak. Her eyes were red and she looked drawn and exhausted. There was an almost intangible air of eldritch power radiating off her.

"The barkeep has gone," Bressinger murmured uncertainly. "Help yourself to ale."

"When is the trial?" August asked without preamble.

"The day after tomorrow," Vonvalt replied.

"I have been watching the Eastmark of Haunersheim," August said. In the circumstances, I took this to mean she had been commanding animals like puppets: birds, foxes, wolves. "There is a host of men moving on Galen's Vale. Most bear the livery of Margrave Westenholtz."

Everyone suddenly straightened up, united in alarm.

"How many men?" Vonvalt asked, incredulous.

"Half a thousand, all in."

"Bloody Nema!" Sir Radomir growled, "'a host of men'? More like a fucking army!"

"From the east?" Vonvalt asked, cutting over the sheriff. "Roundstone?"

"Aye," August said. "They have been lodging with Baron Naumov. At least some of those among the host will be the baron's retainers."

"We knew Claver had been poking around Roundstone when you went up the Relay; we did not know he was conjuring up an army," Sir Radomir said. "Naumov has a reputation for piety, but I did not think it stretched to treason."

"The letters I found in Fischer's private apartment said that Claver had met with the baron," I said. "I did not think anything of it."

Vonvalt sat back, seeming to deflate slightly. "So. He has thrown his lot in with Westenholtz and Claver then."

"It would appear so," August said drily.

Bressinger grunted with disgust. "That is the problem with these old Sovan Hauners. They have spent too long in the Autun's jaws, soaking up the drool of their religion."

Vonvalt rubbed his face with his hands. "How far?"

"No more than a day or two. I will check again in the morning. I've not the energy to keep monitoring them now."

"Nema's tits," Sir Radomir growled. He let out a sigh that reeked so strongly of alcohol a naked flame would have set it alight. "He cannot mean to attack the town, surely?"

No one answered. We sat in silence for a few moments, letting this unwelcome development percolate around the group.

"How many men were in the garrison at Gormogon?" Vonvalt asked Bressinger and Sir Radomir. "When you went looking for Vogt?"

"They had quarters for a few hundred," said Bressinger. He shrugged. "But the interior may have been derelict for all we know. We were not there for long."

"We didn't clap eyes on more than a few dozen men," Sir Radomir added.

Vonvalt let out a frustrated sigh. "There were a hundred at Gresch, but it would take them three days to reach us at least – and that is assuming we could get the message to them immediately."

"What about further up the Tollish border?" August asked.

"The Westmark has no good roads," Sir Radomir said dismissively. "They are close, but the going is worse. A small company of light troops could get to us inside a week, maybe, but in large enough numbers to take on half a thousand men? It would take them a fortnight just to clear the Marches."

Vonvalt grimaced. He turned to August. "Do you have the energy to get messages out to the wayforts at Gresch and Gormogon? And Baron Hangmar at Weisbaum?"

"Aye," August said wearily. "But that is it. If I overtax myself, I will be of no use to anybody."

Vonvalt nodded. "I understand. Thank you, Resi." He thought for a moment, before turning back to Sir Radomir. "How many men do you command?"

"I don't like where this is going," Sir Radomir murmured.

"How many?" Vonvalt asked sharply.

"A hundred, all in," Sir Radomir replied. "Sir Konrad, you are not suggesting—"

"You are right," Vonvalt said. "I am not suggesting. I am ordering. Whatever happens in the next couple of days, those soldiers are not to enter this town."

≈

Our little party broke up not long after that. Sir Radomir returned to his house, wherever that was, and Bressinger made for Lord Sauter's. I elected to use the latrines before the walk back, and on my return through the inn I heard Vonvalt and August talking in low voices. Rather than continue, I crept up to the doorway, my curiosity getting the better of me.

"What do you mean to do?" I heard August ask Vonvalt.

"What do you mean?" Vonvalt replied.

"The Emperor must be told. This is getting out of hand."

"The Emperor will be told," Vonvalt said. His entire tone was different; calm and gentle. "I will have a message dispatched tonight bearing my personal seal."

"Never mind your personal *seal*. Present to him your person."

"I will not abandon Galen's Vale to Westenholtz," Vonvalt said. "I was the one who kicked the wasps' nest. I cannot be the only one to escape the sting."

I peered around the corner. I could not see their heads, for a beam obstructed my view, but I could see the rest of them.

"You do not mean to press on with the trial?" August said.

"Of course I do." Vonvalt shrugged. "If nothing else, it will pass the time."

"Do not jest with me."

"Come, Resi," Vonvalt said. He reached out and took her hands in his. I expected her to shake him off, but she did not, and I wondered what depth of feeling there was between them. Certainly, whatever the strength of their affection for one another, it had survived an absence of several years. And yet, despite all the recent bickering, they seemed so natural in one another's company. It was like seeing an old married couple together. I wondered whether Vonvalt's previous dismissals of her had been for my benefit alone.

They began to talk more quietly and tenderly, and I couldn't hear. It is just as well; I shouldn't have been spying in the first place, but now it felt doubly intrusive. Besides, seeing Vonvalt like this, displaying a tenderness which he had only shown to me on a handful of occasions, aroused a keen sense of jealousy in me, and I was suddenly eager to be out of the inn.

I tramped round the corner gracelessly and towards the main door, lifting my cloak off the peg there. Vonvalt took his hands away from August's the second I appeared. At the time I considered this a strange sort of triumph, though I would feel guilty about it later.

"Good night," I mumbled.

"Good night, Helena," they both replied, and I walked out into the biting cold and made for the mayor's house.

XXIV

Lions and Brothers

"He who asserts must prove."

FROM CATERHAUSER'S PILLARS
OF SOVAN CIVIL LAW

The desperate entreaties for help were sent, but the following day passed with no word from any would-be allies. Vonvalt, Bressinger and Sir Radomir, along with a handful of the town's serjeants and more martially minded council members, walked the walls and planned the town's defences, while I toiled away in the courthouse vaults in tense quiet, only pretending to work. By the end of the day, grief for Matas, fear of the approaching troops and uncertainty about the future of the Empire had frayed my nerves irretrievably; I ate meagrely and turned in having exchanged barely a word with anyone.

That night I had a wretched night's sleep. It felt like I had only finally just drifted off when I was roused, dry-eyed and blurry-headed, by Vonvalt. The man looked as though he had not slept at all, though whether it was because he had spent part of the night with August, or because he had been locked away in urgent meeting after urgent meeting for much of the rest of it, I did not know.

We put on our formal courtroom dress with a heavy sense of foreboding. Another hearty breakfast had been laid out but the only thing any of us took was small beer. The impending arrival of Westenholtz's men had cast a pall over us, making us all tense and irritable and diverting our minds from the task at hand. Lord Sauter put in a brief, sweaty appearance, bade us good fortune, then bustled off to the watch house, where Sir Radomir was briefing the Vale's meagre company of guards. No doubt the mayor regretted us ever having turned up.

We made our way to the courthouse. It was barely an hour after dawn and already there was a press of people outside its gothick frontage – and this in spite of the rumours of an approaching host. It was like the square on market day: people of all social classes filling the streets, trying to secure a place in the public gallery. Of August, there was no sign.

"Where is Justice August?" I asked as innocently as I could.

"She is up on the town walls, watching the Eastmark," Vonvalt replied.

"With birds?"

"Probably," Vonvalt muttered, and that was the end of the conversation.

We pushed through the crowd and the main doors. Beyond the threshold it was so quiet we could have been in another town. None but essential business was being conducted. Because of the disruption, many wardens had pushed their lists to evening hearings or postponed them altogether.

Warden Dietmar was the judge who was to hear our case, and he had reserved the building's largest courtroom for us. It was at the back of the courthouse, a large, rectangular chamber overlooked by a wooden bench on a raised dais. Above it hung an intricately carved and painted Sovan device – the Autun rampant, which put me immediately in mind of Lady Karol Frost.

Next to the warden's bench was a seat for the witness, and in front of the bench were two desks where the lawmen sat, one for the prosecutor and one for the defender. Of the latter there was no sign; the defending lawmen would be down in the gaol with the prisoners taking last-minute instructions.

The only other thing of note in the room was a separate area of seating for the empanelled laypersons, or the jury as they were known in modern Sovan parlance. I did not know how many had drawn duty for the trial, but given the severity of the charges it would be a high number, perhaps fifteen or twenty. A simple majority was needed to convict.

"Helena," Vonvalt said. He looked imperious in his formal robes. "Make sure you take a good note of what is said. I may need to refer back to it at short notice."

"Of course," I said.

"Good. Sit on the end there, will you?" he said, pointing to the furthest seat on the prosecutors' bench. I followed the line of his finger. I should have been thrilled: a seat on the prosecutors' bench. It was the first time I had been afforded such an honour, and in other circumstances I might have accepted this promotion with excitement, or even cocky indifference. As it was, I couldn't conjure up any emotion except trepidation.

My expression must have betrayed me, for he said, "Helena, it is not for you to worry about the approaching host. Put it from your mind for now. Just concentrate on taking notes, and giving your evidence. Understand?"

I nodded. "Yes," I said, though he might as well have said anything. I was hardly going to stop thinking about Westenholtz and his men.

There was little for me to do now but wait. Sir Radomir and Bressinger joined us a short while later, and they and Vonvalt murmured to one another while the courthouse was opened to the public and the inevitable flood of people came rushing in to secure the best seats. I did my best not to turn around and look, but I could still hear the excited conversation and the gasps and whispers, and glimpse the subtle and not-so-subtle nods and points to Vonvalt.

After a little while Warden Dietmar came out. He was a thin rake of a man, wizened and white-haired, with a face like melted wax. Everyone stood, and there was a notable drop in the volume of conversation at his appearance, but not silence. He waved everyone to sit and took his seat on the judicial bench, shuffling through some papers there while we all waited for the accused to appear.

We did not have to wait long. The warden called for silence several times before he got it. Bauer, Vogt and Fischer appeared – in their finest clothing – led by their defending advocates, Garb and Beyers and a town watchman. Garb was a portly man and red-faced, and wore a pair of small and expensive half-rimmed spectacles which told of a busy and profitable mercantile practice. Beyers was also overweight but not by much – stout, rather than portly – and was bald. He had a pronounced lean, like a vulture, and I wondered whether the man had a problem with his spine.

Last to enter were the laypersons that made up the jury. They filed in to little fanfare and took their seats in their allocated area, sixteen in total, which meant Vonvalt would have to convince nine of them – or eight, with the warden casting his vote to break the deadlock. Their appearance has long faded from my memory, but they would have been an ordinary, well-off collection of individuals, given those earning under a certain income were barred from sitting.

Sovan procedure dictated that, as a representative of the Crown, the prosecutor was accorded precedence and would speak first. Accordingly, it was to Vonvalt that Warden Dietmar directed his attention.

"Sir Konrad," he said in a heavy Hauner accent. "Welcome to our courts. It is a rare honour to have a Justice advocate here in the Vale."

"Thank you, Warden. I know that the Vale is as keen to see the Emperor's justice done as I am," Vonvalt said, reminding everyone of his only authority – Emperor Kzosic IV himself.

Dietmar nodded with a tolerant smile. "The defendants have informed me that they contest the indictments and are not guilty of the charges. Thus under the common law they are entitled to be tried by a jury of Sovan citizens. With that in mind, you may proceed with your opening remarks, Justice." Then he invoked the traditional phrase in High Saxan which preceded every trial and which translated as "be as lions in the courthouse, but as brothers in the common room", and which meant in essence that the lawmen were to be professionally courteous to one another.

Vonvalt paused deliberately for a moment, then turned to the jury. I fancied I could hear a general intake of breath.

"Ladies and gentlemen, I am Justice Sir Konrad Vonvalt. I am an Emperor's Justice, a member of the Imperial Order of the Magistratum and empowered by the Crown to investigate, using any and all means at my disposal, those crimes taking place within the borders of the Empire." He pointed to the defenders' bench. "I am before you today because of those three men there: Lord Leberecht Bauer, Obenpatria Ralf Fischer and Mr Zoran Vogt. These three men are responsible, ladies and gentlemen, for a litany of crimes so heinous that they deserve nothing less than death."

A murmur of excitement rippled through the courtroom. The defending lawmen, Garb and Beyers, shook their heads theatrically. The accused sat in stony, anxious silence. I wondered how they must have felt, knowing that in a few hours they could well be dangling from the hangman's noose.

"The tale I am about to tell, ladies and gentlemen, is not some flight of fancy, nor some lawman's conjecture. It is hard fact, solid truth pulled from these men's throats like a difficult calve. I have on the desk in front of me three signed and witnessed confessions, which together tell in detail the full extent of the criminal empire which these men are guilty of running. It matters not what these men say to you today, nor what inventive stories or concoctions they turn out to try and lessen their culpability. The fact stands that they each from their own mouths confessed to these crimes, and in the Emperor Lothar Kzosic IV's name, they should die for them."

My skin broke out in gooseflesh. I could feel Vonvalt's power of speech radiating out of him with that same eldritch energy that Justice August exuded. The jury looked as though they had been jolted by lightning.

"Our tale begins, ladies and gentlemen, two and a half years ago, with Mr Vogt making a trip to the bank. Mr Vogt's financial records will tell you that he went to the Guelan bank Konig and Keller Mercantile Trust, which specialises in shipping finance; but in fact he went to see Obenpatria Fischer in the kloster. Obenpatria Fischer had amassed quite a fortune from the generous handouts sent from the town's coffers, and he had decided to branch out into, shall we say, *investment*.

"Mr Vogt told Obenpatria Fischer that he required a large loan in order to cover the cost of a hundred tonnes of coarse grain. Mr Vogt knew that the Legions along the River Kova were ill-supplied and that the Autun quartermasters were paying over the odds for fodder. Mr Vogt proposed to purchase cheap grain and sell with a substantial margin. With the profits he could pay back Obenpatria Fischer with interest and still line his own pockets with a substantial sum. In fact the grain was so cheap that it was unfit for consumption, but that did not matter. All the men cared about was maximising their profit. Obenpatria Fischer readily agreed to the plan.

"Mr Vogt then did what any prudent fraudster would do: he

arranged to have the cargo guaranteed. Enter Lord Bauer, a well-known and successful figure working in the nascent but lucrative business of merchant assurance. I shall take a moment to explain what that is.

"Let us imagine, for a moment, that I have a shipment of . . . a hundred tonnes of coarse grain." There were some more scattered sniggers. This was what the modern Sovan court was all about, after all: theatre, dramatic and bombastic advocacy – mummery. Vonvalt played the wry man to devastating effect, deploying a joke here and there, getting the crowd on side and then suddenly eviscerating his witness as effectively as any sword swipe. "I want to ship my grain from the wharf here in Galen's Vale all the way to the Kova. It's a long journey and there are many different routes to take, each with its own perils. I might be faced with Grozodan pirates, or Northman raiders, or the Kova Confederation Navy. If I go by sea it will be quicker, but I run the risk of storms. If I go by river, it will be slower – perhaps too slow, and I may miss my delivery window.

"A gambling man would simply set sail and pray to Nema for the best. But luckily – or unluckily – I am not a gambling man. No, I would do what any sensible merchant would do and seek to have my cargo *guaranteed*. And in order to do this I would speak to a *guarantor*, one such as Lord Bauer. A trusted and well-known businessman, like Lord Bauer, would evaluate my ship, my crew, the cargo, my planned route and a dozen other factors, and using his practised eye he would offer to assure the cargo for me. In other words, ladies and gentlemen, I would pay Lord Bauer a sum of money, carefully weighed against the foreseeable risks of my journey, which would ensure that, were the cargo to be lost, Lord Bauer himself would pay me its agreed value as underwriter. A simple and effective transaction in which there are few losers, right?

"Except that that is *wrong*, in our case, because Lord Bauer is a devious, deceitful rogue!" He smacked his palm on the desk for each of the three final words, making half the courtroom start. One of the defending lawmen made to stand, but Vonvalt bade him sit back down with a dismissive wave of his hand. Such was the force of his power and authority that I think the lawman did it almost without thinking.

"Lord Bauer did not know the grain was spoiled of course, but it was his practice to pay a member of the crew to spy for him. It was just as well: that same accomplice informed Lord Bauer via a network of fast riders that Mr Vogt was concealing mouldy grain under good. Lord Bauer now realised that he was at risk of having to pay out under the guarantee – which, at the inflated prices the Imperial quartermasters were paying, would leave him substantially out of pocket. He therefore arranged to have the shipment impounded at the Kzosic Principality border by Imperial customs under the false pretext of Mr Vogt having arranged the incorrect import warrant.

"In doing this, Lord Bauer frustrated Mr Vogt and Obenpatria Fischer's plan on several levels. The first was to stop the grain reaching the Kova at all, which caused not just the conspirators' profit to evaporate, but left them to swallow the initial outlay too, since the grain was completely worthless and could not be sold on to anyone else. The second was to prevent Mr Vogt from claiming the price of the grain back under the terms of the guarantee. Lord Bauer, himself as crooked as a broken back, was able to do this by claiming that Mr Vogt's failure to arrange the correct import warrant invalidated the contract. The fraudsters had been themselves defrauded!"

"Preposterous," Vogt muttered.

"Preposterous!" Vonvalt roared, causing the room again to start. "Preposterous, Mr Vogt says, except we don't have to take my word for it; we can look at the complaint that Mr Vogt himself made to the watch right here in Galen's Vale!"

Here he pulled up the criminal complaints log from the watch house, the one I had pored over several weeks ago. He put his finger to the correct place and began to read.

'On the fifteenth day of the month of Golrich, Mr Zoran Vogt attended the watch house to lodge a complaint against Lord Bauer ... shipment held at Kzosic Principality customs house ... incorrect import warrant from Imperial customs ... Mr Vogt *adamant* he had arranged for the correct warrant ... delay caused termination of contract and left Mr Vogt in debt with Guelan bank ... *Mr Vogt convinced that Lord Bauer arranged for this to happen to withhold a significant guarantee payment.*'

He snapped the ledger closed and returned it to his bench. Sir Radomir moved it to one side. Consternation rippled through the room. "Two days later the complaint had been withdrawn. Mr Vogt had gone from adamant – *adamant* – to withdrawing the complaint entirely. What made him change his mind so completely and so quickly, and over so important a matter?

"It seems strange, does it not, ladies and gentlemen, that a man involved so heavily in a criminal enterprise would approach the town sheriff for satisfaction. The fact of the matter is, these two men were stupid and arrogant enough to believe that their criminal scheme was so beyond detection that they could afford to involve Imperial lawkeepers and still operate it with impunity." I watched the defendants bristle at this. One of the lawmen settled them with a subtle gesture.

"Of course, the pair quickly realised that Lord Bauer was as crooked as the two of them, and clearly a talented fraudster in his own right. The best way to recoup their losses was not to go through the Sovan justice system, but to recruit Lord Bauer and make common cause. How, then, to achieve this? Lord Bauer would never have gone willingly to join them. He had too good a scheme going on himself. But he was a family man. And family men always have a weakness that other, predatory men are quick to exploit."

Vonvalt paused, expertly feigning a kind of avuncular

disappointment. "Some of you may have heard of the death of Lord Bauer's son – perhaps you may even remember it. Taken by a pox, so the story ran. In fact, having exhumed the corpse, and having interrogated these men, we now know that the young boy was in fact murdered."

There were shocked gasps, followed by a hum of conversation. Bauer looked wretched, his comportment completely fractured. The other two remained impassive. I felt a surge of anger that made it difficult to concentrate. Bressinger, too, bristled.

"Quiet, please," Warden Dietmar said, and then, "Silence!"

The hubbub died like a pinched candle flame.

"He was killed by a blow to the head, by a thug employed by Fischer, to serve both as vengeance and a warning to Lord Bauer," Vonvalt continued. "And the message was clear: 'Lord Bauer, you have defrauded some very dangerous people'." He paused, and sighed theatrically. "And then, as if that were not enough, Sanja Bauer was abducted and held in the kloster vaults as further collateral."

There was another eruption, and another series of attempts by Warden Dietmar to silence the chamber. Vonvalt was happy to let the outcry run its course. The mob-hate it was generating could only help his case.

"Sanja Bauer is alive, but she is not here today," he said softly. "She is too exhausted and frightened out of her wits after having been kept a prisoner in the kloster for over two years. But do not be troubled by her absence; it does not bolster the defendants' case. Not only do I have their signed statements by which they confess to having abducted the girl, but I also have three Crown witnesses sitting here next to me who will all give evidence of what they have seen. My clerk here, posing as a novice, infiltrated the kloster and discovered Sanja Bauer living in a filthy gaol cell, half mad with fear. She will relay to you what Miss Bauer told her. You will hear how Sanja was snatched up, visited only occasionally by her father and otherwise left to rot, a different kind of guarantee to keep the man in line and ensure that he shared with his new compatriots the fruits of his assurance fraud – not to mention the fruits of the other criminal schemes the men devised going forwards.

"Lord Bauer was a prize worth taking such extreme measures for, ladies and gentlemen. Not only did he know how to manipulate the shipping trade to his own ends, he was also the town's treasurer. We have obtained a whole trove of ledgers confiscated from the treasury which clearly demonstrate regular and illicit transfers of money from Imperial funds to the kloster, and you will see more sworn statements from the mayor himself and other members of the town council about how these payments were an unauthorised application of this money. There was no effective oversight of Lord Bauer's use of these account books and it is clear he has been able to conceal the siphoning-off of Imperial funds for years, capably and willingly assisted by the assistant treasurer Fenland Graves." Vonvalt paused again. The next part I knew would be delicate.

"Ladies and gentlemen, I have spoken to Mr Graves myself, following his death." There was palpable consternation. There were some uneasy looks being exchanged, even ones of fear and disgust. I watched the defending lawmen take notes. I was still unsure of the wisdom in using the information over simply relying on the defendants' confessions. "I and my retainers attempted to apprehend the man. Unfortunately, he would not yield and suffered a sword cut to the chest from which he did not recover. You may have heard of the powers that I possess as a member of the Order of the Imperial Magistratum. Many rumours and stories surround these powers and their use and shroud them in mystery and fear. Ladies and gentlemen, do not be concerned with the manner of their exercise; concern yourselves only with the information they yield. By its very nature this information can come across as obscure, but to a practised ear like mine the words are loud and clear.

"Graves, when interrogated, warned us with his own tongue that the kloster was a 'dark place for dark deeds'. He referred to Sanja Bauer as the 'guest of a dangerous man', and the name of that man he referred to as the 'water hunter'. Well, it does not take a great mind to see that he was referring to a fisherman, or fisher – and there sits Obenpatria Fischer, the dangerous man to whom Graves was referring."

It was difficult to gauge the reaction to this truncated version of Graves's interrogation. Vonvalt had obviously cherrypicked the more salient points and left out the general horror of that night, but strangely, without the context, I felt that Graves's words seemed to have less impact. Some in the room clearly thought that these excerpts were small rubies in what was otherwise a large shit, but more still seemed discomfited by it all. Irrespective, Vonvalt ploughed on.

"But Fischer, Vogt and Bauer, for all they were bound together by fate, were not easy bedfellows. Fischer was angry that Mr Vogt nearly lost him a substantial amount of coin on their very first attempt at misappropriating Imperial funds. You have heard, too, that Sanja Bauer was held captive in the kloster to keep Lord Bauer in line. Ladies and gentlemen, in my long experience of enforcing Sovan law across the provinces and investigating and prosecuting criminal matters, I have seen plenty of similar examples: men who dislike, perhaps even loathe one another, but who have no choice but to continue, bound by the circumstances they themselves have engineered. These three men are no different. They are not friends. That does not mean they cannot be conspirators. Bear that in mind when you come to hear what they have to say." He raised his voice. "For friends do not murder one another's wives; co-conspirators do. Lady Natalija Bauer, a popular, beautiful and kind woman, was last seen alive shopping for Grozodan velvets on Thread Street. Green velvet to make a dress in the latest fashion." I could see what Vonvalt was doing now. He was adding in little details, reminding the panel that ultimately

Natalija Bauer had been a living, breathing person, and not just a cadaver to be discussed in a courtroom. "Many of you knew her by sight. Some of you knew her socially. I did not have the pleasure to meet her – though I did have the great displeasure of examining her murdered body – and I understand that she was well-liked and good-natured."

This was not entirely true. I understood from what I had heard that Lady Bauer was sullen and withdrawn since her son was killed and Sanja was abducted. Living in constant fear of her husband and grief for her children had crushed her spirit and rendered her a quiet, meek woman.

"She was killed, ladies and gentlemen, on the orders of Obenpatria Fischer and Zoran Vogt." He pointed to the men as he said it. Fischer shrank back as though Vonvalt had aimed a loaded crossbow at him. Vogt remained impassive. "Why? Because for two years Bauer's daughter was these men's captive. *Two years.* For two years, Lord Bauer felt the stress and strain of his empty house, his murdered son, his abducted daughter, and he tried to do something about it. He began to lay plans to break her free of the kloster, and at the same time, break the chains that bound him to Fischer and Vogt.

"Except, foolishly, he had forgotten the full measure of his co-conspirators' wrath. Over the course of two years, he had come to mistake the nature of their relationship. He had forgotten the well-worn adage that there is no honour among thieves. It did not matter how good a job he did for them, how much money he made for them. They would go to almost any length to keep him bound to them. After all, a word in the right ear and Lord Bauer could undo them completely. In the two years since the abduction and imprisonment of Sanja Bauer, the three men had together built up a large criminal empire. Fischer's secret accounts tell of vast holdings of ill-gotten land and goods all guarded by a network of criminal enforcers. For a greedy, unscrupulous man, it is too much to give away."

Vonvalt paused. He was reaching the end of his opening remarks now. When he spoke, it was in a voice pregnant with dismay.

"Lady Bauer was murdered by Zoran Vogt and Ralf Fischer, ladies and gentlemen, on their instruction. She was struck brutally by a man wielding a heavy object – the very same man who two years before had murdered her son. Think on it for a moment: a noblewoman, returning from a shopping trip, taken from the street and smashed around the head by a club. We can only hope that the blow killed her outright, rather than the waters of the ice-cold Gale from which she was pulled."

Vonvalt adjusted his robes, pausing to let the horror of Lady Bauer's murder sink in. "Lord Bauer, insensible with rage, went to Sheriff Radomir and accused Mr Vogt of having his wife killed. For the first time in a long time, Lord Bauer was telling the truth. But, once he had calmed down, he withdrew the complaint. For what choice did he have? His daughter, now the only surviving member of his family, remained a hostage in the kloster. If he were to unravel everything, there is no doubt she too would be killed – or worse. And besides, he bore at least some responsibility for the death of his wife along with Fischer and Vogt. To involve Imperial lawmen in the matter now would be to guarantee his own execution as well as theirs – and Lord Bauer is a coward, ladies and gentlemen, I think that is very much in evidence.

"It seems strange to say this, but the man who struck the physical blow against Natalija Bauer is of no importance in this trial. A mere thug posing as a monk, he was killed but a few days ago by Sir Radomir's men as they stormed the kloster. No, what we are concerned with is these three men here, who, through their common enterprise, may as well have wielded the club themselves. In an indictment for conspiracy, all men may have played different roles, but without their involvement, the ultimate crime cannot have come to pass. They therefore share equal responsibility for its outcome, and you should have no hesitation in condemning them for the senseless and brutal death of this poor woman."

He finished his speech to stunned silence. I didn't know if anyone in the room had been treated to such a forceful bout of advocacy before. It is difficult to convey in words alone the power behind it; I have recreated his speech here from my notes and memory, but how it felt to be in the presence of it . . . it was as though his words themselves had a life of their own, each one a spirit that filled the air with an arcane power.

Eventually, Warden Dietmar stirred.

"Thank you, Justice," he said. Vonvalt had been speaking for a long time, and the warden had been as enraptured by the account as everyone else in the room.

He turned to the bench where the defending lawmen sat. "Sirs; the court is ready to hear your witnesses' rebuttal."

It was Garb, the fatter of the two defending lawmen, who stood up to speak. He cleared his throat with an almighty rumble before gripping his robes in his pudgy hands.

"Ladies and gentlemen, Warden, I do not propose to take up a huge deal of everyone's time like my friend Justice Sir Konrad here," he said. He had a naturally booming tone, one that carried like a roll of thunder effortlessly across the room. Whereas Vonvalt had an affected Saxan accent, an aristocratic Imperial inflection which marked him out as high-born – though which occasionally slipped to eastern Jägelander when he was particularly exercised – Garb had a distinct Hauner twang and was the bass to Vonvalt's baritone. Though I hated to admit it, it was an authoritative and authentic voice.

"Sir Konrad has made much of these men's alleged confessions," he said. "You will of course make up your own mind on the evidence that you hear in due course," he continued, "but before we hear from the various witnesses, I would like to make a few opening remarks of my own.

"The first thing I want to say is this. Justice Sir Konrad is a member of the Imperial Order of the Magistratum. It is an old and powerful organisation based in Sova. Their ways are arcane, and their powers – frankly – are terrifying. Pay attention to the evidence Sir Konrad presents: the words of a dead man, killed by the Justice's own retainer. Words forcefully pulled from a corpse's mouth as his soul struggles to rest in the afterlife.

"Ladies and gentlemen, I do not know about you, but these powers, these prophetic words from a dead man's throat . . . they confuse and frighten me, and require a great deal of interpretation to make any sense of them. Describing the kloster as a 'dark place' may equally mean it is a place of poor lighting than a place of evil!" This caused the room to erupt in laughter. Vonvalt had anticipated this line of attack as regarded Graves's words, and wasn't particularly troubled by Garb's sarcasm. It bothered me more that we had all endured so much mental distress for so little currency at trial.

"It is the same matter with these confessions," Garb continued. "These pieces of paper which Sir Konrad flaunts in front of you. They were obtained by a power known as 'the Emperor's Voice'. Perhaps you are not familiar with this power, but I have done some research into it. 'Tis the power, members of the jury, to compel a man to speak. Sir Konrad need only channel his eldritch abilities and a man will be forced to speak . . . well, whatever a Justice wants him to speak, is that not right?"

Vonvalt did not launch to his feet with the vulgarity of the outraged; rather, he did it with the measured deliberateness of offended authority.

"Warden," he said, but with his eyes on Garb, and his words came out like a sword forged from ice. "I am sure that my friend did not mean to offend the Imperial Crown as profoundly as he in fact did with his last remark. Nonetheless, I invite him to withdraw it. If he has indeed done his research as he claims, then he will know as well as anyone else that the Emperor's Voice compels a man to speak only the truth as he sees it. I can no more twist a man to speak 'whatever I want' as I can wring blood from a stone."

Garb's mask slipped ever so slightly, and he had to catch his words a second time before he could get the sentence out. "An injudicious choice of language, Warden," he said to the equally alarmed adjudicator. "I withdraw the remark."

"Have you satisfaction, Justice?" Dietmar asked.

Vonvalt offered a thin smile. "Indeed," he said, and resumed his seat. A moment later, a liveried messenger who had been moving subtly up the edge of the courtroom took the opportunity to bend Vonvalt's ear. Vonvalt frowned as the man spoke quickly and quietly and then withdrew.

"What is the matter?" Bressinger asked, but Vonvalt ignored him and stood up, interrupting Garb once more.

"My apologies, Warden, there is a matter which requires my urgent attention. May I request a recess?"

The warden frowned. "Justice, we are not an hour into the hearing. How long a recess do you require?"

"I'm afraid I will need the balance of the day."

I looked sharply up at Vonvalt. Once more, whisperings and mutters filled the air behind us. The defending lawmen tutted and rolled their eyes like idiots. The three defendants' expressions were inscrutable. Who knew how they were feeling? Was it an extra day's reprieve, or simply dragging out the inevitable?

"It is most irregular, Justice," Dietmar said, but it was merely for show. There was no way he could deny Vonvalt – or rather, *would* deny Vonvalt. Irrespective of whether the courts were supposed to be supplanting the Order of the Magistratum, few wardens in the Sovan Empire would stand their ground in the face of an Imperial Justice. Everyone in that courtroom – defending lawmen included – were dancing to Vonvalt's tune.

"Trust me, Warden, I would not request it if it were not important," Vonvalt said with a hint of impatience.

Dietmar sighed. "Very well, Justice." He turned to the defending lawmen. "We shall reconvene on the morrow."

"What's going on?" I asked Vonvalt as the room emptied.

"Not here," Vonvalt said. "Come; we've a few hours' ride ahead of us."

XXV

Evening the Odds

*"It is only now, in my twilight years, that I question
the actions I took in my youth. So many decisions
made, so many lives ended. One cannot help but
agonise over every little thing. This power is a curse,
and only the utterly foolish would seek it out."*

JUSTICE LADY ANDREA CONSTANCE

Vonvalt, Bressinger and I rode south on the Hauner road for a
few hours, then took one of its small and ill-kept branches in the
general direction of the Guelan border. The land here was rough
and fractured, not unlike the slopes of the Tolsburg Marches.
Uncultivated grassland and dark, damp forest clung to shallow
rolling hills, and everywhere large slabs of grey rock jutted
from the soil as though someone had swung a morningstar up
through the crust of the earth. In spite of the length of our journey, Vonvalt had not seen fit to divulge any of the details of our
destination or whom we were going to meet.

Our journey came to an end at the edge of an escarpment which overlooked a lengthy tract of farmland and, lost in the early afternoon haze, a small agricultural town. To continue south would have taken us to Weisbaum, the seat of Lord Hangmar, Baron of Osterlen and one of the few friendly noblemen within striking distance of Galen's Vale. To go north would take us to the Eastmark of Haunersheim and Roundstone, while to continue on east would bring us ultimately to the River Kova and, beyond, Kòvosk, or the Graveyard of the Empire, as it was known. It felt somehow prophetic that of the three options, two took us directly to enemies.

Just off to one side, a tent had been erected, though it was a far cry from the shelters one usually saw on the side of the road. This was a large, chamber-sized tent of sturdy waxed fabric, pitched so expertly it could have been a permanent structure. Next to it stood three horses, with a fourth cropping the grass fifty yards away. Further afield, several donkeys were being tended to by a muleteer. Men and women moved about the campsite tending to various tasks – several of them preparing a meal. A pair of lightly armoured guards carrying Sovan short-swords approached us as we drew near.

"Milord," one called out to us. "Your name please, sire?"

"Justice Sir Konrad Vonvalt. I am expected."

Almost immediately the tent flap was thrown open, revealing a man of middling age, with thinning dark-brown hair, shrewd features and a well-exercised frame. The inside of the tent must have been warm, for he was dressed in little more than a loose-fitting shirt and black breeches.

"That you are. Come in, my lord Justice," the man said.

We dismounted and followed him inside. I was amazed at what I saw. It was odd that such temporary accommodation could be made to look so permanent. The man, whoever he was, did not travel lightly, and was clearly exceptionally wealthy. Rugs, wooden chests, a bed and even a shrine to the Soldier were just a few of the concessions to comfort. In one corner I noticed a suit of armour, set behind a shield painted dark blue and with a heraldic creature I did not recognise; it looked for all the world like some kind of scaled badger, rendered in gold.

"'Tis a pangolin, miss," he said, following my eye – and perhaps reading my mind. "The creature on my shield. They are quite common in the lands of the Kasar. I squired there," he added, and with good reason, since few members of the Imperial aristocracy had the good fortune to spend much time among the wolfmen of the southern plains.

"It is quite striking," I said obligingly.

"The Imperial Herald thought so too," the man said. "My peers thought it flippant."

"Let us cut to it, Senator Jansen. You have called me away from important business," Vonvalt said.

I looked at Vonvalt. Sometimes his authority was manifested in overt, obvious ways – the sentencing and execution of a criminal, for example. But to focus on that aspect of his power was to forget that it was also exercised in other, more subtle ways, which were often as effective as the use of naked force. One of those ways, as it transpired, was to speak dismissively to one of the most powerful men in the Empire, for Jansen was no mere functionary – he was a member of the second Imperial Estate. And yet, in spite of this, he was forced to weather Vonvalt's displeasure as though he were a mere serving boy. If there was any doubt as to the pecking order in that tent, Vonvalt had established it with a brief verbal cue.

"I rather think the opposite is true," the senator said. He did not seem put out Vonvalt's tone. In fact, I got the sense that it would take rather a lot to rile him up. "Tymoteusz Jansen," he said for mine and Bressinger's benefit; and then, to the three of us: "Will you take some wine?"

Disarmed by the man's good humour, Vonvalt softened. "Yes, all right," he said.

We decloaked and sat around the table in the corner of the tent while Jansen filled four glasses. "You have the look of a Grozodan," he said, nodding to Bressinger. "This is a good Pjolskimis. Ten years ripe."

Bressinger offered a half-hearted smile. He seemed to be in a sour mood, as he often was when faced with authority. In spite of who he was and what he did, he would never shake his disdain for the Autun. "I'm afraid I've no nose for it."

"Shame," Jansen said. "Well, you will have to take it from me that this one is very good. Your health."

We toasted half-heartedly, and drank. The wine was exceptionally good.

"You have come directly from Sova?" Vonvalt asked.

"I have," Jansen said. "I, and most of the rest of the Senate, have had word that you are tangling with a Neman, Bartholomew Claver. The entire mummery is playing nicely into the hands of your enemies."

Vonvalt pinched the bridge of his nose. "I have just about had my fill of people coming and going and giving me advice about that damned man. He is a menace."

Jansen gestured to Vonvalt with his wine goblet. "He is much worse than that. The way the Nemans talk about him, you would think he was the earthly incarnation of the God Father Himself. Wherever he goes, money and converts come out. I do not think the Templars have ever seen such a swell in numbers."

"I know all too well what Bartholomew Claver is up to. You are not the first person to warn me of him. My intention is to finish prosecuting a case in Galen's Vale and then to head to Sova to undo the damage he and his ilk have wrought there."

"I am very glad to hear it," Jansen said, sincerely. "Given that you are well-informed, you will be aware then that the master of your order is making something of a fool of himself in the capital. It is an open secret that he is treating with the Mlyanars."

"How is it that the Mlyanars have gained so much power?" Vonvalt asked. He was as close to exasperation as he got. "They have been nothing but petty agitators for so many years."

"The ebb and flow of Imperial politics, Justice. The Magistratum has always tried to set itself above our grubby world. But I'm afraid Kadlec has breached the wall between our estates. As it transpires, it was rather a flimsy one."

Vonvalt thought for a moment. "A colleague of mine has been at pains to explain the situation to me, though I fear I still do not grasp its severity. Tell it to me as you see it; explain as though I were a child."

Jansen sighed. "'Tis both as tangled as a spider's web and yet as simple as day versus night." He held up a thumb. "The Haugenates: both the Emperor's familial line and those of us in the Senate who owe him our loyalty." Now he held up his index finger. "The Mlyanar Patricians: wealthy, landed and 'petty agitators for years'. For the longest time, a substantial minority in the Senate – now a precarious majority – and professional complainers." Now he held up his middle finger. "The Neman Church: much like your Magistratum – aloof, concerned only with ministering to the ever-expanding volume of Imperial subjects. And of course, complaining about having all of their magickal powers taken away." He let his hand drop, and shrugged. "An uneasy but functional equilibrium that, apparently, it takes little more than a single man to upset. The Mlyanars and the Savarans have of course historic ties, and with Claver sending rivers of gold and men and women into the Templar's coffers and ranks, the Mlyanars have become predatory. Emboldened. The Nemans see a way of getting their powers back, and have thrown their lot in with Claver, adopting him with retroactive effect, which is both awkward and amusing since they spent so long distancing themselves from him and his radicalism." Now he gripped his thumb and index finger together. "So you see, we Haugenates are being overwhelmed.

The Magistratum, which should be an ally, is being neutered by Kadlec's actions, infuriating the Emperor. His Imperial Majesty is all but alone."

Vonvalt took a drink of his wine. He thought for a moment. "I see the complexity; I do not see the simplicity."

"Power," Jansen said simply. "It is about power. Claver wants power for his Templars, and himself. The Nemans want their magickal powers back from the Order. The Mlyanars want to depose the Emperor while they control the Senate. They are like a room full of philosophers, with each of them considering themselves smarter than the next man. They all think they are about to outmanoeuvre one another, but the truth is we are heading for a calamitous fall. I am trying to do what I can to soften the blow, but one of our great institutions of state will not see out the year – of that I am confident. 'Tis like kicking out one of the legs from a stool; it does not take long for the thing to topple over."

Vonvalt sat quietly for a few minutes. He was no fool – though he had been foolish. Jansen had not told him anything August hadn't, and he was not blind to the weight of evidence as regarded the situation in Sova. Rather, for the longest time he had been trying to manage what he had considered to be competing priorities. Sitting in that tent with the senator, I think it finally dawned on him that he – like so many others – had badly miscalculated.

"Why is Kadlec treating with the Nemans?" Vonvalt asked. "He has always been a sensible, if uninspiring master. He paid his religious dues to the extent his office required it, but I never got the sense that he was a true believer."

"Kadlec has always been a Neman at heart," Jansen said, dismissive. "Particularly in his advancing years. I and many of my colleagues are not surprised to see he has chosen that particular ring in which to throw his hat. But it is not just Kadlec. There are plenty of Justices whom the Mlyanars have their claws in. Their biases are bleeding through into their work – finding against the Crown, cutting tithes for those lords in the Empire who are under the yoke of the Patricians, recusing themselves from common-law matters in favour of canonical adjudicators ... My retainers unearth secret networks between members of the Neman Church, the Mlyanars and the Magistratum near daily, all working to undermine the Emperor and transfer power to the Senate, which they seek to control."

Vonvalt remained admirably impassive, but I knew that hearing the senator dismiss so many Justices as corrupt would have both shocked and offended him. In Vonvalt's eyes, to be a Justice was to be beyond reproach, an exemplar of incorruptibility and fairhandedness. In that respect, he was quite naïve.

"Is it so bad?" Vonvalt asked eventually. He was in a surly, contrary mood, perhaps because Jansen was so demonstrably better-informed, and did what he often did when he felt like he was on the back foot: retreated to academic, juridical arguments where he could reassert his superiority. "A group of representatives ruling the Empire, rather than the whim of one man? A collection of men and women, tempering one another's more extreme predilections, governing what has become a gigantic and unwieldy nation?"

Jansen sent back, smiling humourlessly. "So, you are Kasivar now? Summoning sprites out of the ether to distract us from the main argument? Or are you actually suggesting that the Mlyanars stuffing the Senate with loyalists and putting a puppet on the throne – or worse, Claver himself – is a good thing? A collection of men and women the Mlyanars may be, but representatives they are not."

"You have been speaking to Resi," Vonvalt muttered. He was not used to being put in his place, and he reacted with uncharacteristic sullenness.

"Infrequently," Jansen said. "Why, has she been telling

you the same thing? Is she the colleague you referred to a moment ago?"

Vonvalt nodded once.

"I am surprised you required me to bolster her entreaties; her reputation is formidable."

"It is not a question of her intellect or her judgement," Vonvalt said. "Tell me why you have brought me here. This conversation, as enlightening as it has been, could have taken the form of a letter."

I could not help but feel bad for Justice August. Whatever the nature of Vonvalt's and her relationship – and I had no doubt that it was complex – Bressinger had been right: it had clearly coloured Vonvalt's opinion of the ill tidings she had brought with her from Guelich. My guess was that Vonvalt thought August's warnings had come from a place of concern for Vonvalt himself – from a place of love and affection – whereas Jansen's bore the hallmark of cold, hard and self-serving political machination. The former was easy to dismiss – quite wrongly, in the event – as inflated by sentiment; the latter, not so much.

"This is an appropriate juncture to discuss it actually, since we are already talking about her. I had word yesterday of your predicament in the Vale. A note carried by a blackbird, bearing Justice August's seal. A fortunate coincidence, since I have not made my travel plans widely known."

"You know, then, that the Mlyanars are already moving?" Vonvalt asked.

"I do now. I would not be surprised, however, if Westenholtz and the Baron of Roundstone are on a frolic of their own. Powerful though our enemies may be, I did not have the sense when I left Sova that the Mlyanars were in a position to take such bold action." He shrugged. "Either way, there is blood about to be shed."

"Am I to take it that you are in a position to help?" Vonvalt asked.

"I hope that I already have," Jansen said. "But a small piece of bad news first: there is no one to be taken from Gormogon – the garrison has already made west for Denholtz."

"That is bad news."

"But not fatal. What is much better news is that Lord Hangmar, Baron of Osterlen, is taking a company of Imperial soldiers from the Twenty-eighth Legion west from Weisbaum to replace them. His plan, as far as I am aware, is to hollow out the garrison at Gresch as well. If they are where they should be, and they have received my message, then this should give you a fairly sizeable force – larger, if you are able to supplement it with town watchmen and perhaps a company of volunteers."

Vonvalt leant forwards sharply. "How many men? Where are they?"

Jansen held out a hand for calm. "Only three hundred to Westenholtz's five, and these are garrisoneers, not the Emperor's finest. But they have some cavalry, and are well placed to help, as chance – or Nema – would have it."

"Why is Baron Hangmar travelling west at all?"

"They are staging at Gormogon in case more soldiers are required in Denholtz." He gestured dismissively. "Some pagan rebels or something – who knows? There are so many these days. What is important is that they can be spared. I have dispatched my fastest rider to catch up with them – would that I had Justice August's power, I would have sent a bird. Notwithstanding, I have no reason to think that my man will not succeed – if he has not already. With a tailwind and a bit of luck, Hangmar can reach the Vale inside a day or two."

"They might as well be marshalled on the Gvòrod Steppe if they cannot get to me inside of two days," Vonvalt said.

"Well, you know what they say about beggars. I had planned to make an appearance myself, have a tilt at some of your rebels, but I cannot say with honesty that you have enamoured me to your cause."

Vonvalt sighed. He took a long draw of wine. "I am sorry,

Tymoteusz. I am being ... extraordinarily ungrateful. There is no excuse."

The senator appeared to have no difficulty with accepting this apology. "It is just as well you are an old friend, or I might have been offended by your bad grace," he said wryly. "In any event, I hope it is enough to make a difference. Perhaps Westenholtz will be frightened off."

"I don't know," Vonvalt said uncertainly. "He acts as one who is extraordinarily comfortable in his position."

"He has plenty of allies in Sova; you may rest assured of that. Do you even know what it is the man is planning to do?"

"My guess is that the work I have undertaken in Galen's Vale will disrupt the amount of money his and Claver's scheme is receiving. I had not set out to do it, of course, though I am pleased that I have."

"What scheme is that?"

"Money being siphoned off from the town's treasury, funnelled through miscreants in the Neman kloster and ultimately making its way into the hands of the Templars. It is as twisted and complex as anything happening in Sova; would that I had more time, I would tell you about it in detail."

Jansen waved him off. "Then I am glad you do not have more time."

Vonvalt laughed despite himself. "And as for you yourself, why are you this far north of Sova? Has the Emperor favoured you with some governorship in the northern Haunersheim?"

"Would that he had," Jansen said. "It is a dangerous time to be a senator in Sova. I was on my way to Hasse, on some trivial diplomatic function. I must admit the thought of getting my sword red in the Vale sounds much more appealing. Westenholtz always was such a bastard."

Vonvalt smiled. "Thank you for your help, Tymoteusz. But please, do not put yourself in harm's way on my account. I cannot face being responsible for the death of a senator."

"Enough of that, mother hen," Jansen scolded. It was the first time I had seen his composure fracture. "I shall do as I please, for the glory of the Two-Headed Wolf."

Vonvalt looked grim. "I do not know what is going to happen in the next day or so – but of one thing I'm certain: there is going to be nothing glorious about it."

We made our farewells and parted ways with the senator and his retinue in the late afternoon. By the time we reached the Vale, it was well after dark, and I was exhausted from a hard day's riding.

"Mayor Sauter is looking for you," Sir Radomir called out to us as we trotted through the Veldelin Gate. He was standing up on the gatehouse, having spent the balance of the day preparing the town's defences. He looked grim and tired in the dancing firelight of the braziers.

Vonvalt sighed. I knew he had been avoiding Lord Sauter. The mayor was, understandably, very worried about what was going to happen to his town – but it did not make his constant questioning any less irritating.

"Helena, Dubine," Vonvalt said to us. "Head to the mayor's house. Tell him whatever he wants to know. As far as I am concerned, nothing we discussed this afternoon needs to be kept from him."

"Aye," Bressinger said gruffly.

"Where are you going?" I asked Vonvalt as we trotted past him.

"I am going to find Justice August, and see if she has seen anything further today," he said, somewhat guardedly.

"I wouldn't bother," Sir Radomir called down. "She is gone out ranging."

Vonvalt's mouth formed a thin line. "Fine. Then I will be in my chambers in the courthouse."

"You do not mean to continue with the trial tomorrow?" I asked, incredulous.

"Of course I do. I will not let Westenholtz put an end to everything we have worked so hard to achieve. It is precisely because he is on his way that we must continue. The law is the law; the day we abandon it for the sake of bloodshed is the day we abandon ourselves."

And with that, he made for the courthouse, leaving us to spend a long and sleepless night without his counsel.

XXVI

A Light to the Touchpaper

❦

The trial did indeed continue the following morning. I was not the only one who was surprised. Sir Radomir and his watchmen had spent all of the previous day stockpiling arrows and missiles, checking and testing the town gates (the Segamund Gate had been closed for the first time in years) and drafting companies of armed volunteers from the general population. These activities had hardly gone unnoticed.

But in spite of all this, the town's council had not issued any formal proclamation. After all, Westenholtz's actual intentions were not known. We had assumed the worst, but not everyone else had. For most, it was business as usual; and by the time we were back in the courthouse, the streets outside were thronged with the usual crowds going about their daily lives.

I sat at the prosecutors' bench with my ledger opened, scribbling away with my quill, though there was no conscious link between my mind and my hand. As on the day before, I could only focus on the threat of impending violence.

Garb was continuing very much where he had left off the previous day, attacking Vonvalt and the Order of the Magistratum rather than the case against his clients. It was a singularly irritating and unintellectual argument, and also entirely irrelevant, which was probably why it seemed to be having such a powerful effect on the courtroom.

"Think on it, as you sit there," he said in his rumbling basso. "By what right does this man, this *nobleman*, with his expensive estate on the Summit of the Prefects in Sova, judge my clients? He does not know the intricacies of life in Galen's Vale. His people are not our people; his ways are not our ways. He will seek to baffle and impress you with books written by members of his Order, and he will seek to turn you against my clients with intricate and clever points of law. He will urge you to hang these three men not because he is right, but because he thinks that the time he spent being tutored in philosophy and legal theory and other bookish pursuits makes him cleverer than you.

"Ladies and gentlemen, you are not beholden to him just because he is a Justice. Despite how he may come across, he is no better judge of character than you are. Trust your instincts; do not be swayed by his sorcerer's ways and impressive-sounding legal arguments. He is but a man, flesh and blood, no more an expert on what is right and wrong than you are."

These arguments were also infuriating because of the rank hypocrisy. Garb himself was a wealthy and educated man, and enjoyed all the privileges in life that came with those things; and yet he prattled on like he was a member of the lowliest class of villein, as though he were tilling the fields in between his trips to the courthouse. I could see through it, as could Vonvalt, who weathered this stream of sewage from the lawman imperturbably. What was worrying was that these risible appeals to the prejudices of the commonfolk in that room were actually working. Had the trial been allowed to continue for longer than it did, I would have been genuinely worried about the prospects of our success – and that in spite of the fact that we had three signed confessions.

". . . and let us not forget, ladies and gentlemen, that the very practice of having Justices as the ultimate arbiters of one's guilt is itself coming to an end – and with very good reason. Soon it will be the case that all people will be tried by a jury of their peers, rather than the whim of a single man or wom—"

He was cut off, and in any other circumstances I would have been thrilled. But it was the alarm bell from the watch house. Being only a building away from the courthouse, its crashing toll rang loud and clear in the crisp morning air and diverted everyone's attention.

Vonvalt turned sharply to Sir Radomir.

"The host from Roundstone," the sheriff said, his eyes wide. "They must be here."

The room filled with a sudden outburst of nervous chattering. We left the prosecutors' bench with neither permission nor ceremony and hurried outside. Immediately I saw that the Veldelin Gate had been lowered shut, its thick iron lattice barring all but the most well-equipped and determined besieger. Crowding atop the town walls were watchmen in the mustard-yellow and blue livery of Galen's Vale, the wan morning sun catching their kettle helms and pike tips with watery grey light. I saw, amid them, a solitary figure, motionless and clad in a tired-looking waxed cloak.

"There's Resi," Vonvalt said, pointing. Behind us, the courtroom crowd swelled from the building like wine gurgling out of a bottle neck.

"Get away, all of you!" Sir Radomir shouted. "Back to your homes, now!"

They dispersed, but slowly, each craning to see what was through the gate. They chattered away like idiots, pointing and clamouring like they were watching games in the Sovan arena. I recall being staggered by how untroubled they were, as though large armed hosts of men routinely pitched up at the town walls. But one has to remember that these people did not know what we knew; they had not been privy to our misgivings, nor did they know what great forces were at work within the Empire.

"Dubine, see that the accused are taken back to the gaol," Vonvalt said. "I don't want them slipping away in the confusion."

"Aye, sire," Bressinger replied.

"You two, come with me."

Sir Radomir and I followed Vonvalt down the street to the gatehouse.

"Make way, there," Sir Radomir shouted, as we made our way briskly up the stooped, narrow staircase that led to the top of the wall itself. Watchmen, uneasy to a man, parted to allow us through.

"Nema's blood," Vonvalt said as we reached the top of the wall. Beyond, wending its way down the grassy approach, was a host of five hundred armed and armoured men in the dark-blue livery of Margrave Westenholtz's household. About a quarter of the company was mounted; the rest tramped through the muddy fields on foot. They sang an old Hauner marching song as they walked, which carried on the cool morning breeze.

At the head of the host was Westenholtz himself, unmistakable atop his caparisoned white destrier and clad in a full suit of expensive black plate. He wore a dark blue surcoat over it which was embroidered with his device – a gull with its wings displayed.

Next to him, riding a palfrey, was Claver, looking ridiculous in his threadbare purple robes.

Vonvalt pushed up to August. Behind us, I was vaguely aware of Sir Radomir barking commands to his men.

"Resi," he said. "Are there more coming or is this it?"

August didn't stir. She stood as motionless as a statue, her eyes glassy and vacant. It did not take a Justice to sense that something was wrong.

"Resi," Vonvalt said, moving closer. He waved a hand in front of her eyes. I saw a few watchmen glance over at us nervously. "How long has she been like this?" Vonvalt demanded of the closest.

"For as long as I've been here," the man replied.

"And how long is that?"

"Since dawn, milord. Is something the matter? I assumed it was something to do with her powers."

Vonvalt waved the man off and took a deep breath.

"What's wrong?" I asked as he placed a hand on August's shoulder.

"Gods!" Vonvalt shouted, snatching his hand away. He clutched it like he'd just picked up a hot coal.

"What?" I shouted.

"They have me," August said. I looked over to the Justice. Still she remained motionless. "See the fox," she murmured. I watched a bead of sweat trickle down her forehead. Whatever it was that was happening, it was taking all of her effort and might to control it.

Vonvalt pressed himself up against the battlement. The advancing men were perhaps quarter of a mile away. I watched Vonvalt squint.

"There," he said, pointing. "Look at the man behind Westenholtz."

I raised my hand to shield my eyes, and followed the line of Vonvalt's finger.

"Yes," I said, confused. "I see it." A knight, riding behind Westenholtz, had a caged fox strapped to his saddle.

"Rune . . . of . . . Entrapment," August murmured.

"What is going on?" I asked. My heart was hammering. Surely the man was not about to storm Galen's Vale. Even with everything that had happened, it was unthinkable.

Vonvalt rubbed his face. I had not seen him look so worried

since . . . in fact, I think that was the first time I had seen him look properly, profoundly concerned. It frightened me more than the approaching soldiers.

"She has been using the fox to spy on the margrave's men as they approached," Vonvalt said. There was a sense of helplessness in his voice which made me shiver. "They have caught the fox and bound her mind within using the Rune of Entrapment." He waved his hand. "It's a tool in the *Grimoire Necromantia* for binding a soul before they can stray too far into the afterlife. I have never known it used in this way."

"How?" I asked. I felt sick. "How do they know how to use it?"

Vonvalt shook his head. "I do not know. It is something I am privy to only by virtue of my position and my powers. It is a rare enough thing even within the Order. The runes are ancient Draedist magicks."

I shuddered. I couldn't take my eyes off the approaching soldiers. "They are so powerful, and so quickly," I murmured. "How did this happen?"

"Either Master Kadlec has been trading away more than he has let on," Vonvalt said, "or there is someone else in the Order working against us." I saw his hands shaking with anger, and he gripped a stone merlon to steady himself. "They have gone much too far this time," he said. "I should not have tarried in the Vale. We will have an end to this, here and now."

The company was close, now, a straight-shot arrow's distance from the wall. Westenholtz held up a hand and the soldiers behind him clattered to a stop. Their song died away. Now, the only sound was the wind as it whistled across the embrasures and rustled the long grass.

Westenholtz urged his destrier forwards and raised his visor. Claver remained where he was.

"What is the meaning of this?" Vonvalt shouted down. His voice rolled across the field like late-summer thunder.

"You are a man of books and procedure," Westenholtz called

up. "So I shall give you a choice. We can do this your way, or . . ." He gestured expansively to the armed host behind him. ". . . we can do it mine."

"You have a hold over Justice August," Vonvalt snapped. "What you are doing is treason. Release her immediately. Then we shall talk."

Westenholtz ignored him. "Patria," he said, nodding to Claver. I could see that Claver had a heavy book of legal procedure in his hands. I recognised it: *The Conflict of Canon and Civil Law: Precedents and Procedure*, written by one of the Order's most celebrated old jurists, Marck Kandall.

"Obenpatria Fischer is in your custody, Justice," Westenholtz called up. "Has he confessed all?"

Vonvalt's fingers clenched. "He has. And he will die."

"Fischer is an obenpatria of the Order of Saint Jadranko," Claver shouted. His voice was thin and reedy in the wake of Westenholtz's. "His confession to the sins of fraud and murder render him a chattel of the Neman Church. Under Sovan canon law he falls within its exclusive jurisdiction, to be adjudged by a panel of canonical adjudicators."

"Don't be absurd," Vonvalt snapped. "Margrave Westenholtz, your presence here is an insult to the Emperor and rides roughshod over all notion of Sovan law and procedure. Remove yourself and your men from here at once!"

"Insulting the Emperor," Westenholtz said with dark amusement. He reached out his hand and one of his men placed a scroll – one I instantly recognised as the indictment-pending-execution I myself had drafted – in his gauntlet.

Westenholtz unfurled it with mock ceremony.

"'On this charge and pending execution of this indictment, Margrave Waldemar Westenholtz shall stand to be tried, on which date and by which manner to be determined, and if found guilty of the charge shall have no recourse but the Emperor's mercy.' My second insult to the Emperor, then, is it?"

"For Nema's sake, Margrave, explain yourself immediately!" Vonvalt roared. He was losing control of the situation, and I knew from past experience that that did not sit well with him.

"Your trial, these *proceedings*, such as they are and whatever stage they may be at, are over," Westenholtz said. "Obenpatria Fischer has confessed. He is subject to the canon law and will be taken into my custody. Patria Claver here and a panel of canonical adjudicators will decide the most appropriate sentence. Release him immediately."

"You talk of procedure and the law yet you spit in the face of the Emperor," Vonvalt shouted. "If you truly have legal submissions to make you will address them to me via the proper channels! Not at the head of an armed host of men!"

"I will not be lectured on due process by a man who took the head off one of my men on the Hauner road!" Westenholtz roared, suddenly furious. I winced. The men around me stirred.

"You have no authority here, Margrave," Vonvalt said. "Take your men and go."

"Sir Konrad, *this* is my authority," Westenholtz said, pulling his sword free of its scabbard.

"You threaten an Emperor's Justice with a blade? I knew you for a fool, Margrave, but this is something else. I had plenty of cause before, but you will hang for this alone."

Westenholtz shook his head condescendingly. "My dear Justice," he said, trading a vile grin with Claver. "You *really* ought to pay Sova a visit sometime. Remind me, when was the last time you were there?"

Vonvalt said nothing. I could see his jaw working. He should have paid closer attention to Justice August. He should have heeded her warning with greater alacrity, and he knew it.

Westenholtz sighed. "Here," he said, tossing the indictment with his free hand to Claver. The priest made a show of tearing it up and throwing it to the floor. "This is the difference between a piece of paper and steel. If you have not learned by now, you will soon enough." He turned to the knight behind him who had the caged fox strapped to his saddle. "Kill it," he said.

"No!" I shrieked.

"By Nema, Westenholtz, stop this madness immediately!" Vonvalt thundered in the Emperor's Voice. The margrave and Claver were unaffected, but the men around them faltered, hit by the force of it.

"For Nema's sake, give it here," Westenholtz snapped at the dazed knight. He wrestled the thrashing fox from the man's gauntlet.

Vonvalt turned desperately to August. "Resi, break free, you must!" he said frantically.

August strained. Sweat sheened her brow. "'Tis hopeless," she murmured through gritted teeth. "I haven't the power."

"Please!" Vonvalt said, gripping her arm. But the same force that had thrown him off before threw him off again. It was as though the rune which bound August was like a wall of fire to him.

"You . . . are a good man, Konrad. I was always so fond of you. Save the Order. See . . . that justice is done."

I turned back to Westenholtz. He pressed the blade to the fox's throat.

"Wait!" Vonvalt shouted over the battlement, his hands gripping the cold stone merlon. "Just wait a minute! Damn you, man, wait!"

But there was nothing he could say. Westenholtz drew the blade across the struggling animal's neck. It took but a moment. The thing screeched briefly, then died, its head almost completely severed. The margrave's features creased in distaste as rich arterial blood spurted out of the gash, staining his horse's caparison. He tossed the fox to the ground and wiped his sword.

I looked back to August. Her eyes went wide, she made a brief choking sound, then collapsed into Vonvalt's arms. Several watchmen leapt forwards to stop her cracking her head on the embrasure. For a moment I thought that she had died; then, with a hatefully hopeful heart, I thought that she had not only survived, but had managed to transfer her mind back into her human body. Yet after a few moments, the excruciating truth was laid bare. Her mind had gone, killed as surely as the fox which had housed it. Her eyes kept that glassy stare, the spark of consciousness extinguished. She had been transformed, in a stroke, into a drooling simpleton.

Vonvalt was overwhelmed. He sank to his knees and would do nothing but stroke August's face with a trembling hand and apologise over and over. It was not just the death of a close friend and former lover; it was what it represented. It was a return to the evil days of the Reichskrieg, when law and order came a distant second to who had the largest army. A time of evil men and dark deeds.

Vonvalt clearly had not expected matters to escalate to the state that they had reached. I think he truly believed that he could control Claver and Westenholtz, to eventually try them and bring them to justice. Perhaps one of the small rubies to be prised from the situation was that it killed off that naïveté in Vonvalt's mind – but, as I and many others would come to find, it killed off a few other of his better qualities too.

"Men of the town watch," Westenholtz called up to the battlement. "I am Waldemar Westenholtz, Margrave of Seaguard and a lord of Haunersheim. This is Patria Bartholomew Claver. We are here to take Obenpatria Fischer into custody. I do not know what your masters here have told you, but that is our sole concern. You need not fear me or my men. I ask only that you open the gates so we may recover our charge and leave."

"Don't you touch that fucking winch, Jakob Beekman!" Sir Radomir shouted to the anxious young lad manning the gate.

Westenholtz cocked his head in amusement. "And who are you, sir?" he called up.

"Fuck off!" Sir Radomir growled.

I watched Claver briefly bend the margrave's ear.

"Sheriff Radomir Dragić," Westenholtz said. "Your reputation is not that of a foolish man – but then, neither was Sir Konrad's. I have told you who I am."

"I don't give a fuck who you are," Sir Radomir shouted back. I looked at the sheriff with awe. I felt in that moment that I could follow him into the fires of Kasivar's realm. "Fischer is guilty of a list of crimes as long as my arm. The only place he's going is from his cell to the afterlife."

Westenholtz sighed. His amused expression gave way to one of intense irritation.

"Men of the town watch!" he called. "I have told you why I am here and who I seek. I am a fair man. If you open the gate now, all of your lives will be spared. There will be no punishments for disobeying the sheriff. I will recover the obenpatria and leave you all to get on with what remains of the day.

"You will see that behind me are five hundred soldiers and cavalrymen. They are Reichskrieg veterans to a man. If you deny me, I will smash that gate down and ensure that every last one of you is drawn and quartered. You do not stand a chance. Make your decision: do you obey your liege lord, or a Justice? Be quick about it; I have business elsewhere to attend to."

I looked around at the watchmen. A collection of young and old local men, well-equipped, but more accustomed to breaking up bar fights and keeping the curfew than fighting battles. Some looked nervous; others, terrified. At the time I felt angry and helpless, but looking back, I cannot blame them. They were constables with pikes, not soldiers.

"You guarantee our safety?" one of the serjeants called down.

Sir Radomir whirled on him. "Shut your fucking mouth, Leon!"

"On my honour," Westenholtz called back.

"Don't do it!" I found myself shouting. "He is an evil man and a liar! They have not the means to break down the gate!"

"Shut it, girl," another watchman spat.

"Aye," another chimed in. "I'm not getting killed for the sake of some crooked priest."

"Sir Konrad!" I shouted, but the man remained oblivious to my desperate entreaties. "Sir Radomir!"

"Go on then, Jakob. Open the gate," the serjeant shouted, at the same time that two of the watchmen grabbed Sir Radomir.

"In the name of Kasivar, leave it be!" Sir Radomir roared, struggling violently against the men holding him. "You idiots, you damn us all!"

"Shut up!"

"Get it open!"

"Come on, Jakob, turn the winch. Let's be done with this. 'Tis fucking freezing up here."

I watched with horror as the lad started slowly turning the winch. The gate began to rise. Westenholtz nodded, and motioned for his men to move up.

"Sir Konrad," I said, shaking his arm. The man ignored me, broken and inconsolable. "Sir Konrad, we need to leave!"

"Helena!" Sir Radomir hissed at me. "Get to Dubine!"

I looked at Sir Konrad, then back up at the sheriff.

"For fuck's sake," he snapped, rolling his eyes. "Go!"

"Nema's arse," I cursed. I ran across the wall, into the gate-house and down the steps. Behind me the gate clanked fully open. Westenholtz's soldiers advanced quickly. The watchmen might have been fooled, but if the margrave had truly wanted Fischer and Fischer alone, he didn't need five hundred soldiers to do it. There was only one way this was going to go.

I sprinted across the cobbles. Despite Sir Radomir's orders, there were still dozens of people and watchmen milling about the street, trying to catch a glimpse of what was happening.

"Move!" I shouted, shouldering my way through the crowds. A barrage of curses followed me as I pushed my way to the town gaol. I thrust the door open so hard the handle cracked the plaster on the wall behind.

"Dubine!" I shouted.

Bressinger appeared from the next room. "What?" he shouted, his features creased in confusion. "Where is Sir Konrad?"

Then we both turned sharply as the first screams and the ringing of steel on steel filled the air.

"What's going on?" Bressinger asked, his hand going to his sword hilt.

"Westenholtz murdered Lady August!" I said breathlessly. "They are coming to get Fischer!"

Bressinger's eyes were wide as he watched the margrave's soldiers pour into the town. Perhaps two dozen made it through before the watchmen had the presence of mind to let the gate fall closed again. Immediately the soldiers started fighting their way up the gatehouse stairs. I watched Sir Radomir frantically directing men to fight.

"What do we do?" I asked, breathless with fear.

"We must guard the prisoners," Bressinger said. "'Tis what Sir Konrad would expect."

I groaned, on the verge of frustrated tears. "Must we always stick so rigidly to the rules?"

Bressinger pulled out his dagger and handed it to me. His expression was firm. "I was a soldier in the Reichskrieg, Helena," he said. "I have seen what the world is like without the rules."

Then he slammed the door closed and barred it.

XXVII

A Taste of Battle

I do not know how long we waited in that damp, cold gaol, but
it could not have been more than a few minutes. I admit that I
spent most of the time crying and praying to Nema. The sounds
of fighting, of screaming, of swords and pikes clashing, of horses'
hooves on the cobblestones – all of it was a hellish cacophony that
drove me near insane.

Fischer and Vogt shouted to us the whole time from their cells
in the next room. Once they realised that Bressinger was not
going to simply execute them, and emboldened by their pending
rescue, they began to taunt us with all manner of threats. I shall
not waste expensive ink repeating them here, but suffice it to say
their words revealed plenty of their vile and ungodly natures. Of

the three of them, only Bauer remained silent. He was a broken man, full of hate and regret.

The first blow on the door made me scream out. After that, the pounding was loud and constant. I clutched the dagger until it felt as though the skin of my fingers would burst. The door bulged against its hinges, fracturing under the force of the battering. Bressinger placed himself between it and me, his Grozodan blade held out in front of him.

"Fear not, Helena," he said over his shoulder. "I will not let anything happen to you."

The door was finally smashed off its hinges. Armoured fingers yanked the splintered wood away and the bar was pulled from its brackets. Three of Westenholtz's men burst through the door, their surcoats already stained with blood. Beyond I watched cavalry charge through the streets, gleefully cutting down townsfolk.

Bressinger wasted no time. He dispatched the first man with a sword thrust through his eye socket. He collapsed to the floor like a sack of manure. The other two cursed violently. One of them swung his sword and landed a lucky blow on Bressinger's left arm which took it most of the way off. Bressinger roared as he killed the man in turn with a flick of his side-sword across the throat.

Bressinger shuffled backwards away from the third soldier, gasping and swearing in Grozodan as his arm swung lifelessly from a thin strip of flesh. Blood ran from the wound like a crimson brook. I realised in that moment that if we were to have any hope of surviving I would have to put myself in harm's way, as deeply offensive as it was to all my instincts. In a sudden flash of mad energy I screamed and charged the third soldier from the side, distracting him enough to allow Bressinger, with a classic Imperial sword gambit, to stab him under the armpit and straight into his heart. The soldier's eyes widened, and a large exhalation of his foul breath hit me in the face as he collapsed to the floor.

"*Nyiza!*" Bressinger swore, before letting out a stream of Grozodan I could not understand, and following it up with "Fuck it all!" in Saxan over and over again, looking at his severed arm with horror.

"Dubine!" I shouted. My body felt as though it had been struck by lightning. I was trembling and nauseous, but also felt a strange sense of exultation.

"Get it off," Bressinger said, nodding at his arm. "Quick, before I feel the pain of it!"

I backed away, revolted by the thought. "I can't," I murmured.

"You must!" Bressinger snapped. An appalling amount of blood was leaking from the wound, soaking his dangling arm and creating a large pool on the floor. "Quick, or I'll die!"

"Oh ... shit," I groaned. I darted forwards and quickly and inexpertly cut through the strip of flesh like I was a butcher slicing fillets. The arm flopped to the floor like a large dead trout. Blood splattered my dress and I felt my gorge rise. But I had no time to dwell on it.

"Behind you!" I managed. Another soldier appeared in the doorway. Bressinger parried the man's spear once, twice, then took the blade off the end of the haft. The man dropped it and tried to pull his sword from its scabbard, and Bressinger took the cap of his head off so that his brain was left steaming in the cold afternoon air like an opened boiled egg.

"Tie it off, quick!" Bressinger said, presenting the jetting stump to me again. With fumbling, shaking hands, I tore off a strip of my dress and tied it around the remains of his arm.

"Tighter!" Bressinger shouted. The veins on his neck were bulging. I could not imagine how much pain he was in. "Tighter!" he screamed.

I pulled the knot as tight as I could. The blood stopped trickling out. Bressinger's face looked eerily white, his lips blue. He turned and sat against the desk. "No. No, I think that's done for me," he said. He sounded tired.

"No," I said, frantic with fear and worry. "No, Dubine, you must be strong. Remember what you said, eh? That you wouldn't let anyone hurt me? Well how can you do that if you're dead?"

He smiled. "Aye, I said that." Then he shoved me out of the way as another man appeared in the doorway.

"Stop!" he shouted. I whirled around. It was Vonvalt. He had a watchman's sword in his hand and he had stripped off his formal robes. His white court blouse and breeches were stained with blood.

"Sir Konrad!" I shouted, a thrill of elation running through me.

"Dubine!" Vonvalt said, taking in the man's ghastly wound and the corpses of the soldiers lying about the place. He looked visibly dazed. "Are you all right?"

Bressinger actually emitted a short bark of laughter. "Aren't you supposed to be clever?"

"Your arm's off," Vonvalt said.

"Aye, now you have it. But the prisoners are alive."

Vonvalt gripped his old friend's good shoulder. His expression turned murderous. "Well done. We must move quickly. Sir Radomir's men are fighting bravely, but I do not know which way the day will go. It is only thanks to that expensive plate Sauter has clothed them all in that they have not all already perished."

He strode past me and into the chamber where the cells were. I heard bolts being slid open.

"Out!" he shouted. Fischer appeared in the doorway, looking frightened and confused. I took great pleasure in watching Bressinger grab him with his remaining hand and throw him across the room. Fischer tripped over the corpses and fell clumsily to the floor, crying out pathetically.

Then I froze. Bloodcurdling screams filled the air. For a moment I thought it was the battle cry of a pair of soldiers charging the gaol, but I quickly realised with horror that it was Bauer and Vogt.

"What?" I murmured to myself, frightened and confused. The

screaming stopped, replaced with gurgling and choking and the grotesque sound of steel on flesh.

I pushed my way into the next room. The strong smell of shit and blood hit me first, then the scene which engendered it. It is something I can remember with perfect clarity to this day. Vonvalt stood over the corpses of Bauer and Vogt. The men had been hacked to pieces. Their arms were in shreds where they'd tried vainly to defend themselves. Blood marked the walls in great arcs. It wasn't an execution, even an unlawful one; it was butchery.

"It is the Emperor's justice," Vonvalt said when he saw my horrified expression. "Fear not, Helena. I was within my rights. We do not have the time or strength to take them with us."

Now, finally, I was sick. The meagre breakfast I had eaten and half a mugful's worth of marsh ale sprayed the floor, adding to the mix of revolting smells. Vonvalt paid me no heed. He wiped his sword on the side of his leg and walked back into the main room.

"Sir Konrad—" I heard Bressinger start, but he was cut off. I turned and staggered back into the reception chamber, to see Vonvalt advancing on the cowering obenpatria.

"Don't," I called out hoarsely. It was strange. I thought I would relish in the deaths of these men. But this was evil work. The loss of August had seen Vonvalt come untethered from everything he believed in. I wanted no part in it. I would have seen both Vogt and Bauer released in an instant if it meant having the old Vonvalt back.

Vonvalt spat as he approached the miserable priest. *"What is your connexion with Claver?"* The Emperor's Voice hit Fischer like a battering ram. Blood jetted from the man's nose. He gasped.

"I have been paying him," he wheezed.

"How much?"

"Too – too much to say! *Nngg – thousands of marks!*"

"Why?"

"To fund an army of Templars!" Fischer screeched.

"*What is the purpose of this army?*" Vonvalt roared, but he had gone too far. Fischer clutched his chest and his eyes rolled back into his head.

"You've killed him," I whispered, tears streaming down my face.

"Don't be dramatic, Helena, I have done no such thing," Vonvalt said. He pointed his sword at the man's chest. "Look: he is still breathing."

He turned sharply as the sound of approaching battle reached us through the door.

"Nema," Vonvalt swore. He turned back to Fischer, then to the door again. He grimaced. "I would have more out the wretch."

"Please," I said, itching to leave the gaol house. "We need to go." I did not want to watch Vonvalt kill Fischer while he lay crumpled on the floor.

Vonvalt sighed, and rammed the sword into the scabbard hastily buckled about his hips. "We shall have to hope that he is still here when we return." He took a step towards me. "It is time to go." He made to grab my hand, but I pulled it away.

"What about Dubine?" I asked, my voice breaking. Vonvalt looked over to Bressinger, who had keeled over and was lying awkwardly on the table. Despite my best efforts, his shirt was soaked through with rich red blood and his skin was as white as a sheet. There was no doubt in my mind that the man was dead.

"He is gone," Vonvalt said, almost baffled by my question. He could have been talking about a complete stranger.

"We cannot leave him here," I said. The tears came now, running freely down my face. At least part of the reason I was crying was out of guilt, for however much I loved Bressinger, even I knew that we wouldn't make much headway dragging his heavy corpse through the streets.

Vonvalt looked at me askance. He gestured roughly to his old friend. "The man is dead, Helena. Unless you want to join him in the afterlife, we must leave immediately."

There was no denying Vonvalt's brutal logic, but I was appalled by it all the same. Reluctantly I held out my hand, and without another word, Vonvalt grasped me roughly by the wrist and pulled me through the splintered wooden door.

Outside it was exactly as chaotic as my imagination had predicted. Westenholtz's men had hacked through the meagre town watch and were now going about setting the place ablaze as though they were pagan rebels in the Northmark. The citizens of Galen's Vale, Sovans to a man, were being killed where they stood. Of Sir Radomir's volunteer companies there was no sign. I watched a woman of middling age walking as though in a daze, seemingly untouched until she turned and I saw that most of the side of her head had been sheared clean off by a cavalry sabre. Beyond the courthouse, I saw a small group of men-at-arms taunting a man on fire as he thrashed and screamed and vainly tried to douse the flames that were immolating him. Further on, near the Veldelin Gate, I saw a town watchman square off in a fit of reckless bravery against one of Westenholtz's armoured knights wielding a two-handed greatsword. The knight took both of the watchman's legs off in one terrible sweep, so quickly that the watchman's legs from the knees down were left standing upright while the rest of him clattered to the floor. He was dead before he hit the cobbles.

I had always wondered, listening to Vonvalt and Bressinger's brief and undetailed stories of the Reichskrieg, how I would react in such a situation. I was a resourceful person, and naturally brave, and I had always imagined myself fighting with valour. Besides, I had been in scrapes; the fight in Graves's office in the town treasury, for example, or just a few minutes before in the gaol with Bressinger. I had not performed incredible martial feats, but I hadn't run away.

But as it transpired, there was some quality to battle – or rather, a massacre, as it was at that point in time – which overrode one's senses entirely. I was overwhelmed in the face of these horrors. I could look at a corpse on a slab in a physician's basement without flinching, or watch an execution until the end. But these things, each appalling in its own way, were brief flashes in time, with one's mind hardened in advance. Watching Westenholtz's men brutalise the watchmen and citizens of Galen's Vale paralysed me. I do not think I had felt so vulnerable, felt such animalistic fear, as I did in those moments. One would think that the compulsion to flee would be overwhelming, but the reverse was true. My legs felt as though someone had attached lead weights to them, my arms felt weak and my chest felt heavy, as though each breath was a great labour. I realised then that I was as much a dead weight on Vonvalt as Bressinger's lifeless body back in the gaol.

"Helena, get down!" Vonvalt roared, and from the tone of his voice, not the first time. He tackled me as a sabre sang through the air where my neck had been but seconds before. In my reverie, I had not even heard the thunderous clattering of the destrier's hooves.

The impact of cobblestones against my elbows was what jolted me from my trance. I looked about wildly, my breath rasping in my ears. Vonvalt was lying on the floor next to me, rubbing the back of his head, and for a horrible moment I thought the sabre had nicked his skull. But he examined his hand, and to both his and my relief, there was no blood there.

"Come on," he said. He looked grim, as though attending to an unsavoury task, but never ruffled or frightened. His imperturbability was a foil to my own fear, and suddenly I understood how celebrated battlefield commanders were able to drive their soldiers to such incredible feats. Those two words, uttered with something approaching indifference, had a transformative effect on me. With every nerve in my body vibrating like a plucked string and my blood singing in my veins, I found myself latching onto him with an almost worshipful dependence. So many years after the event, I can still remember that charge of emotion, an even more powerful sense than that I had felt when watching Sir Radomir tell Westenholtz and his five hundred soldiers to fuck off from the town walls.

I pressed myself up off the ground and dashed after Vonvalt. Although initially it had looked as though Westenholtz's men had killed everyone in sight, now I saw that small fights were taking place all around us. Those few surviving watchmen, as well as disparate groups of armed volunteers, were trying desperately to stem the flow of Westenholtz's men into the town, though they were also paying a heavy price. For every corpse bearing Westenholtz's livery I saw, there were two or three citizens of the Vale around them.

We reached the end of the street, where a large limestone Neman temple reared into the sky. A man-at-arms made a wild thrust at Vonvalt with his pike, which Vonvalt cut in half with his short-sword. The key, he had once told me, was to get inside a pikeman's guard as quickly as possible and so to neutralise the advantage of range, and I watched this play out as Vonvalt barrelled into the man inexpertly but effectively, knocking him off his feet. From there it was an apparently simple matter of stabbing him repeatedly in the chest and neck until he died. It was a far cry from the expert swordplay I had seen Vonvalt employ in sparring sessions with Bressinger. Much like how I had seen Sir Radomir fighting in the kloster, real-life battles seemed to be chaotic and almost amateurish, with lots of clumsy hacking and stabbing and none of the flourish that abounded in training.

Another nearby knight turned away from a fresh corpse and made to move on Vonvalt. I screamed and without thinking threw my dagger at him. It hit his helmet hilt-first with a loud metallic clang, and bought Vonvalt a few valuable seconds in which he was able to right himself and stab the man just underneath the groin on the inside of the thigh. It was a vicious cut which saw the knight collapse onto his knees, and Vonvalt took his head off shortly after.

Vonvalt staggered back to his feet, sword in hand, heaving air deep into the pits of his lungs. I followed his gaze to see that the knights and men-at-arms of Westenholtz's company were regrouping. The Veldelin Gate was now fully open, the gatehouse and surrounding walls littered with bodies bearing the blue and mustard yellow of Galen's Vale. It was hopeless.

"This is it, isn't it?" I asked, entranced by the bright orange flames roiling into the grey sky. There was an eerie quiet. Those citizens who had been unfortunate enough to be in the street had been butchered, while the rest had fled or gone into hiding. Now, only the sounds of hooves and sabatons on cobblestones and the crackling of timber beams burning filled the cool, early-afternoon air.

"Yes, I should think so," Vonvalt said. I turned to him. I hadn't necessarily expected a rousing oration, but that threw me. I should have known better. Vonvalt was at his core an unsentimental and pragmatic man.

Our only route of escape, further into the town towards the eastern closure, was now blocked by a sizeable company of men-at-arms. With their initial bloodlust sated, and recognising Vonvalt for who he was, they made no move to engage him. Rather, they manoeuvred to box us in until more senior officers arrived.

"Helena," Vonvalt murmured. He was half-crouched in a ready position, sword gripped in his right hand, dirt and blood crusting a once-pristine white court blouse. Sweat dripped off his forehead; his hair and beard looked wild and unkempt. "I don't think I need to tell you that this will be unpleasant. They will go to great lengths to make this as painful and wretched a death as possible. And knowing soldiers as I do, I'm sorry to have to say that killing you will not be the first thing on their minds." He stood up fully, dropping the sword slightly. He looked me dead in the eye. "I can put an end to it now, if that is what you would prefer."

I couldn't believe what was happening. When I spoke, I felt as though I were choking. "You mean to *kill* me?" I asked. My voice sounded brittle, as though I were on the verge of insanity.

"It would be a mercy," Vonvalt said, calmly and patiently, as though he were explaining a complex point of law. "You would not feel a thing. Helena, please understand that nothing would break my heart more, but I would rather it was me, and cleanly. They will do unspeakable things to you."

I looked around for any avenue of escape, but of course there was nothing. "We may be out of it yet," I said uncertainly – desperately, even. The fact of the matter was, I did not want to be killed by Vonvalt or anybody else, in spite of the obvious truth of what he was saying.

Our attention was diverted to a procession of armoured knights making their way up the road towards us. They boxed in a diminutive figure which could only be Claver, though quite who they sought to protect him against Nema only knew.

"Sir Konrad," Claver called out as the knights parted to reveal him fully. He gestured about him with both hands held wide. "Look what your intransigence has brought on this town. Your heresy."

Vonvalt grimaced. He resumed his half-crouch, his grip on his sword tightening. "I have no intention of trading mindless jibes with you, priest," Vonvalt spat. "If mine is the last murder you need to accomplish here in order to conclude your godless business, get on with it."

Claver smirked. "You err, my lord Justice. Just as you once told me that you, and you alone, would decide on what made a mockery of the laws of Sova, so I, and I alone, will decide what is and what is not godless. And this—" he gestured to the burning buildings and hacked-up corpses around him "—this is the Goddess's work."

Vonvalt snorted with disgust. "I do not know what poison you have poured into these men's ears to get them to follow you so, but a blind man could see the Prince of Hell's red hand at work here." He pointed the tip of his sword at the company of knights surrounding Claver. "Come now; have your tame idiots dispatch me. I cannot bear to hear you squeaking like a rat any longer."

Claver drew himself up. He was losing this exchange, and it clearly infuriated him. Even with half a thousand soldiers at his back, he could not outdo Vonvalt's natural authority.

"What makes you think I want to kill you?" he said with affected amusement. "You are to accompany us back to Sova. An example must be made of you." He pretended to think for a second. "Perhaps a gibbet, strung from the Wolf Gate."

Vonvalt shifted slightly, and I knew instantly what was coming. Before I could say or do anything, Vonvalt was charging directly at Claver. It was clearly hopeless; it would achieve nothing except his own death, but of course that was the point.

An overdue scream was about to escape my throat, when Vonvalt stopped. He did not stop in the sense of deliberately abandoning his charge and slowing to a halt; nor did he stop because he had been killed, like a man impaled on the tip of the pike might stop dead. He simply . . . stopped, mid-stride, as though a giant invisible hand had fixed him in place.

A collective gasp went up from the assembled soldiers. I blinked, then rubbed my eyes. It was as though the turning of the world – as though time itself – had simply halted, but in a way that was localised entirely to Vonvalt. I looked around frantically to see what might have happened, until I noticed that Claver had taken on an expression of intense concentration. The veins in his forehead were bulging and his entire body was trembling, as though he was carrying an immense physical weight.

Vonvalt was locked in place much as August had been on the walls of the town. He too was trembling slightly, and I could see that his entire body was rigid, as though every single muscle had been engaged for maximum effort. Only his eyes seemed to be free of the spell. They rolled around in his skull like marbles, and for the first time in a long time, he looked truly panicked.

"Sir Konrad," I breathed, shaking my head in disbelief.

Then the impossible happened: Vonvalt began to rise into the air. Another gasp penetrated the air. Armour, swords and shields rattled as everyone watching took a step back. Faces were contorted into rictuses of disbelief and alarm. A strange throbbing sound filled the air like the rumbling of a distant earthquake. I could taste blood in my mouth. Eldritch energy radiated away from Claver like tendrils of intangible darkness. Whispers, like the chittering of insects, buzzed in my ears.

"You ... cannot even ... begin to imagine ... the ... horrors that await you," Claver gasped. His eyes had gone completely white. He shook as though he were having a seizure. Every vein in his body bulged, like his entire blood system was trying to tear free of his skin. What had Westenholtz's men unleashed on the world? What dark powers had they unfettered?

If there had been a strange, eerie quiet before, now there was complete silence. I knew that the Order of the Magistratum had a number of codices with powerful magicks contained between their covers, kept under lock and key in the Law Library in Sova; but the power to control a person with nothing but one's mind – it made Claver the most dangerous man in the known world. If there had been any lingering doubt about the importance of stopping him, it was completely obliterated in that moment.

And then everyone was jolted from this collective trance by the sound of a war horn, which punctured our shock like a dagger through a lung.

Baron Hangmar had finally arrived.

XXVIII

In Lady Bauer's Wake

The note carried through the late-afternoon air like the roar
of a gigantic beast. Soldiers and knights turned sharply. Claver,
already overtaxed, seemed almost relieved to release his devilish
grip, and Vonvalt collapsed to the cobblestones like the severed
counterweight of a trebuchet.

The horrified silence was now replaced by the unmistakable
rumble of hooves on earth, which did not take long to turn into
the clatter of hooves on cobbles; then more sounds – the whin-
nying of injured horses, the screams of smashed men, the ring
of steel against steel – carried on the air. From where we were
we could see none of it, but the story needed only sound for
the telling.

The soldiers around me rushed back down the road. Despite

the fact that Claver was on their side, they clearly preferred to launch themselves into the crucible of combat than spend any longer in his presence. In but a few seconds, the priest was abandoned, exhausted and bewildered. The position could not have reversed more fully.

I rushed to Vonvalt's side and crouched down next to him. To my immediate relief, he seemed intact. He was clearly exhausted, but whether from the fighting or from having been immobilised I did not know. I wiped his lank, sweat-soaked hair from his brow, and cradled his head as he surfaced to consciousness. A confusing mixture of emotions clashed in my heart. Not long before I had been revolted by his actions and the abandonment of his personal ethics. Now, with the very real threat of his death, I felt a cold, visceral fear. It was not just a fear of being alone again, as I had been in Muldau; my feelings for the man ran deeper, though it was not the time nor the place to explore their full nature.

"Sir Konrad?" I asked as his eyes opened. "Are you all right?"

"Kadlec," Vonvalt said. For a second I thought he had seen the man; I even looked around, as though the Master of the Order of the Magistratum was about to stride through the smoke thickening the air.

My features creased in confusion. "What?"

"Kadlec," Vonvalt said. He pressed himself into a sitting position, and recovered the sword that he had dropped nearby. "Kadlec has given them the old lore. The codices from the Master's Vaults." The sword grated against the cobbles as Vonvalt stood. "Those books have remained untouched for centuries – and with very good reason."

I took a step backwards as Vonvalt advanced on Claver, but haltingly, as one who has only recently recovered the use of his legs. Claver emitted a small squeal and tried to push himself away, but he seemed to be pinned in place by Vonvalt's glare. This time, however, there were no magicks involved – just the power of Vonvalt's cold fury.

"Bartholomew Claver," Vonvalt growled. "You have assaulted an Emperor's Justice. You have committed the crime of treason."

My attention was suddenly drawn to a commotion down the road. A detachment of knights on foot must have hived itself off from the enemy rear guard at the Veldelin Gate, and was now making its way back towards us. I recognised the man at the head of the group immediately: it was the unmistakable form of Waldemar Westenholtz in his black plate armour. But he was no longer resplendent, as he had been on the back of his caparisoned destrier in front of the town walls. Now his dark-blue surcoat was spattered with gore and mud, while his armour was gouged and scratched.

I do not know whether Vonvalt had seen Westenholtz and his men and was simply ignoring them, or whether he was so wrapped up in his own rage that he had not noticed them, but he continued to advance on Claver heedless. "By His Most Excellent Majesty the Emperor Kzosic IV, I, His Justice Sir Konrad Vonvalt, adjudge you guilty . . ."

"Sir Konrad!" Westenholtz called out, lifting the visor of his helmet. His features were grimly set. He turned to say something to the men around him, and they broke into a run.

Vonvalt was nearly on Claver now. It was impossible to know who would reach the priest first. I was tempted to snatch the short-sword out of Vonvalt's hand and finish the job myself, but as I had already learned, it required a vast store of courage to voluntarily place oneself in harm's way.

Vonvalt reached Claver and raised his sword. " . . . and sentence you to die."

Claver screamed as the sword whistled through the air towards his face. I also found myself screaming as the foremost of Westenholtz's knights closed with the pair. For a second it looked as though Vonvalt was going to kill Claver, and in doing so lose his own head; then I felt a tremendous blast of air at my back, and an armoured company of heavy cavalry thundered past me, obscuring my view of both Vonvalt and Claver.

I staggered backwards, overawed. I immediately recognised the pangolin device of Senator Jansen on a broad, dark-blue shield. One of the knights riding next to him wore a two-headed wolf pelt like a cloak, with each head, its lower jaw removed, fixed to the crown of his helmet. Instead of a lance, he carried a standard, a red bull's head against a white background, which must have been the device of Baron Hangmar.

They smashed bodily into Westenholtz and his men. This was no arcane, elemental power drawn from ancient magickal tomes or siphoned off from the astral planes; it was naked force, raw, powerful and brutal. I found the effect enthralling. I felt as though I were at the centre of a storm, the thunder exploding through me, energising my blood as powerfully as any herbologist's concoction. I was filled with the bizarre urge to laugh, as though I had been overstimulated by excitement.

I watched as the head of one of Westenholtz's knights was speared by a lance like an arrow through an apple and whisked cleanly from his shoulders. Another man was taken in the chest and the lance emerged through his back carrying what seemed like a gallon of viscera with it. A third was cut from shoulder to navel by a cavalry sabre and blood lashed the cobblestones behind him like water from a thrown pail. He took three halting steps before clattering bodily to the ground.

Westenholtz himself was battered to the cobbles by one of the gigantic destriers. The other knights around him were similarly thrown. The air was filled with the sound of crunching steel, breaking bones and the gruesome squelch of pulverised organs. I craned my neck, desperate to see whether Vonvalt had survived the onslaught unscathed, filled with a sudden horror that the mounted knights had mistaken him for another enemy and lopped him into uneven parts. Indeed, once the company of cavalry had passed, as unstoppable as a tidal wave, and run on into the enemy rear guard, I saw that Vonvalt was there, lying face down and covered in blood. Next to him was Claver, bewildered but unhurt.

"No!" I shrieked at this cosmic injustice, and started forwards – but halted so abruptly I nearly skidded over. A small group of soldiers had emerged from an alley and, having not sated their blood- and other lusts, immediately started moving towards me.

"Here, girl!" one of them shouted to me. In a strange way I was glad that he did, for it jolted me from my horrified stupor.

Now, finally, it was time to run. I cast one last forlorn look at Vonvalt's prostrate form, and then, with a hot feeling of guilt and shame, I turned tail and fled. I paused only to snatch a discarded short-sword from the cobbles outside the temple, though quite what I hoped to achieve with it I did not know.

I sprinted madly through the streets, making for the eastern closure. From the windows I heard people shouting at the soldiers to stop, even going so far as to throw things at them – bits of food, pots and pans, logs normally reserved for burning in fireplaces. These impromptu missiles clattered to the street, but their only effect was a mild annoyance. I recall at the time being angry that these people would not do more to help me, but of course, what could they do? It is always easy to begrudge people's inaction in situations such as this, without appreciating that they would fare no better against armed men.

Given that the soldiers were encumbered with armour, they were considerably slower than me, and the run for them much more tiresome. I should of course have ducked into a side street and hidden, or leveraged my superior knowledge of the town to lead them on a merry chase. But much like our would-be assassin from many weeks before, I found that my panicked flight was completely bereft of imagination. Looking at a map of Galen's Vale, one could have plotted my attempted escape with a more or less straight line, and in doing so I squandered any advantage in speed that I had. It seems ridiculous with hindsight, but of course I was not thinking clearly.

It was not long before I found myself running through the thick mud that preceded the River Gale for a hundred yards at the northern edge of the closure. Whereas before it had been mostly frozen and only occasionally soft, now, as we approached spring, it was like cake, engulfing my legs up to the calf. This part of the eastern closure was completely unmolested by the fighting, and had the town's bells, ringing in a demented chorus of panic, not sent everyone scurrying into their houses, one would be forgiven for thinking it was just another day.

I reached the bank of the Gale and turned, breath rasping in my throat, sword dangling uselessly in my grip. The soldiers were still doggedly approaching. There were only two of them now, though even just one would have been more than a match for me. Bressinger and Vonvalt had taught me the rudiments of swordplay, and sparring had formed an oft-neglected part of my syllabus, but I might as well have been a child with a toy sword against a Reichskrieg veteran.

Exhausted, frightened and with no hope of escape across the stinking, claggy mud, I lifted the short-sword up with trembling hands and held it out in front of me. I suddenly wished that I had taken Vonvalt up on his offer of a clean, quick death. There was no doubt in my mind about what I was about to endure. These men had not chased me simply to kill me.

But slowly, like ice held over a candle, I found my fear giving way to anger. I had been through so much over the course of my life, only for it to end ignominiously at the hands of a pair of murderers and would-be rapists. Moreover, it just didn't seem *right*. Not right in the sense of what was right and wrong – clearly these men were about to commit a sequence of heinous crimes. But Justice August had said that I had become entangled in great, world-shaping events. My spirit, in whatever form it took, was being whisked along the great currents of history. Being hacked to pieces in the mud did not sit comfortably with that theory.

I found myself steeled by this. I did not know how, but I was going to survive – I felt it. And even if I were not, I would make a damned good account of myself. I put aside Helena the Imperial clerk and brought forwards Helena the orphaned reprobate from Muldau. These men would regret having chased me down. I resolved to attack them with as much ferocity as I could muster.

"Come now, girl," the man closest to me said. He had the accent and features of a man from the Eastmark of Haunersheim, right on the border of the River Kova. In short, he was ugly and stupid, and it was with a profound sense of dismay that I realised that I might well be killed by such a person. "Drop the sword."

"Fuck off," I said breathlessly. Behind me I could hear the Gale gurgling and lapping against the muddy banks. I briefly turned my head, wondering if I would fare better in the water than the man who had tried to kill us with snakes.

"You'll freeze," the other soldier said.

"I rather freeze than be touched by you," I snapped.

"Ugh," the first man said, "fuck me blind, I hate Tolls. Your voice is like nails on slate. I think I'll cut your tongue out so I don't have to listen to you for the next few hours."

At least they wanted to take me alive, which gave me a small advantage. He would try and disarm me first, which meant attacking my sword rather than my body.

"I think I'll cut your cock off – if I can find it," I said. I lowered the sword so that it was pointing at the man's crotch, though I was careful to hold it inexpertly, as though it were a weight in my hand. If he thought he could disarm me easily, it would make his attempt lazy, which I could exploit. It would probably be the only chance I had to do anything.

"You are a mouthy bitch," he grunted. "I shall enjoy this."

The first man lunged at me. As I had predicted, he made to hit my sword out of my hand with a forceful right-to-left swipe. Instead of letting our blades clash, I let my own sword drop flat so that his passed through the air above it. It was a very neat little trick, and he let out a grunt of surprise as he overbalanced and then slipped on the mud.

I hadn't expected it at all, but I did not waste the opportunity.

The man was armoured, but his neck was exposed and I thrust into the meat of it. I was surprised and revolted at how far the sword went in. The tip of it must have been stopped by his neck-bone for it came to a stop against something hard. The man's eyes bulged and his face went bright red. He clawed at the wound ineffectually as I withdrew the blade, and he made the most awful gurgling and choking noises as blood rattled in his windpipe.

The second man shouted incoherently. Of course it was easy to assume that these two soldiers were soulless automatons, but for all they deserved death and hate, they experienced emotion as keenly as I did, and had probably been close friends. It made the second man reckless with anger, and he charged at me, this time smashing the sword out of my hand with ease and tackling me bodily down the bank of the Gale.

My head came to a stop so that my hair was actually in the river, with the rest of my body pointing back up the bank. I felt cold water soak into my clothes. The soldier pinned me with his armour-laden body so that his legs dug painfully into my thighs, and he raised his fists to beat me.

"Get the fuck off me!" I shrieked, struggling violently under-neath him. The mud here, already treacherously slippery, was coated with scum from the river, making it even greasier; and thanks to my frantic thrashing I was able to squirm part way out from under him. Unfortunately, this meant I slid further into the river, and I had to lift my head to stop the rancid waters from closing over my face.

The soldier grabbed a fistful of my dress and yanked me back out, and punched me square in the nose. Pain exploded through-out my face and neck as my head whip-cracked backwards. This time I fell bodily into the Gale, grasping fruitlessly at the mud about my waist.

It was no use. I could see immediately what Bressinger had been talking about all those weeks ago. Though it was approach-ing spring, the water was still perilously cold, and the breath was knocked immediately from my lungs. I could swim, but I was exhausted, and with a heavy, waterlogged dress I doubted I would be able to stay afloat for longer than half a minute. It was a strange quirk of fate that the death that had brought us to Galen's Vale – that of Lady Bauer – was the same death I was about to experience. It seemed almost poetic, like a pair of bookends to this wretched tale.

My grip on the bank began to fail. My fingers were like icicles as they sank into the cold mud, desperate for any purchase; but all I ended up doing was pulling clumps of the stuff into the water. Already I could feel those treacherous, infamous currents tugging at me. The effect was quite terrifying – so terrifying, in fact, that I abandoned all reason and even tried to get my murderer to help me.

"Please," I called out hoarsely.

"Shut up," was all the man said, and kicked me into the water.

I tried once again to pull myself out of the river, but my strength was flowing out of me in much the same way the Gale was flowing out of the town. The soldier seemed content to simply watch as I slowly succumbed, and I found myself despising him with every fibre of my being. Then I remembered what Vonvalt had said about people dying in a miasma of negative emotion and attracting predatory entities in the afterlife, and I was filled with a sudden and overwhelming sense of terror so strong that I begged the soldier to save me. I realised in that moment that any life was better than the death that awaited me.

"Please," I said. "I will do whatever you want. Just please don't let me die like this."

"Girl, there is nothing I want more in this world right now than to watch you drown," he replied.

They were his last words. A long, thin sword suddenly cut two-thirds of the way through his neck, and he collapsed to the floor. Slowly, almost sedately, his body slid into the river and sank like a stone.

"There is a battle on, and here I find you swimming,"

Bressinger said. Someone had dressed his wounds – or at least made a good go of it – but he still looked every bit the reanimated corpse. He reached out to me with his single remaining hand and dragged me unceremoniously back onto the mud. Then he sat down heavily, and took a few moments to catch his breath. "I told you I would not let anything happen to you."

"You have let a few things happen to me," I said.

He pulled a very Grozodan expression, a simultaneous down-turning of the corners of the mouth and a raising of the eyebrows that was part indifference, part *mea culpa*.

We sat without talking for a few minutes as the sounds of distant battle died away, and not long thereafter, the tolling of the bells also ceased. Not for the first time, a strange quiet filled the town. The woodsmoke smell of burning buildings and the sickly-sweet stench of burning corpses drifted in fits and starts on the breeze.

"You are not dead, then," I said, though my eyes remained on the River Gale.

"Not yet," he agreed.

I began to tremble all over as the horror and excitement of the day faded and I realised that I had survived it. A curious mixture of sorrow and elation overtook me, and I felt like laughing and crying all at once.

"You'll freeze," Bressinger remarked, looking at my soaking, muddy form. "We'd best get you in front of a fire. Nema knows there are enough of them about."

We stood with difficulty and made our way up the slippery bank using our hands and feet, clambering up the mud like apes. I paused at the crest to vomit, and Bressinger did his best to keep the hair on the left side of my head, that which had survived Mr Maquerink's shears, free of the sick. Although he did it roughly, it was Bressinger's attempt at tenderness.

"I do not feel well," I said, as though it were not obvious. "I cannot stop shaking."

Bressinger grunted. "It will pass," he said. "'Tis your first taste of battle." He nodded to the corpse of the first soldier who had made to attack me. "From the look of it you have acquitted yourself exceptionally. Sir Konrad will be proud."

"He is alive?" I asked, realising with no small measure of guilt that I had forgotten about him completely.

"Last I saw," Bressinger said. "Come on. I've no blood left to warm me."

"You've less body to keep warm, though," I said.

Bressinger barked out a laugh and shoved me. "You are a fine one. I'm glad you lived."

And with that, we trudged back across the mud as the afternoon turned into evening and the light drained from the sky.

XXIX

The Butcher's Bill

*"Power does things to a man's mind. It unlocks his baser
instincts which the process of civilisation has before
occluded. Powerful men are closer in mind to wild beasts
than they are to their supposed human inferiors."*

SIR WILLIAM THE HONEST

❧

"Tell me how he did it."

Westenholtz looked up. Stripped of all his expensive plate
armour, sallow from several days without food and with the
gaunt expression of one being slowly crushed under the weight
of a death sentence, he looked a far cry from the man who had
received us at Seaguard.

He briefly regarded Vonvalt and me. It was as though an
apothecary had managed to distil the very essence of contempt
and infuse him with it. He blinked a few times, slowly, and then
turned back to the window which sat high up in the gaolhouse
wall. The only view was of a fresh and featureless blue sky, but

he looked at it fixedly as though it were the most fascinating vista in the Empire.

"Tell me how he did it," Vonvalt asked again. There was no thunderous mental battering from the Emperor's Voice, nor a relentless barrage of angry questions as might have been put by Sir Radomir's investigators. He simply asked the same question over and over again.

Westenholtz invariably ignored us. Initially he had laughed with incredulity; then he had sneered. Then, as the energy left him, he simply turned away. It was easy to imagine what he was feeling. To be in such a position would have humbled any nobleman, let alone a man who had pretensions to the Imperial throne. But to add insult to injury, Vonvalt's father had taken the Highmark. Westenholtz was a purebred Sovan. The margrave's contempt for Vonvalt was rooted in prejudice, and this reversal of fortune had fixed within him such a depth of resentment that I wondered whether he could even physically bring himself to speak.

These fruitless sessions of questioning were the only times I saw Vonvalt in the days immediately after the battle. Once the ritual was complete, Vonvalt would make his way back to the vaults underneath the courthouse, and he would spend all day there, poring obsessively over every old lore book he could lay his hands on, trying to make sense of Claver's newfound powers. The ability to suspend and lift a person into the air by the power of words or thoughts alone was not one of the Order's typical gifts – but of course, it had come from somewhere. As well-stocked as the courthouse vaults were, however, it was clear that only the Law Library in Sova would give him the answer.

I have no doubt that Vonvalt was consumed by his quest for knowledge, but it did also have the benefit of keeping him out of sight of the people of Galen's Vale. Perhaps understandably, though quite misguidedly, they had turned on him, viewing him as one of the authors of their current misery. I also think Vonvalt wanted somewhere private to mourn Justice August. On those rare occasions when he did emerge, it was clear from his red-eyed and pale expression that at least some of this time in solitude was given over to grieving.

The cruel irony was, of course, that Resi August was not dead – not in any physical sense at least. We ended up transferring her to the hospice in the Galen's Vale kloster, a quiet, peaceful and well-appointed establishment, to be taken care of by the nuns there. I think the sole reason we lingered in the Vale for as long as we did was so that Vonvalt could make sure he would not miss a surprise recovery. Alas, in spite of the efforts of Haunersheim's best physicians, she never regained any semblance of consciousness, and I received word that her physical body died around ten years later, as lifeless and vacant as the day Westenholtz had stolen her mind. It is difficult to overstate the effect this had on Vonvalt. He was never the same man afterwards.

Bressinger also lived – though he very nearly did not – thanks to the careful ministrations of Mr Maquerink and the Vale's best barber surgeons. His "disarmament", as he liked to subsequently call it, did dent his character somewhat, and he was surlier and more ill-tempered as a result, though fortunately his flamboyant Grozodan fighting style required only his right hand. The barber surgeons informed us that the length of his convalescence would be dependent on the slow replenishment of his blood, which in the event took some weeks. He spent much of this time ill-advisedly drunk.

The watchmen who had died – around two-thirds of the town's force in the battle, with more succumbing to wounds and poxes later – were buried in a mass grave. Lord Sauter and Sir Radomir led the funeral rites, and it was a passionate and painful affair which was hardly surprising given the depth of anger felt by the town's inhabitants. I can remember standing there in the cold breeze, trying and failing to comprehend what had happened and how matters had reached a head so quickly. Normally in such times I would have relied on Vonvalt's steadfastness, but that was gone, his mind elsewhere. That lack of leadership frightened me to my core and made the process of coming to terms with August's "death" and the sacking of the Vale a rudderless and desperate affair.

Of course, the ramifications of Westenholtz's attack on Galen's Vale were not consigned to a handful of members of Vonvalt's itinerant court and sixty town watchmen. With the margrave's hand laid bare, wheels across the Empire were now put in motion which would turn for years to come and would reshape the world as we knew it. News of the attack on the Vale spread quickly through Haunersheim and the neighbouring provinces, and the news that came back with the peddlers and merchants, tantalisingly obscure and freighted with fear, was that something bigger was stirring in Sova: talk of power struggles in the Senate, of problems with the Kova Confederation to the east and the pagans on the Frontier, of powerful Imperial lords positioning themselves and of fractures already beginning to show in the nascent Empire of the Wolf.

But I shall come on to all of that in due course.

We left Westenholtz's cell and made our way back into the street. As anticipated, Vonvalt turned to make his way to the court-house, but this time we were intercepted.

"My lord Justice."

We both looked up to see the senator, Tymoteusz Jansen, standing in the street. Like Vonvalt, he cut an impressive figure in his Imperial finery – though that was not necessarily difficult, given that a good portion of the buildings behind him were a charred ruin. I had not seen him since the battle, though he seemed unhurt. I was pleased; for all his slightly grating wryness, I sensed a decent and brave man in him. It was easy to respect a politician who put himself in harm's way.

"Senator," Vonvalt replied, apparently able to muster some courtesy in spite of his black mood.

Jansen gestured to the gaol as he approached. "Has he said anything?"

"Not yet."

Jansen nodded. He reached us and put a hand on Vonvalt's shoulder. I could see sympathy in the senator's eyes. "We are having a meeting shortly – well, another one. Myself, Lord Hangmar and the mayor. I know you have been busy looking into this . . . occult matter, but would you consider joining us? It will not take up a great deal of your time."

Vonvalt nodded. I could tell that he did not like having the man's hand on his shoulder. "Yes."

"At noon, in the mayor's residence. I understand you are lodged there, though one would scarce believe it, given the amount of time you have spent in the courthouse vaults."

"Someone has to find out exactly how Claver has acquired his power," Vonvalt replied. "I am best placed to do it."

Jansen looked at him with a measure of reproach. "Come, Justice. There is more at play here than the magickal intrigues of one Neman priest. You think the rest of us are sitting around idly?"

"No, I did not say that," Vonvalt said. He drew himself up slightly, for he had been sagging – though not entirely from sullenness. It was easy to forget that he had been badly battered during the senator's cavalry charge. He sighed. "You must forgive me. I am not myself at the moment."

Jansen waved him off. "I do not see that there is anything to forgive. I would not trouble you at all, unless it were important."

"You are heading there now?" Vonvalt asked. "It cannot be much before noon already."

"I am. Shall we walk together?"

We made our way through the streets to the mayor's house.

"I hear your clerk dispatched one of Westenholtz's rogues," Jansen said by way of conversation. "What was it, miss? A sword cut to the neck?"

I felt a strange mixture of emotion. The killing of the man

on the bank of the Gale, though entirely justified, had revolted and horrified me. I could still see the man's shocked, desperate expression in my mind's eye, and feel the grating of steel against bone as the blade thrummed in my hand like a tuning fork. But, at the same time, I felt hardier and more resilient, closer in mindset to the girl I had been in Muldau than to the young woman I had become in Vonvalt's employ. Knowing that I was physically capable of killing in self-defence, especially after my hesitation in the bowels of the kloster when squaring off against Vogt with the watchman's pike, was a curious source of comfort.

"Aye," I replied eventually, for want of anything better to say. To bask in the man's praise seemed vulgar; to ignore the compliment, rude.

"You must be proud of your apprentice," Jansen said to Vonvalt. "I imagine not everyone has the stomach for the sharp end of the profession."

"Indeed," was all Vonvalt said.

I looked at him, but he did not meet my eye. I don't know what I had expected his response to be. Given that swordsmanship formed part of our syllabus, and he and Bressinger infrequently sparred with me – though that was probably more of an excuse to keep their own eyes in than to train me – I thought he would have been eager to take his share of the credit. If nothing else, he should have been proud of me for defending myself. Nema knew he had been relieved to see that I had survived.

With hindsight, I think he was disappointed that I had had to go to such lengths to protect myself at all, and ashamed that he had offered to kill me – albeit quickly and mercifully. But at the time, I found myself disappointed by his lack of recognition.

Jansen, too, was visibly taken aback.

"In my experience it is best to get these things out of the way early in life," he continued with affected brightness. "How did they use to do it in the Lodge? Take the Order's initiates down to the Palace gaol and have them slice the heads off the condemned?"

Vonvalt sniffed. "They used livestock in the first instance."

It was too much even for the conversational talents of Jansen. The three of us lapsed to silence, and I found myself wishing that the senator had not suggested he accompany us, for it was from that point on an awkward journey, marked by uncomfortable silence.

Baron Hangmar and the mayor were already there, waiting for us in the great hall. The mood was palpably sombre, and though a great spread of food had been laid on for these high lords of state, it might as well have been a funeral feast.

"Justice, Senator," Sauter said nervously. He gestured to some chairs around the table. "Please, come and help yourselves to food and wine."

The three of us made our way to the table. I lifted up one of the platters in front of me and loaded it up with some venison pie, and filled my goblet from one of the wine jugs about the table. I watched Jansen do the same, but Vonvalt did not touch any of the food.

"I have heard word from the town physician as to the final tally of dead," Baron Hangmar said. He was a big, barrel-chested man, possessed of a thick head of blond hair and a close-cropped blond beard. In the wake of the battle, I had seen him briefly in the street, his plate armour black like Westenholtz's, but his surcoat was white and embroidered with a crimson bull's head.

"Aye?" Jansen asked.

"Sixty from the town watch. A hundred from my own men killed, another hundred wounded."

"And of the margrave's men?"

"Two hundred and fifty killed. Of the prisoners we have taken, thirty have gone to the noose. We will clear the balance in the next day or two."

"If I may ask, what accounts for the disparity in the numbers?" Sauter asked. "Westenholtz had the greater force. Not that I am displeased with the result, of course."

"Cohesion," Hangmar grunted. "My men were organised. They were not. Too busy pillaging the place like bloody Draedists."

"But did the margrave not say they were Reichskrieg veterans?" Sauter pressed.

Hangmar shrugged. "What man is not?"

"They were retainers," Jansen said. "No match for legionnaires."

I frowned. I was not really permitted to speak, on account of my low rank, but I sensed an ally in Jansen, and my curiosity was too piqued to let the point slide.

"What is the difference?" I asked.

Everyone looked at me. Vonvalt looked slightly irritated that I had breached protocol, but the man could drink brine. I was still smarting from the snub he had dealt me en route to the mayor's house.

As I suspected, Jansen was happy to indulge me. "Westenholtz's men belonged to Westenholtz – and probably a large number from Baron Naumov's household, too. The Legions belong to the Emperor. A lord may keep a number of men on retainer, though they require a royal licence to do it. But such men are no match for the Imperial armies. Good at terrorising the countryside like bandits, and not much else."

"I have not heard of the practice," I said. "It seems rather outdated, does it not?"

"'Tis on the wane, like many other things," Hangmar said. He seemed to glance over at Vonvalt as he said it. "It is mostly confined to the countryside. I expect it will be outlawed entirely after this sorry episode."

"Indeed," Jansen said. "More pressingly, is there any sign of our priest? I have asked Sir Konrad here specifically to hear your news."

Hangmar grunted. He took a long draw of red wine. "My scouting parties report that the body of Westenholtz's surviving troops have made for Roundstone. Claver was among them, as well as the other one . . . " He snapped his fingers. "What was his name?"

"Fischer," Vonvalt said. "Obenpatria Ralf Fischer."

"That was it," Hangmar said.

"And what precisely is your plan to deal with them?" Vonvalt asked. His face was a mask of displeasure. "I guarantee they will not remain in Roundstone for very long."

Jansen and Hangmar exchanged a look. Much like the senator, the baron was subordinate to Vonvalt, and was bound by protocol to endure his bad moods.

"Word has been sent to Count Maier of Oldenburg, and His Highness Prince Gordan," Hangmar said. Gordan Kzosic was the Emperor's third son and the Prince of Guelich. I knew that word had been sent to the Emperor as well, but given that Guelich bordered Haunersheim, the Prince would almost certainly receive the news first. "I am confident His Highness will strike north in force. You have seen what a few hundred wayfort garrisoneers can do; wait until you see what a full Imperial Legion is capable of. Roundstone and Seaguard will be bled dry."

Hangmar seemed satisfied with his own answer, but Vonvalt said nothing, and there followed a silence, which stretched unbearably.

"Sir Konrad?" Jansen prompted.

"I'm thinking," Vonvalt replied.

There was another silence, until eventually Sauter cleared his throat. "What will you do now, Sir Konrad?" he asked. "I don't imagine there is much to keep you here in the Vale."

"Once my business is finished with Westenholtz, I will make for the capital," Vonvalt said. "Clearly, matters are reaching a head within my Order – and in such a way as to require my personal attention."

"Indeed," Jansen said. "I will give you the names of a few senators to call on. The situation is precarious, but you are not without allies. There is still time. Westenholtz's actions here will reflect catastrophically on the Mlyanars – not to mention Claver's on the Nemans. I daresay you will have the wind at your back."

"Aye," Hangmar agreed. "When Sova hears that a Mlyanar has sacked one of the largest and most important towns in Haunersheim, it will be poison to their cause. There will be outrage in the capital."

But Vonvalt was immune to such optimism. "Senatorial politicking will count for nothing soon enough. The Emperor would do well to send the Legions south and destroy the Templars before Claver is able to reunite with them. And smoke out Claver from Roundstone and destroy Naumov's entire household while he's at it."

"Roundstone will be taken care of," Hangmar said. "And the Emperor is no fool, Justice. He will not allow the Savarans within a hundred miles of Sova."

Vonvalt looked up at the baron, as though he had only just noticed him at the table. He regarded the man in silence for a long time; but unlike before, there was a leaden quality to this deliberate pause that meant no one moved to prompt him.

And then, slowly, Vonvalt began to smile.

Hangmar, disarmed, smiled back uncertainly. Even Jansen, who was the only one close to Vonvalt's intellectual equal, seemed compelled to smile as well, as though preparing himself for the punchline to a joke he didn't quite understand. Sauter went as far as to chuckle, in his sweaty, anxious way.

Vonvalt continued to smile, but I was the only one who could see it for what it was. It was the cold, helpless smile of a man who has just lost a high-stakes game he might otherwise have won had he just paid more attention. For the first time, Vonvalt saw his own naïveté reflected back at him. He might as well have been looking into a mirror. He saw in Hangmar and Jansen exactly what August had seen in him: an unshakeable yet entirely misplaced confidence in the permanence of the state. In spite of all the evidence to the contrary, they were still willing to believe that because the Empire was geographically vast, and had armies and a complex bureaucracy and a religion and all the other great institutions that came with it, it would simply . . . endure. That it was an entity greater than the sum of its parts, rather than a huge collective delusion that required constant maintenance at gigantic expense of treasure and blood. The Empire's power was drawn entirely from its subjects' perception of it. We had just witnessed how a couple of rogue lords and a deranged priest could nearly destroy one of its towns in an afternoon. It was not a great leap of the imagination to see how Claver, given another few weeks and set at the head of five or ten thousand men, could undo the world as we knew it.

The effect on Vonvalt was transformative. It did not rob him of his bitterness, nor did it realign his personal ethical code – as I would come to discover but a few weeks later. But it did infuse him with a sudden sense of purpose that, for now at least, provided a decent simulation of both.

He stood, and we all stood with him, though our obeisance was slightly delayed on account of how wrong-footed we were. "Westenholtz will die at dawn. I have decided to bring his execution forwards." Vonvalt turned to Sauter. "Please erect a scaffold in the market square, tonight."

"Uh – at once, my lord," Sauter spluttered, but Vonvalt was already sweeping out of the room.

"Come, Helena," he called over his shoulder. "Make preparations for our departure."

XXX

Leaving the Vale

"To meet a Justice is often to meet a dispassionate
automaton, so robbed of any human nature it is like
conversing with a walking textbook. And yet, one cannot
help but question the wisdom of entrusting unlimited
power to any class of person. Can the Order really be
so successful in stamping out every last partiality,
every last prejudice and quirk of the human soul?"

FROM CHUN PARSIFAL'S TREATISE,
PENITENT EMPIRE

❧

"Tell me how he did it."

It was dawn, and heavy rain lashed the Vale. Vonvalt and
I stood in the margrave's cell, this time accompanied by Sir
Radomir. Our cloaks dripped with rainwater, and more water
trickled down the stones of the wall where a rash of mould had
sprung up overnight. Given that, under the common law, a person
was not guilty of a crime until declared so by a jury or a Justice,
Sovan ordinances commanded that gaols were to be constructed

robustly, and in such a way as to provide some measure of comfort to their occupants. After all, not everyone who entered them exited having been adjudged guilty. But, perhaps unsurprisingly, of all the Imperial decrees around the legal process, it was the most neglected. Vonvalt once told me that the effectiveness of a state's criminal justice bureaucracy was entirely congruent with the compassion of its citizens, and the Sovans were a vengeful mob. It was one of life's great ironies that the better treated the criminal class, the less crime there was overall, but that is a hard sell to the parents of a murdered child, or the peddler who has just been violently robbed on the highway.

Westenholtz was very much a victim of this wilful oversight. Freezing cold, starving and with his meagre clothes concealing all manner of bruises, he was a broken man. I was surprised at how much pity I felt for him. I detested him, of course, and had done from the moment we had met. He was a loathsome creature, and deserved nothing other than death. Yet, to look at his pale and emaciated form, my overwhelming emotion was one of sadness. How could we claim any moral superiority over him when we allowed him to be kicked by his gaolers or starved of victuals?

"There is nothing left for you," Vonvalt said. "It is over. Your estates and titles have been revoked. Your household disbanded. The Imperial Herald has erased your device. Any goodwill you have built up as the guardian of the northern shores of this Empire has been obliterated." Vonvalt took a step forwards, and squatted down. When he spoke again, his voice had softened somewhat. "Do some good now. Salvage *something*. Don't take it with you. Tell me how he did it. Tell me where he got the knowledge from. Tell me who helped you."

Westenholtz opened his mouth to speak, but only a dry rasp came out. Vonvalt turned to the gaoler. "Bring some ale in here," he said, and a few minutes later Westenholtz's throat was moistened enough to speak.

"But you are wrong. It is not over," he said. He spoke quietly, but with absolute conviction. Rather than break him, the last few days seemed only to have hardened his resolve. The sincerity in his voice frightened me. "It is only just beginning."

"Oh for fuck's sake," Sir Radomir muttered, and spat on the floor. He gestured roughly to the margrave. "Sir Konrad, you are wasting your time. He has naught but trite prophecies in him."

Vonvalt did not take his eyes off Westenholtz. "Is Sir Radomir right? Are your final words really to be so unimpressive?"

"You'll not goad me into confessing anything," Westenholtz said, irritably, as though Vonvalt were a beggar hassling him on the street. He turned to look out of the window again. "My fate is in Nema's hands."

Sir Radomir sighed angrily. "If I wanted to listen to this shit there are a dozen madmen outside the temple who preach it better. I'll see you at the scaffold." And with that, he left.

Vonvalt regarded Westenholtz for a long minute. Outside, the rain intensified. One thing was certain: it was going to be a dramatic execution.

"You are not special," Vonvalt said. He spoke as though he were simply listing facts. "Martyrdom does not await you. You will die a dishonourable death as a hated man, your only legacy that of a butcher."

Westenholtz rolled his eyes. "If you are going to kill me, then get on with it."

Now Vonvalt sighed, and smiled sadly. He seemed to be lost in thought for a few moments; then he shook his head, as though he were having some internal conversation with himself. When he spoke, it was quietly.

"I have been there. I have seen what is on the other side." He brought his face in close to the margrave's, his voice freighted with haunted authority. "If you knew what awaited you, you would not be so eager to die."

For the first time, Westenholtz's composure fractured. Now he could not keep the fear from his face. Nema, even my skin broke out in gooseflesh at Vonvalt's cold delivery. But of course, I had been there. I had seen the truth of it for myself.

"What do you mean? What is there?" Westenholtz whispered, wide-eyed and in spite of himself. Claver must have filled his head with all sorts of nonsense, which he was only now beginning to see for what it was – empty exhortation. He reminded me of myself, calling out to the soldier on the bank of the Gale. Even such debasement was better than the alternative. Faced with the enormity of death and an afterlife as dark and vast and filled with predatory entities as the oceans of the world, it was not surprising that the man cracked. The only thing that was surprising was how long it had taken. But, in my experience, people are able to deny the reality of their situation in the face of quite overwhelming evidence.

Vonvalt stood, and turned to leave. "I have given you ample time to assist me. You will find out very shortly."

"What is there, Justice?" Westenholtz called. His voice was louder now, and urgent, but he was speaking to our backs. "Justice? What is there? Justice!"

But he did not get his answer – at least, not from Vonvalt.

❧

We stepped out into the street, and made our way to the market square. Rain lashed down around us, overwhelming the shit-ditches either side of the road, which now overflowed with effluent. Without winter to chill the air, the Vale was coming alive with unpleasant smells, and I knew the place would be unbearable in summer.

We reached our destination after ten minutes of brisk walking. There, a scaffold had been erected per Vonvalt's instructions. Above, the sky was dark and filled with bloated black cloud, and thunder pealed through the air. In spite of this, a huge crowd had turned out, and there was a palpable sense of tension and excitement in the air.

We pressed our way through the throng. No one quite had

the temerity to shout at us, though there was plenty of angry and resentful muttering in our wake. I was largely oblivious to it. Thoughts of divination and the afterlife clamoured for attention in my head. I could not help but think that the weather was some kind of divine expression of displeasure – but how could the elemental gods not be pleased with what was about to take place? Vonvalt was a great believer in the Natural Law, the idea that morality and ethics were absolutes irrespective of human-made laws, and if this were truly the case, then by any measure, Westenholtz deserved to die. Perhaps the answer lay in the works of Justice Kane and his theory of Entanglement. Although we were taking immediate succour in revenge, perhaps Westenholtz's execution was objectively the wrong thing to do, an action which would shunt us onto a different temporal pathway and doom the Autun to destruction. Perhaps it was not so much an expression of displeasure as a warning?

Or perhaps it was simply some bad weather.

Vonvalt had not given me anywhere specific to stand, so I joined him on the scaffold. We were joined shortly after by Sir Radomir and Lord Sauter, the former with a sense of grim anticipation, the latter with a sense of abject misery. A few months ago I might have been surprised by Sauter's reaction, but my opinion of him had changed over time. There was cowardice in his honour. His light-touch approach was not born of a desire to do the right thing; it was a consequence of his weak moral foundation. As he would be glad to see the back of us, so I would be glad to see the back of him. Once we left the Vale, our paths would never cross again.

We were not long on the platform when a great jeer went up from the crowd, and I turned sharply to the end of the street. There I saw Westenholtz being led to the scaffold by a pair of burly executioners' assistants and a Neman priest. He seemed to come compliantly enough – for what choice did he have? – but when he saw the noose, he baulked. I saw him stiffen with resistance. He started shouting something, but it was not the raving of a man who has gone insane with fear. He seemed angry about something.

I leant towards Vonvalt, and asked quietly, "What is the matter with him?"

Vonvalt did not look at me, but his face was grim set. "The man was a lord. He will say he is entitled to a lordly death."

"By law?"

Vonvalt nodded. "Aye."

"What manner of death is he entitled to?"

"The sword."

"But you are hanging him?"

"I am hanging him."

It was as though we were back on the Hauner road, and Vonvalt was striding towards the Templar, about to strike his head from his shoulders in violation of the common law. This was a lesser transgression, but it was still unlawful – and petty. It reeked of vendetta. Perhaps I had been naïve to expect anything else.

"But if the law says—"

"Peace, Helena."

I fell silent. What could I say? What could I do? Even if I had the means to intervene, I wasn't exactly about to dart forwards and chop the man's head off. I doubted I even had the strength to do it. And what a ridiculous scene that would be, the Justice's clerk snatching up a sword and beheading the condemned.

No. I was forced to weather it like so many other things. There would be a time to air my concerns, but that time was not now. No citizen of the Vale was about to object to Westenholtz hanging. Indeed, many of them would relish a much more prolonged end. I just hoped that Vonvalt was hanging Westenholtz for some principle, perhaps as a mark of disrespect for the violations of his oaths of office, rather than as an indulgence to the crowd. The former I could understand, even if I didn't like it; the latter would take Vonvalt into the realms of populism, the very antithesis of Sovan legal doctrine.

I was jolted from my unhappy reverie by Westenholtz surmounting the scaffold. He struggled against the iron grip of his escort.

"I'm entitled to an honourable death," he spat. The fear which Vonvalt had instilled in him in the gaol had given way to anger again.

"Waldemar Westenholtz," Vonvalt said, ignoring him. His voice boomed like the thunder overhead. "On the twenty-eighth day of Ebbe, you led a large company of your own retainers into the town of Galen's Vale and killed, or caused to be killed, without lawful justification and under the Emperor's peace, numerous of the Emperor's subjects therein. In doing so you have committed the crimes of murder and treason, and I so indict you.

"I further indict you with the murder, or its incitement or authorisation thereof, of Sir Otmar Frost, Lady Karol Frost and the other inhabitants of the village of Rill, located in the province of Tolsburg, on a date unknown but nevertheless falling within the month of Goss.

"On these charges, His Most Excellent Majesty the Emperor Lothar Kzosic IV, through me, His Justice, Sir Konrad Vonvalt, does adjudge you guilty, and on this, the seventh day of Wirter, you are sentenced to die by hanging. Have you anything to say?"

"I'm entitled to an honourable death," Westenholtz repeated. Despite his gaunt and bedraggled form, he still managed to summon every ounce of venom remaining in his system and direct it at Vonvalt.

"You are entitled to a death," Vonvalt said. "If you wanted an honourable one, you should have conducted yourself honourably."

"That is not what the law says!" Westenholtz shouted, once more struggling fruitlessly against the men holding him. "You're not permitted to hang me!"

Vonvalt leant in close. He spoke quietly, intending for only

Westenholtz to hear him, but I was close enough to catch the words.

"This is the difference between a piece of paper and steel. If you have not learned by now, you will soon enough."

When Vonvalt took a step backwards, Westenholtz's expression had changed. The realisation that nothing he could say or do would alter his fate finally hit him. I watched as the man's soul snapped like an overtaxed bowstring. He sagged, and had to be physically held up.

Vonvalt nodded to the two executioners.

Lightning split the sky dramatically as Westenholtz was dragged towards the noose. I turned to Sir Radomir, but his face was grim set, and I knew I would not find an ally in him. He was an uncomplicated man, in favour of uncomplicated justice, and did not agonise over the intricacies of the common law.

The crowd was now jeering again. Some, presumably those who had lost family members or friends, were screaming bloody exhortations until they were hoarse. As a display of collective rage, it was powerful – and who could blame them? I was not so high-minded that I felt no satisfaction watching Westenholtz die. I hated him, and did not deny that the living world was a better place without him in it. It was just that any succour I may have taken from his execution was being tempered by the effect I knew it was having on Vonvalt. It seems strange to quibble about it – a death, after all, was a death, an execution an execution. What did it matter if Westenholtz was beheaded or hanged?

Well, the answer is that it couldn't have mattered more. The Reichskrieg had claimed the lives of tens of thousands, yet the consequentialist philosophers and jurists of the day considered it justifiable because the great forces of civilisation that had followed in its wake had improved the lives of *millions*. Under the watchful gaze of the common law, every person from the lowliest peasant to the highest nobleman was rendered equal. So many had sacrificed so much, so many lives had been extinguished upon its altar, that to abandon its tenets now rendered the whole thing worthless. Take away a representative senate, the Magistratum, and a set of laws common to all persons, and the Reichskrieg had been no more than an end in itself, a mere sequence of bloody conquests.

One of Vonvalt's favourite quotes was, "All may be judged by the law, so all may uphold it", and I spoke it once to Matas when I was trying to be clever. But that is not the full quote. The full quote is, "All may be judged by the law, so all may uphold it; but all those who uphold the law may not judge it." It was for Vonvalt to apply the law as it stood, in spite of himself, not to further his own designs.

The noose went around Westenholtz's neck, and the executioner to whom Vonvalt had delegated the task turned the winch. Westenholtz was hoisted into the air no more than twelve inches. His feet kicked and his body convulsed. His face turned an incredible shade of purple. Every so often he would emit a screeching, choking sound as his throat opened and spasmed. I looked around the crowd, waiting for someone, perhaps Claver, to suddenly rush to the man's rescue. But of course, there was no one.

Vonvalt lost interest after a few minutes and left the scaffold. Sauter, pleased to be able to do so, hurried after him and headed home. Only Sir Radomir remained, watching Westenholtz dispassionately.

I myself watched the entire gruesome spectacle. I felt it was somehow important, like I was witnessing history being made – which of course, I was.

Eventually it was over. By the tolling of the bell, the man had taken perhaps ten minutes to expire. His death could not have been more ignominious. Urine dripped from his lifeless legs. His eyes were almost black where every single blood vessel had ruptured. Thick spittle foamed around his mouth, and his tongue thrust out gruesomely.

Once it was clear Westenholtz had expired, I left the scaffold. I heard Sir Radomir cut him down behind me.

The crowd let out a great cheer as his lifeless body thumped on to the boards.

≈

Another day and night passed before I saw Vonvalt again. For the first time in a long time, he looked fresh. His hair had been cut, his beard trimmed, and his face looked fleshier, as though he had eaten and drunk well. I must admit that despite everything that had happened recently, this simple transformation had a powerful impact on me, and served to obscure many of my misgivings.

"It is time to leave for Sova," he said. We were standing in Vonvalt's chambers in the upper levels of the courthouse. Vonvalt was drinking a goblet of red wine, and looking out over the town. Already many of the houses which had been burned were being rebuilt, and I did not doubt that Galen's Vale would return to something resembling business as usual in a few days' time. Vonvalt sat quietly for a little while, then drained the last of his wine. "I will not achieve satisfaction for Resi in this place." He looked around the town as though it were a pagan relic constructed on unholy ground.

"Have you decided?" he asked after another silence.

"Have I decided what?" I asked.

"What you want to do. The death of Matas changes your circumstances somewhat, I should imagine, but . . . " He shrugged. "You may want to stay in the Vale anyway. Or part ways with me and Dubine."

To my shame, I had not thought of Matas for some time, so preoccupied was I with recent events. I was surprised that Vonvalt had so badly misjudged the source of my unhappiness – for I was clearly unhappy with how Vonvalt was changing. But I did not have the courage to confront him about it, and I really did not have any other option except to accompany him.

"I will stay with you," I said. I paused. I felt wretched, and

I did not want to cry, and so took a half-minute to compose myself. Vonvalt did not look up. "There is so much left to do, so many wrongs to set right. I can only do that if I come with you to Sova."

"Do you want to accompany me for vengeance, or do you want to accompany me to learn how to become a Justice?" Vonvalt asked.

I took a deep breath. There was no sense in lying to him. "I do not know," I said. "The former. Perhaps both. I cannot say for sure that I want to become a Justice."

"Perhaps it is for the best," Vonvalt said, surprising me. "It would appear that now is a dangerous time to be associating with the Order anyway."

I looked at my hands. "My loyalty is to you, not the Order," I said quietly.

"My dear Helena," Vonvalt said. I looked up. He was smiling, albeit sadly. "You owe me nothing."

"I owe you everything," I said.

"I have . . . misused you. Put you in danger. Asked things of you I should not have."

"I am an adult. I could have refused."

"Were it not for me, Matas would still be alive."

"It was Vogt who murdered him," I said simply.

"My actions created the circum—"

"I don't want to discuss it particularly," I said.

"No," Vonvalt said. "No, that is fair."

We sat in silence for a moment.

"I wish to speak to Sir Radomir before we leave," Vonvalt said. "I sense he feels he has lost his place here. He is a good man with a keen sense of justice. He is a doughty fighter, too. He might be persuaded to join us. Gods know we could use an extra sword arm." His eyes widened as he realised what he had just said. "You take my meaning," he added.

"Yes," I said.

"Go then. Ready your things and have our horses and the ass prepared. Then inform Dubine that we will be on our way today, and ask him if he feels capable of joining us."

⚬

"You would have me accompany you?" Sir Radomir asked later that morning.

We were standing in the sheriff's office, the fire for once unlit on account of the unseasonably mild weather. Sir Radomir looked gaunt, and his wine-stain birthmark looked redder and more inflamed. He offered us drinks, which we refused on account of our impending departure.

The man was drunk, but lucid. Since the attack on the Vale, his drinking appeared to have increased in both volume and intensity. "With respect, Sir Konrad, it seems like something of a demotion. I am the sheriff of a town. By its ordinances I am entitled to employ a hundred men."

"A hundred men?" Vonvalt asked.

"Aye," Sir Radomir said.

"How many do you answer to?"

"I answer to the mayor."

"And certain other lords?"

"Indirectly."

"And Lord Sauter answers to?"

Sir Radomir shrugged.

"Lord Hangmar," Vonvalt said. "Eventually."

"The Lord of Haunersheim?"

"The Baron of Osterlen," Vonvalt corrected. "And who does Baron Hangmar answer to?"

"I know not."

"Count Maier, of Oldenburg and Lord of the Southmark. Who in turn answers to?"

"Some high lord I should imagine," Sir Radomir said dourly.

"Duke Hofmann, foremost lord of Haunersheim. And Duke

Hofmann answers to His Highness Gordan Kzosic, Prince of Guelich, who answers to his father, His Imperial Majesty."

"I take your meaning," Sir Radomir grumbled.

"Who do I answer to?" Vonvalt persisted.

"Nema?"

"The Emperor Himself. Directly. And that is no hollow honour; it is as fundamental to the constitution of the Empire as that beam is to the structure of this watch house. I am offering you a singular honour, Sir Radomir," Vonvalt said. "As my retainer you would be second only to me. And I have just told you who I am second to."

"Aye," Sir Radomir said. "That you have."

"And your hundred men become a hundred million. Across the whole of the Empire."

"Gods," Sir Radomir muttered. "No man should have so much authority."

"I can think of several men who would agree," Vonvalt remarked.

Sir Radomir's face was grim. "What would my duties be?"

"Investigations. Arrests. Protection. Prosecution. Anything in furtherance of my ultimate objective: justice."

"Does revenge fall within that remit?" Sir Radomir growled. He leant in slightly.

There was a dangerous silence. I looked at Vonvalt, expecting – hoping – to see him shake his head like a parent gently chiding a child. But to my great sadness, Vonvalt nodded.

"Aye," he said. "That would fall within justice."

"What is the procedure? If I were to accept?" Sir Radomir asked.

"It is as simple as a signature on a piece of paper, and that is only to ensure that you are paid."

There was silence as the sheriff thought. "I will need time to prepare. To set things in order. 'Tis true I have no family here, but I have ... acquaintances, if you take my meaning. I should not like to leave unannounced."

"You have the balance of the morning. We will be leaving

at noon. Meet us by the Veldelin Gate at the twelfth bell and no later."

"Where are we going?"

"To Sova, Sir Radomir. To the seat of the Empire and the beating heart of the civilised world."

Epilogue

The Emperor's Justice

*"Justice is not vengeance, and vengeance is not
justice. But the two often overlap. The state is as
capable of vengeance as any individual, for what
is the state if not the people that comprise it?"*

SIR RANDALL KORMONDOLT

A week later we were plodding down a muddy track through an
open stretch of hilly Guelan farmland. Warm rain thrummed on
my hood and I could feel the slow but inevitable surrender of my
waxed cloak to full saturation.

We had spent the time travelling briskly south, avoiding the
Hauner road wherever possible, stopping only for Vonvalt or Sir
Radomir to make enquiries at the various waystations and inns
on the way. Bressinger lay in the Duke of Brondsey's cart, covered
over in waxed cloaks, drinking and sleeping. Though his convalescence was ultimately successful, it would be a while before he
was ready to engage in the banter and raucous behaviour I had

been used to. I think he resented, too, the inclusion of Sir Radomir into Vonvalt's retinue.

I did not really appreciate what was happening until it came to me suddenly that afternoon. I pieced together the various strands: our route, which conspicuously avoided the Hauner road and the Imperial Relay; and the frequent stops for information which did not involve me.

I urged my horse forwards until it was trotting next to Vincento.

"Where is he?" I asked Vonvalt. I had to raise my voice above the rain.

"Ossica," he replied simply. He looked grim and uncharacteristically unkempt, his black beard tangled like a bird's nest, his hair long and lank in the mild wet weather.

I tried to think of the right words. "He cannot be—"

"I know, Helena," Vonvalt replied.

We carried on. I urged my horse up again so that it was level with Vonvalt.

"The jury did not—"

"I know, Helena."

His face was inscrutable.

"So why are we—"

"Enough. You have worked it out, despite my efforts. I should have known you would. You are not to be a part of it. It is a minor detour, then we will be on our way south. We need information."

"Just information?" I pressed.

Vonvalt did not respond.

"You are talking about—"

"I said *enough*," he snapped. "I do not want to discuss it with you."

I lapsed into silence, both wounded and troubled, and resumed my place in the line.

We carried on for the rest of the day while the sun slowly set. Twilight crept up on us in the late afternoon. Still, the watch fires of Ossica, another large merchant town connected to

Galen's Vale by the same wide, deep river, glowed on the horizon like beacons.

We reached the town long after nightfall, and it was only by Vonvalt's authority that we were able to gain entry through the main gate. I could feel the eyes of the nightwatchmen following us as we clattered along the cobbled streets. It was as if they could sense why we were there.

We found an inconspicuous inn and had the horses stabled. I saw Vonvalt pay the keeper an exorbitant sum by the flash of silver in the firelight. The common room was filled with unsavoury types but none spared us a second glance.

Vonvalt spoke quietly to the innkeeper for a few minutes, then we turned to leave.

"Stay here with Dubine, Helena," Vonvalt said as we reached the door. "I have booked you a room upstairs."

"Mm," I replied noncommittally. Bressinger slumped next to me, only half-conscious thanks to the pain in his arm stump and his inebriation.

"Bolt the door and do not come out. I will come and find you in a few hours or so."

I made some show of protestation, but I knew that if I wanted any hope of following them I would have to play along. I dallied for a little while, then departed upstairs to our room. I helped Bressinger into the bed and shot the bolt once I was inside.

I watched Vonvalt and Sir Radomir from the window. The moment they rounded the corner I dashed back out of the room, downstairs and out the common-room door. Outside, I followed Vonvalt's route down the unfamiliar streets until I picked them up a minute or so later. I kept to the shadows and followed them for around a quarter of an hour. Their route took them away from the lantern-lit cobbles of the main streets and into the back alleys, where whores waited in doorways and called out to them and where men gave them appraising looks and decided that robbing them would be unwise.

Eventually they stopped outside the door of a brothel, and for a horrible moment I wondered whether I had got it all wrong and they were just out to achieve an entirely different kind of satisfaction. Then I saw a man in the doorway, and I recognised him immediately as one of Sir Radomir's men from Galen's Vale. They exchanged a few quiet words, then the man slunk off and Vonvalt and Sir Radomir entered, closing the door behind them.

I looked about. There was no way I would be able to gain entry, but the surrounding houses were dilapidated and tumbledown and easily scaled. My time on the streets of Muldau had made me an excellent climber and given me a good eye for it, and in no time I had hoisted myself up on to the thatch of the adjacent roof. I looked through a few windows and quickly found what I was looking for: Obenpatria Fischer, being ridden with false enthusiasm by a bored whore.

Seconds after I had taken my place in the shadows, the door to the priest's room was kicked in. Sir Radomir and Vonvalt entered, swords drawn. The girl pulled out a knife from nowhere and pressed it to Fischer's throat. I watched as a brief stand-off ensued while Vonvalt took over proceedings; then the girl recovered her clothes – and a purse of coin from Sir Radomir – and left.

My heart pounded. I moved closer until I drew within a few feet of the window. The glass was of poor quality and fit, and the conversation bled easily through the gaps and into the cool night air.

"What in Kasivar's name is this all about, Justice? It is over. Let me be on my way and we shall forget about this," Fischer said. His voice was shaky and weak.

"Put some clothes on," Vonvalt said to the priest. The man hastily complied, pulling on his undergarments and purple habit. "Sit down. This will not take long."

"Sir Konrad, please – you already have my confession."

"Shut the fuck up," Sir Radomir snapped.

Silence fell. Vonvalt took a breath.

"How did you get here from Roundstone?"

The Emperor's Voice. It hit the air like a thunderclap. I jumped. I found it impossible to acclimate to that initial force.

"By boat . . . down the Kova."

"Did you travel with Claver?"

"Y-yes!"

"Where is he?"

"Further south!" Fischer gasped. The words came out hoarsely, dragged from his unwilling throat like a fish from a river. "To the Frontier!"

"Where? Südenberg? Keraq? Zetland?"

"Yes . . . *gnn* . . . one of those!"

"Which one?"

"I know not!"

"What is the name of the boat?"

"I do not know!" The man was gasping like he was on the rack.

"Where did Claver get his powers from?"

"Gah! Please! Stop!"

"Where? Is there a member of the Order working with him?"

"Y-yes! I don't know the name, please!"

"Who?"

"I don't know!" Fischer gasped. Blood trickled from his nose. His eyes were as wide as saucers.

Silence. Fischer fell to quietly weeping. Vonvalt and Sir Radomir stood there. Vonvalt lowered his sword and then took a seat in the corner. Sir Radomir continued to point his at the priest, but the man was in no shape to try anything.

Vonvalt pressed the tip of his sword into floorboards between his feet. He rested his hands on the pommel and his chin on his hands. When he spoke, it was quietly. Using the Voice used up a great deal of energy, but it was not just that. The man was tired, and, I think, profoundly melancholic. I had to strain to hear him.

"When I was a boy in Jägeland, before the Reichskrieg arrived, we had a very old saying: 'The Justice of Kings'. Like all very old sayings it had taken on a number of meanings over the years, but my father was a lawman himself, and he told me that the Justice of Kings actually had a very specific meaning. You see, like the Sovans, we Jägelanders had a system of justice whereby guilt was decided by a jury drawn from the accused's town. But if someone was adjudged innocent by that jury, the king could still be petitioned to intervene. Even if your peers, the commonfolk, had absolved you of all criminal culpability, the king could still have you executed if he thought the wrong decision had been reached." He paused, briefly lost in thought. He shook his head. "The Justice of Kings," he murmured to himself.

Then he stood, and walked towards Fischer.

"Of course, it is the Emperor's Justice, now."

The priest barely had time to shriek. He was still half-stupid from being battered by the Voice. He tried to leap up and parry the sword with his hands, and ended up losing both of them. He stared at the geysering stumps of his wrists with wide eyes, and let out a single grunt of horrified surprise, before Vonvalt's short-sword plunged into his neck, severing his spine cleanly in two. He collapsed and banged unceremoniously off the bed before coming to a bloody stop on the floor.

That I had expected it did not make it easier to witness. In spite of my hand being clamped firmly over my mouth, a muted screech did escape.

Vonvalt called out to me without taking his eyes from Fischer's corpse.

"Helena: get back to your room. We have an early start tomorrow."

❧

With the benefit of long hindsight, it is easy to say that the murder of Obenpatria Fischer, with Vonvalt's blood two weeks cooled, was the point at which he turned. He did not become a bad person, or change fundamentally overnight. But between the

Vale and Ossica there had been time for him to step back from the brink and take stock, to realign himself with the forces of absolute good. Instead, the extrajudicial killing of Fischer set in stone the relaxation of Vonvalt's personal and professional code which would change how he approached the question of justice – and of being a Justice – for the rest of his life.

The death of Fischer in any event marks the end of this part of my story. We all found ourselves changed by it, and it represented a capstone for our time in Galen's Vale. I too, changed, for I did not speak out. I did not chastise Vonvalt for the slayings of Vogt and Bauer either, for although they had deserved to die, without the jury's verdict, Vonvalt had committed the crime of murder. And before them, too, was the Templar on the Hauner road. I wish I had acknowledged the signs earlier, the signs of his moral decline.

The following morning I was roused at dawn. We did not discuss what had happened the night before. I allowed myself to be led, wordlessly, to the stables. There Vonvalt and Sir Radomir were already packed and mounted, and Bressinger was in the cart, still half-stupid from pain and wine.

"Our destination remains Sova," Vonvalt said to me without preamble. "Will you come? Decide quickly."

I nodded. There was nothing to say – or rather, there were too many things to say. I mounted my horse, and soon we were on our way. In two weeks it would be the month of Sorpen and the first day of spring, and indeed a new beginning for all of us, for better or worse.

There followed many adventures. Some had happy outcomes; others were dreadful and their ramifications are still being felt to this day. I shall get to committing as many of them to paper as my time permits. The story of Sir Konrad Vonvalt, after all, is the story of the rise and fall of the Sovan Empire.

But I am an old woman now, and my eyes are sore, and my hand needs a rest.

The story continues in...

Book Two of the Empire of the Wolf

Keep reading for a sneak peek!

Acknowledgements

This is the second novel I have submitted to Orbit for publication. The first, *Celestial Fire*, was an epic space opera I co-authored when I was fifteen with a school friend called George Diggory. Agentless, clueless and talentless, we posted the book in hard copy (it is extraordinary to think that only seventeen years ago the internet was still largely redundant) to Orbit, where it no doubt languished on the slush pile before being dismissed by an editor as too dangerous, too provocative and too ahead of its time for commercial publication.

Seventeen years later (and probably about seventeen novels too) I have returned to Orbit, agented, clued-up and moderately talented, with *The Justice of Kings*. That this has happened is down to me (sort of), the vagaries of Fate and the interventions of a number of people whom it is only right to acknowledge here.

In the first instance, I would like to thank George Lockett, Will Smith and Tim Johnson, my brain trust of beta readers, for their insights, recommendations and in some instances needlessly scathing feedback. You have each brought something to this book, and I am grateful for it.

The second order of thanks belongs to my agent, Harry

Illingworth, for his own editorial efforts (pace!), patient assistance and savvy advice. Thank you, Harry, for cracking open the gate and letting me in to the world of traditional publication – it's somewhere I've wanted to be for a very long time.

Penultimately, thanks go to the Orbit team, and specifically to my editor, James Long, for, well, editing the book, and everything that goes with it. It is not controversial to say that *The Justice of Kings* would be much worse, much shorter and much less published without you.

Finally, thank you to my wife, Sophie, for making sure I have the time – often at the expense of your own – to write. I could not have written this book without your support.

The Justice of Kings is dedicated to my friend and mind-clone Will, who was there at the very beginning of my writing journey, and, troublingly, might very well be there at the end of it too.

Richard
London, April 2020

extras

orbit

meet the author

Photo Credit: Robert Lapworth

RICHARD SWAN was born in North Yorkshire in the United Kingdom and spent most of his early life on Royal Air Force bases in Yorkshire and Lincolnshire. After studying law at the University of Manchester, Richard was called to the bar in 2011. He subsequently retrained as a solicitor specializing in commercial litigation.

When he is not working, Richard can be found in London with his wonderful wife, Sophie, where they attempt to raise, with mixed results, their two very loud sons.

Find out more about Richard Swan and other Orbit authors by registering for the free monthly newsletter at orbitbooks.net.

if you enjoyed
The Justice of Kings
look out for

Book Two of the Empire of the Wolf

by

Richard Swan

I

ON THE ROAD TO SOVA

"No event simply occurs. Each is the culmination of countless factors that trace their long roots back to the beginning of time. It is easy to bemoan an era of great upheaval as a sudden commingling of misfortunes – but the discerning eye of history tells us that there are few coincidences where the schemes of man are concerned."

—Justice Emmanuel Kane, *The Legal Armoury: Entanglement, Necromancy and Divination*

"Do you think he's dying?"

"Sir Konrad?"

"Aye."

"The way he carries on, you'd think so."

It was a warm, drizzly spring morning in the Southmark of Guelich, and Sir Radomir, Bressinger and I were standing fifty yards from a tumbledown herbalist's cottage. Vonvalt had been inside for most of an hour, and the three of us were trading bored, tired jibes, trying to get a rise out of one another.

"There is certainly something the matter with him," I said.

Both men turned to me.

"You said yourself the man is easily het up on matters of health," Sir Radomir said.

"Nema, keep your voice down," I muttered. Bressinger looked at me chidingly. He had always had a reproachful streak, but since the loss of his arm, his humour had worsened. Now his hackles were quick to rise, especially when he felt Vonvalt's character was being called into question. Once, these nonverbal reprimands would have plagued me with guilt. Now I was beginning to give these chastisements short shrift.

"I don't think anyone can sensibly argue he is not," I said, glancing at Bressinger. "But this is different. I have not seen him like this in a long time."

"Aye," Bressinger murmured eventually, in what was a rare concession. "This is not his usual fussiness."

I turned back to the cottage. It was a ramshackle place, a daub-and-timber construction sagging under the weight of its thatch. The place was mostly concealed behind a riot of wildflowers and other plants, and a strong herbal scent, intensified by the drizzly wetness, suffused the air and had led to no end of both human and equine sneezing.

We had been on the road from Ossica for most of the month of Sorpen, and were now but a few days' ride from the outskirts of Sova itself. Guelich was one of the three principalities which surrounded Sova like the white around a yolk, and was ruled by the Emperor's third son, Prince Gordan Kzosic. His castle, the fortress at Badenburg, was just visible on the distant horizon, a towering fastness of grey stone that caught the sun—and the eye—from thirty miles away.

Our journey was not supposed to have taken this long. Had Bressinger not lost an arm in Galen's Vale, we would have left our horses and equipment in that city, and then taken the Imperial Relay for a hundred and fifty miles south as far as the Westmark of Guelich. From there we could have simply taken the Baden road due east to Sova itself, for a total journey time of perhaps a week with good weather, or ten days in bad.

In fact, had Vonvalt not insisted on tracking down and then murdering Obenpatria Fischer, we could have simply hired a ship to take us down the Gale, since the river was a tributary of the Sauber, which flowed directly to Sova. But this is as much a digression as the route itself.

In any event, Vonvalt's illness had scuppered any plans to make haste. It had come on suddenly one night. He had complained of light-headedness, which we had all attributed to the wine, but it had persisted the following day. Vonvalt, learned as he was in ailments, blamed vertigo – until he began to suffer, too, from a deep-seated sense of dread, which he could not place. The emergence of this second symptom had confused all of us, since fearfulness was not amongst his faults. But the nebulous dread continued, and then not long after, tiredness, which itself turned into bouts of crippling fatigue.

The Empire was lousy with self-proclaimed medical men, and Vonvalt could pick out a quack—and prosecute them, since displaying the blue star without proper training was a crime—in seconds. But this particular herbalist had a good reputation, and so after our infuriatingly slow journey south, we had diverted another few tens of miles so that our lord and master could be plied with medicines.

"What he needs is a good fuck," Sir Radomir proclaimed with great sincerity after a period of silence. He took a long draw from his flask, which I knew to contain watered-down wine.

I said nothing. I liked Sir Radomir, but I didn't really want to engage with such vulgarities.

We continued to wait. There was no way to tell the time beyond our innate sense of its passage; even the sun was obscured by banks of raincloud, each one intent on testing the limits of our waxed cloaks. And then, eventually, Vonvalt reappeared, carrying a parcel no doubt filled with powders and potions. He looked pale and drawn, and his bearing reminded me of the way he looked and acted after a séance.

"The herbalist has found you a cure?" Sir Radomir asked. His voice was gruff, but there was a trace of optimism in it. As with Bressinger and I, Sir Radomir took great comfort from Vonvalt's stable and predictable temperament, and the man's abrupt decline had unnerved him.

"We can but hope," Vonvalt muttered. It was clear the ailment embarrassed him, particularly given that the rest of us rarely took ill.

He swept past us to his horse, Vincento, and he stashed the parcel away in one of the saddle bags; then he mounted up.

"Come, then," he said, sitting upright with some effort. "We'll make Badenburg tonight with a tailwind."

The rest of us exchanged a brief look at this absurd optimism; then we, too, mounted our horses. My attention was stolen by the harsh caw of a rook which had perched on the rickety fence at the boundary of the herbalist's land.

"'Tis a portent of spring," Sir Radomir remarked.

"'Tis not a portent if it has already come to pass," Bressinger said with scorn. He nodded towards the bird. "A single rook is death."

I scoffed. "I didn't think you were superstitious, Dubine," I said. I tried to inject some levity into my voice, for we had become a miserable little band, crushed under the weight of our mission and the doom and gloom it represented.

Bressinger simply smiled thinly, and then kicked Gaerwyn to a trot.

"Nema," Sir Radomir murmured to me as his own horse trotted past. "He needs a good fuck and all."

❧

We did not reach Badenburg until almost noon the following day, thanks in large part to the Duke of Brondsey, our donkey, and the cart full of legal accoutrements and our own personal effects that he pulled. With the benefit of hindsight, it was a burden we should and could have done away with, but I think Vonvalt thought that, like Bressinger a month before, he might have needed it as a litter—or worse, a bier. Besides, Vonvalt had long before arranged for a liveried company of messengers to dispatch the ill tidings from Galen's Vale – and we were hardly the sole source of the news.

The countryside here in the tip of the Southmark of Guelich was a hilly, rocky, forested place, the earth not quite as fractured as in the Tolsburg Marches, but nonetheless full of feature. Guelich had long had a reputation as a province of exceptional beauty, filled with fragrant pine forests, clear rivers, and abundant wildlife, to which lords from all over the Empire made pilgrimage for an unparalleled hunting experience. The castle of Badenburg reared up into the sky out of all of this beauty like a carbuncle, a jagged, blocky, functional fortress of grey stone. Cast in the unimaginative pre-Imperial style, it lacked all modern gothick ostentation – though what it lacked in beauty, it made up for in impregnability, designed and located as it had been to keep the Hauner armies from penetrating into the Grozodan peninsula. Given Haunersheim's subjugation a half-century before, and the subsequent vassalisation of both Venland and Grozoda, the castle had become all but obsolete as a base for military operations, and now existed mostly as a dwelling for the Emperor's third son.

By the flags above the keep, however, it was clear that Prince Gordan was not in residence; and by the churned mud of the fields outside the front gates, the wild pigs and foxes rootling for bones in the muck, and the unmistakable stench of a mass latrine, it was also clear that a great host had marshalled there until very recently.

"He has gone east, milord Justice," the duty serjeant said. "Not a day ago. Left with the Sixteenth Legion."

"The Sixteenth Legion?" Vonvalt asked. "Nema. Where were they garrisoned?"

"As far as I know, sire, they came from Kolsburg."

"How many men?"

"Thick end of five thousand, sire. I believe the prince is to take on siege specialists from Aulen and then make sail up the River Kova."

"Siege specialists?"

"Aye, sire. They are making for Roundstone, in Haunersheim, and then on to Seaguard. The Emperor has had word that some of the lords in the north have turned traitor. Baron Naumov is one. I believe Margrave Westenholtz is another."

Vonvalt grimaced at this. "Aye," he said. He tapped himself on the chest. "It was me who sent the news. We have come from Galen's Vale directly."

"I heard the Vale was sacked," the serjeant asked. "'Tis true, then? The Prince could scarce believe it."

"Indeed," Vonvalt said absently. He looked up about the battlements. "I need to leave some things here. My donkey and cart, for one."

The serjeant nodded. "Whatever you need, sire."

"And you say the prince is heading east?"

"Aye, sire. Are you heading to Sova?"

"Mm."

"I daresay you'll overtake him in a day or two. They are keeping to the Baden road."

Vonvalt nodded. "Thank you, serjeant," he said, and we moved off.

⁂

Despite Vonvalt's illness, we now rode hard down the Baden road. The evidence of the Sixteenth Legion's progress was everywhere; farms stripped bare, food waste picked over by scavengers, human, horse and donkey shit in vast quantities, and of course the sides of the road trampled to stinking, cake-soft mud. Given we were but four people, mounted and riding on a paved road, I expected to reach the tail end of the army within a couple of hours, let alone the day that the duty serjeant had guessed. Five thousand men – around four thousand of them on foot, if the Sixteenth

Legion were a typical one – would normally be a cumbersome host, after all, lucky to make ten or fifteen miles a day in rainy conditions.

I was wrong. Vonvalt had often talked about the capabilities of the Imperial Legions, and I had often privately dismissed what I considered to be the more outlandish claims. After all, they might have had a reputation as an élite force, but they were still human beings, with all the fallibilities that came with it.

But we rode for the balance of the day, made camp, struck camp before dawn, and rode on again for another half-day before we caught up with the rearmost section of the baggage train. By that time the countryside had opened up considerably, and we were on the final approach to Sova itself.

Another half hour's riding saw us to the head of the host, clearly identifiable by the knot of flagbearers, musicians and Imperial Guard—and of course, Prince Gordan himself. We had to come off the road and urged our exhausted horses through the mud to get past the long tailback of dismounted knights and soldiers. I marvelled at how uniformly well-equipped they were, with mail, surcoats in the bold red, yellow and blue Autun colours, and kettle helms for the majority. The knights, a fraction of the total force, all owned plate of varying expense, but did not wear it on the march, since they did not want to die of exhaustion or otherwise over-burden their horses.

Prince Gordan himself had the classic red hair and beard of the Haugenate line, the former of which was covered over by a flat-topped helmet and crown, the latter close-cropped. He wore a mail hauberk with an expensive-looking surcoat quartered in the colours of the Empire and resplendent with a black Autun rampant. He had a pleasant, handsome face, and appeared to be in good humour as we approached, laughing at a comment or joke from one of his retainers.

"Your Highness," Vonvalt called out. He drew the attention of Prince Gordan, as well as that of every man in the immediate vicinity.

The prince squinted at Vonvalt for a few moments whilst Sir Radomir, Bressinger and I made sudden and energetic obeisance; then his face broke into a grin. "That's not...Konrad, is it? By Nema!"

"The very same, Highness," Vonvalt said, touching his forehead out of respect rather than requirement – as a Justice, after all, Vonvalt outranked even the Emperor's third son. Even after years travelling with Vonvalt, and becoming fully acquainted with every aspect of his practice, it was still easy to forget just how much power he enjoyed.

"Faith, man, it's been – what, three, four years? When were you last in Sova?"

"About that," Vonvalt said, nodding in the direction of the capital. "But I make for it now."

"And not a day too soon," Prince Gordan replied. His tone was serious, but his face retained its levity. It is easy to forget, having long since met and rubbed shoulders with the highest-ranking nobles in the Empire, that initial sense of awe and fear; but at the time I was near breathless with it. Riding but ten yards from me, after all, surrounded by all the extravagant trappings of state and tailed by an Imperial legion, was one of the three princes of the Empire.

"You make for Roundstone?"

"Aye," Prince Gordan said pleasantly. "Baron Naumov has apparently the will to suicide and has chosen a curiously long and expensive way to commit it." The lords and retainers around him laughed with varying levels of sincerity.

"And then on to Seaguard?"

"Aye, you are well-informed."

"It was me, Highness, who uncovered the treachery," Vonvalt said, "and sent word to His Majesty."

"Ah!" Prince Gordan said. "My father did not mention you by name, only that a Justice had tipped him off to the rebellion being fomented in the Hauner lands. You are in his favour, Sir Konrad; you would do well to capitalise on it, for 'tis a fleeting thing!"

More bombastic laughter. I wondered if being the retainer of a prince was exhausting.

"I plan to pay your father a visit soon."

"Good man," Prince Gordan said. "Though I wonder if you would not prefer to accompany me? Your reputation as an accomplished swordsman precedes you – and I always have space for wise counsel."

Vonvalt bowed deferentially. "Would that I could, Highness. Alas, it would appear the Order is in some turmoil – and I myself am no spring chicken."

Prince Gordan gave him an appraising look. "Aye," he said. "You do look a little green around the gills. Have you eaten something bad?"

"I know not what ails me, Highness – only that it is not contagious."

He added the last part to assuage the prince and his men, for armies were far more susceptible to a rampant pox than they were to any enemy action.

"Well, see that you avail yourself of the Royal Physician, sir, though I daresay she will do little more than have half your blood out and a good gulp of piss to boot."

Vonvalt bowed again. "I am grateful, Highness. May I ask, is that the sum of your plans? Has there been any news of further rebellion? Westenholtz is hanged, but Naumov may have drawn others to his banner."

Prince Gordan shrugged. I could tell in that moment that he was a simple man, capable of commanding a legion in battle, but someone who did not trouble himself to ask too many questions or seek to understand wider events. I imagined him as one who enjoyed hunting and carousing with a close circle of friends more than the daily burdens of government.

"I sometimes forget that you Justices are lawmen in your bones, with your questions! I know not the intricacies of the traitors' movements or plans, sir, only to kill them and confiscate their lands." He waved a hand dismissively, and for the first time in this encounter,

I saw the stirrings of discontent amongst the prince's retainers – an exchanged glance, a raised eyebrow. "You would do better to speak to my father; I have not his shrewdness, I am afraid."

"I am sure that is not the case," Vonvalt said.

Prince Gordan chuckled. "Well, do not let me detain you further, Justice," he said. "Give my regards to my father, would you? I imagine it will be a year before I am back in the capital, perhaps longer."

"I will, Highness," Vonvalt said, touching his forehead once more. The prince tapped the rim of his helmet in reply, and then we were back on the Baden Road and charging ahead to put some distance between us and the inexorable advance of the Sixteenth Legion.

"Well, that takes the sting out of it," Vonvalt said as we slowed to spare the horses.

"What do you mean?" Sir Radomir asked.

Vonvalt gestured back down the road. "A Legion to crush whatever remains of Naumov and Westenholtz's rebellion and restore order in the Northmark of Haunersheim." Already I could see the effect this piece of good news was having on Vonvalt. He looked calmer and more relaxed – and healthier for it. I wondered then whether his ailment was simply the result of the incredible stresses on him.

"I am surprised it can be spared," Bressinger muttered.

Vonvalt shook his head, patting the side of Vincento's neck. "Haunersheim is the spine of the Empire. Were it another province, I would agree with you." He took in a deep, invigorating breath. "There is still plenty to be done, but at least we can stop worrying about this. It is precisely the sort of decisive intervention I had hoped for."

Vonvalt's sudden optimism was infectious. I remember looking back at the five-thousand-strong host of Reichskrieg veterans with their expensive arms and armour, led by one of the Emperor's own sons, and allowing myself to feel some of that good cheer, too. After all, the Emperor was known to have around fifty legions of Imperial troops in varying states of readiness across the Empire.

What damage could Claver, the Mlyanars, the Templars, or anyone really do against such a weight of numbers?

In fact, it was the last we – and most others – would ever see of both Prince Gordan and the Sixteenth Legion. In a few short months they would disappear into the forests of Haunersheim, and thereafter from the face of the earth.

But I must not get ahead of myself.

if you enjoyed
The Justice of Kings
look out for
The Pariah
Book One of
The Covenant of Steel
by
Anthony Ryan

The Pariah *begins a new epic fantasy series of action, intrigue, and magic from Anthony Ryan, a master storyteller who has taken the fantasy world by storm.*

Born into the troubled kingdom of Albermaine, Alwyn Scribe is raised as an outlaw. Quick of wit and deft with a blade, Alwyn is content with the freedom of the woods and the comradeship of his fellow thieves. But an act of betrayal sets him on a new path—one of blood and vengeance, which eventually leads him to a soldier's life in the king's army.

Fighting under the command of Lady Evadine Courlain, a noblewoman beset by visions of a demonic apocalypse, Alwyn must survive war and the deadly intrigues of the nobility if he hopes to claim his vengeance. But as dark forces, both human and arcane, gather to oppose Evadine's rise, Alwyn faces a choice: Can he be a warrior, or will he always be an outlaw?

PART I

"You say my claim to the throne was false, that I began a war that spilled the blood of thousands for nothing. I ask you, Scribe, what meaning is there in truth or lies in this world? As for blood, I have heard of you. I know your tale. History may judge me as monstrous, but you are a far bloodier man than I."

From *The Testament of the Pretender Magnis Lochlain,*
as recorded by Sir Alwyn Scribe

CHAPTER ONE

Before killing a man, I always found it calming to regard the trees. Lying on my back in the long grass fringing the King's Road and gazing at the green and brown matrix above, branches creaking and leaves whispering in the late-morning breeze, brought a welcome serenity. I had found this to be true ever since my first faltering steps into this forest as a boy ten years before. When the heart began to thud and sweat beaded my brow, the simple act of looking up at the trees brought a respite, one made sweeter by the knowledge that it would be short lived.

Hearing the clomp of iron-shod hooves upon earth, accompanied by the grinding squeal of a poorly greased axle, I closed my eyes to the trees and rolled onto my belly. Shorn of the soothing distraction, my heart's excited labour increased in pitch, but I was well schooled in not letting it show. Also, the sweat dampening my armpits and trickling down my back would only add to my stench, adding garnish for the particular guise I adopted that day. Lamed outcasts are rarely fragrant.

Raising my head just enough to glimpse the approaching party through the grass, I was obliged to take a deep breath at the sight of the two mounted men-at-arms riding at the head of the caravan. More concerning still were the two soldiers perched on the cart that followed, both armed with crossbows, eyes scanning the forest on either side of the road in a worrying display of hard-learned vigilance. Although not within the chartered bounds of the Shavine Forest, this stretch of the King's Road described a long arc through its northern fringes. Sparse in comparison to the deep forest, it was still a place of bountiful cover and not one to be travelled by the unwary in such troubled times.

As the company drew closer, I saw a tall lance bobbing above the small throng, the pennant affixed beneath its blade fluttering in the breeze with too much energy to make out the crest it bore. However, its gold and red hues told the tale clearly: royal colours. Deckin's intelligence had, as ever, been proven correct: this lot were the escort for a Crown messenger.

I waited until the full party had revealed itself, counting another four mounted men-at-arms in the rearguard. I took some comfort from the earthy brown and green of their livery. These were not kingsmen but ducal levies from Cordwain, taken far from home by the demands of war and not so well trained or steadfast as Crown soldiery. However, their justified caution and overall impression of martial orderliness was less reassuring. I judged them unlikely to run when the time came, which was unfortunate for all concerned.

I rose when the leading horsemen were a dozen paces off, reaching for the gnarled, rag-wrapped tree branch that served as my crutch and levering myself upright. I was careful to blink a good deal and furrow my brow in the manner of a soul just roused from slumber. As I hobbled towards the verge, keeping the blackened bulb of my bandaged foot clear of the ground, my features slipped easily into the gape-mouthed, emptied-eyed visage of a crippled dullard. Reaching the road, I allowed the foot to brush the churned mud at the edge. Letting out an agonised groan of appropriate volume, I stumbled forwards, collapsing onto all fours in the middle of the rutted fairway.

It should not be imagined that I fully expected the soldiers' horses to rear, for many a warhorse is trained to trample a prone man. Fortunately, these beasts had not been bred for knightly service and they both came to a gratifyingly untidy halt, much to the profane annoyance of their riders.

"Get out of the fucking road, churl!" the soldier on the right snarled, dragging on his reins as his mount wheeled in alarm. Beyond him, the cart and, more importantly, the bobbing lance of the Crown messenger also stopped. The crossbowmen sank lower on the mound of cargo affixed to the cart-bed, both reaching for the bolts in their quivers. Crossbowmen are always wary of leaving their weapons primed for long intervals, for it wears down the stave and the string. However, failing to do so this day would soon prove a fatal miscalculation.

I didn't allow my sight to linger on the cart, however, instead gaping up at the mounted soldier with wide, fearful eyes that betrayed little comprehension. It was an expression I had practised extensively, for it is not easy to mask one's intellect.

"Shift your arse!" his companion instructed, his voice marginally less angry and speaking as if addressing a dull-witted dog. When I continued to stare up at him from the ground he cursed and reached for the whip on his saddle.

"Please!" I whimpered, crutch raised protectively over my head. "Y-your pardon, good sirs!"

I had noticed on many occasions that such cringing will invariably stoke rather than quell the violent urges of the brutishly inclined, and so it proved now. The soldier's face darkened as he unhooked the whip, letting it unfurl so its barbed tip dangled onto the road a few inches from my cowering form. Looking up, I saw his hand tighten on the diamond-etched pattern of the handle. The leather was well worn, marking this as a man who greatly enjoyed opportunities to use this weapon.

However, as he raised the lash he paused, features bunching in disgust. "Martyrs' guts, but you're a stinker!"

"Sorry, sir!" I quailed. "Can't help it. Me foot, see? It's gone all rotten since me master's cart landed on it. I'm on the Trail of Shrines. Going to beseech Martyr Stevanos to put me right. Y'wouldn't hurt a faithful fellow, would you?"

In fact, my foot was a fine and healthy appendage to an equally healthy leg. The stench that so assailed the soldier's nose came from a pungent mix of wild garlic, bird shit and mulched-up leaves. For a guise to be convincing, one must never neglect the power of scent. It was important that these two see no threat in me. A lamed youth happened upon while traversing a notoriously treacherous road could well be faking. But one with a face lacking all wit and a foot exuding an odour carefully crafted to match the festering wounds this pair had surely encountered before was another matter.

Closer scrutiny would surely have undone me. Had this pair been more scrupulous in their appraisal they would have seen the mostly unmarked skin beneath the grime and the rangy but sturdy frame of a well-fed lad beneath the rags. Keener eyes and a fraction more time would also have discerned the small bulge of the knife beneath my threadbare jerkin. But these unfortunates lacked the required keenness of vision, and they were out of time. It had only been moments since I had stumbled into their path, but the distraction had been enough to bring their entire party to a halt. Over the course of an eventful and perilous life, I have found that it is in these small, confused interludes that death is most likely to arrive.

For the soldier on the right it arrived in the form of a crow-fletched arrow with a barbed steel head. The shaft came streaking from the trees to enter his neck just behind the ear before erupting from his mouth in a cloud of blood and shredded tongue. As he toppled from the saddle, his whip-bearing comrade proved his veteran status by immediately dropping the whip and reaching for his longsword. He was quick, but so was I. Snatching my knife from its sheath I put my bandaged foot beneath me and launched myself up, latching my free hand to his horse's bridle. The animal reared in instinctive alarm, raising me the additional foot I required to sink my knife into the soldier's throat before he could fully draw his sword. I was proud of the thrust, it being something I'd practised as much as my witless expression, the blade opening the required veins at the first slice.

I kept hold of the horse's reins as my feet met the ground, the beast threatening to tip me over with all its wheeling about. Watching the soldier tumble to the road and gurgle out his last few breaths, I felt a pang of regret for the briefness of his end. Surely this fellow with his well-worn whip had earned a more prolonged passing in his time. However, my regret was muted as one of many lessons in outlaw craft drummed into me over the years came to mind: *When the task is a killing, be quick and make sure of it. Torment is an indulgence. Save it for only the most deserving.*

It was mostly over by the time I calmed the horse. The first volley of arrows had felled all but two of the guards. Both crossbowmen lay dead on the cart, as did its drover. One man-at-arms had the good sense to turn his horse about and gallop off, not that it saved him from the thrown axe that came spinning out of the trees to take him in the back. The last was made of more admirable, if foolhardy stuff. The brief arrow storm had impaled his thigh and skewered his mount, but still he contrived to roll clear of the thrashing beast and rise, drawing his sword to face the two dozen outlaws running from the treeline.

I have heard versions of this tale that would have you believe that, when confronted by this brave and resolute soul, Deckin Scarl himself forbade his band from cutting him down. Instead he and the stalwart engaged in solitary combat. Having mortally wounded the soldier, the famed outlaw sat with him until nightfall as they shared tales of battles fought and ruminated on the capricious mysteries that determine the fates of all.

These days, similarly nonsensical songs and stories abound regarding Deckin Scarl, renowned Outlaw King of the Shavine Marches and, as some would have it, protector of churl and beggar alike. *With one hand he stole and the other he gave,* as one particularly execrable ballad would have it. *Brave Deckin of the woods, strong and kind he stood.*

If, dear reader, you find yourself minded to believe a word of this I have a six-legged donkey to sell you. The Deckin Scarl I knew was certainly strong, standing two inches above six feet with plenty of muscle to match his height, although his belly had begun to swell in recent years. And kind he could be, but it was a rare thing for a man does not rise to the summit of outlawry in the Shavine Forest by dint of kindness.

In fact, the only words I heard Deckin say in regard to that stout soldier was a grunted order to, "Kill that silly fucker and let's get on." Neither did Deckin bother to spare a glance for the fellow's end, sent off to the Martyrs' embrace by a dozen arrows. I watched the outlaw king come stomping from the shadowed woods with his axe in hand, an ugly weapon with a blackened and misshapen double blade that was rarely far from his reach. He paused to regard my handiwork, shrewd eyes bright beneath his heavy brows as they tracked from the soldier's corpse to the horse I had managed to capture. Horses were a prize worth claiming for they fetched a good price, especially in times of war. Even if they couldn't be sold, meat was always welcome in camp.

Grunting in apparent satisfaction, Deckin swiftly turned his attention to the sole survivor of the ambush, an outcome that had not been accidental. "One arrow comes within a yard of the messenger," he had growled at us all that morning, "and I'll have the skin off the hand that loosed it, fingers to wrist." It wasn't an idle threat, for we had all seen him make good on the promise before.

The royal messenger was a thin-faced man clad in finely tailored jerkin and trews with a long cloak dyed to mirror the royal livery. Seated upon a grey stallion, he maintained an expression of disdainful affront even as Deckin moved to grasp the bridle of his horse. For all his rigid dignity and evident outrage, he was wise enough not to lower the lance he held, the royal pennant continuing to stand tall and flutter above this scene of recent slaughter.

"Any violence or obstruction caused to a messenger in Crown service is considered treason," the thin-faced fellow stated, his voice betraying a creditably small quaver. He blinked and finally consented to afford Deckin the full force of his imperious gaze. "You should know that, whoever you are."

"Indeed I do, good sir," Deckin replied, inclining his head. "And I believe you know full well who I am, do you not?"

The messenger blinked again and shifted his eyes away once more, not deigning to answer. I had seen Deckin kill for less blatant insults, but now he just laughed. Raising his free hand, he gave a hard, expectant snap of his fingers.

The messenger's face grew yet more rigid, rage and humiliation flushing his skin red. I saw his nostrils flare and lips twitch, no doubt the result of biting down unwise words. The fact that he didn't need to be asked twice before reaching for the leather scroll tube on his belt made it plain that he certainly knew the name of the man before him.

"Lorine!" Deckin barked, taking the scroll from the messenger's reluctant hand and holding it out to the slim, copper-haired woman who strode forwards to take it.

The balladeers would have it that Lorine D'Ambrille was the famously fair daughter of a distant lordling who fled her father's castle rather than suffer an arranged marriage to a noble of ill repute and vile habits. Via many roads and adventures, she made her way to the dark woods of the Shavine Marches where she had the good fortune to be rescued from a pack of ravening wolves by none other than the kindly rogue Deckin Scarl himself. Love soon blossomed betwixt them, a love that, much to my annoyance, has echoed through the years acquiring ever more ridiculous legend in the process.

As far as I have been able to ascertain there was no more noble blood in Lorine's veins than mine, although the origin of her comparatively well-spoken tones and evident education are still something of a mystery. She remained a cypher despite the excessive time I would devote to thinking of her. As with all legends, however, a kernel of truth lingers: she was fair. Her features held a smooth handsomeness that had survived years of forest living and she somehow contrived to keep her lustrous copper hair free of grease and burrs. For one suffering the boundless lust of youth, I couldn't help but stare at her whenever the chance arose.

After removing the cap from the tube to extract the scroll within, Lorine's smooth, lightly freckled brow creased a little as she read its contents. Captured as always by her face, my fascination was dimmed somewhat by the short but obvious spasm of shock that flickered over her features. She hid it well, of course, for she was my tutor in the arts of disguise and even more practised than I in concealing potentially dangerous emotions.

"You have it all?" Deckin asked her.

"Word for word, my love," Lorine assured him, white teeth revealed in a smile as she returned the scroll to the tube and replaced the cap. Although her origins would always remain in shadow, I had gleaned occasional mentions of treading stages and girlhood travels with troupes of players, leading me to conclude that Lorine had once been an actress. Perhaps as a consequence, she possessed the uncanny ability to memorise a large amount of text after only a few moments of reading.

"If I might impose upon your good nature, sir," Deckin told the messenger, taking the tube from Lorine. "I would consider it the greatest favour if you could carry an additional message to King Tomas. As one king to another, please inform him of my deepest and most sincere regrets regarding this unfortunate and unforeseen delay to the journey of his trusted agent, albeit brief."

The messenger stared at the proffered tube as one might a gifted turd, but took it nonetheless. "Such artifice will not save you," he said, the words clipped by his clenched teeth. "And you are not a king, Deckin Scarl."

"Really?" Deckin pursed his lips and raised an eyebrow in apparent surprise. "I am a man who commands armies, guards his borders, punishes transgressions and collects the taxes that are his due. If such a man is not a king, what is he?"

It was clear to me that the messenger had answers aplenty for this question but, being a fellow of wisdom as well as duty, opted to offer no reply.

"And so, I'll bid you good day and safe travels," Deckin said, stepping back to slap a brisk hand to the rump of the messenger's horse. "Keep to the road and don't stop until nightfall. I can't guarantee your safety after sunset."

The messenger's horse spurred into a trot at the slap, one its rider was quick to transform into a gallop. Soon he was a blur of churned mud, his trailing cloak a red and gold flicker among the trees until he rounded a bend and disappeared from view.

"Don't stand gawping!" Deckin barked, casting his glare around the band. "We've got loot to claim and miles to cover before dusk."

They all fell to the task with customary enthusiasm, the archers claiming the soldiers they had felled while the others swarmed the cart. Keen to join them, I looked around for a sapling where I could tether my stolen horse but drew up short as Deckin raised a hand to keep me in place.

"Just one cut," he said, coming closer and nodding his shaggy head at the slain soldier with the whip. "Not bad."

"Like you taught me, Deckin," I said, offering a smile. I felt it falter on my lips as he cast an appraising eye over the horse and gestured for me to pass him the reins.

"Think I'll spare him the stewpot," he said, smoothing a large hand over the animal's grey coat. "Still just a youngster. Plenty of use left in him. Like you, eh, Alwyn?"

He laughed one of his short, grating laughs, a sound I was quick to mimic. I noticed Lorine still stood a short way off, eschewing the frenzied looting to observe our conversation with arms crossed and head cocked. I found her expression strange; the slightly pinched mouth bespoke muted amusement while her narrowed gaze and drawn brows told of restrained concern. Deckin tended to speak to me more than the other youngsters in the band, something that aroused a good deal of envy, but not usually on Lorine's part. Today, however, she apparently saw some additional significance in his favour, making me wonder if it had something to do with the contents of the messenger's scroll.

"Let's play our game, eh?" Deckin said, instantly recapturing my attention. I turned back to see him jerk his chin at the bodies of the two soldiers. "What do you see?"

Stepping closer to the corpses, I spent a short interval surveying them before providing an answer. I tried not to speak too quickly, having learned to my cost how much he disliked it when I gabbled.

"Dried blood on their trews and cuffs," I said. "A day or two old, I'd say. This one—" I pointed at the soldier with the arrowhead jutting from his mouth "—has a fresh-stitched cut on his brow and that one." My finger shifted to the half-bared blade still clutched in the gloved fist of the one I had stabbed. "His sword has nicks and scratches that haven't yet been ground out."

"What's that tell you?" Deckin enquired.

"They've been in a fight, and recently."

"A fight?" He raised a bushy eyebrow, tone placid as he asked, "You sure it was just that?"

My mind immediately began to race. It was always a worrisome thing when Deckin's tone grew mild. "A battle more like," I said, knowing I was speaking too fast but not quite able to slow the words. "Something big enough or important enough for the king to be told of the outcome. Since they were still breathing, until this morn, I'd guess they'd won."

"What else?" Deckin's eyes narrowed further in the manner that told of potential disappointment; apparently, I had missed something obvious.

"They're Cordwainers," I said, managing not to blurt it out. "Riding with a royal messenger, so they were called to the Shavine Marches on Crown business."

"Yes," he said, voice coloured by a small sigh that told of restrained exasperation. "And what is the Crown's principal business in these troubled times?"

"The Pretender's War." I swallowed and smiled again in relieved insight. "The king's host has fought and won a battle with the Pretender's horde."

Deckin lowered his eyebrow and regarded me in silence for a second, keeping his unblinking gaze on me just long enough to make me sweat for the second time that morning. Then he blinked and turned to lead the horse away, muttering to Lorine as she moved to his side. The words were softly spoken but I heard them, as I'm sure he intended I would.

"The message?"

Lorine put a neutral tone to her reply, face carefully void of expression. "You were right, as usual, my love. The daft old bastard turned his coat."

Deckin ordered the bodies cleared from the road and dumped deeper in the forest where the attentions of wolves, bears or foxes would soon ensure all that remained were anonymous bones. The Shavine Forest is a hungry place and fresh meat rarely lasts long when the wind carries its scent through the trees. It had been dispiritingly inevitable that it would be Erchel who found one of them still alive. He was just as hungry as any forest predator, but it was hunger of a different sort.

"Fucker's still breathing!" he exclaimed in surprised delight when the crossbowman we had been dragging through the ferns let out a confused, inquisitive groan. Jarred by the unexpectedness of his survival, I instantly let go of his arm, letting him slump to the ground, where he continued to groan before raising his head. Despite the holes torn into his body by no fewer than five arrows, he resembled a man woken from a strange dream as he gazed up at his captors.

"What's happened, friend?" Erchel enquired, sinking to his haunches, face drawn in an impressive semblance of concern.

446

"Outlaws, was it? My fellows and I found you by the road." His face became grim, voice taking on a hoarse note of despair. "What a terrible thing. They're naught but beasts, Scourge take them. Don't worry—" He set a comforting hand on the crossbowman's lolling head. "—We'll see you right."

"Erchel," I said, voice edged with a forbidding note. His eyes snapped to meet mine, catching a bright, resentful gleam, sharp, pale features scowling. We were much the same age but I was taller than most lads of seventeen, if that was in fact my age. Even today I can only guess my true span of years, for such is the way with bastards shucked from a whorehouse: birthdays are a mystery and names a gift you make to yourself.

"Got no time for your amusements," I told Erchel. The after-taste of murder tended to birth a restless anger in me and the exchange with Deckin had deepened the well, making my patience short. The band had no formal hierarchy as such. Deckin was our unquestioned and unchallenged leader and Lorine his second, but beneath them the pecking order shifted over time. Erchel, by dint of his manners and habits, foul even by the standards of outlaws, currently stood a good few pegs lower than me. Being as much a pragmatic coward as he was a vicious dog, Erchel could usually be counted on to back down when faced with even marginally greater authority. Today, however, the prospect of indulging his inclinations overrode his pragmatism.

"Get fucked, Alwyn," he muttered, turning back to the cross-bowman who, incredibly, had summoned the strength to try and rise. "Don't tax yourself, friend," Erchel advised, his hand slipping to the knife on his belt. "Lay down. Rest a while."

I knew how this would go from here. Erchel would whisper some more comforting endearments to this pitiable man, and then, striking swift like a snake, would stab out one of his eyes. Then there would be more cooing assurances before he took the other. After that it became a game of finding out how long it took the benighted wretch to die as Erchel's knife sliced ever deeper. I had no stomach for it most days, and certainly not today. Also, he had failed to heed me which was justification enough for the kick I delivered to his jaw.

Erchel's teeth clacked as his head recoiled from the impact. The kick was placed to cause the most pain without dislocating his jaw, not that he appreciated my consideration. Just a scant second or two spent blinking in shock before his narrow face mottled in rage and he sprang to his feet, bloodied teeth bared, knife drawn back to deliver a reply. My own knife came free of the sheath in a blur and I crouched, ready to receive him.

In all honesty, the matter might have been decided in favour of either of us, for we were about evenly matched when it came to knife work. Although, I like to think my additional bulk would have tipped the scales in my direction. But it all became moot when Raith dropped the body he had been carrying, strode between us and crouched to drive his own knife into the base of the crossbow-man's skull.

"To be wasteful of time is to be wasteful of life," he told us in his strange, melodious accent, straightening and directing a steady, unblinking stare at each of us in turn. Raith possessed a gaze I found hard to meet at the best of times, the overly bright blue eyes piercing in a way that put one in mind of a hawk. Also, he was big, taller and broader even than Deckin but without any sign of a belly. More off-putting still were the livid red marks that formed two diagonal stripes across the light brown skin of his face. Before clapping eyes on him during my first faltering steps into Deckin's camp, I hadn't beheld one of Caerith heritage before. The sense of strangeness and threat he imbued in me that day had never faded.

In those days, tales of the Caerith and their mysterious and reputedly arcane practices abounded. Never a common sight in Albermaine, those who lived among us were subject to the fear and derision common to those viewed as alien or outlandish. Experience would eventually teach us the folly of such denigration, but all that was yet to come. I had heard many a lurid yarn about the Caerith, each filled with allusions to witchy strangeness and dire fates suffered by Covenant missionaries who unwisely crossed the mountains to educate these heathen souls in the Martyrs' example. So, I was quick to avert my eyes while Erchel, ever cunning but rarely clever, was a little slower, prompting Raith to afford him the benefit of his full attention.

"Wouldn't you agree, weasel?" he asked in a murmur, leaning closer, the brown skin of his forehead briefly pressing against Erchel's pale brow. As the bigger man stooped, his charm necklace dangled between them. Although just a simple length of cord adorned with bronze trinkets, each a finely wrought miniature sculpture of some kind, the sight of it unnerved me. I never allowed my gaze to linger on it too long, but my snatched glances revealed facsimiles of the moon, trees and various animals. One in particular always caught my eye more than the others: the bronze skull of a bird I took to be a crow. For reasons unknown, the empty eye sockets of this artefact invoked more fear in me than its owner's unnaturally bright gaze.

Raith waited until Erchel gave a nod, eyes still lowered. "Put it over there," the Caerith said, nodding towards a cluster of elm a dozen paces away as he slowly wiped his bloodied blade on Erchel's jerkin. "And you can carry my bundle on the way back. Best if I don't find anything missing."

"Caerith bastard," Erchel muttered as we heaved the crossbow-man's corpse into the midst of the elm. As was often his way, our confrontation now appeared to have been completely forgotten. Reflecting on his eventual fate all these years later I am forced to the conclusion that Erchel, hideous and dreadful soul that he was, possessed a singular skill that has always eluded me: the ability to forgo a grudge.

"They're said to worship trees and rocks," he went on, careful to keep his voice low. "Perform heathen rites in the moonlight and such to bring them to life. My kin would never run with one of his kind. Don't know what Deckin's thinking."

"Mayhap you should ask him," I suggested. "Or I can ask him for you, if you like."

This blandly spoken offer had the intended effect of keeping Erchel's mouth closed for much of the remainder of our journey.

However, as we progressed into the closer confines of the deep forest, drawing nearer to camp, his tongue invariably found another reason to wag.

"What did it say?" he asked, once again keeping his voice quiet for Raith and the others weren't far off. "The scroll?"

"How should I know?" I replied, shifting the uncomfortable weight of the loot-filled sack on my shoulder. The bodies had all been stripped clean before I could join in the scavenging, but the cart had yielded half a meal sack, some carrots and, most prized of all, a pair of well-made boots which would fit me near perfectly with a few minor alterations.

"Deckin talks to you. So does Lorine." Erchel's elbow nudged me in demanding insistence. "What could it say that would make him risk so much just to read it?"

I thought of the spasm of shock I had seen on Lorine's face as she read the scroll, as well as her contradictory expression as she stood and watched Deckin coax deductions from me. *The daft old bastard turned his coat*, she had said. My years in this band had given me a keen nose for a shift in the varied winds that guided our path, Deckin always being the principal agent. Never fond of sharing his thoughts, he would issue commands that seemed odd or nonsensical only for their true intent to stand revealed later. So far, his guarded leadership had always led us to profit and clear of the duke's soldiers and sheriffs. *The duke . . .*

My feet began to slow and my eyes to lose focus as my always-busy mind churned up an insight that should have occurred to me back at the road. The messenger's guards were not ducal levies from the Shavine Marches but Cordwainers fresh from another battle in the Pretender's War. Soldiers in service to the king, which begged the question: if his own soldiers couldn't be trusted with escorting a Crown agent, which side had the Duke of the Shavine Marches been fighting on?

"Alwyn?"

Erchel's voice returned the focus to my gaze, which inevitably slipped towards Deckin's bulky form at the head of the column.

We had reached the camp now and I watched him wave away the outlaws who came to greet him, instead stomping off to the shelter he shared with Lorine. Instinct told me neither would join us at the communal feast that night, the customary celebration of a successful enterprise. I knew they had much to discuss. I also knew I needed to hear it.

"There's something I feel you should know, Erchel," I said, walking off towards my own shelter. "You talk too fucking much."

Follow us:

 /orbitbooksUS

 /orbitbooks

 /orbitbooks

Join our mailing list
to receive alerts on our
latest releases and deals.

orbitbooks.net

Enter our monthly
giveaway for the chance
to win some epic prizes.

orbitloot.com